# Windfall

"*Windfall* is about all of my favorite things—a girl's first
big love, her first big loss, and—her first big luck."
—**JENNY HAN,** *New York Times* bestselling author of
*Always and Forever, Lara Jean*

"*Windfall* is perfectly named; reading it, I felt like I had
suddenly found something wonderful. It's a story about love,
and luck, and the way our lives can change in an instant.
I laughed and cried and bought a lottery ticket the very
next day." —**MORGAN MATSON,** *New York Times*
bestselling author of *Since You've Been Gone*

"*Windfall* is rich with the intensity of real love—in all its
heartache and hope." —**STEPHANIE PERKINS,** *New York Times*
bestselling author of *Isla and the Happily Ever After*

"If you're looking for your next great read, then you're in 'luck'!
Smith combines humor and emotion to capture these characters'
life-changing story, while teaching us all a bit about luck, love,
kindness and the true meaning of home." —*JUSTINE*

"Younger readers and adult readers alike will fall in love with
this charmer about luck, love, and fortune." —*POPSUGAR*

"This compelling read, gracefully told, raises issues seldom
explored in popular fiction. How can we rationalize life's
inequalities? What do we owe, and to whom, when blessed
with good fortune? Smart and entertaining, as to be expected
from Smith." —*KIRKUS REVIEWS*

# Windfall

# Windfall

Jennifer E. Smith

EMBER

Text copyright © 2017 by Jennifer E. Smith Inc.
Cover photograph copyright © 2018 by Rennie Solis
Cover art by Maggie Edkins

All rights reserved. Published in the United States by Ember, an imprint of Random House Children's Books, a division of Penguin Random House LLC, New York. Originally published in hardcover in the United States by Delacorte Press, an imprint of Random House Children's Books, a division of Penguin Random House LLC, New York, in 2017.

Ember and the E colophon are registered trademarks of Penguin Random House LLC.

Visit us on the Web! GetUnderlined.com

Educators and librarians, for a variety of teaching tools, visit us at RHTeachersLibrarians.com

The Library of Congress has cataloged the hardcover edition of this work as follows:
Names: Smith, Jennifer E., author.
Title: Windfall / Jennifer E. Smith.
Description: First edition. | New York : Delacorte Press, [2017] |
Summary: "Alice loves Teddy, her best friend, but has never told him. When she buys him a lottery ticket that turns out to be a winner, their lives are changed forever and their friendship is put to the ultimate test"— Provided by publisher.
Identifiers: LCCN 2016034305 | ISBN 978-0-399-55937-2 (hardback) |
ISBN 978-0-399-55939-6 (glb) | ISBN 978-0-399-55938-9 (ebook)
Subjects: | CYAC: Love—Fiction. | Friendship—Fiction. | Lotteries—Fiction. |
Luck—Fiction. | Wealth—Fiction.
Classification: LCC PZ7.S65141 Wi 2017 | DDC [Fic]—dc23

ISBN 978-0-399-55940-2 (tr. pbk.)

Printed in the United States of America
10 9 8 7 6 5 4 3 2 1
First Ember Edition 2018

For Andrew,
my lucky charm

*Pause you who read this, and think for a
moment of the long chain of iron or gold,
of thorns or flowers, that would never have
bound you, but for the formation of the first link
on one memorable day.*

—CHARLES DICKENS, GREAT EXPECTATIONS

*windfall (noun): a piece of unexpected good
fortune, typically one that involves receiving a
large amount of money*

—OXFORD AMERICAN DICTIONARY

# Part One

JANUARY

# One

When the man behind the counter asks for my lucky number, I hesitate.

"You must have one," he says, his pen hovering over the rows of bubbles on the form. "Everyone does."

But the problem is this: I don't believe in luck.

At least not the good kind.

"Or it could be anything, really," he says, leaning forward on the counter. "I just need five numbers. And here's the trick. The big secret. You ready?"

I nod, trying to look like I do this all the time, like I didn't just turn eighteen a few weeks ago, like this isn't my first time buying a lottery ticket.

"You have to make them really, really good ones."

"Okay then," I say with a smile, surprised to find myself playing along. I planned to let the computer decide, to put my faith in randomness. But now a number floats to the surface with such ease that I offer it up to him before thinking better of it. "How about thirty-one?"

*Teddy's birthday.*

"Thirty-one," the man repeats as he scratches out the corresponding bubble. "Very promising."

"And eight," I tell him.

*My birthday.*

Behind me, there's a line of people waiting to buy their own tickets, and I can practically feel their collective impatience. I glance up at the sign above the counter, where three numbers are glowing a bright red.

"Three-eighty-two," I say, pointing at the display. "Is that millions?"

The man nods and my mouth falls open.

"That's how much you can win?"

"You can't win anything," he points out, "unless you pick some more numbers."

"Right," I say with a nod. "Twenty-four, then."

*Teddy's basketball number.*

"And eleven."

*His apartment number.*

"And nine."

*The number of years we've been friends.*

"Great," says the man. "And the Powerball?"

"What?"

"You need to pick a Powerball number."

I frown at him. "You said five before."

"Yeah, five plus the Powerball."

4

The sign above the counter clicks forward: 383. It's an amount nearly too big to mean anything—an impossible, improbable figure.

I take a deep breath, trying to shuffle through the numbers in my head. But only one keeps appearing again and again, like some kind of awful magic trick.

"Thirteen," I say, half-expecting something to happen. In my mind the word is full of voltage, white-hot and charged. But out loud it sounds like any other, and the man only glances up at me with a doubtful look.

"Really?" he asks. "But that's unlucky."

"It's just a number," I say, even though I know that's not true, even though I don't believe it one bit. What I know is this: Numbers are shifty things. They rarely tell the whole story.

Still, when he hands over the slip of paper—that small square of illogical math and pure possibility—I tuck it carefully into the pocket of my coat.

Just in case.

# *Two*

Outside, Leo is waiting. It's started to snow, the flakes heavy and wet, and they settle thickly over his dark hair and the shoulders of his jacket.

"All set?" he asks, already starting to walk in the direction of the bus stop. I hurry after him, skidding a little in the fresh snow.

"Do you have any idea how much this ticket could be worth?" I say, still trying to get my head around the number.

Leo raises his eyebrows. "A million?"

"No."

"Two?"

"Three hundred and eighty-three million," I tell him, then add, in case it isn't entirely clear: *"Dollars."*

"That's only if you win," he says, grinning. "Most people get nothing but a piece of paper."

I feel for the ticket in my pocket. "Still," I say, as we arrive at the three-sided shelter of the bus stop. "It's kind of crazy, isn't it?"

We sit down on the bench, our breath making clouds that hang in the air before disappearing. The snow has a sting to it, and the wind off the lake is icy and sharp. We scoot closer together for warmth. Leo is my cousin, but really he feels more like my brother. I've been living with his family ever since I was nine, after my parents died a little more than a year apart.

In the hazy aftermath of that horrible time, I found myself plucked out of San Francisco—the only home I'd ever known—and set down halfway across the country with my aunt and uncle in Chicago. Leo was the one to save me. When I arrived I was still reeling, stunned by the unfairness of a world that would take away my parents one at a time with such coldhearted precision. But Leo had decided it was his job to look out for me, and it was one he took seriously, even at nine.

We were an odd pair. I was wispy and pale, with hair like my mother's, so blond it took on a slightly pinkish hue in certain light. Leo, on the other hand, had inherited his liquid brown eyes and messy thatch of dark hair from his own mom. He was funny and kind and endlessly patient, whereas I was quiet and heartsick and a little withdrawn.

But right from the start, we were a team: Leo and Alice.

And, of course, Teddy. From the moment I arrived, the two of them—inseparable since they were little—took me under their wing, and we've been a trio ever since.

When the bus appears, its headlights hazy in the whirling snow, we climb on. I slide into a seat beside the window, and Leo sinks down next to me with his long legs stretched into the empty aisle, a puddle already forming around his wet boots. I reach into my bag for the birthday card I bought for Teddy, then hold out a hand, and without even needing to ask, Leo passes over the heavy fountain pen he always carries with him.

"So I ended up stealing your idea," he says, pulling a pack of cigarettes from his coat pocket. He twirls them between his fingers, looking pleased with himself. "Another perk of turning eighteen. I know he doesn't smoke, but I figure it's still better than the IOU for a hug he gave me."

"You got a hug?" I say, looking over at him. "I got one for a free ice cream, which I somehow ended up paying for anyway."

Leo laughs. "Sounds about right."

I pin the card against the seat in front of me, trying to keep it steady against the bouncing of the bus. But as I stare at the blank interior, my heart starts to hammer in my chest. Leo notices me hesitate and shifts in his seat, angling himself toward the aisle to give me some privacy. I stare at his back for a second, wondering whether he's just being polite or whether he's finally guessed my secret, a thought that makes my face burn.

For almost three years now, I've been in love with Teddy McAvoy.

And though I'm painfully aware that I probably haven't been hiding it very well, I usually choose—in the interest of self-preservation—to believe that's not the case. The one consolation is that I'm pretty sure Teddy has no idea. There's a lot to love about him, but his powers of observation are questionable at best. Which is a relief in this particular situation.

It took me by surprise, falling in love with Teddy. For so many years, he'd been my best friend: my funny, charming, infuriating, often idiotic best friend.

Then one day, everything changed.

It was spring of freshman year, and we were on a hot dog crawl, of all things, a walking tour that Teddy had mapped out to hit all the best spots on the North Side. The morning had started off cool, but as the day wore on it became too warm for my sweatshirt, which I tied around my waist. It wasn't until our fourth stop—where we sat at a picnic table, struggling to finish our hot dogs—that I realized it must have fallen off along the way.

"Wasn't it your mom's?" Leo asked, looking stricken, and I nodded. It was just an old Stanford hoodie with holes in both cuffs. But the fact that it had belonged to my mother made it priceless.

"We'll find it," Teddy promised as we began retracing our steps, but I wasn't so sure, and my chest ached at the thought of losing it. By the time it started to pour we'd only made it halfway back through the day's route, and it was quickly becoming clear that the sweatshirt was a lost cause. There was nothing to do but give up on it.

But later that night my phone lit up with a text from Teddy: *I'm outside*. I crept downstairs in my pajamas, and when I opened the front door, he was standing there in the rain, his hair dripping and his jacket soaked, holding the wet sweatshirt under his arm like a football. I couldn't believe he'd found it. I couldn't believe he'd *gone back* for it.

Before he could say anything, I threw my arms around him, hugging him tight, and as I did I felt something crackle to life inside me, like my heart was a radio that had been full of static for years, and now, all at once, it had gone suddenly clear.

Maybe I'd loved him long before then. Maybe I just hadn't realized it until I opened the door that night. Or maybe it was always meant to happen this way, with a shivering boy holding a damp sweatshirt on my front stoop, the whole thing as inevitable as day turning to night and back to day again.

It hasn't been easy, loving him; it's like a dull throb, constant and persistent as a toothache, and there's no real cure for it. For three years I've acted like his buddy. I've watched him fall for a string of other girls. And all this time, I've been too afraid to tell him the truth.

I blink at the card in front of me, then jiggle the pen in my hand. Out the window the night is cloaked in white, and the bus carried us farther from the heart of the city.

Something about the darkness, all those flecks of snow hurrying to meet the windshield, dizzying and surreal, makes me feel momentarily brave.

I take a deep breath and write: *Dear Teddy*.

Then, before I can second-guess myself, I keep going, my pen moving fast across the page, a quick, heedless emptying of my heart, an act so reckless, so bold, so monumentally stupid that it makes my blood pound in my ears.

When I'm finished I reach for the envelope.

"Don't forget the ticket," Leo says, and I slip it out of my pocket. It's now bent, and one of the corners has a small tear, but I lay it flat against my leg and do my best to straighten it out. As Leo leans in to get a better look, I feel my face flush all over again.

"Teddy's birthday?" he says, peering at the numbers, his glasses fogged from the warmth of the bus. "Kind of an obvious one . . ."

"It seemed appropriate for the occasion."

"Your birthday. Teddy's basketball jersey." He pauses. "What's eleven?"

"A prime number."

"Very funny," he says, then his eyes flash with recognition. "Oh, right. His apartment. And nine?"

"The number of years—"

"That you guys have been friends, right," he says, then turns to the final number. I watch his face as it registers—that awful, conspicuous thirteen—and he snaps his chin up, his dark eyes alert and full of concern.

"It doesn't mean anything," I say quickly, flipping the ticket over and pressing it flat with my hand. "I had to think fast. I just . . ."

"You don't have to explain."

I shrug. "I know."

"I get it," he says, and I know that he does.

That's the best thing about Leo.

He watches me for a second longer, as if to make sure I'm really okay; then he sits back in his seat so that we're both facing forward, our eyes straight ahead as the bus hurtles through the snow, which is thick as static against the windshield. After a moment, he reaches over and places a hand on top of mine, and I lean against him, resting my head on his shoulder, and we ride like that the rest of the way.

# Three

The inside of Teddy's apartment is warm and almost humid, the small space filled with too many bodies and too much noise. Beside the door, the old-fashioned radiator is hissing and clanging, and from the bedroom the music thumps through the walls, making Teddy's school photos tremble in their frames. The single window by the galley kitchen is already fogged over, and someone has written *TEDDY MCAVOY IS A* across it, the last word rubbed out so that it's impossible to tell just what exactly he is.

I stand on my tiptoes, scanning the room.

"I don't see him," I say, shrugging off my coat and throwing it on top of the haphazard pile that's sprung up on the floor. Leo picks it up, knotting one of his sleeves to one of mine so that our jackets look like they're holding hands.

"I can't believe he's doing this," he says. "His mom is gonna kill him."

But there's more to it than that. There's a reason Teddy doesn't usually have people over, even though his mom works nights as a nurse. Their whole apartment is only two rooms—three if you count the bathroom. The kitchen is basically just a small tiled area tucked off in the corner, and Teddy has the only bedroom. His mom sleeps on the pullout couch while he's at school, a detail that makes it glaringly obvious they don't have the same kind of money as most of our classmates.

But I've always loved it here. After Teddy's dad walked out on them, they had to give up their spacious two-bedroom apartment in Lincoln Park, and this was all they could afford. Katherine McAvoy did what she could to make it feel like home, painting the main room a blue so bright it feels like being in a swimming pool, and the bathroom a cheerful pink. In Teddy's room each wall is a different color: red, yellow, green, and blue, like the inside of a parachute.

Tonight, though, it feels less cozy than crowded, and as a cluster of junior girls walk past us I hear one of them say, her voice incredulous, "It's only a one-bedroom?"

"Can you imagine?" says another, her eyes wide. "Where does his mom sleep?"

"I knew he wasn't rich, but I didn't realize he was, like, *poor*."

Beside me I can feel Leo bristle. This is exactly why Teddy never has anyone but us over. And why it's so strange to see dozens of our classmates crammed into every available inch of space tonight. On the couch, five girls are wedged together so closely it's hard to imagine how they'll ever get up, and the hallway that leads to Teddy's room is clogged by the better part of the basketball team. As we stand there, one of them comes barreling past us—his cup held high, the liquid sloshing onto his shirt—shouting, "Dude! Dude! Dude!" over and over as he elbows his way toward the kitchen.

"*Dude,*" Leo says in a voice that makes me laugh, because it doesn't matter what season it is, whether it's soccer or basketball or baseball—we always feel slightly out of place among Teddy's teammates. Sometimes it's like he has two separate lives: the one where he spends Friday nights hitting game-winning shots in front of the whole school and the one where he spends Saturday nights watching stupid movies with me and Leo. We always go to his games and cheer him on and show up at the parties afterward because he's our best friend. But I like it better when it's just us.

"There he is," Leo says, and I close my eyes for a second, keenly aware of the card in my bag, a secret still lit with possibility, like something about to bloom.

*It's only Teddy,* I remind myself, but then I spin around and there he is with that enormous grin of his, lifting a hand to motion us over.

The thing about Teddy McAvoy is that there's nothing particularly exceptional about him. If I had to describe him, it would be difficult to find something defining enough to pin him down. He's average height: a few inches taller than me and a few inches shorter than Leo. And he has ordinary

15

brown hair that's cut in a completely ordinary way. His ears are normal-sized, and his eyes are plain brown, and his nose is unremarkable. But somehow, taken as a whole, he's beautiful.

"Hey," he says, his face lighting up as we squeeze past the girls who have positioned themselves at the edge of the kitchen. "You're late."

I open my mouth to say something, anything, but before I can he sweeps me into one of his bear hugs, my feet parting ways with the sticky linoleum floor, my heart flying up into my throat. When he sets me down, I blink at him.

"Aren't you gonna wish me a happy birthday?" he asks, wiggling his eyebrows, and something about his teasing tone makes me snap back.

"Stop fishing," I say with a grin. "I've already said it a million times today."

"Yeah, but that was at school. Not at my party."

"Well then, happy birthday," I say, rolling my eyes. "About time you caught up."

Without warning he loops an arm around my neck, putting me into a friendly headlock. "Just because you've been eighteen for ages now—"

"Weeks," I correct, trying to squirm away from him.

"—doesn't mean you get to act like you're so much older and wiser than me."

"It's not acting," I say, laughing now, and he lets me go.

"It's tough being the youngest," he says with an exaggerated sigh. "Especially when I'm obviously so much more mature than you guys—"

"Obviously," I say, shaking my head.

Leo reaches for a handful of M&M's from a bowl on the counter. "So I thought this was gonna be at Marty's tonight."

"His parents' flight got canceled because of the snow," Teddy says, "and there were no other options. So I figured we might as well move it here."

He flashes a smile, but there's an effort behind it. Even six years later, he's still embarrassed by the run-down building, the single bedroom, the absence of his father.

"So," he says, clapping his hands. "Since neither of you greeted me with balloons this morning—which was a real letdown, by the way—and there wasn't any confetti when I opened my locker, I *know* you must've brought me something tonight."

"You make it sound like our presence isn't enough," Leo teases him.

"Really, what do I get?" Teddy asks, looking between us. "Actually, wait. Let me guess. Leo probably made me something computer-y—"

"That's not a word."

"Maybe a cartoon about the adventures of Teddy McAvoy? Or a pixelated portrait? Or a website of my very own?"

"Sure," Leo says, nodding. "You can find it at www.Teddy IsAnIdiot.com."

"And Al," Teddy says, turning to me, "I bet you went out and bought something really amazing, then promptly gave it away to someone who needs it more."

17

"You know," Leo says with a grin, "she *was* at the soup kitchen earlier tonight."

"And probably the nursing home too."

"And picking up garbage in the park."

"And walking dogs at the shelter." Teddy laughs. "She totally gave my birthday present to a dog. Was it at least a cool dog? Like a Doberman or a basset hound? Please tell me you didn't give it to a poodle or a Chihuahua."

I roll my eyes at them. "You guys are the worst."

"Here," Leo says, pulling the pack of cigarettes out of his back pocket and handing it over to Teddy, who stares at the box in his palm.

"What're these for?"

"You're eighteen now. Just one of the perks."

"What," Teddy jokes, arching an eyebrow, "no *Playboy*?"

"I figured you were probably pretty well stocked in that department."

He laughs, then turns to me. "So what else do I get?"

Just over his shoulder, the refrigerator is covered in photos from when he was little, smiling to display a missing tooth or half-buried in a pile of leaves, and I try to remember what it was like when I knew him then, when I could look at him without feeling this way, without loving him so desperately. I've very nearly managed to capture it again— the flatness of it, effortless and uncomplicated—when I raise my eyes to find him watching me expectantly, and I give up.

It's different now. And there's no going back.

When I take his card out of my bag, I notice that my

hand is shaking, and I realize—swiftly and suddenly—that I can't do this. How in the world did I think I could?

This envelope—this small, thin rectangle of folded paper—is heavy with hope and possibility. I've tucked my whole heart inside of it. There's no way I can stand by and watch him open it. Not here. Not now. Maybe not ever.

But before I can change my mind, before I can make up some excuse and shove it back into my bag, Teddy snatches it out of my hand.

"For me?" he says sweetly. "Thanks, Al."

He's the only one who ever calls me that, and he always has. But hearing it now, I'm overcome by a panic so strong I think I might tackle him to get it back.

"No," I say, my voice a little choked as I reach for it. But Teddy holds it high with one long arm, oblivious to the look on my face. Out of the corner of my eye I see Leo register what's happening, and to my relief he points at the card.

"I think that's the wrong one, actually," he says, and Teddy lowers it with a puzzled expression.

"But it has my name on it." He runs a finger underneath my tiny handwriting. "See? Ted E. Bear."

It's my old nickname for him, one I haven't used in years, and something about seeing it there on display, clutched in his hand, makes me go queasy.

"I forgot to sign it," I say, trying to push the alarm out of my voice, but he isn't listening anymore. He's too busy opening the envelope.

I glance over at Leo, who gives me a helpless shrug, then back at Teddy, who is now flipping open the card. I'm so nervous about what I've written that I've actually forgotten about the lottery ticket, which is right there on top of my words—my awful, misguided, humiliating words—but Teddy holds the ticket up with a smile.

"Hey, look," he says. "I'm gonna be rich."

"*Really* rich," says one of the basketball players—an enormous guy wearing a bow tie that may or may not be ironic—as he tries to elbow his way past us to get another drink. "They were just talking about it on the news. It's a monster jackpot."

As he continues to push toward the makeshift bar, he manages to bump into Leo, who stumbles into Teddy, who then drops the card, and for a brief, frozen moment I watch it happen as if in slow motion: the way it falls from Teddy's hand, sailing to the floor, where it slides underneath the refrigerator with all the grace and purpose of a paper airplane.

We stare at the spot where it disappeared.

"Nice shot," says Leo, raising his eyebrows.

"Sorry," says the guy, backpedaling away from the scene.

"Oops," says Teddy, dropping to his knees.

I stare dumbly as he crouches on the floor, his hand scraping at the thin gap between the bottom of the refrigerator and the tiles.

"Someone grab me a fork or something," he says, still hunched over.

"A fork?" Leo asks. "Are you planning a meal down there?"

"No, but I think if I could just—"

"It's fine," I say, placing a hand lightly on his back. "Really. It wasn't anything important."

Teddy looks worried as he springs to his feet. "You sure?"

"Yes," I say, trying not to sound as relieved as I feel.

He wipes his hands on his jeans, then stoops to grab the ticket, which came to rest on the floor near my shoe. "Better the card than the ticket, right?"

"Right," Leo says, laughing at this. "I'm sure that refrigerator was the only thing standing between you and the jackpot."

# *Four*

Teddy tends to be the center of attention even when it isn't his birthday. So tonight it's almost impossible to get any time with him. He's surrounded by other friends, and there always seem to be more lingering off to the side, waiting to say hello or give him a hug.

I watch from across the room as he bends his head low to say something to Lila, his ex-girlfriend. They only broke up a few weeks ago, after dating for nearly three months, which is right around when it usually happens. There's a method to Teddy's madness when it comes to girls: after winning them over, they date for a little while, then when he's ready to move on he starts acting so distant, so frustratingly unavailable, so entirely checked out, that *they* eventually break up with *him*.

"You're awful," I said over Christmas break when he told me Lila had finally given up on him.

"Or am I kind of a genius?" he said with that trademark grin of his.

I'm not anything like the parade of overly perky girls who usually go after him. I'm supposed to fall in love with someone like Nate from my advanced calculus class, who is going to MIT next year, or David, who volunteers with me at the nursing home, or Jackson, who writes poetry so beautiful my heart speeds up when he reads it aloud during our English class.

The truth is, Teddy McAvoy isn't my type at all. He's a little too smooth, a little too confident, a little too pleased with himself. He is—basically—a little too Teddy.

Even so, I watch miserably as Lila rises onto her tiptoes to whisper something in his ear and he throws his head back in laughter.

"You know," Leo says, following my gaze, "the traditional way to pass the time at events like this would be to talk to someone." I open my mouth to respond, but he holds up a hand before I can. "Other than me."

"I know," I say, pulling my eyes away from Teddy. "Sorry. I don't know what's wrong with me. I promise I'll be more fun."

"Let's try for something more realistic," he teases, giving me a pat on the shoulder, "like mildly talkative or even just mostly present."

"What's that?" Teddy asks, coming up behind us. "More presents?"

I roll my eyes.

"I'm going out to see the snow," he says. "You guys wanna come?"

"Too cold," Leo says, and I'm silently grateful for this as I turn to Teddy with what I hope comes off as a casual shrug. He holds out his arm to me. "Shall we?"

As soon as we step outside the apartment, the party feels distant, the music muffled and far away. At the end of the dimly lit hallway, Teddy pushes open the heavy door to the fire escape and we're met with an icy blast of air. Outside, the snow is still coming down hard, the wind tossing it around like bits of confetti. I tuck my hands into the sleeves of my sweater and walk over to the railing.

There isn't much of a view from up here, just the windows of the buildings all around us, which are mostly dark at this point. Below there's a single set of footprints in the snow, and even those are quickly fading. It's nearly midnight, and the world is quiet.

Teddy bends down and scoops up a handful of snow with his bare hands, leisurely packing it into a perfect ball. Then he winds up, adopting a pitcher's stance, and looks out toward the street as if to launch it over the side of the fire escape. But at the last minute he spins around and tosses it at me.

"Hey," I say, giving him a look of mock outrage as I brush the snow from my sweater, but he just smiles.

"Had to be done," he says, stepping up to the rail beside me. He leans in and bumps my shoulder gently with his. "It's tradition."

I can't help smiling at this. My face is already stinging with cold, and my hands are frozen, so I shove them into the pockets of my jeans, trying not to show it. Because the last thing I want right now is to go back inside, to step out of the snow and the dark and the stillness. Below us the door to the building opens, then closes, and a few people spill out, their voices hushed. In the cone of light from the streetlamp the snow falls steadily, and Teddy turns to face me, his smile slipping.

"So," he says. "He didn't call."

I shake my head. "I swear . . ."

"Before you get annoyed—"

"I'm not annoyed," I correct him. "I'm mad. And you should be too."

"You know how he is."

"That's the whole point," I say. "I do know. He's been doing this to you for years now, and it sucks. If he wants to disappear the other three hundred sixty-four days, that's fine. But on his son's birthday, he could at least—"

"Al."

I shrug. "I'm just saying."

"I know," he says, looking almost amused. "And I appreciate it."

"Well, I bet he's thinking of you today, wherever he is."

"Sure," Teddy says with a bitter laugh. "Probably in between hands of poker."

"You don't know that," I say, but he gives me a stern look.

"Let's not kid ourselves. He'll probably remember he missed it next week and send something ridiculous to make it up to me, then ask for it back the minute he stops winning and needs to cover his debts. We both know how this works."

"Maybe it's a good sign," I say, because I can't stand to see him looking so dejected. "Remember last year, when he sent all those honey-baked hams?"

"Yeah," he says with a frown. "And the set of knives the year before."

"Exactly. He only sends stuff when he's on a hot streak," I say, remembering the way, when we were little, that Charlie McAvoy used to burst through the door with bags of presents for Teddy, telling Katherine about all the overtime pay he was getting for his job as an electrician. It wasn't until later that they discovered he'd been at the racetrack most of that time. "So maybe this means things are better. Maybe it means he's getting help."

Teddy doesn't look convinced, and I can't really blame him. It's been six years since Charlie gambled away their family's entire life's savings during a three-day bender in Vegas. They haven't seen him since.

"But," I say, shaking my head, "it's still not fair."

He shrugs. "I've gotten used to it."

"Teddy," I say, turning to meet his eyes, because I want to make sure he knows this, really knows it: that it's okay to be upset, that he doesn't always have to pretend everything's fine. "That doesn't make it any better."

"I know," he says quietly.

In the whirl of snowflakes and the blur of the lights behind him, there's something almost dreamlike about him right now. His eyes are very bright, and his hair is flecked with snow, and there's a quietness to the way he's looking at me. I realize we're standing very close and I'm shivering, though it's not because of the cold. Just now the cold feels beside the point. It's because of the jumbled, chaotic thought that's working its way through me: all of a sudden I want to tell him about the card, about all those things I said in it and just how much I meant them.

But then the door opens behind us, and the light from the hallway comes spilling out to reveal a group of sophomore girls, all standing there giggling in their stylish coats and fancy boots. "Hi, Teddy," one of them says as they step outside. "Okay if we join you?"

He hesitates, just for a moment, before pulling his eyes away from mine, and all at once the spell is broken. "Sure," he says, giving them a smile, and before he can say anything else, before he can mangle my heart any worse, I clear my throat.

"I'm gonna go find Leo," I say, but Teddy's attention has already shifted, already started to wander off in some other direction. Just as it always does.

Just as it always will.

# Five

Back inside, as I search for Leo, I trip over a garbage bag near the kitchen. I pick it up automatically, dragging it back through the crowd and out into the empty hallway. For a moment I just stand there, looking around at the dirty linoleum floors and the flickering lights on the ceiling. To the left is apartment thirteen, where the crooked brass numerals on the door always seem to be watching me, and to the right is the fire escape, where Teddy is still outside with those girls.

I should've said something to him about the card before we were interrupted. I should've figured out a way to make him see me, really see me, to come to his senses and realize he loves me too. Sometimes it feels like if I wish for it hard enough, it might just come true. But I know that's not the way it works. Life doesn't bend to anyone's will. And it doesn't run on credit either. Just because the world stole something from me doesn't mean it owes me anything. And just because I've stockpiled a whole lot of bad luck doesn't mean I'm due anything good.

Still, it doesn't seem like all that much to ask: that the boy I love might love me back.

With a sigh I haul the garbage bag over to the chute and listen to it clatter all the way down. Back inside I find Leo sitting on the old leather armchair in the corner of Teddy's bedroom, his head bent over his phone. He's shed his green sweater and is now wearing the Superman T-shirt I gave him for Christmas, though with his thick glasses he looks more like a rumpled version of Clark Kent.

I nod at the phone. "Max?"

He shakes his head, but not before a smile crosses his face, the same one he gets whenever anyone mentions his boyfriend. They'd only been together about six months when Max left for college in Michigan at the end of last summer, but they'd moved swiftly from *I kind of like you* to *I think this might be something* to *I'm completely in love with you*. And along the way I'd fallen for Max too, the way you do when you witness someone discovering all the amazing things about a person who means a lot to you.

"No," Leo says, looking up at me. "Just Mom."

"Let me guess. She's panicking about the snow?"

My aunt Sofia has never exactly adjusted to Chicago winters. She spent her childhood in Buenos Aires before her family moved to Florida when she was eight, and this type

29

of weather is pretty much the only thing that ever slows her down, sending her straight into hibernation mode.

"She's worried about the roads," he says. "She thinks we should stay over."

It's been a while since we've slept here. We used to do it all the time, the three of us. When we were younger and Teddy still needed someone to watch him while his mom worked nights, we'd convince Mrs. Donohue, the old woman from next door, to let us stay too. While she snored on the couch, we'd line up the two sleeping bags on the floor, and then Teddy would hang over the edge of the bed, his face looming above ours, and we'd talk until our eyelids grew heavy and our words started to taper off.

"I can't exactly tell her everyone else is leaving," Leo says with a sheepish grin, "because she thinks we're the only ones here. So . . ."

"So," I say, looking around the room at the piles of discarded clothes, the books stacked on the dresser, and the lone sock sticking out from under the twin bed.

Teddy's bed. The place where he sleeps every night.

I swallow hard. "I guess we're staying, then."

Which is how—a few hours later—we end up traveling back in time.

Teddy offered me the bed, but I refused, so we are—once again, after all these years—arranged in our old familiar formation: Teddy lying with his chin propped on his hands, peering over the edge at me and Leo, who are curled up on the floor beneath a random collection of blankets.

"You guys," Teddy says, a hint of laughter in his voice. "You guys, you guys, you guys."

This was twelve-year-old Teddy's never-ending chorus, and hearing it again now gives me a jolt of nostalgia so strong that I feel a little light-headed.

Leo chimes in with his typical, slightly weary response. "Yes, Theodore?"

"Remember when we convinced you to draw us a mural?" Teddy thumps a fist against the wall beside his bed, which was once white—a perfect canvas, it seemed to us when we were eleven—but is now painted a dark blue. "I paid you in lollipops."

"Best commission I ever got," Leo says. "Even if we did have to paint over it the next day."

"You can still see the outline of the penguins in the corner," I say with a smile. "And that fish you drew on the back of the door."

Teddy is quiet for a moment, then his voice—uncharacteristically tentative—breaks through the dark again. "So do you think it went okay tonight?"

"It was great," Leo says, the last word swallowed by a yawn. "I think you might've set a world record for most people per square inch of space."

"It was a little crowded," Teddy admits. "Do you think people noticed there's only one bedroom?"

"No," I say firmly. "They were much too busy having fun."

"Someone broke my mom's vase," he says. "I'm hoping

she won't notice, since there's no way I'll be able to afford a new one till I start working again this summer."

"We'll chip in so you can get one now," I say. Then before he can argue, which I know he will, I add, "You can pay us back later."

"I take Visa, MasterCard, and lollipops," Leo says.

This makes Teddy laugh. "Thanks. You guys are the best."

Leo yawns again, louder this time, and we slip into silence. I stare up at the plastic stars on the ceiling, the familiar constellations they make. The faint light from the windows is bluish, the snow still falling outside. After a few minutes I hear the soft whistle of Leo's breathing, and I reach out in the dark and gently remove his glasses, setting them on the floor between us. From above, Teddy watches me.

"Hey," he says. "Remember when—"

But I put a finger to my lips. "Don't wake him."

"Then come up here so we can keep talking," he says, and there's a rustling as he scoots over to the far edge of the bed. "It's still my birthday. And I'm not tired yet."

"Well, I am," I say, even though that isn't true at all.

I've never been more awake in my life.

"Come on," he says, patting the side of the bed, but I lie frozen on the floor, feeling stupid for hesitating, for thinking twice. All he wants is to talk to his best friend the way we've been doing since we were little.

I rise to my feet, moving carefully so as not to wake Leo, then climb into the bed beside Teddy. It's narrow, certainly not meant for two people, but when we lie on our sides, facing each other, there's just enough room.

"Hi," he says, grinning at me through the dark.

"Hi," I say, my heart beating fast.

His breath has the minty scent of toothpaste, and he's so close that I can only bring one of his features into focus at a time: his nose or his mouth or his eyes. I stop there, because he's watching me with a curious look.

"What's wrong?" he asks.

I shake my head. "Nothing."

"Don't recognize me now that I'm eighteen?"

"Guess not," I say, reaching deep for some sort of witty comeback, the kind of banter that usually flows freely between us. But there's nothing. My thoughts are scrambled by the nearness of him, and my chest aches with something deeper than love, something lonelier than hope.

*Teddy*, I think, blinking at him, and it takes everything in me not to say it like that, the way it sounds in my head: like a sigh or a question or a wish.

"Did you have fun?" he asks, and I nod, my hair sparking with static against his pillow. "I thought it was pretty good. I mean, not like my sixteenth, but who has the stamina for that kind of thing anymore?"

"Old man," I say softly, and he laughs.

"I do feel kind of old," he admits. "Eighteen. Man."

"Do you realize we've known each other for half our lives now?"

"That's crazy," he says, then shakes his head. "Actually, it's not. It's weirder trying to remember a time when we didn't know each other."

I'm quiet for a moment. It still hurts too much to think

33

about that time before: the whole first half of my life, when I lived with my parents in San Francisco and we ate breakfast together and went to the park and read bedtime stories like a normal family. Trying to remember it feels like staring at the sun for too long. It's red-hot and flashing, and still, half a life later, it burns like hell.

Teddy reaches out and rests a hand on my arm. I'm wearing one of his sweatshirts, but even through the fabric I can feel the heat of his touch. "Sorry," he says. "I didn't mean to—"

"No," I say, drawing in a breath. "It's fine. I wasn't thinking about that."

He gives me a skeptical look. "You can talk to me, you know."

"I know," I say automatically.

He shakes his head. His eyes are wide and unblinking, and as he shifts, his foot brushes against mine. "I mean the way you talk to Leo. You open up to him about this stuff. But you can talk to me too."

I bite my lip. "Teddy . . ."

"I know it's really painful," he says, rushing ahead. "And I don't mean to push. But I know you think all I do is joke around. That I'm not serious enough. That I can't be there for you when it comes to this kind of stuff. But I can."

"That's what you think?"

"Well, yeah," he says. "That's always how it's been. You go to Leo when you want to remember. You come to me when you want to forget."

I stare at him, my throat tight. There's a truth to his words that hasn't ever occurred to me.

"All I'm saying is that I can be there for you too, if you let me."

"I know."

"I can be a good guy too."

"You already are."

"I'm not," he says. "But I want to be. For you."

The words linger there in the dark and I press my eyes shut, wanting to offer him something, wishing it were easier to let him in. He finds my hand, closing his around it.

"Sometimes," I say after a moment, "it feels like I'm starting to forget them."

"Impossible," he whispers.

"When I think of them now, it's like I'm watching a movie of this happy family. But none of it seems real anymore."

"It's because you're thinking big-picture," he says. "That'll knock the wind out of you every time. You have to take it in pieces." He pauses. "Like, my dad used to draw smiley faces with toothpaste on the bathroom mirror for me."

"Really?" I say softly, and he nods.

"Or he'd write little messages, like *Today's the day!* and *Look out, world!*"

The way he says this—sad and solemn and a little bit wistful—it's almost like his dad is gone too. Which, of course, he is. Just in a different way. But right then I feel a surge of recognition, of shared experience, unknowable to the outside world, and I give Teddy's hand a squeeze.

"I mean," he says ruefully, "that was just on the mornings he wasn't having breakfast at some seedy riverboat casino. But still. I think about it sometimes."

I take a deep breath, wanting to share something with him too. "My dad used to make heart-shaped pancakes on Sundays," I say finally, and I feel a spike of pain in my chest at the memory. "They were always burnt on the bottom. But I still like them best that way. And my mom . . ." I trail off, biting my lip. "My mom used to sing while she washed the dishes. She was kind of terrible."

"See?" Teddy says, his eyes still fixed on mine. "Little things."

Our faces are very close together now, our hands still clasped, our socked feet touching. We're so close I can feel his breath on my face, and for a few long seconds we stay there like that, just looking at each other. I'm not sure what's happening, exactly; my thoughts are too muddled to make sense of it. He's just being a friend. He's just being there for me. He's just being a good guy. That's all.

But then he inches a little closer, and it feels like something is short-circuiting inside me. I want so badly for him to kiss me, but I'm terrified of what will happen if he does. I'm scared that everything will change, and scared that it won't, scared that when the lights come on tomorrow morning we won't be able to look at each other, scared that it will be a huge mistake and that it might ruin nine whole years of friendship.

Teddy leans forward a bit more so that his nose brushes against mine and it's like the focus shifts, the lens pulling in tighter so that the edges of the world go blurry, and right here, right now, there's only us. Outside, the snow is caked against the windowsill, everything muffled and quiet, the storm beginning to settle. Inside, his room is cozy and warm, our own private igloo.

Our noses touch again—a prelude, a prologue—and my heart tumbles toward him, the rest of me desperate to follow it. But just before our lips meet, just before the whole world shifts, there's a bright crack, followed by a crunching sound, and when we both bolt upright at the same time, peering down toward the foot of the bed, it's to find Leo, rumpled and not quite awake, fumbling for his broken glasses.

# Six

When I open my eyes the next morning, I'm greeted by a scattered array of red plastic cups. Beyond them the sun is just starting to push through the frosted window, the room still steeped in shades of blue. I blink a few times, trying to remember where I am and how I ended up on the couch, then sit up with a yawn.

Still, it takes a moment for it to come rushing back.

Teddy's face, so close to my own. The way his nose brushed against mine. The thump of our two hearts loud in my ears.

And then Leo rubbing his eyes and asking what time it was, and me leaping awkwardly out of the bed, and Teddy looking like someone who had been sleepwalking only to snap abruptly awake.

I squeeze my eyes shut again.

Nothing happened. Not really. But in that moment of confusion, the slow and bewildering aftermath, I could see it in the way he looked at me across the darkened room. It had—for him, anyway—been a near miss.

And the worst part is I know he's probably right to be relieved. Because I didn't just want him to kiss me. I wanted so much more than that. I wanted him to fall in love with me. And that isn't Teddy.

Behind me the door to his room swings open and I take a deep breath, steeling myself before turning around to face him. But it's only Leo.

"Morning," he says. Without his glasses he looks much younger, but he's squinting and shuffling down the hallway like someone very old. His snow boots are dangling from one hand, and he drops them on the floor in front of the couch, then motions for me to scoot over. I tuck my legs beneath me, waiting for him to say something about last night, but he only yawns as he bends to tie his laces.

"You're leaving?" I ask, and he nods.

"I need to get a new pair of glasses. Or at least find my old ones. And I've got a bunch of other stuff to do too."

"Design stuff?"

He shakes his head. "Applications."

"Which ones?"

"Michigan," he says without looking at me. "It's due Monday."

This is a bit of a sore point between us. Ever since Leo's art began to migrate from his notebooks to his computer, the graphic design program at the School of the Art Institute

39

here in Chicago has been his dream. But now that Max is at Michigan, his focus seems to be shifting.

"Well," I say, my voice a few octaves too high, "I think that's great."

I've been trying to keep my feelings on the subject to myself, since it's obviously a decision he needs to make on his own. But we know each other too well for that, and my disapproval keeps shining through in spite of my best efforts.

"No, you don't," Leo says. "But it's fine. I'm just keeping my options open."

"I know."

"It's not like I don't still want to go to—"

"I know."

"It's just that I really miss—"

I smile. "I know that too."

We're both quiet for a second.

"Okay," he says, standing up. "Want to head back with me?"

I look around the room, which is a disaster. There are cups everywhere, half-eaten bags of chips strewn around, and a bottle of soda tipped over on the counter, still dripping down the cabinets. Pretty much every surface is covered with sticky ring stains, and the overflowing garbage bin is surrounded by dented cans and balled-up paper towels.

"I should probably help him clean up before his mom gets home," I say, glancing at the clock; it's almost eight, which means she'll be back soon. "Just to make sure he gets to see his nineteenth birthday."

"Don't worry," Teddy says, padding down the hall behind us. I twist to look at him, then flick my eyes away, remembering again. He's wearing nothing but a pair of gray sweatpants, a green T-shirt tossed over one shoulder, and the sight of his bare chest is almost too much to take this morning. "My mom just called to say she has to cover the morning shift. I guess the snow's screwing everything up down there."

"Best birthday present you could've gotten," Leo says as he grabs his coat.

Teddy tugs his shirt on, then ambles over to the kitchen counter, lifting the tinfoil off the cake his mom made for him. They had their own celebration last night before she left for work, and what was left over was pretty much demolished at the party last night. But he scrapes some crusted frosting off the side of the dish with his finger, then walks over to drop onto the couch beside me.

It takes me a second to brave a sideways glance at him. The need to know what he's thinking is nearly overwhelming. But as soon as Leo puts a hand on the doorknob, I feel a surge of panic at the thought of being alone with him and decide maybe it's best not to know after all.

"Sure you don't want to wait a bit?" I ask, my voice strained. "I bet the roads aren't great, and you don't even have your glasses."

"I'll be fine," Leo says, then spins around and bumps

into the coatrack, grabbing it to steady himself and squinting at it in mock confusion. "Teddy?"

"Very funny," I say as he takes a little bow. Then he gives us a wave, opens the door, and walks out into the hallway. And just like that we're all alone.

# Seven

As we stand in the kitchen tossing cups into a garbage bag, neither of us mentions what almost happened last night. Even so, it hangs in the air between us.

"Here," Teddy says, stepping in just as I bend to grab a paper towel that's fallen to the floor. He picks it up, then drops it into the bag with an overly solicitous smile. "I got it."

"Thanks," I mutter, turning my attention to a different corner of the room, but again he's right there, following me around, offering to take over even the simplest tasks, hovering and helping and just generally trying way too hard.

This only makes it worse.

Nothing even happened and, still, something has changed.

This isn't how we are together. And this certainly isn't

Teddy. Teddy is the guy who teases me about my do-gooding and throws snowballs at me and never bothers to help clean anything up. When he gives me a hug, he always lifts me off the ground so that my toes dangle a few inches from the floor, and sometimes he draws little alligators in honor of his nickname for me, which matches mine for him: Al E. Gator.

He isn't careful with me. And I'm not polite with him.

Until now.

And it's driving me nuts.

"What in the *world*," I say, exasperated, as we try to pass in the small kitchen, sidestepping like shadows of each other, moving this way and that at the exact same time, hopelessly out of sync, "are you doing?"

He looks surprised at my impatience. "I was just gonna help—"

"Why don't you work on the living room and I'll finish up in here?"

"Okay," he says with a shrug.

But the apartment feels too small even for this. The kitchen is open, so I can see him over the counter, flopping down onto the couch, remote control in hand.

"How is that helping?" I ask, and he swivels around with a grin.

"I'm double-tasking," he says. "I clean better when the TV's on."

I roll my eyes. "I bet."

As he begins to flip through the channels, I straighten

up the kitchen, rinsing glasses and wiping down counters. Every so often I stop and glance at the back of his head, willing him to turn around, to say something, to look me in the eye. But he doesn't. The room feels charged with an awkwardness so foreign that I want to cry, and I almost wish I could take it back, what nearly happened last night.

Almost.

In the next room Teddy pauses on the local news, which is showing pictures of cars that have skidded off the road and snowdrifts nearly as high as the reporters.

"Look at this," he says, gesturing at the screen. "A foot and a half. We should go sledding when we're done."

"I have to leave when we're done."

Teddy gives me a wounded look. "But it's my birthday."

"Not anymore."

"Well, it's my birthday *weekend*."

I shake my head. "I've got homework."

"It's senior year."

"And applications."

"You're a shoo-in."

"Not if I don't apply."

He laughs. "Fair enough."

On the screen the focus has shifted back to the newscaster, who announces that they'll return with the results of last night's lottery drawing right after the commercial break. I turn back toward the kitchen, and Teddy tips his head to look at me.

"Don't you want to watch? We could be rich."

"*You* could be rich."

"Maybe, but if it's a winner . . ."

"Yeah?"

"I hope I can find the ticket."

"You lost it already? That was quick, even for you."

"I mean, I'm sure it's here somewhere," he says, waving a hand, and I glance around at the place, the tables and counters cleared off and wiped down, the floors mostly spotless and the garbage bags lined up near the door, ready to be taken out.

"It's fine," I say with a shrug, because ticket or not, the odds are against us. "Do you have any idea what the statistical probability of winning the lottery is?"

He shakes his head.

"I don't either," I admit. "But I once read that you have a better chance of getting struck by lightning or being attacked by a shark or becoming president one day."

Teddy laughs. "So . . . pretty likely."

"You have a better chance of being killed by a falling vending machine too."

"Now, *that* seems totally possible," he says, turning back to the TV as the weekend anchor, a young woman with close-cut dark hair, returns to the screen.

"Lottery officials have confirmed there were three winning tickets sold in last night's four-hundred-twenty-four-million-dollar Powerball jackpot," she begins, and I find myself walking over to the living room so I can hear better, feeling kind of ridiculous even as I do. "And you could

46

be a winner if you bought yours in Florida, or Oregon, or right here in Chicago." The image changes to show a small shop with a red awning. "The lucky local has yet to come forward, but the winning ticket was sold at Smith's Market in Lincoln Park."

My mouth falls open.

"Isn't that place right by you?" Teddy asks, turning around, and when he sees my face, his eyes widen. "Wait, that's where you bought it? Whoa. Maybe we really are millionaires."

On the screen, they're now showing footage of the man from the store, the one who helped me fill in the numbers just last night. But too quickly they switch back to the newscaster. "Elsewhere, the owner of a winning ticket sold in Oregon has chosen to remain anonymous, and a third ticket holder in Florida has yet to come forward. Last night's jackpot was the seventh-largest in Powerball history at a whopping four hundred twenty-four million dollars. The winners will split the pot three ways for a pretax total of 141.3 million dollars each, which can of course be taken as a lump sum or split into annual payments."

Teddy is standing up now. "There's no way."

"No," I say, shaking my head.

"I seriously have no idea where the ticket is," he says, half-laughing as the shot pans out on-screen to include the weatherman, the two of them bantering about how they wished they'd thought to buy a ticket. "Do you remember the numbers?"

I don't answer, my eyes still glued to the TV. It would

be easier to tell him they were random, that they didn't mean anything, that none of this did. The only way he'd find out is if we won. If *he* won. And the odds of that are absurd.

But I don't want to pretend anymore. And so I nod.

"Yes," I say quietly, just as the newscaster turns back to the camera.

"And those numbers, again," she says, "were twenty-four . . ."

Teddy raises his eyebrows. "My lucky number."

"Eight . . ."

"Your birthday."

"Thirty-one . . ."

He looks a little pale now. "And mine."

"Nine . . ."

Before he can even ask, I say, "When we met."

"Eleven . . ."

At this he crinkles his brow.

"Your apartment," I whisper, my heart racing.

"And the Powerball," the newscaster says cheerfully, "was a very unusually lucky number thirteen."

This time there's no need to say anything. We both know the significance of that one. I bow my head, unable to look at him.

My parents died thirteen months apart from each other.

My mom, after a short battle with breast cancer, on July 13.

And my dad, just over a year later, in a car accident on August 13.

*Thirteen.*

*Thirteen.*

*Thirteen.*

It's a cliché, of course: the unluckiness of that number.

But for me it's more than that too: it's a trip wire, a land mine, a scar.

And now, maybe, something more.

As a kid I won the worst kind of lottery possible. The odds of that had to be almost as long as these, the chances at least as unlikely. But now here I am, staring at the television screen, where the numbers I chose are laid out across the bottom like a math problem I can't possibly begin to solve.

Teddy is staring at me. "Thirteen?"

"Thirteen," I repeat numbly. My mouth is so dry it's almost hard to say the word. I blink at him several times, then—in as calm a voice as possible—I say, "You can still find the ticket, right?"

He steps around the couch, walking over to me, but not the way he normally does, not with his usual Teddy strut. There's something tentative about him now, something a little jangly. I notice for the first time that his shirt has a shamrock on it, the word LUCKY stamped in faded white letters just beneath it. "Are you saying . . . ?"

"No," I say quickly.

Teddy breathes out, looking almost relieved. "No."

"Except . . . yes."

"Al, come on," he says. "Yes or no?"

I swallow hard. "I need to check to be sure. I don't want to . . . I don't want to get your hopes up. But . . ."

49

"But?"

"I think . . ."

"Yeah?"

"We might've . . ." My heart is thundering. "I think you might've won."

Teddy stares at me for a second, uncomprehending, then his eyes get big and he lets out a loud whoop, pumping his fist and whirling around. "Are you kidding?" he asks, punching at the air again. "We won?"

"I think—"

Before I can finish, his arms are around me and he's lifting me off the ground the way he always does, both of us laughing as he spins, my face pressed against his lucky green T-shirt, which smells of sweat and detergent and sleep, and I fold my arms around his neck and let myself go dizzy.

When he sets me down again, his eyes are shining the same way they were last night.

"We really won?" he asks softly.

I smile. "Happy birthday."

And then, before I even quite realize what's happening— before I have time to memorize the look on his face and the shape of his lips, all the things I know I'll want to remember later when I replay this in my head—he leans down and kisses me, and all the dizziness of before, of last night when his face was so close and a moment ago when I saw those numbers on the screen, of the way the world tilted when the newscaster said the word *thirteen* and the way all the colors of the room blurred when he twirled me around, they're nothing compared to this.

My heart is a yo-yo, whizzing up and down, and he's the one pulling the string. Only I didn't ever know it could go this high.

In all the times I imagined this, I didn't know.

He's all electricity right now—like a balloon about to pop or a soda about to fizz over—and I can feel it in his kiss, in the way he presses his lips against mine, the way he tightens his arms around my waist, pulling me as close as possible.

Then, just as quickly, he lets go.

I take an uneven step backward, still reeling.

"This is crazy," he says, practically skipping away. He lopes over to the kitchen, then paces back toward the TV, running his hands through his hair so that it stands out all over like someone has shocked him. For a second I think he's talking about the kiss, but then realize—of course—he means the lottery.

I stare at him, still somewhere else entirely.

*He just kissed me,* I think, my head too crowded for anything else, even something as big as millions of dollars. *Teddy McAvoy just kissed me.*

Maybe last night wasn't a mistake after all. Maybe it wasn't a fluke.

Maybe it was a beginning.

The thought sends a thrill through me.

"What are you supposed to do when this happens?" he

asks, and when I simply blink at him he gives me an impatient look. "Al. C'mon. Focus. What do we do? Call a lawyer or something, right? Or hide the ticket? I think I heard you're supposed to put it in a safe, maybe? We don't have a safe. We only have a cookie jar. Maybe we should Google this and figure out what to do."

"I think the first thing," I say, snapping back again, "is to actually *find* the ticket."

"Right," he says, and stops abruptly. "Right!"

But he just stands there as if awaiting further instruction.

"Why don't you go check your pockets from last night?" I suggest, my heart still pounding, and without answering he bounds off toward his room, emerging a few seconds later with a look of utter despair.

"It's not there," he says, his face ashen. He puts both hands on his head and lets out a strangled groan. "I don't know where . . . I have no idea what I did with it. I'm such an idiot. *Such* an idiot."

"It's fine," I tell him. "It has to be around here somewhere, right?"

We search the entire apartment in a kind of frenzied scavenger hunt, undoing—room by room—all the work we've just done to clean it up. We fish through drawers and check under his bed, tear open cabinets and toss around clothes. We dump out the garbage can in the bathroom and scan the contents of the kitchen shelves. We even sift through the trash bags stacked neatly by the door, though I'm the one who filled them and I'm certain the ticket isn't there. We just can't think of anything else to do.

Every now and then, we brush against each other as we move from room to room and I think it again: *Teddy McAvoy kissed me.* It's all I can do not to grab his hand, drag him back over to me, stand on my tiptoes, and kiss him again.

But when he tries to look for the ticket under the fridge, a different memory rushes up and I lunge at him, practically shoving him out of the way and offering to do it myself. "I have smaller hands," I explain, my face burning against the cool of the tiled floor as I feel around beneath it, coming up empty-handed.

Teddy frowns at me as I stand up again. "I'll check the shower."

"The shower?" I follow him into the bathroom. "You haven't taken one."

"I know, but it's the last place I can think to look," he says, yanking back the curtain and stepping into the tub. I can see the panic in his eyes as he stoops to pull the plug out of the drain and I put a hand on his shoulder.

"Teddy," I say. "I doubt—"

"We're talking about millions of dollars here," he says, standing up fast, his face pinched with worry. "What if I just threw it away?"

Something clicks then and I thump my head against the doorframe.

Teddy steps out of the bathtub. "What?"

"I know where it is," I say with a groan. "It's the only place we haven't looked."

"Where?"

"Get your coat."

"What?"

"Get your coat," I repeat, already walking away. "We've got some digging to do."

# Eight

Outside, we stand facing the blue dumpster. A thin layer of snow has covered the plastic bags piled on top like powdered sugar sprinkled over some kind of strange, lumpy dessert. The bin itself is filthy, slick and wet and speckled with brown spots and spills. As we stare at it, neither of us quite ready to dive in yet, there's a loud noise from above, then the sound of something banging its way down the chute. A moment later a pizza box lands on top with a thud.

Teddy takes a step closer. "Wrong bin, you idiot," he calls up, cupping his hands around his mouth, then he shrugs at me. "That's clearly recyclable."

I laugh at this, then tip my head at the dumpster. "You ready?"

"Why me?"

"Because it's your ticket."

"But you bought it," he says. "And you're the one who threw it away."

"I'm the one who took the garbage out," I say, aware of how quickly, how automatically, we've already returned to our usual dynamic. "*You're* the one who threw it away. And you're the one who's gonna be rich if we find it."

He blows out a sigh, his breath frosty in the bitter air. The sky is clear and bright this morning—it stopped snowing sometime in the night—but the plows haven't yet reached the alley behind the building, where the drifts are nearly up to our knees.

Teddy wipes his nose with the sleeve of his jacket as he stares down the dumpster. "What did the bag look like?"

"It was a garbage bag. What do you think?"

"Right, but black or white, paper or plastic."

"White plastic," I say, walking over to stand on my tiptoes a few inches from the bin, where dozens of indistinguishable plastic bags poke out beneath the snow.

"Great," Teddy says as he steps up beside me, "at least it won't blend in."

"Want a hand?" I ask, but he's already thrown himself up and over the edge of the dumpster, dangling there like a monkey, his boots banging loudly against the metal side. He uses one arm to balance as he roots around, digging out two white trash bags and tossing them over the side. I scoot away just before one of them can hit me, and Teddy drops to the ground, scattering the snow.

Together we fumble with the ties, opening the bags and

56

peering inside. In the first there are broken eggshells and an apple core and some torn envelopes made out to an A. J. Lynk; we don't go further than that. The second is mostly full of shredded paper: old bills and bank statements and pieces of envelopes.

"Recycling again," Teddy says, tossing it into the next bin. He wipes his hands on his jeans and glances back at me. "What are we even looking for?"

"I don't know. I didn't pack it up or anything. It was just there last night, so I took it out. But I'm pretty sure it's the only one since the party."

He puts his hands on his hips. "Is this all just a trick to get me to jump in there?"

"What?" I let out a laugh. "No!"

"Were those really even the numbers?"

"Just get in there," I tell him, pointing at the dumpster, and he gives me a salute, then hoists himself up again. Only this time he throws one leg over the side, then the other, and with a groan, he rolls into the bin and out of sight.

For a second it's quiet. I walk over to the edge, rising onto my toes again. But it's too tall, and all I can see is the stained blue metal. This close it smells like rotten fruit and damp coffee grounds and something sour, and I wrinkle my nose. "Teddy?"

There's a faint rustling but no answer. I crane my neck, trying to get a better look, wondering if he could've hurt himself when he tumbled over. I'm about to call out to him again when an arm appears, and before I can react a snow-ball is cracked over the top of my head like an egg, clumps of ice falling from my hat into the collar of my coat.

"Gross," I say, shuddering and laughing as I wipe at my face. "Garbage snow."

"Only the best for you," Teddy says cheerfully, then disappears again.

"Hey," I say a few minutes later, rubbing my hands together as I wait for more bags. "Remember that time we got busted trying to steal lottery tickets?"

"They were just scratch-offs," he says, his voice muffled from inside the dumpster. "And you're the one who got us kicked out of the store. You have no poker face whatsoever."

"C'mon," I say. "I was nervous. It was my first heist."

"First and last. You were never very good at playing it cool. Even as a twelve-year-old."

"*Especially* as a twelve-year-old."

He tosses another bag out, and as I poke through it I think about that ill-conceived expedition. It was just after Teddy's dad left, after he'd lost all their savings and more, and Teddy had become obsessed with money. *What would you do if you had a million dollars?* he'd ask us constantly, casually, as if it was nothing more than a trivia question, an idle thought; as if he wasn't thinking about what that kind of money could mean, with his dad's debts still hanging over them and his mom working long hours at the hospital and him coming home to an empty apartment after school.

Even then it always broke my heart a little.

"So," I say, kicking at the snow. "What *would* you do if you had a million dollars?"

Teddy's head pops up and over the rim of the metal container. He squints down at me, looking uneasy. "I can't think about that yet. Not until we find the ticket."

"I remember what you always used to say. . . ."

"What?" he says, but there's a catch in his voice and it's clear he already knows the answer.

"You wanted to get your old apartment back," I say. "For your mom."

He smiles almost involuntarily, remembering the solemn vow he made to us, and for a second he looks like he's twelve years old again, dreaming about untold riches.

"That," he says, "and a pinball machine."

"I'm pretty sure there was talk of a pool table too."

"At least it was better than Leo's idea. He just wanted a puppy."

"A boxer," I remind him. "Because he thought boxing was cool. Oh, and a thousand colored pencils."

Teddy laughs at the memory. "Doesn't exactly add up to a million dollars."

"Leo has always been a man of simple tastes."

He leans an elbow on the edge of the dumpster, gazing down at me. "And you—you'd never tell us what you wanted."

He's right. I never played along the way the boys did, losing themselves to their daydreams. The things I want most in the world can't be bought with money.

Except, maybe, for one thing. Standing there in the snow,

I think about the photograph I keep on my dresser, a picture of my parents in Kenya, where they met in the Peace Corps. In it, the two of them are gazing at each other as the sun sets behind them, the savanna bathed in golden colors, a lone giraffe silhouetted in the distance.

That, I think, would be my wish. To travel there myself.

But all these years later I still can't bring myself to say it out loud.

"I always knew anyway," Teddy says, and I look up at him, surprised.

"You did?"

He nods. "It's the only logical thing. If you had a million dollars and you could buy anything in the world, I'm one hundred percent positive that you would absolutely, without a doubt choose to have your very own . . . ostrich."

It's so completely random—so utterly ridiculous—that I begin to laugh. *"What?"*

"An ostrich," he says, like this should be obvious, like *I'm* the one talking nonsense. "You know. The giant bird."

"Why in the world would you think I'd want an ostrich?"

"Because that's how well I know you," he says, deadpan. "I'm probably the only person on the planet who realizes you wouldn't be happy unless you owned an enormous flightless bird."

I shake my head, but I'm still laughing. "You're so weird."

"That's why you love me," he jokes, which sobers me right up again. My smile falls, and my face gets hot, and I have to concentrate to keep from bringing a hand to my lips, to the place where he kissed me less than an hour ago.

But Teddy doesn't notice. He just grins, clearly pleased with himself, then disappears back into the piles of trash.

After that we work in silence for a while—him throwing the bags out one at a time and me searching each one for something that might have come from the McAvoys' apartment—until finally I see it.

"Teddy!" I call, and there's a quick bang, then his head appears. I look down at an envelope with the name Katherine McAvoy on it, which had been buried beneath a mess of red plastic cups from last night's party. "I think this might be it."

"The ticket?" he asks, a little breathless as he vaults back out of the bin, sliding gracelessly down the side and slipping on the snow as he lands.

"No, just the bag," I say, handing him the envelope. "Should we take it inside?"

He looks torn and I understand. Part of me wants to rip it open right now, to dump it all out and begin the frantic search in spite of the cold and the damp and the wind. But there's another part of me that understands what might be about to happen—that our whole world could very well be cracked wide open—and I'm not sure I'm quite ready for that yet.

Teddy is breathing into his hands and stamping his feet, waiting for me to tell him what comes next. I meet his eyes from beneath my woolen hat, and when he looks back at me I feel suddenly numb.

"Inside," I say, and so we go.

# Nine

We sit across from each other on the kitchen floor. Our cheeks are still pink from being outside and our fingers are still stiff with cold, but we've shed our boots and coats and now face each other solemnly, the garbage bag between us: a strange and unlikely arbiter of our fate.

Teddy nods at me. "You look."

"You stink more," I point out, nudging the bag in his direction.

He rips open the top, then stands up. "Okay," he says, dumping the contents onto the floor just as I scramble to my feet, narrowly avoiding the landslide. "Here we go."

We stare at the pile of dirty napkins and empty bags of chips and soggy slices of pizza, which go skidding onto the recently spotless floor. Teddy is the first to dig in, squatting like a kid playing at the beach as he sifts through the papers. I kick aside a tangle of stained napkins and poke at the pile with my toe.

In the living room the TV is still on, and I can hear the tinny laughter of a sitcom. Outside, the voices of a few kids rise up through the steam-covered windows as they tussle in the snow. But I'm suddenly aware of how quiet it is in the kitchen: just me and Teddy and the hum of the refrigerator, which is still steadfastly guarding my note to him.

Looking again at the pile of trash, I'm struck by the urge to reach out and grab his hand, to stop him before he can find that little slip of paper that will change everything.

Because how many times can one life be split into a before and an after?

*It was just a joke,* I want to tell him. *None of this was supposed to happen.*

But I can't bring myself to squash his excitement. It wouldn't just be money to Teddy; it would be safety and security, possibility and promise. With one little ticket, his life could become completely unrecognizable.

All because of me.

No matter what he said last night, I know that in some ways Teddy understands me better than Leo ever could. Leo has two loving parents and a house with enough beds for an extra kid. They take vacations and go to nice dinners and buy new clothes without thinking about what they might have to give up because of it. They're kind and generous, my aunt and uncle, and I'm unbelievably grateful to have landed there.

But it makes Leo different from me. He's one of the lucky

ones. He still lives in a world where the ground beneath his feet is solid.

Teddy and I, on the other hand, have grown up in quicksand. And though we're there for different reasons, and though we rarely talk about it, something about that simple fact has always bound us together.

So now I watch him search for his ticket to the other side with a terrible, mounting dread, which comes from the darkest, most selfish corners of my heart. But I can't help it. Already it feels like a kind of loss.

Because just now he looks like he's about to turn into someone else entirely.

He looks like someone whose ship is about to come in.

He looks like the luckiest person in the world.

Suddenly he goes very still, everything about him frozen for a few beats, before looking up at me. I don't have to ask. The moment our eyes meet, I know.

For a long time neither of us says anything. Then he picks up the ticket—carefully, gingerly, as if it might break—and sits back, staring at it with wide, disbelieving eyes.

I clear my throat once, then again, but I can think of nothing to say. It's too big, what's happening, too staggering. I can't seem to find the words to fit.

Teddy lowers the ticket, looking at me in shock.

And then—without warning—he begins to laugh. It's quiet at first, but then his shoulders start to shake, and as it rises in volume I feel myself start to give in to it too. Because it's hilarious all of a sudden, this crazy, improbable, ridiculous stroke of luck that's been set down smack in the middle of our utterly ordinary lives. And because the two of us are crouched here on the floor, panning for gold in a river of trash.

And, most of all, because we've found it.

Teddy is tipped over on his side now, clutching his stomach with one hand and the ticket in the other, and I lean back against the cabinets, breathless and giddy, the sound of our laughter filling the tiny space, echoing off the walls and cupboards, making everything warmer and brighter.

When he sits up again there are tears in his eyes, and he wipes at them as he takes a few gulping breaths. I shake my head, still grinning, but my smile fades as I see him pause, staring down at the ticket resting in his flattened palm.

"So," he says, looking up at me, his face suddenly solemn. "What now?"

# Part Two

FEBRUARY

# Ten

The lottery websites are all very clear about what to do first. Without exception, each and every one of them suggests calling a lawyer.

Instead we decide to call Leo.

"Hey," Teddy says into the phone, looking like he's trying very hard not to laugh, the news bubbling up inside him, threatening to boil over at any moment. I'm sitting beside him on one of the barstools at the kitchen counter, so close that our knees are touching, which makes it hard to concentrate on anything else. At least for me. Teddy is clearly too distracted to notice. He winks at me as he presses the phone closer to his ear. "Yeah, so . . . you have to get back here, okay? We need your help with something."

There's a long pause, which is no doubt Leo grumbling that he's only just gotten home.

"Something happened," Teddy says finally, then shakes his head. "No, nothing like that. It's just—no, it's something good. I swear. Yeah, she's here. She's fine. No, listen. Can you please just—"

He lowers the phone, setting it on the counter between us, then punches the speaker button so that Leo's voice crackles out into the kitchen.

". . . and do you have any idea how cold it is?" he's saying. "It's like the Arctic out there. And the roads are a mess. Plus, I've got a bunch of stuff to do, and I can't do any of it until I find my old glasses."

"Dude," Teddy says, leaning forward. He has an odd smile on his face, one that I've never seen before: it's strangely serene and kind of punch-drunk at the same time. His eyes are on the cookie jar that's sitting on the counter between us. It's ceramic and blue and shaped like a very portly hippo, and to get inside you have to decapitate the poor creature. I reach out and pull it over to me; then, for what feels like the thousandth time in the past few minutes, I peek inside.

The ticket is there at the bottom, alongside a few dark crumbs from the Oreos we had to dump out (and then, of course, eat) to make room for it. All the articles online instructed the winner to sign the back of the ticket. So after checking and double-checking the numbers, Teddy scrawled his name there, then dropped it inside. Afterward I placed the lid on firmly, keeping my hand pressed against the hippo's head as if I'd just bottled a genie or some other kind of strange and unknown magic. Which in a way I suppose I had.

"Just trust me," Teddy is saying to Leo, who has gone silent on the other end of the phone. "You *want* to come over."

"Can't you just tell me now?" Leo asks wearily. "It's gonna take me forever to get back there."

"Leo," I say, leaning forward. "Just come, okay?"

He hesitates, and I know then that he will. "Yeah?"

"Yeah," I say, and Teddy flashes me a grateful smile.

"Okay," Leo finally says with a sigh. "Then I guess I'll just . . . I'll be there as soon as I can. But you owe me."

Teddy laughs. "I'll give you a million dollars."

"How about brunch?" Leo suggests. "I'm starving."

"We'll meet you at the Lantern," Teddy says, then hangs up and turns to me. "Will you babysit while I get dressed?"

It takes me a second to understand that he's talking about the cookie jar.

"Sure," I say, thinking it's a bit early for him to start acting paranoid about his newfound fortune. But when he returns a few minutes later in jeans and a striped sweater, his hair damp where he combed it flat, it turns out I'm reluctant to let the jar out of my sight too.

"Changing of the guard," I joke as I stand up, sliding it back in his direction.

I realize the likelihood of anything happening to it during the six minutes it takes to brush my teeth and change back into yesterday's clothes is very small. But still, that ticket is essentially a hundred-and-forty-million-dollar bill, and that seems like an awful lot of pressure to put on such a little piece of paper, especially since Teddy has a tendency

71

to lose things. So when I walk back out to find him scrolling through his phone with one hand, the other resting on the hippo's head, I'm a tiny bit relieved.

"It says we're supposed to call a tax guy too," he says without looking up. "And a financial adviser."

"Who says that?"

"I don't know." He shrugs. "The Internet."

"Are you sure you don't want to call your mom?"

He raises his eyes to meet mine. "I sort of do, but I think I need a minute to process all this first. Plus, I'd rather do it in person. Can you imagine the look on her face when I tell her?"

I smile, thinking of Teddy's expression when he held up the ticket not so long ago. "I can, actually."

"She'll be home in a couple hours anyway. Let's just go meet Leo and figure out what the hell we should be doing next." He stands, looking dazed, then grabs the cookie jar and tucks it under his arm. "You ready?"

I stare at him. "You're not bringing that to the diner."

"The ticket?"

"No, the cookie jar."

Teddy studies it as if he isn't quite sure how it came to be resting in the crook of his elbow. "Well, what else should we do with it?"

"I don't know, but I think that looks a little suspicious."

He tilts his head at me. "You think someone's gonna see me with a cookie jar and assume there's a winning lottery ticket in there?"

"I don't think it's entirely out of the question," I say, trying to keep a straight face.

He lifts the lid and reaches inside for the ticket, which he holds carefully between two fingers. It seems impossibly flimsy and extraordinarily fragile. "So what do you propose we do with it, then?"

"Your wallet?"

"I don't know. The Velcro is kind of worn out, and—"

"I think the bigger problem," I say, laughing, "is that your wallet has Velcro at all."

"Not the point."

"Okay," I say, eyeing the ticket. "Maybe we should leave it here."

"Well, what if there's a break-in?"

"What are the odds that after living here for six years, the very first break-in happens this morning?"

Teddy gives me a look. "What were the odds of us winning the lottery?"

"Good point," I say, walking over to the drawer beneath the microwave and pulling out a plastic sandwich bag. I take the ticket from him and slip it carefully inside. "Here. This'll keep it safe from the snow."

"We can't just carry it like that," he says, alarmed. "Everyone can see it."

"I'll keep it in my bag."

He looks warily at the black canvas messenger bag that's sitting on the coffee table. "Is there, like, a pocket or something?"

"With a zipper and everything."

"Okay," he says as we grab our coats from the hooks near the door. "But you know this means I can't let you out of my sight."

I smile as I step into my rubber boots.

"I mean it," Teddy says. "I'm gonna be your shadow. You couldn't lose me if you tried."

"Believe me," I tease him, "I've tried."

When he bumps me with his elbow, my heart gives a little hiccup. I shove him right back and he sidesteps away from me, laughing. It all feels so normal between us, like the kiss was some sort of distant dream, and I'm not sure whether to be relieved or disappointed by this.

Once we're ready, and the plastic-clad ticket is zipped securely into my bag, Teddy reaches for the doorknob. But just before opening it, he pauses and turns back to face me. His mouth is twisted up to one side, like he's trying to hold back a smile.

"Hey, Al?"

"Yeah?"

"We just won the freaking lottery," he says, his voice filled with awe, and I laugh, because it's ridiculous and incredible and true. Somehow I picked not just one or two or even three of the numbers, but all of them. The odds of that happening have to be astronomical. Yet here we are.

Teddy's watching me, his eyes shining, and I grin back at him.

"*You* just won the freaking lottery."

He puts a hand on the doorknob then lets it slip off. "Al?"

"Yeah?"

"Thanks," he says, turning to fold me into a hug, and there's something about it—the wonder in his voice or the thud of his heartbeat through his jacket or the way his chin rests against the top of my head—that causes a lump to rise in my throat.

Outside, the sun is bright against the hard-packed snow, the world blinding and full of glitter. The sidewalks aren't plowed yet, but a set of deep footprints forms a path up the street toward the Lantern, our favorite diner, and I walk ahead of Teddy, one mittened hand clutching the strap of my bag.

As we make our way through the snow I look around, trying to decide if the world seems different this morning. There are people shoveling their walks, and kids running by with plastic sleds, and dogs bounding through the mountainlike drifts made by the plows. It's the first day of February, the morning after a snowstorm, a Saturday in Chicago like any other.

Except for the ticket that's burning like a coal deep in the pocket of my bag.

Behind me I can hear the crunch of Teddy's boots and the ragged sound of his breathing. "Next time," he says, "we'll be able to take a cab."

"It's only three blocks," I say, but he's right, of course. Next time we won't have to trudge through the snow or wait outside in the icy wind for a bus. From now on we can afford to take a taxi. Or at least Teddy can.

I know how silly it is to feel a pang of loss over this.

For starters, rich people probably don't even take cabs; they probably skip right to limos or maybe even helicopters. But even though a taxi is a pretty pitiful excuse for a lottery fantasy, it's always been a luxury for us, the kind of thing we dream about on days like this.

And it's the first small sign that things will soon be different.

As we near the Lantern, I can see Leo sitting at our favorite table by the window, his head bent over a menu. When Teddy pushes open the glass door, a familiar bell rings out and we're greeted by a burst of warmth and the sweet smell of waffles.

Together we walk toward the table, and when we're both standing over it Leo lowers his menu, squinting up at us through an old pair of glasses.

"This better be good," he says, and Teddy smiles.

# Eleven

Once the whole story comes out, Leo simply stares at us.

"Why in the *world*," he says finally, "are you telling *me*?"

Teddy blinks at him in confusion. "Uh, 'cause you're my best friend, and I just figured—"

"No," Leo says, lowering his voice like a shifty character from a heist movie. "I mean, why aren't you talking to a lawyer or something right now?"

"Oh," Teddy says. "Because I figured you'd know what to do."

After that Leo doesn't even let us order. Instead he marches us straight out of the diner.

"Sorry," Teddy calls to the baffled waitress as we abandon our table. "I promise I'll leave a really big tip next time."

She just rolls her eyes, which is fair enough, considering

he usually leaves her a pile of lint-covered coins. But it makes him laugh all the same.

Back at the apartment we kick off our boots and shed our coats, then sit three in a row on the couch, staring at the plastic bag with the ticket while we wait for Teddy's mom and Leo's parents—whom they called on the snowy walk back from the diner—to come over and take charge. Katherine McAvoy was just finishing up her extra shift at the hospital, and Aunt Sofia and Uncle Jake promised to be there as soon as they dug out the car. None of them have a clue why they're being summoned, since Teddy is determined to deliver the news in person.

As we wait for them, it occurs to me for the first time that between the three of us, we have exactly half the usual number of assigned adults. Three parents. Three kids. Two patched-together versions of a family.

Leo is the one to keep breaking the silence. "This is bonkers," he repeats every so often, looking at the ticket in awe. "Totally bonkers."

"I know," Teddy says, a little wild-eyed.

"Bonkers," I agree, still slightly numb.

"You won the *lottery*," Leo says to Teddy, as if this fact might've slipped his mind. He drops his head into his hands, mussing up his dark hair, then turns to me. "And you bought the ticket. This has to be the craziest thing that's ever happened. Ever."

By the time Katherine McAvoy shows up, we're all wired too tight. Teddy is pacing, I'm making coffee, and Leo is on his phone, looking up what happens when you win the lottery. As soon as we hear a sound at the door, we all freeze. And then Katherine appears, still wearing her green scrubs, her short blond hair falling over her eyes as she fumbles with the keys, bleary after working back-to-back shifts.

She stops short when she sees us all staring at her.

"Hi," she says, drawing out the word in a way that suggests our efforts to look normal have failed. She arches an eyebrow. "What's up, guys?"

Teddy takes a step forward. He looks like a little kid trying to wrestle with a big secret, his face practically glowing with the news. "Hi, Mom," he says, leaning one arm on the couch in a futile attempt to seem casual. "We've, uh, got something to tell you, actually."

From where she's still standing by the door, I can see Katherine stiffen; it's clear from the set of her jaw that she's steeling herself. But Teddy sees this too, and he immediately shakes his head.

"No, it's okay," he says, hurrying over. He grabs her hand and half-drags her to the green armchair beside the couch. She's still wearing her coat, and when she sits down it puffs up all around her so that she has to stuff it back down. "It's a good thing, I promise."

"Teddy," she says wearily. "It's been a long night."

"I know, but believe me, you're gonna want to hear this. Listen, do you remember that time we tried to steal—actually, never mind. Remember how you used to tell me never to—"

"Teddy," I say, setting down my coffee mug. "Just tell her."

79

"Yes," Katherine says. "Please. Just tell me."

Leo picks up the plastic bag with the ticket inside, holding it out to Teddy. He takes it carefully between two fingers, then hands it to his mom with a look of pride.

"Here," he says, unable to contain a smile now, and Katherine frowns at it for a few seconds, uncomprehending, before a flicker of annoyance crosses her face.

"You know," she says finally, "the lottery isn't any better than gambling, right?"

"Mom," Teddy says with a groan. "Relax. It's not the same thing at all."

But Katherine sits forward, newly energized. "Of course it is," she tells him. "It's just a socially acceptable form of it. It's a bunch of people who can't really afford to be playing just throwing their money into a game where the odds are—"

"Alice is the one who gave it to me," Teddy says, pointing in my direction, and Leo bursts out laughing.

"We all know Alice is a terrible influence," he says, and I roll my eyes at him.

"It was for his birthday," I explain to Katherine, walking over to join them in the living room. "It was just a joke. You know, for turning eighteen." I almost add that Leo got him cigarettes but decide that's beside the point right now.

"It doesn't matter anyway," Teddy says, stooping in front of the armchair so that he's eye level with his mom. "This has nothing to do with Dad. This is about us. It's about, well . . ." He lets out a sudden laugh. "The thing is . . . we won."

She stares him. "Won . . . ?"

"The lottery. We won the lottery.

"Like . . ."

"Like we hit the jackpot. The big one."

Her eyes are wide now. "How big?"

"It's 141.3 million dollars," Leo says, glancing down to check this on his phone. "Would've been more if there hadn't been two other winners. But that should still be about fifty-three million after taxes. Or 2.8 million a year if you go for the annuity. Though who wants an annuity? You can't take over the world on an allowance, right?"

Nobody is paying attention to him. Katherine is still staring at Teddy, her face now a grayish color. She looks utterly gobsmacked, which is almost as weird a sight as anything else that's happened today.

"You're serious," she says, but it isn't a question.

He nods. "I am."

"This isn't a joke? Because I'm exhausted, and if this is one of your—"

"Mom," he says, putting a hand over hers. "This isn't a joke. I swear. We won the lottery. Alice picked the winning numbers. She won us *millions*."

It's strange to watch it happen, to see her face move from wariness to incredulity to shock, then finally slip into something I haven't seen from her in a long time: joy.

"Millions?" she repeats, shaking her head, and Leo passes over his phone, where the numbers from the lottery website match the ones on the ticket in her hand. Katherine opens her mouth as if to say something more, then seems to change her mind; instead she stands up, moving straight past Teddy and over to me. She's a few inches shorter than I am, but she grips my shoulders so that I have to bend a little, and there's something steady in her eyes, something almost fierce in the way she's looking at me.

"Alice," she whispers. *"Thank you."*

"It was nothing," I say automatically, because this is the truth. It was five minutes in a convenience store. It was as easy as picking up a pack of gum or a tube of toothpaste. It was a gag gift, a token, an afterthought. It was just a birthday present, and a pretty lame one at that.

But still she folds me into a hug so tight it's almost hard to breathe.

"It was everything," she says.

# Twelve

When the intercom buzzes, Leo hurries over to answer the door.

"Password is 'jackpot,'" he says into the speaker, and there's a pause—filled by a crackle of static—before Aunt Sofia's voice emerges.

"Leo?"

"Hi, Mom," he says, punching the button. "Come on up."

Teddy turns to Katherine, who is still looking kind of dazed. "We thought we might need a lawyer," he explains. "So we asked Sofia to come over."

"And Uncle Jake," I add with a grin. "Just in case we needed an office-supply salesman. You never know."

Katherine laughs. "Stranger things have happened today."

While they climb the stairs, Leo and I stand waiting near

the open door of the apartment. "No rush," he shouts when we hear their footsteps. "Take your time."

"Hey," Uncle Jake calls back. "We're not all eighteen here, okay?"

At the top he slumps against the banister in mock exhaustion, mopping his forehead with the sleeve of his flannel shirt. "Okay, I'm here," he says with a grin I still think of as my dad's, even after all these years. The similarities between them are startling: the reddish hair, the round blue eyes, the same booming laugh. Uncle Jake was older by a few years, and it flattens me still on each of his birthdays, knowing my dad will never reach that same age.

"I've now climbed approximately six million stairs," he says. "And I'm missing the Bulls game. And I had to drive three miles through ice and snow with the biggest scaredy-cat on the planet. So if you guys want to fill us in at any point, that would be fantastic."

"I heard that," Aunt Sofia says, finally making it up too. She walks straight over to Leo and me, pulling us both into a hug. I can almost feel the relief radiating off her. "You two could be a little more selective with your use of the word *emergency*."

"I told you everything was okay," Leo says, holding up his phone as proof, but Aunt Sofia only shakes her head. She's wearing jeans and an oversized Northwestern sweatshirt, her long dark hair pulled back into a low ponytail so that she looks much younger than usual, her face still full of worry.

"Well, a bit more information would've been nice,"

she says, but the sternness is melting away now that she's clapped eyes on us. "It still would."

"Sorry," I begin, ready to explain, but then Teddy pokes his head out the door.

"Actually it's my fault," he says, smiling broadly at them. "Turns out I could use some legal advice."

"It was only a matter of time," Uncle Jake stage-whispers to me, and I laugh, because he's not totally wrong. But suddenly I can't wait for them to hear the real reason that they're here, the incredible, impossible news.

Aunt Sofia is frowning at Teddy. "What happened?"

"Let's talk inside," he says, ushering us in and closing the door.

As soon as Katherine sees my aunt, she pulls her into a hug. Then she gives my uncle a quick kiss on the cheek and offers them a cup of coffee, her hands shaking. By the time we're all settled in the living room, Teddy is practically bursting to tell them the story. The rest of us have arranged ourselves on the couch or pulled over chairs, but he's still standing in front of the coffee table, ready to hold court.

"So what's going on?" Aunt Sofia asks. "How can I help?"

Teddy rubs at his jaw, trying to look serious. "Well, like I said, a situation has come up, and I could really use some legal advice, and I know you're a great lawyer—"

"An environmental lawyer," she reminds him. "So unless you spotted a polar bear in need this morning, I might not be of much use."

"I know," Teddy says, nodding. "But I figured you could

help us with all the legal jargon, and maybe you'd know someone at your firm who could—"

Aunt Sofia is starting to look anxious again. "What exactly happened?"

"Don't worry," I tell her. "I promise we didn't rob a bank or anything."

Leo snorts. "Might as well have."

"Seriously," Uncle Jake says with a hint of impatience. "What's going on?"

"I don't know if you saw the news about the big lottery drawing this morning," Teddy says, beaming at them. "But, well . . . I won."

Uncle Jake stares at him. "You won?"

"The lottery?" Aunt Sofia asks, dumbfounded.

I can't help laughing, because this is now the third time we've had this conversation, and it's gone exactly the same way each time.

"He won *millions*," I say. "Like, millions and millions." I pause. "And millions."

"All because of Alice." Teddy smiles at me, and the way he says my name—my real name—sends a jolt through me. "She picked the numbers."

My uncle looks over at me with wonder. "Well, nice going there, kid," he says, then turns to wink at Katherine. "I taught her everything she knows."

"Wow," Aunt Sofia says, still absorbing this information. She stands abruptly, then crosses the room to hug him. "Teddy, that's amazing. Congratulations."

"We're so happy for you," Uncle Jake says, popping up

as well. He gives Teddy one of those handshakes that turn into a shoulder bump that turn into a hug. "Couldn't have happened to a better guy."

"And we're here to help however we can," Aunt Sofia says, looking at Katherine now. "Whatever you need. Lawyers, financial planners, anything. Just let us know."

Katherine has been listening to all this with a thoughtful expression, but now she sits forward. "You're eighteen now," she says to Teddy, who grins at this; with all the excitement, his birthday party feels like a long time ago. "And that means the decisions are all yours to make. But I just hope—"

"Mom," Teddy says, laughing. "This *just* happened. No lectures yet, okay?"

"I'm just saying that money comes and goes," she continues, and it's obvious she's thinking about his dad. "I know you'll want to have some fun with it, and you should. But I hope you'll be responsible too."

He nods impatiently. "I will."

"And I think the first thing we should do," she says, "is set aside some money for college."

Teddy hesitates, and I sit up straighter, watching him carefully. He's always dismissed the idea of going straight to college, and while I've been hoping he might change his mind, I also understand his reasoning. He's spent so many years watching his mom try to get out from under his dad's debts that the last thing he wants is to take out a loan. But as soon as Katherine says it, I realize she's right: this is his chance.

"Mom," Teddy says, shaking his head, "you know my plan is to—"

"I know," Katherine says, her voice sharp. "Work for a year or two, then apply to community college. But I'm worried you'll end up spending the rest of your life as an assistant manager—"

"Associate manager," Teddy says, looking embarrassed to be making the distinction. He's spent the last three summers working at a nearby sporting goods store, and they've promised him the promotion after graduation.

"But that's just it," she says, leaning forward. "It doesn't matter anymore. You have the money for a real college now. One with a great coaching program. And you don't have to wait."

"I'm not sure if . . . ," Teddy begins, then trails off. "My grades might not even be good enough to . . . I mean, this only just happened, so I haven't really thought about . . ."

"It's okay," Katherine says, relenting. "We can talk about it more later. But a college fund is definitely going to be our first priority." She pauses and her gaze shifts to me. "And I think we should arrange one for Alice too."

There's a brief silence where I feel my face go prickly.

"What?" I say, blinking at her. "No, you don't need to—"

"Alice," Katherine says with a smile. "You're the one who bought the ticket. This is all because of you."

Across the room Teddy has gone stock-still. He's staring at me, his arms limp at his sides, his face ashen. The triumphant look he's been wearing all afternoon has disappeared entirely. "I can't believe I didn't . . . ," he begins, then stops and shakes his head. "I feel awful. It's just that today's been such a whirlwind, and I wasn't thinking. . . ."

"It's fine," I say quickly. "Really."

He walks over and sits on the coffee table across from me so that his knees bump up against mine. His face is very serious. "You bought the ticket," he says in a low voice. "And you picked those numbers. I'm so sorry. I should've thought of this right away."

His brown eyes are focused on me with unnerving intensity, and he takes a deep breath, then sticks out a hand. I stare at it for a moment. There's something strangely formal about the gesture, and I think again of our kiss this morning, the way his arms closed around me so tightly, the way we fit together so perfectly.

"Half of it's yours," he says, his hand still outstretched, and I hear my aunt breathe in sharply. Beside me on the couch Leo tenses. "It's only fair."

"Teddy . . . ," I say, though I'm not sure how to finish that.

His arm sags a little, but he's speaking fast now, the way he does when he's excited about something. "You're the one with the lucky numbers. You're the one who made this all happen."

"It was just—"

"It was all you," he says, pushing ahead. "So you should be part of this. How about it? You and me?" He smiles crookedly. "Just a couple of millionaires?"

Numbly, I shake my head, my eyes still on his open palm. "I can't," I say quietly. "It was a gift."

"What?" he says, standing up fast, and when I look up at him his face has hardened slightly. "You can't just pass this up, Al. It's a once-in-a-lifetime thing."

The others are all watching us; I can feel it. But it might as well just be me and Teddy in the room, our eyes locked and our jaws set.

"Teddy," I say. "Really. The ticket is yours. So are the winnings. Thank you for offering, but—"

He frowns. "Thank you for offering? It's not a stick of gum, Al."

"I know that."

"Then what's the problem?"

"There's not a problem," I say, lifting my chin, trying to seem calm in spite of the panic that's starting to bloom inside me. "I just don't want it. I'm sorry."

"Don't be *sorry*," he says with a scowl. "I mean, you're the one who'll be missing out. Who turns down twenty million dollars?"

"Actually, it'll probably be more like 26.5 if you take the payout," Leo interrupts, and we both turn to glare at him. He holds up his hands. "Just saying."

I rub my eyes, suddenly tired. "Can we please just drop it?"

"No," Teddy says, "because you deserve it at least as much as me, and I don't think it's so crazy that I'd want to—"

"Teddy," I say, cutting him off. He stops short, and I take a deep breath. "It's not crazy. And it's so generous. But I don't need it."

He stares at me. "What? Why not?"

"My parents," I begin, but my mouth is suddenly chalky. "My parents . . ."

"Her parents had a life insurance policy," my aunt says, and I glance over at her gratefully. Her gaze is fixed on me, her eyes full of warmth. "Most of it will go to college, but there'll be a little left over for when she turns twenty-one."

Teddy lowers his eyes, and for a second I think it's over. But then he looks up at me again. "I'm glad they took care of you," he says, and in spite of my frustration I feel a surge of affection for him. "But it's not the same as what I'm trying to do. Don't you want a safety net? After everything that's happened to you? Don't you want to know you'll be taken care of for the rest of your life? No matter what?"

I blink at him, suddenly less certain. For a second, I'm almost tempted to give in, to say yes, to agree to whatever he wants. But something holds me back.

"I can't," I say, and his frown deepens.

"What your parents left for you," he says, clearly anxious to be understood, "that's great. But it's just . . . it's a pile of snow. I'm offering you a whole iceberg."

"Teddy," I say wearily, but he's still not finished.

"I don't get it. I don't get *you*. After all the awful things that have happened to you, this is something good. Something *incredible*. And you don't want any part of it?"

My eyes are burning now, and the room feels much too small. I shake my head, unable to look at him, desperate for this conversation to be over.

"We're talking about millions of dollars here," he says, as if I'm not quite grasping the scope of it. "You'd never have to worry about anything again. It's the kind of money that would change everything. *Everything*."

These last words rattle me. I close my eyes and take a deep breath and wonder if everyone can hear the sound of my heartbeat. I try to swallow the sob that's in my throat, but when I open my mouth my voice comes out watery and muddled, heavy with the threat of tears: "Teddy, please," I say. "Don't."

His eyes widen slightly, but his face doesn't change; he still looks wholly uncomprehending. There's a long silence, then Aunt Sofia clears her throat.

"Okay," she says with a note of finality. "I think maybe that's enough."

When I look up, they're all watching me—she and Uncle Jake and Leo and Katherine—with slightly stunned expressions. The room is quiet.

"That's really kind of you, Teddy," Aunt Sofia says, looking around. "But there's a lot of other stuff we need to talk about too, so maybe we should move on for now."

Teddy grunts, retreating to a chair on the other side of the room, where he folds his arms across his chest with a look of frustration. Nobody else moves.

After some time passes, Uncle Jake sits up. "Food," he says, so suddenly that Leo jumps a little. "I think we need some food, right? Anyone else getting hungry? Maybe Alice and Leo could go grab a couple of pizzas. . . ."

"Sure," Leo says, glancing sideways at me. "That sounds great."

Uncle Jake starts to dig for his wallet, but Teddy beats him to it. "I've got it," he says, walking over to the kitchen; he pulls a few bills from the drawer where they always keep a small amount of cash for emergencies. As he leans over to hand it to Leo, he avoids my eyes. "Gotta spend all this money somehow."

# Thirteen

It only takes two blocks for Leo to say it.

"What were you *thinking*?" he asks, his eyes wide beneath his red woolen cap. "How could you turn down twenty-six million dollars just like that?"

He snaps his fingers and I wince.

I don't have an answer for him. The enormity of what happened is just beginning to settle over me. My response was quick and automatic, a purely knee-jerk reaction. It's only now dawning on me that I just politely declined a literal fortune.

"I don't know," I say as I breathe into my hands. "I guess I didn't expect him to spring that on me—"

Leo raises an eyebrow. "Come on," he says. "You guys found the ticket, like, five hours ago. It must've crossed your mind that he'd offer you some of it."

"It didn't," I say truthfully. "It's his ticket. Not mine."

"Yeah, but you bought it."

"As a gift," I say, exasperated. "Why does nobody get that?"

"Because," Leo says, looking at me with amusement, "I don't think anyone else would ever think that way."

"What do you mean?"

He shrugs. "Most people would be dreaming of all the things they could buy or thinking about how awful the economy is or how they wouldn't have to worry so much about getting a job one day. Most people would be busy looking out for themselves."

"And you think I should be too," I say flatly. "Since I have nobody *but* myself."

He turns to me, brow furrowed. "What? No. That's not what I meant at all."

"It's what Teddy was trying to say too. That I need a safety net." I keep my eyes straight ahead as I say this, unable to look at him. "Because I'm on my own."

"That's not true," Leo says, and though he means it to sound comforting, there's a hint of annoyance in his voice. "You have me. And my parents. You know that."

"But it's not the same as it is for you. I'm eighteen now, which means they're not technically responsible for me anymore." I can tell he's about to interrupt me, so I hurry on. "I know they'll always be there if I need them—I do. But it still makes me an island."

Leo comes to a stop, turning to face me. "That's what you think?"

95

I shift from one foot to the other. We're standing in an inch of slush and I can feel my toes growing cold even in my rubber boots.

"You're not alone." He looks wounded. "You have us. Forever."

*Forever,* I think, closing my eyes for a second.

It seems like such a brittle promise.

"You've been here nine years," he says. "That's, like, thousands of family dinners. But you still think of San Francisco as home. It's not that you're actually an island, Alice. It's just that you still act like one. And nobody can change that but you."

I dip my chin, staring down at my boots, then blow out a puff of frozen air. The words have a sting to them, and I realize that's because they're true.

"I know," I say in a small voice, and Leo gives me an officious nod, like this is all he wanted to hear. Then he begins to walk again, picking his way around the puddles.

"Besides," he says over his shoulder, "if anything, you're more of a peninsula."

"Like Florida?" I ask, which makes him laugh.

"Something like that."

We walk in silence for another block, our heads bent against the wind, and when we pause at an intersection I glance over at him. "Teddy wasn't totally wrong," I admit. "If I was smart, I probably would've taken the money. But it doesn't feel like mine to take."

"Yeah, but—"

"The ticket belongs to him," I say. "Which means the money belongs to him. That's all there is to it."

"Right, but—"

"Leo," I say with a sigh. "It was the right thing to do, okay?"

He gives me a look I know well. The one that suggests I'm not telling him everything. When the light turns green, we make our way across the icy crosswalk. Leo's jaw is set and his hands are shoved into his pockets, and even though it might look for all the world like he's lost in thought or simply ignoring me, I can tell he's really just biding his time, waiting for me to admit the true reason.

"Fine," I say eventually. "Maybe I'm a little afraid of it too."

"Why?"

"Because," I say with a shrug, "you heard what Teddy said. It's the kind of money that could change everything."

"Ah," he says, a look of understanding passing over his face.

"Everything in my life has already changed once before," I tell him, trying to sound matter-of-fact. "And I don't really have any interest in that happening again."

This time when Leo stops and turns to me, his brown eyes are clear and bright. "I get it," he says. "Your parents died, and your life got turned upside down, and now all you want is for things to be normal."

I blink at him. "I guess."

"And you got a bunch of money out of it too," he

continues. "Which you'd trade in a heartbeat for more time with them. Right?"

"Right," I say cautiously, not sure where this is going.

"So now the last thing you'd ever want is *more* money," he says, like he's just solved some sort of mystery. "Especially a *lot* more money."

"Leo," I say with a frown. "Stop trying to psychoanalyze me."

He laughs. "I'm just trying to figure out where you're coming from," he says as we start to walk again. "I do get it. At least somewhat. But I still think you're nuts for turning down the money."

I shrug. "Maybe I am. But it just feels like . . . I don't know. It's almost too much, isn't it? I mean, I'm so happy for Teddy, and for Katherine, because I know they really need it. But if you had the choice, would you honestly want millions and millions of dollars, just like that, out of nowhere?"

"*Yes,*" Leo says, so emphatically that we both laugh. "I think if you asked a hundred people that question, they'd all say the same thing. They'd also fully expect to split the ticket, by the way. Which would be totally fair."

"Isn't it enough just to be excited for Teddy?"

"Maybe," he says, softening. "But the universe owes you the same way it does him. Probably a lot more."

I shake my head. "That's not how it works."

"You only think that," he says, watching me intently, "because you've never had any faith in the world. Which makes sense, since it's let you down in some really horrible ways. But what if this money was supposed to make it up to you? What if it was supposed to balance things out?"

"Leo," I say, frustrated again. "Come on. You know there's not enough money in the world for that. And besides, not everything happens for a reason. There's no grand plan here. All I did was buy a ticket. And it wasn't even for me. The whole thing was a complete coincidence."

"Right," he says insistently, "but it happened. So now you'd be crazy to miss out, especially just because you're being stubborn."

"I'm not being stubborn."

He grins. "She says stubbornly."

"Leo," I say with a groan. "Enough."

"Fine," he says, holding up his hands. "If this is what you really want . . . then I guess I can live with it."

"Thanks," I say, shaking my head as the pizza place comes into sight, the awning weighed down by snow and the window foggy with steam. "That's really big of you."

"It would've been fun, though, you know?" he says as he hops up the steps to the entrance. "All those piles of money. Caribbean vacations on private jets. Skyboxes at Wrigley Field. Fancy cars. A stupidly big yacht. Our very own camel."

I laugh, thinking about Teddy's theory that I'd want an ostrich.

"I feel like that's a thing, right?" Leo says. "Rich people all have weird pets."

"Uncle Jake won't even let you get a dog."

He shrugs as he pulls open the door. "That's because he's

allergic. I'm sure he'd be thrilled with a camel. It'd save him from having to mow the lawn."

Leo stands there waiting for me to walk inside, but I've stopped short, suddenly deep in thought. Because the minute I said Uncle Jake's name, the realization came crashing over me: that less than an hour ago I was offered millions of dollars, and in my rush to turn it down, I somehow forgot to consider the two people who had welcomed me into their home all those years ago with no expectations whatsoever.

Leo is frowning at me. "Are you coming?"

From inside the restaurant there's a blast of warm air and the scent of garlic. But I hesitate, suddenly panicky. "Actually, I'm gonna run next door and get some gum."

He shrugs. "Sure."

"Want anything?"

"Yeah," he says, cracking a smile. "How about a lottery ticket?"

I give him a withering look. "Funny."

But as I walk to the convenience store at the end of the block, my stomach is churning. I try to remember what Aunt Sofia's face looked like after I refused the money, whether Uncle Jake seemed angry with me. After nine whole years of supporting me, of breakfasts and lunches and dinners, beach vacations and summer camp, ski trips and school fees, doctor visits and phone bills, books and computers and music—all those things that make up a life, all of which come at a price—how could they not be interested in a portion of that money? And how did it not occur to me to ask them?

Leo was clearly right. If I'm an island, there's no one to blame but myself.

My aunt and uncle have always done everything they can to make me feel like part of their family. But as much as I try, it's never been easy for me to completely let them in. In my experience families are fragile things. And being part of something—really part of it—means it can be taken away. It means you have something to lose. And I've already lost way too much.

Maybe it's true that I'm more of a peninsula now—attached but apart, connected but separate—but that can be a lonely business too. And I want more than that. I want to be absorbed into their little continent. I want to stop thinking that the worst could happen if I am. I want to be more daughter than niece.

I want to belong.

But that means trying harder. It means letting them in and including them when it comes to the big stuff—like turning down tens of millions of dollars. And maybe the fact that I *didn't* is a sign. Maybe it means I'm even further adrift than I thought.

Once, not long after I arrived in Chicago, I heard Leo ask his mom if I was an orphan. They were reading Harry Potter before bed, as they did every night. Aunt Sofia had offered to start again from the beginning so that I could follow along too, but I told her I thought the books were stupid—even though the truth was that I'd already read the first three with my dad and just couldn't imagine returning to those pages without him.

"Harry's parents died," Leo was saying that night as I passed by his room on my way to brush my teeth, "and that made *him* an orphan, so . . ."

"Yes," Aunt Sofia said, her voice brisk. "But it's different, because Alice has us."

"Harry had an aunt and uncle," Leo reminded her. "But they didn't want him."

"Well, we want Alice," she said. "Very, very much."

"So she's not an orphan, then?"

There was a short pause, then Aunt Sofia cleared her throat. "Tell me this," she said. "When you think of Harry, what's the first word that comes to mind?"

Leo's answer arrived right away: "Wizard."

"Exactly. So he's an orphan *and* a wizard. Both things are true, right?"

"Right."

"Well, that's how it is for all of us. We have all sorts of words that could describe us. But we get to choose which ones are most important."

Leo paused to consider this. "So Alice could be a wizard too?"

"I suppose it's possible," Aunt Sofia said, laughing softly. "But maybe it'll be something else entirely, some other word we don't know about just yet."

"Like what?"

"That," she said, "is up to Alice."

# Fourteen

Just after third period on Monday I run into Leo at our lockers, which are side by side. "Have you seen him yet?" he asks as I pull a few books off the top shelf.

"No, but he texted earlier," I tell him. "He seemed disappointed it was mostly just paperwork. I think he was expecting a little more fanfare."

"What, like balloons and confetti?"

I laugh. "Probably."

"So does this mean it's all official?" Leo asks, keeping his voice low, though nobody around us seems particularly concerned about what we're saying.

"I think so. The ticket is claimed. The money will be here in six to eight weeks. And guess what? It turns out he's the youngest winner ever."

Leo's eyes widen behind his glasses. "Really?"

"Well, he did win, like, twelve hours after turning eighteen," I say, like it's no big deal, though the wonder of it still hasn't worn off for me either.

For the rest of the weekend, in between calls and texts from Teddy, I daydreamed about all the amazing things he could do with this money, all the doors it could open, all the people it could help. Last night he finally decided to take the lump sum, which means he'll be getting a check for a little more than fifty-three million dollars soon.

*Fifty-three million dollars.*

The population of Chicago is only 2.7 million, which means Teddy could now afford to give every single person in the city—every postal worker and firefighter and nurse, every intern and bus driver and retiree—a twenty-dollar bill. I can't remember the last time Teddy had even *one* extra twenty. And now this.

Leo shakes his head, still looking awed. "Has he started telling people yet?"

"I don't know," I say, glancing behind me down the crowded hallway, which is filled with voices and laughter, slamming lockers and loud conversations about the weekend. "It doesn't seem like it. But I'm pretty excited to see everyone's faces when he does. Can you imagine?"

"I doubt you'll have to wait long," Leo says. "He's never been much for keeping things bottled up."

The color rises in my cheeks as I think about how Teddy still hasn't mentioned our kiss the other morning. I'm starting to wonder if he's forgotten about it entirely, whether such a thing is even possible. More than anything, I wish I knew if it meant something to him, the way it did to me. So far it's been impossible to tell.

On the back of Leo's locker door, there's a black-and-white photo of him and Max from last summer, their heads bent close in laughter. I nod at it.

"Have you told Max about the big win yet?"

"I was waiting till it's official," Leo says, stooping to unzip his backpack, "which I guess it is now."

"But it's Max. I just figured you would've—"

"I know, but I didn't want to jinx anything."

"Teddy already won," I say, giving him a funny look. "You're way too superstitious."

"I'm not," he insists, but when I tilt my head at him, he shrugs. "I mean, it's not like I'm afraid of black cats and broken mirrors and the number thirteen—" He stops short when he realizes what he's said. "Sorry, I didn't—"

"It's fine," I say. "I probably shouldn't be teasing you about this when I've got my own weird superstition, right?"

He gives me a sympathetic smile. "I'd say yours is pretty justified."

I turn back to my locker, staring at the small Stanford pennant that hangs inside the door: a reminder of my mother, who bought it for me just after she'd been accepted to a graduate program there—a program she never got to attend because she died on the thirteenth day of July.

The bell rings and around us our classmates begin to scatter.

"Maybe it's not such bad luck anymore," Leo says, looking hopeful. "Not since it was one of the winning numbers."

I manage a smile as I shut my locker. "Maybe," I say, but I'm not so sure.

It isn't until sixth period that I start hearing the rumors about Teddy, which means he must be back by now. Just before the bell rings, Jack Karch taps me on the shoulder. "Were you really the one who bought the ticket?"

Before I can answer, Kate McMahon swivels around in her seat. "Is it true he's dropping out of school?"

"What?" I ask, my voice so loud that our English teacher, Mrs. Alcott, glances over with a frown as she walks into the room.

"I heard he's gonna sail around the world for a year," Kate says, more quietly now. "On a forty-foot yacht."

"Captain McAvoy," says Jack, laughing. "Now there's a scary thought."

Beside me, Ian Karczewski leans in. "I heard it's just a big prank. That all he really won was twenty bucks on a scratch-off."

They all turn to look at me, waiting for answers, hoping for gossip, and I'm relieved when Mrs. Alcott begins the class by reading the first few lines of a poem.

When the period is over I'm quick to gather my books, and as soon as I step out the door I can already feel it. There's a strange energy in the hallway, an undercurrent of excitement as the news winds its way from one person to another.

"Hey, Alice," says Mr. Tavani, my math teacher, as I hurry past him. "I hear you've got a knack for picking numbers. Must be all those calc quizzes, huh?"

I give him an awkward wave, anxious to find Teddy, but when I arrive at his locker the only one there is Leo. He's staring at a cluster of posters and balloons taped to the drab green door with a baffled expression. It's not unusual for decorations to appear there on game days, so it takes me a second to notice these are different.

"Whoa," I say, gawking at a sign that reads *We love you, Teddy!* Below that, another one says *You've always been a winner to us!* "How'd they do this so fast?"

Leo shakes his head in amazement. "They're like elves."

"Grammatically incorrect elves," I say, pointing at a sign that says *Congratulations Moneybags!* "They forgot the comma."

"I doubt there are any left in the whole city of Chicago," Leo says with a grin. "They must be using them all for Teddy's check."

I glance at my watch, realizing seventh period is about to start. I have physics, which is my only class with Teddy, and he usually stops here to switch out his books beforehand. But there's still no sign of him.

"I should go," I say, but just as I do I spot him at the far end of the hallway, walking with the principal, Mr. Andrews, who gives Teddy a hearty pat on the back before turning into the stairwell.

"What was that about?" Leo asks when Teddy makes his way over to us.

"He just wanted to say congratulations on behalf of the administration," he says, clearly delighted. "And to remind me that the auditorium is in desperate need of repair."

Leo laughs. "Man, is he ever barking up the wrong tree. You've never sat through a play in your life."

"Yes, well, now that I'm a man of means," Teddy says in a borderline English accent, lifting his chin and peering over his nose at us in a vaguely aristocratic fashion, "it's not out of the question that I might become a patron of the arts."

"So how'd it go this morning?" I ask, aware of how eager I sound but unable to tamp down my excitement. "Were they psyched to meet you? Do you feel different?"

"It was mostly just paperwork," he admits. "But it was definitely the most exciting paperwork I've ever filled out."

"I bet," I say, as behind us Ms. Hershey, the French teacher, pokes her head out of her classroom and raises a finger to her lips. Teddy winks at her and she shakes her head at him, but she's smiling. Not even teachers are immune to his charms.

"We should probably get going," I say, pulling at his arm, and he lifts his other hand to give Leo a wave as we start to head off in opposite directions.

"See you later, *Moneybags*," Leo calls out, and Teddy laughs, then turns back to me with a slightly dreamy expression.

"This is the best day ever," he says. "I've only been here a couple hours and the whole school already knows. Oh, and I've been telling everyone how I owe it all to you, and now they all want to give you money for more tickets."

I laugh. "I'm not sure there's much chance of lightning striking twice."

"That's okay," he says, slinging an arm around me, drawing me close so that his words ruffle my hair. "I kind of like having you as my own personal lucky charm."

I smile into his chest, listening to the thump of his heart. "I think that's the first time anyone's ever called me lucky."

Teddy stops walking, his arm slipping from my shoulders as he turns to me. "Al," he says, his face suddenly very earnest. "You're the luckiest thing that's ever happened to me. You know that, right?"

I feel a rush of warmth, a fizzy lightness that makes me want to stand on my toes and kiss him again. "Teddy," I begin, not completely sure what I'm going to say, but it doesn't matter anyway, because I hear a voice behind me.

"Hi, Teddy," says a freshman girl, her friends dissolving into giggles behind her. "Heard the big news. Congrats."

As soon as he glances over at them, the moment between us is gone. "Thanks," he says, giving them a crooked smile.

I shake my head once they've walked past. "I think you have a fan club."

"I've always had a fan club," he jokes, and I narrow my eyes at him.

"You better not lose your head over this, Teddy McAvoy," I say as sternly as possible, but he's grinning at me, and I'm grinning at him, and it's hard to take any of this too seriously, even though I know perfectly well this is only the beginning.

It won't be long before this will all get bigger. The news will travel even farther: it will be in the papers and on TV, it will light up the Internet and become public knowledge, a fact, forever a part of Teddy's identity. Soon there will be even less of him to go around. And I know that will be too much to bear.

"I think we should make a deal," he says, offering his hand, which I automatically take, nodding without even knowing what he's about to suggest, which is exactly why I can't trust myself around him.

"What kind of deal?"

"I promise not to let all this lottery stuff go to my head," he says, gripping my hand. "As long as you promise to yell at me if it does."

I laugh. "You know I'd yell at you even without the handshake, right?"

"Yeah," he says, looking at me fondly. "I'm sort of counting on it."

I hold his gaze a beat too long. "Okay, then. You've got yourself a deal."

When we finally get to Mr. Dill's classroom, we peek through the square of glass in the door. If it was just me I'd turn the knob carefully, hoping it didn't make any noise, then hurry to my desk, wishing I was invisible. But Teddy has never been much for keeping a low profile; he throws open the door so hard that it bangs against the wall and comes bouncing back at him. He catches it with an open palm, then grins at the twenty-two faces turned in his direction.

"Howdy," he says, and Mr. Dill—who is standing at the board, his glasses askew and his gray hair messy—lets out a long sigh.

"Mr. McAvoy," he says, sounding tired already. "Thanks for joining us."

"Sorry," I say, inching inside the classroom just behind Teddy.

"And Ms. Chapman too. We're honored."

Teddy gives him a little salute, then stands there for a few seconds, and I realize he's waiting for Mr. Dill to say something about the lottery. I glance at our classmates, who are watching the exchange with unusual alertness, and it occurs to me they are too.

But Mr. Dill clearly either doesn't know or doesn't care, and in that moment I sort of love him for it. "Did you want to sit down," he says, looking at Teddy over his glasses, "or were you planning to stay in the cheap seats?"

Teddy shakes his head. "No," he says, uncharacteristically contrite. "We'll sit."

We file over to our desks, but it isn't until we're both seated that Mr. Dill turns back to the board, where he writes *SENIOR PHYSICS PROJECT*, then underlines it three times.

"This is the big one, folks," he says. "The one you've all been waiting for . . ."

"Boats," someone whispers behind me.

"It's the Twelfth Annual Cardboard Boat Regatta!" Mr. Dill says, grabbing a pile of papers from his desk and handing them out. "We'll be applying all the principles of physics we've learned so far. Buoyancy, surface tension, density, et cetera. Your only supplies will be cardboard and tape, and this will have to be enough to get two of you across the length of the swimming pool. So I hope you're up for the challenge."

Teddy turns around in his seat and raises his eyebrows. "Partners?" he asks, though he doesn't really have to, since we always pair up for these types of projects.

"Of course," I say, already looking forward to the hours we'll be spending together, working as a team, building something from scratch. He gives me a thumbs-up before swiveling back around, and it's only then I notice that Jacqueline—the gorgeous French exchange student—is scowling at me, and Lila—Teddy's ex-girlfriend—is gazing at him with obvious disappointment. I'm afraid to turn around and see how many other girls were hoping to be his partner.

I have a sinking feeling there are more today than there would've been last week.

# *Fifteen*

It isn't until later, when I walk into the soup kitchen where I volunteer after school, that the day starts to feel normal again. I stand in the doorway for a minute, watching the familiar preparations: the chopping and sorting and simmering, the hustle and hurry and noise. It's only three-thirty, but already the whole place smells like tomatoes and garlic.

I'm always reminded of my parents, being here. There was a soup kitchen not far from where we lived in San Francisco, and the three of us used to go often, bringing grocery bags full of fruits and vegetables and loaves of crusty bread.

Other kids played soccer or video games growing up. Not me. I spent my weekends trailing after my parents—who each ran their own nonprofit—on all their other philanthropic pursuits: wading through dirty streams in my wellies as my mom picked up trash, handing out cups of water at a 5K to raise money for Alzheimer's research, donating my Halloween candy to a homeless shelter, and grooming ponies at the therapeutic riding center where my dad volunteered.

So I know they'd be happy that I'm carrying on the family tradition. What I don't know—what I never know—is whether it's enough.

"Alice," says Mary, the sprightly sixty-something who runs the place, shoving a box of cans down the counter in my direction. "Can you help Sawyer with the sauce? He always adds too much salt."

"Sure," I tell her, looking over at the industrial-sized stove, where a tall boy with shaggy blond hair and a green apron is stirring a giant pot.

"Sawyer?" I say, setting the box down beside the burners.

He glances over at me with a smile. "Hey."

"I'm Alice."

"I know."

"Oh," I say, realizing we must have worked together before. The problem is that I've been volunteering here two nights a week since I was twelve, and after so many shifts and so many faces, it's all become something of a blur. "Sorry, have we—"

"We go to school together."

I look at him more carefully. He's tall and spindly, with clear blue eyes and ears that are just a bit too big. "You go to South Lake?"

"Yeah, but I'm a junior."

"Ah," I say. This makes more sense. The school isn't huge, but it's big enough that I don't even know everyone in my grade, much less the ones below me.

"And I'm in your art class."

I blink at him. "You are?"

"I am," he confirms, leaning to turn the heat down on the burner. "I'm the one who made that phenomenal sculpture of a castle last week."

"A castle?" I ask, giving him a blank look.

"Yup. It was brown? And had spires? And turrets?"

"That was a castle?" I say, suddenly remembering. "I thought it was a porcupine. You must be going through an abstract period."

"Something like that," he says, grinning as he gives the sauce a stir. "I'm not much of an artist."

"Well, I wouldn't beat yourself up about it. I'm sure there's a porcupine-shaped castle somewhere in the world."

He laughs. "I know a *lot* about castles, and I haven't come across one yet."

"Oh yeah?" I ask, starting to unpack the box of cans. "Why, are you secretly the prince of some tiny country just pretending to be an American high school student for security reasons?"

"Yes," he says with a laugh. "But don't feel like you have to call me Prince Sawyer or anything like that. Your Royal Highness will do just fine."

"Seriously."

"Seriously? I'm kind of a history nerd," he says, looking a little embarrassed. "I've been tracing my family roots to

115

a castle back in Scotland, and I'm saving up for a trip there after I graduate."

"If you're trying to save, shouldn't you get a job that pays something?"

He drops the spoon and turns to me with mock horror. "You mean I'm not getting paid here?" he asks, starting to untie his apron. "Well, this is a complete outrage."

I laugh, stepping in to pick up the spoon, which is starting to sink in the bubbling sauce. "Don't worry, this place has some other things going for it."

Sawyer refastens his apron. "Such as?"

"Well," I say, looking over his shoulder as Mary approaches. "You couldn't ask for a better supervisor."

"She'd be a lot better if she trusted me with the sauce," Sawyer says, and to my surprise Mary reaches up to give his shoulder a quick punch.

"Sorry," she says, winking at me. "Gotta keep my grandson in line."

Sawyer rolls his eyes at me good-naturedly, then passes her a spoonful of the sauce. "What do you think?"

"Not too salty for once." Mary glances over at me with a hint of a smile. "You must've distracted him."

"We were just talking," Sawyer says quickly, but his face has turned a deep red, and he looks relieved when Mary heads off to check on the pasta.

As I set to work opening up more cans of sauce, I can feel his eyes on me. But it's a few minutes before he gathers the nerve to say anything.

Finally, he clears his throat. "I thought of another."

"Another what?"

"Job perk."

"Yeah?" I say, looking up at him, and something about the way he's watching me makes my stomach flutter.

"Yeah," he says with a little smile. "Good company."

# Sixteen

Later, once the food has been served and the kitchen cleaned up, Sawyer suggests we get a cup of coffee, and just as I'm about to say no, I realize to my surprise that I kind of want to say yes. So I do.

We've kept up a steady, easy conversation all afternoon, but as we stand in the vestibule at the back of the church, putting on our hats and gloves, we're both suddenly quiet.

Sawyer gives me a shy smile. "There's something I should probably tell you."

"What's that?" I ask as I wrap my scarf around my neck.

"I don't actually like coffee. I'm mostly in this for the cocoa."

I laugh. "Fair enough."

When we're ready, he pushes open the door and we both wince at the blast of freezing air. It's dark now, the streetlights making the snow sparkle, and the concrete steps are icy. I'm so busy trying not to slip that it takes me a moment to notice that someone is standing a few feet away in the shadows. It isn't until Sawyer stops short beside me that I look up to see Teddy.

"Hey," I say, my voice full of surprise. "What are you doing here?"

It looks like he's been out in the cold for a while; his hands are shoved deep into the pockets of his coat, and his face is pale beneath his hat, and I can see that he's shivering. His eyes move from me to Sawyer and back again.

"I wanted to see if you were free for dinner," he says, and my first instinct is to look around for Leo. But then I realize he means just the two of us, and my heart does a little flip-flop.

Before I can say anything, Sawyer steps down off the stairs, his hand outstretched. "Hey," he says. "I'm Sawyer."

Teddy accepts his handshake in an overly serious manner. "Teddy," he says. "You work here too?"

"Well, it turns out the position is unpaid," Sawyer jokes. "But yeah, I volunteer sometimes."

Teddy raises his eyebrows. "Like, serving soup?"

"Sure," Sawyer says, looking less certain now. "I mean, all sorts of things, really. We do bag lunches for the kids, and have support groups, and collect donations of toiletries and—"

"He knows," I say, giving Teddy a pointed look. "I've told him a million times."

Teddy ignores this. "So," he says to me, raising his eyebrows. "Dinner?"

119

I hesitate, looking from one to the other.

"If you guys need to . . . ," Sawyer says. "I mean, we can do this another time."

"Do what?" Teddy asks with a look so dark it makes me want to laugh; this act he's putting on right now—this vaguely menacing, swaggering guy in a back alley—is such a far cry from the real Teddy it's almost comical.

But I also realize what it means: that he must be jealous. And the shock of that, the mere idea of it, is enough to send a thrill through me.

"Just coffee," Sawyer says quickly. "But we don't need to—"

"It's fine," I tell him, then turn back to Teddy. "Can we just get dinner tomorrow instead?"

His face shifts, and he gives me a pleading look. "C'mon, Al. I had a whole thing planned . . . ," he says, then trails off. "Please?"

"It's fine," Sawyer says, stepping away. "Really. I'll take a rain check. Next time we're both here, we'll grab that coffee, okay?"

"Cocoa," I remind him, and he smiles.

"Cocoa."

He waves one last time and I watch as he walks away, a thin figure disappearing into the darkness. Once he's gone, I turn to face Teddy.

"You didn't have to be a jerk about it," I say, raising an eyebrow, and he holds up both hands in defense, surprised.

"I wasn't. It's just . . . I had this whole big plan for tonight, and I didn't expect—"

120

"What plan?" I ask, and he offers his arm with a grin.

"You'll see."

As we walk, I can feel his mood lightening. I press myself closer to him as we turn onto Lincoln Avenue, the sound of our breathing drowned out by the crunch of our shoes on the snow and the music drifting from a nearby bar, which is quick and full of tempo, matching up with the beating of my heart.

I have no idea where we're going, but this is part of the fun of being with Teddy. We could end up sledding at a nearby park or bowling at the sketchy place up the block or walking down to the frozen harbor. You just never know how the night will turn out.

So when he comes to a stop in front of a fancy French restaurant, all I can do is stare at him. "This is where we're going?"

He nods, gesturing proudly at the sign, which is written in a cursive so elaborate it's hard to read. "This is it."

I peer into the window to see that the place is filled with middle-aged couples in pearls and jackets and ties. The decor is stuffy, and the tables are decorated with white cloths and skinny candles. I look at the menu, which is framed just outside the door.

"The prices aren't even listed," I say, "which means it's expensive. So expensive it would be awkward to have them hanging out here for all the world to see."

Teddy seems entirely unruffled by this. In fact, he smiles. "I *know*."

"But you don't actually have the money yet."

"I might've signed up for a few extra credit cards," he says with a shrug. "I figure by the time the bills come, I'll have the money to pay them off."

"Teddy," I say, starting to understand. "You don't have to do this."

His eyes are bright in the wash of light from the restaurant. "It's a thank-you."

"You don't need to thank me," I say, putting my hands on his shoulders in the familiar way I always do, which now feels almost too intimate. "Especially not like this."

"Like what?"

"Well," I say, dropping my hands to point at the menu. "At a place that serves stuff like rabbit and duck and squab. I don't even know what squab *is*."

"Pigeon," he says. "I looked it up."

"You want us to go to a fancy restaurant and eat pigeon?"

"Well, you can always get steak or lobster or something else," he says with a grin. "But yes to the fancy restaurant part. We just won the lottery. I think the very least we can do is treat ourselves to a nice meal, right?"

"Right, but—"

"C'mon," he says, grabbing my hand and pulling me toward the door. "Let's argue about this over some pigeon."

# Seventeen

We're shown to a small table for two near the back, where the napkins are folded in the shape of swans and the plates are trimmed with gold. Most of the diners are gray-haired, and they smile indulgently at us as we walk past in our jeans and sneakers.

"It's always so hard to choose between the bone marrow and the caviar," I say when we open our menus, trying to keep a straight face. "I can never decide."

Teddy strokes his chin thoughtfully. "Well, as you know, I'm partial to truffles."

"Of course," I say. "I've heard they're *marvelous* here."

"Ooh, and there's escargot. Have I ever told you the one about the snail?" he asks, not bothering to wait for an answer. "This snail gets mugged by a tortoise. But when the police ask him to describe the suspect, he says, 'I don't know. It happened so fast.' "

I want to groan or roll my eyes at him, but I'm having way too much fun for that and I find myself laughing instead. "Nailed it."

"Always," he says with a grin.

When the tuxedoed waiter arrives to take our orders, Teddy closes his menu and leans back in his seat. "We'll have one of everything."

"Pardon me, sir?" the man says, his mustache twitching.

Teddy winks at me. "We want to try it all. Especially the squab."

The waiter's pen is still poised above his notepad. "Perhaps the tasting menu, then, sir?"

"Sounds great," Teddy says good-naturedly, and when the waiter is gone he turns back to me. "I'm starving."

"Teddy," I say in a low voice, leaning forward so that my breath makes the candle between us gutter. "Did you see how much it cost?"

"The tasting menu?"

"It's two hundred dollars a person. Plus tip."

His face pales just slightly. "That's okay. I'm pretty sure I have enough to . . ." He leans forward and pulls a thick stack of credit cards from his back pocket, which he fans out in front of him. The couple at the next table look over with raised eyebrows. But Teddy doesn't notice. "I think this one has a three-hundred-dollar limit, but I can't remember how much is left," he says, holding up a blue card.

"And this one is at least two hundred, but I think I've already spent some of it, so—"

He stops abruptly when the manager—a short man with a shiny bald head and thick glasses—appears at our table.

"Good evening to you both," he says in an English accent. His eyes fall on the credit cards arranged like game pieces on the table. "I just wanted to stop by this evening to make sure—"

"We can pay," Teddy interrupts, sweeping the cards back into his hands. "If that's what you were going to ask. We have enough."

The manager looks startled. "Of course not, sir. I would never presume—"

"I just won the lottery, actually, but the money hasn't come through yet, and we wanted to celebrate, which is why all the cards," Teddy explains, talking much too fast. "But I've got it covered."

I can't help cringing at this, all of it: the defensive tone and the way he's broken out in a sweat, the embarrassment on the manager's face and the quiet that's fallen across nearby tables as the other diners crane their necks in our direction.

Suddenly I can see how it looks to everyone around us: two teenagers woefully out of place in such a lavish restaurant, grandly ordering one of everything while rambling about a lottery win.

But the worst part is watching Teddy notice it too. He snaps his mouth shut, glancing at me with a slightly deflated look. Then he musters a weak smile for the manager.

"Sorry, I just didn't want you to think . . . I wanted you to know it'll be fine."

The manager gives a curt nod. "Certainly, sir. And if there's anything we can do to make your meal more enjoyable, please do let me know."

As soon as he's gone, I lift my eyes to meet Teddy's. "Don't worry about it," I say quickly. "It doesn't matter."

His gaze shifts to the nearby tables, where—except for a few sidelong glances—people have resumed eating. "Yeah, but—"

"They're just jealous."

He frowns. "Of what?"

"Of how many credit cards you have," I say with a grin, and in spite of himself Teddy laughs. But a second later his smile falters.

"I shouldn't have said all that. I got rattled."

"You'll get used to this sort of thing," I say, but it occurs to me that maybe I don't want him to get used to restaurants like these, a life like this, full of extravagant meals and regular indulgences and extreme privilege, all of it so vastly different from anything we've ever known.

"I guess I should've just waited till I had the money. This will all be so much easier when the news is public and my name is out there, and I don't feel like I have anything to prove." He shuffles the credit cards in his hand. "Did I tell you my mom wanted me to stay anonymous?"

"I thought you couldn't do that."

"You can in some states. That's what the winner from Oregon is doing."

"But not here?"

"Not here," he says. "She was trying to convince me to hold the check over my face at the press conference so nobody would know who I am. I told her it wouldn't work. People would figure it out anyway. Plus, where's the fun in that?"

"It's not the worst idea," I tell him. "You'd still have all the money, but then you wouldn't have to deal with—"

"I know, I know. All the vultures who are going to be coming out of the woodwork asking for donations and investments and handouts. I've already gotten this speech from my mom. And your aunt. It doesn't matter. There's no way I'm gonna hide behind a giant piece of cardboard and miss out on everything."

Our waiter appears with a small plate, which he sets down without quite looking at us. "Toasted brioche with crème fraîche and caviar."

When he leaves, Teddy smiles, his spirits lifted by the sight of the food. "Now we're talking."

The room around us seems to grow dimmer and the candles brighter as we pick at the caviar. There's classical music playing softly in the background, and nearby the maître d' pops open a bottle of champagne. Across the table Teddy is smiling at me, and there's something so romantic about the whole scene that when he leans forward and says, "So I have a proposal for you," my heart stops for a second.

"What?"

He laughs at my expression. "Not that kind of proposal."

127

"Of course not," I say, my voice a little shaky. "So what, then?"

"Well," he says, "I wanted to see if you'd reconsider about the money."

"Right," I say, but there's a heavy feeling in my chest because I understand now he didn't bring me here as a thank-you at all. He brought me here because he still feels like he owes me. "I already told you—"

"I know," he says. "And I heard you. But what about at least part of it? Even just, like, a million dollars? That would be enough to—"

"Teddy."

"What?" he asks, his eyes wide. "I don't get it. What's so wrong with trying to make sure you're taken care of? Why shouldn't you get something out of this too?"

I lower my gaze, thinking again of Aunt Sofia and Uncle Jake, knowing they might also want to get something out of this. It's selfish, not asking them. I realize that. But what if all this time they've been taking care of me, it turns out they've just been hoping the universe would figure out a way to pay them back? I'm not sure I could bear it.

I draw in a shaky breath and force myself to look up at Teddy. "It's really nice of you," I tell him. "And I know how much you mean it. But I meant what I said the other day too. I just don't want it."

He shakes his head. "I don't understand. How could you not?"

Because, I want to tell him, this money is going to turn our lives into a snow globe, tipping the whole world upside down. It's going to change everything. And to me there's nothing scarier.

But I can't say that to him. Not when he's been floating a foot off the ground ever since we found that ticket. I don't want to be the one who brings him back down to earth.

"I just don't," I say, more firmly this time, and there's a finality in my voice that makes him sit back hard in his chair with a sigh.

"Fine," he says, reaching for the last circle of brioche. "But fair warning: if you don't change your mind soon, I might spend your half on caviar."

"It's not my half," I say with a little smile. "And you can do better than caviar."

He glances up at me, his eyebrows raised. "How do you figure?"

"Squab," I say. "Obviously."

"Obviously," he says, grinning. "Maybe I'll open up a whole squab restaurant. Or better yet: a chain. I'll bring squab to the masses."

"Just what they want, I'm sure."

"We'll call it McSquab's. It'll be a surefire hit. And then I'll be this giant restaurant tycoon, and I'll open up a big office in New York or L.A., and I'll travel around on my private jet to places like Tokyo and Sydney and Beijing, and . . ." When he sees my expression, he trails off. "What?"

"Nothing," I say, shaking my head. I know he's joking. Of course he is. But still, it feels like he's already preparing to fly away from this place.

"Hey," he says, reaching for my hand across the table. "It's gonna be okay, you know."

My answer is automatic: "I know."

"Nothing's going to change," he promises. "Not really."

And like an idiot I believe him.

# Part Three

MARCH

# Eighteen

The money arrives on a rainy day in the middle of March.

For the past seven weeks, Teddy has been doing a very convincing impression of a contestant on one of those game shows where they set you loose in a store with a bucket of cash and a ticking clock. With his growing assortment of credit cards, he's already managed to run up a debt so big it would've given pre-jackpot Teddy a heart attack.

But now his big win is about to become official, so Leo and I skip eighth period and head downtown for the press conference in the lottery offices. His mom is there, of course, and we stand in the back with her, behind the reporters with their microphones and the news crews with their cumbersome equipment, watching as Teddy accepts the enormous check with a smile nearly as big.

"Teddy," a reporter calls out when it's time for questions. "What are you planning to do with the money?"

"I'm not sure yet," he says as the cameras flash all around him, and Leo rolls his eyes at me because we both know that's not quite true. He's already tried his best to make a nice little dent in it. "For now I'm still just getting used to the idea."

"You're the youngest winner ever," says someone else. "Still in high school. Does this change anything for you?"

"Other than my math grade?" Teddy jokes, and there's a roar of laughter.

I can see it happening: the glint in his eyes, the obvious pleasure he gets when a crowd starts to warm to him. It doesn't matter whether it's a gaggle of reporters or a group of high school students: Teddy knows how to win people over, and a press conference is nothing more than a larger stage and a bigger challenge.

As he hoists the check up higher, it slips from one of his hands and a lottery official reaches out to help. But Teddy side-eyes him and steps away, holding on to it even tighter and giving his audience a look of exaggerated concern.

"No way am I letting go of this thing," he says as the crowd chuckles, and I can't help smiling too. He looks so handsome up there in his checked button-down, his hair combed neatly to tame the piece that always sticks up in the back. He's all boyish enthusiasm and barely concealed joy, and even if I weren't so stupidly in love with him, I'm sure I'd still find it nearly as charming as I do now.

"It's been reported that a friend of yours bought the ticket as a gift," someone says. "Can you comment on that?"

I feel the heat rise in my face, and Katherine reaches over to give my hand a little squeeze. From the podium Teddy winks at me, a movement so fast you wouldn't catch it unless you were looking for it. Which I was.

"That's true," he tells the audience. "Which only proves I'm the luckiest guy in the world in more ways than one."

Without quite meaning to, I put a hand over my heart.

From up onstage, Teddy smiles at me.

When it's over, he finds us waiting for him in the back. "How'd I do?" he asks, grinning in a way that makes it clear he already knows.

"When did you get to be such a pro at this?" Katherine asks, beaming at him.

He laughs. "I think I was born for this."

"Careful," Leo teases him, "or your head is gonna get bigger than that check."

"You were great," I say, aware that I'm staring at him. But I can't help it. Maybe it was the lights or the cameras, or maybe it was seeing him handle those questions like he's been doing it his whole life, but something about him looks different to me now.

"Thanks, Al," he says. "And thanks for being here."

"Of course. I wouldn't cut class for just anyone."

He smiles. "That means a lot."

One of the lottery officials calls his name then, waving him over, and Teddy gives us an apologetic shrug before hurrying off. There are more interviews for him to do, more people to talk to, more hands to shake. Katherine stays behind to wait for him, but Leo and I say goodbye, walking back outside to find that it's raining. We stand beneath the overhang of the building, the air around us smelling of spring, and wait for it to let up.

"Well," Leo says, looking at me sideways.

I laugh. "Well."

"That was . . . something."

On the street, people struggle with their umbrellas. We peer out at the sky, which is low and heavy, a deep gunmetal gray that matches the buildings around it.

"Are you going home now?" Leo asks as he pulls up the hood of his jacket.

I shake my head. "Nursing home."

"Right," he says. "Wouldn't want to miss pinochle."

"Gotta keep my winning streak alive," I say with a grin. "What about you?"

"I've got an application to finish."

"Michigan?"

He shakes his head, his eyes on the rain. "No, Art Institute. Michigan was due a while ago."

There's a catch in his voice, but I let it pass. I twirl my umbrella, listening to the steady patter of rain and the rush of cars on the wet roads.

Leo glances over at me. "Do you think Teddy'll even go now?"

"To college? Of course," I say, but he looks skeptical. "He

was always planning to go at some point; it was just a matter of when."

"No," Leo says, "it was a matter of money."

"Which isn't an issue anymore."

"Right, because he's a millionaire."

"So? It's not like he's gonna spend his days swimming around in a pool of cash. He wants to be a coach—a *college* coach—and you need to go to school for that. I already printed a bunch of applications for him, and he promised to look. A lot of them have rolling admissions, so there's still time. He'll go. I know he will."

"If you say so," Leo says, though he doesn't seem convinced. "And what about you? Have you figured out what you're gonna do if—"

"I don't get into Stanford?" I say, attempting a smile. "Not really."

"But what happens if—"

"I don't know," I tell him. "I just have to get in."

I applied for early decision back in the fall, but my application was deferred. Which was better than being rejected. But it was still a huge disappointment. I've since applied to a bunch of other schools too—eight in all—because Aunt Sofia wants to make sure I cover my bases. But there's no backup plan for me. Not really. Ever since I was little, Stanford has been the goal.

I remember the night my mom found out she got into a program there for nonprofit leaders. My dad and I made her a cake to celebrate; he even let me help draw a shaky approximation of the Stanford seal across the top, and she laughed when she cut into it and saw that it was red velvet in honor of the university's colors.

"School pride?" she asked, and my dad had leaned across the table to kiss her.

"All sorts of pride," he said, his eyes shining.

But in the end she never made it. A few months later she found out she was sick, and my life started to unravel one thread at a time.

Now I have a chance to do what she never could. To follow in her footsteps. To go back to the West Coast. To find my way home again.

"I have to get in," I repeat, more quietly this time.

Leo nods. "You will. I just wish it wasn't so far away."

"It's not *that* far. Besides, you could be in Michigan."

"Which is also really far away."

"Hardly," I say, and he groans.

"When your boyfriend's there, it feels like a million miles."

"Well, the good news," I tell him, "is that you get to see him in less than a week."

Leo smiles at this. "I still can't believe my parents are letting me—"

"Spend your whole spring break alone with your college boyfriend?" I ask with a grin. "I can. They love Max. And they trust you. Plus, you'll be on your own soon anyway. You might even be in Michigan."

His expression dims, just slightly. "Maybe."

"It's gonna be great," I say, making an effort to keep

my voice light, though it's hard to get excited about spring break when he and Teddy are both leaving me behind.

Months ago Teddy assured me that we'd make the best of it, since he wasn't going anywhere either. "You and me," he promised. "We'll paint the town."

"Red."

"What?"

"I think it's *paint the town red.*"

"Why red?" he asked. "Why not blue? Or green?"

"We can paint the town blue if you want."

"Okay," he said with a nod. "Then it's settled. We'll paint the town blue."

But then he won the lottery. And plans changed. Now he's taking the entire basketball team to Mexico, where he rented a private bungalow at a fancy hotel. All his treat, of course. And I'll be staying behind, the town to remain unpainted.

"Don't make me feel guilty about leaving you here," Leo says, smiling at my expression. "Not when you could've gone to Mexico."

I give him a look. "Oh yeah. Me and Teddy and the entire basketball team. Sounds like a dream vacation."

He laughs. "I'm actually a little jealous. Apparently the place has a hot tub and a private pool. With a waterslide."

"Of course it does," I say, not the least bit surprised by this. Teddy might've only gotten the check this afternoon, but this is just the latest in a long string of big purchases: a new phone and a new computer, new sneakers and a new jacket with too many zippers, a hoverboard he can't figure out how to ride, and a watch so expensive it took him a week to work up the nerve to wear it. And all this from a guy who used to agonize over whether to pay extra for guacamole on his burrito.

At school a few weeks ago, the television in Ms. McGuire's room gave out in the middle of a video about World War II, and to the teacher's delight Teddy ordered a better one right there on the spot. Then last week he stood on a table in the middle of the cafeteria and waved around a thick manila envelope.

"Season tickets," he called out. "Who wants to see the Cubbies with me?"

For the remainder of the lunch period, there was a kind of makeshift draft while Teddy doled out tickets with a magnanimous smile.

The next day he bought pizzas for everyone in the cafeteria. And the next there was a coffee cart outside the school, free to anyone who wanted a cup.

"Teddy McAvoy for president," one girl said as she walked away with a steaming macchiato, which seems to be the general consensus these days.

"He just won the lottery," Leo says now, as if I need reminding. "You can't really blame him for living it up."

"I don't. I just—"

"You think he's going overboard," he says, looking out at the gray drizzle.

"And you don't?"

"Honestly? I think he's just getting started."

I nod, staring down at my damp shoes.

140

"Here's the thing you have to remember," Leo says. "If you give a tiger a cupcake, you can't be annoyed with him for eating it."

In spite of myself, I laugh. "Why would you give a tiger a cupcake?"

"Why not?" he asks with a shrug.

But the problem is this: I'm not annoyed with Teddy for eating the cupcake.

I'm annoyed with myself for giving it to him in the first place.

# Nineteen

The next morning I'm a few blocks from school when I hear someone honking. I turn around, alarmed to see a bright red sports car—the kind you might find in a cheesy eighties movie—coasting leisurely behind me.

When I realize it's Teddy at the wheel, I burst out laughing.

He leans out the open window with a grin. "What do you think?"

"I think," I say, unable to resist teasing him, "that you might be having a midlife crisis."

"If I am, you should really join me. It's pretty fun."

"I'm not sure mine would involve a sports car," I say, walking around to the passenger side and climbing in beside him.

"Well, I guess we'll never know, since you didn't want

the money," he says. "But if you change your mind, I saw one in blue I think you'd love."

I roll my eyes. "Tempting."

"C'mon," he says. "There must be *something* you want."

"How about some help with our physics project?" I say, giving him a pointed look. "It's fifty percent of our grade, and we haven't even—"

"I know," he says impatiently, drumming his hands on the wheel. "It's just that I have a lot on my plate right now, and—"

"What, like car shopping?"

He at least has the good sense to look contrite. "We'll get it done. I promise."

"When?" I ask, raising an eyebrow. "It's due right after spring break."

"Soon," he says, which is what he always says about things like this. Teddy tends to be all initial enthusiasm and no follow-through. He flashes one of his trademark smiles. "How about this? I'll help you build a boat if you let me buy you a car."

"You have to help with the boat anyway," I say. "But I appreciate the offer."

"Worth a try," he says, putting on a pair of sunglasses, though the sky is overcast. "So really, what do you think?"

I breathe in the new-car smell and run a hand over the soft leather interior. Honestly, it's a cliché on wheels. But I can see how happy it makes him, so I nod approvingly. "It definitely beats the bus," I say, which is true enough.

When we pull into the parking lot behind the school,

everyone stops to watch Teddy swing the car into a spot, and the moment he steps out he's surrounded by a crowd of admirers. The lottery might be old news around here, but the press conference—plus the new set of wheels—seems to have sparked a second wave of excitement.

"Saw you on the news last night, man," says Greg Byrne, giving Teddy a half hug. "You were awesome."

"My mom read about you in the paper this morning," Caitie Simpson says. "She couldn't believe I know you."

A few others give him high fives as they walk by, and a freshman girl even asks to take a selfie with him. Teddy happily obliges, smiling and flashing a peace sign.

"I'm gonna head in," I say, and he gives me a distracted wave, busy with his adoring fans.

As I cross the pavement toward the double doors at the back of the building, I pass a group of guys I don't recognize; they're standing in a half circle, looking off in Teddy's direction. "Is he joking with that thing?" one of them asks, eyebrows raised. "He gets one lucky break and thinks he's a movie star."

"Did you seem him wearing those sunglasses in the cafeteria yesterday?" says another with a bark of a laugh. "What a jackass."

I keep my eyes straight ahead as I walk by them, but my face floods with heat, and I can't help feeling a little embarrassed on Teddy's behalf.

I have art for first period, and I dash in just as class is starting. Afterward, Sawyer appears by my side. "You have some paint on your forehead," he says, crooking a finger at me, and I bring a hand to the spot where he's pointing.

"Guess I'm going through *my* abstract period," I tell him with a sheepish grin as I begin to scratch at it.

"Right," he says. "I know it well."

We haven't spoken much since that night at the soup kitchen. In class he sits with a cluster of juniors on the other side of the room, while I muddle through each project alongside some of the girls I became close with back in sixth grade, when the divide between boys and girls briefly unsettled my usual trio.

Sometimes I catch Sawyer watching me and we smile at each other, but that's about it. After meeting him that night at the church as he made spaghetti sauce, so friendly and open, it's odd to observe him in school, where he's a little more reserved, a little more drawn into himself. I wonder if he thinks the same of me.

"So what are you doing for spring break?" he asks as we set off down the hallway together. "Anything wild and crazy?"

"Wild and crazy," I say. "That's me."

He laughs. "Same here. I'll be spending most of the week helping my grandma at the soup kitchen."

"Then I'll probably see you there," I tell him, and he brightens.

"You still owe me that cocoa."

"I do," I say as we turn a corner, coming face to face with Teddy and Lila so suddenly that we all stop short, staring at each other.

My stomach drops as I notice that Teddy's arm is around her shoulders, but when he sees my face he quickly lowers it. He's wearing a new sweater, which is pale blue and clearly expensive, and he looks older in it, self-possessed in a way that goes beyond his usual boyish confidence. There's a little alligator logo on it—right over his heart—which reminds me of his old nickname for me. Somehow, this makes me feel worse.

"Hey," he says, avoiding my eyes.

I nod. "Hey."

Lila smirks at Sawyer, and for a second I can see what she must see: a nerdy junior with too-short corduroys and a too-eager smile. "Who are you?"

"That's Sawyer," Teddy supplies, giving him a friendly pat on the shoulder. "Nice to see you again, man."

"You too." Sawyer clears his throat. "And congratulations. I heard about your . . . good luck."

"Thanks," Teddy says. "I owe it all to Al."

"Really?" Sawyer asks, looking over at me. He has to be one of the only people in the whole school who doesn't know this. I've spent the past six weeks dodging questions about whether I get part of the money and gritting my teeth when people try to rub my head for good luck.

"It was a birthday gift," I explain. "The ticket."

"Hard to live up to that one," Lila says, arching an eyebrow. "I mean, what are you gonna get him next year?"

"Two lottery tickets?" I suggest, which makes Teddy laugh. Our eyes meet for a second before I look away again.

"So do you guys have class together or something?"

Teddy asks, glancing from me to Sawyer, whose gaze travels back in my direction.

"Yeah, we just had art," he says. He's answering Teddy but he's looking at me, his blue eyes shiny with amusement. "Alice and I are big fans of the abstract kind."

"You could say we're both aficionados," I agree, and when I look back at Teddy he's frowning. There's nothing mean or malicious about it; he looks more confused than anything, puzzled and a little out of sorts in a way that's totally foreign to him.

"Actually," he says, "Al and I have an art project of our own."

I tilt my head at him. "What's that?"

"The boat," he says with a note of impatience.

"I wouldn't really call that an art project."

"Well, who says we can't make it look nice too?"

"We?" I ask, raising my eyebrows.

"Yes, of course *we*," Teddy says. "You and me."

"Mine's already done," Lila says. "Stef and I finished last week." When nobody answers, she adds: "It's pink and green."

"Does it float?" Sawyer asks politely.

Lila gives him a scathing look. "That's the whole point."

Teddy's eyes are still on me. "So maybe we should get together tonight."

There's a part of me that wants to shoot him down, if only because he was so annoying about the whole thing this morning. But another part of me suspects his reasons for suggesting it and can't help feeling flattered.

Beside me Sawyer shifts awkwardly from one foot to the other. Lila is now glaring at the floor. Teddy gives me a hopeful look.

"Fine," I say, and he smiles.

"Yeah?"

"Yeah. What time? And where?"

He laughs. "Whatever floats your boat."

# Twenty

When I show up at Teddy's building that evening, there are two men waiting outside the door. It's too dark to make out their faces, but one of them is blowing on his hands to keep warm and the other is busy adjusting something on his camera.

"Excuse me," I say, since they're standing in front of the buzzer. They step back from the concrete stoop, but when I hit the button for number eleven they exchange a look.

"Are you here to see Teddy McAvoy?" one of them asks, looking excited at the prospect. He's wearing a winter cap that's pulled low, and his jacket is zipped up so high that all I can see are his eyes. Without answering I hit the button again, my heart pounding. It's cold and dark, and this isn't the greatest neighborhood, and I don't like the way these guys are staring at me.

The second man takes off his Sox cap and scratches his head. "Are you the one who bought the ticket for him?"

I press my lips together and turn back to the buzzer, only this time when I press it I leave my hand there, letting it ring and ring until the door finally clicks. I grab the handle, yanking it open and slipping into the entryway without a word, still shivering and grateful to be inside.

Upstairs the door to the apartment is open, and I walk in without knocking. Katherine is standing in the kitchen wearing her scrubs, and she looks up with a smile when she sees me.

"I don't know if you realize," I say, "but there are a couple of men outside—"

"They're back?" she asks, her expression darkening. "They were here yesterday. I think they're trying to get pictures of Teddy."

"That's kind of a shady way of doing it."

She's gathering her things, getting ready to leave for work, but she pauses to give me a long look. "Maybe you can talk some sense into him. I'm worried he's a little too enamored with this whole circus. It's been nonstop since yesterday, with all these calls about morning shows and requests for interviews, and I'm just not sure—"

"Is she freaking out about the reporters again?" Teddy asks, walking into the room. He's wearing a Michigan hoodie—which Max brought home for him at Christmas—a pair of old sweatpants, and mismatched socks, one of which has a hole in the toe. He looks, much to my relief, like himself again.

Katherine gives him an exasperated look as she puts on her coat. "You can't possibly expect me not to worry about the fact that there are grown men stalking my teenage son."

"That's because your teenage son is so incredibly rich and good-looking."

"And modest," she says, then gives him a stern look. "Just be careful, okay? And listen to Alice. She's always had a lot more sense than you."

"Totally untrue," Teddy says cheerfully.

"And be sure to walk her out at the end of the night."

"I'll get her a taxi," he promises. "Even better: I'll buy her a taxi!"

"No need to get crazy," Katherine says as she steps out into the hallway. "Good luck with the project, you two."

When she's gone, I turn to Teddy. "Do you think she'll keep working nights?"

"You mean now that her son's a multimillionaire?" he asks with a grin. "I don't know. I told her she could quit, but she says her patients need her. She did promise to cut back a little, though. And she's putting in a request for the day shift."

"You think she'll get it?" I ask, because I know she's tried to switch before without any luck.

"I have a feeling it'll be a lot easier to negotiate now that her son's a multimillionaire."

I shake my head. "I'm gonna start making you put a quarter in a jar every time you say the word *multimillionaire*."

"A quarter?" He swats this away. "*Pfft*. Make it a hundo."

"We might need a jar for that one too," I say, rolling my eyes at him. "Your mom's right about those reporters, you know."

"Nah, she's just worried about bad press," he says dismissively. "Trust me. She'll be a lot happier about all this once I get her out of here."

My heart seizes. "You're moving?"

"Yeah, I'm gonna buy her a place."

"You are?" I ask, blinking at him. My first thought is *That's more like it.* And my second is *Please don't let it be far away.*

"I am," he says proudly. "And not just any place."

My eyes widen. "No."

"Yes," he says, smiling at my reaction.

"Your old apartment?"

"Even better," he says. "The whole building."

"Really? You can do that?"

He grins. "Thanks to you."

I can hardly believe it. I know how much it hurt to give up their home when his dad lost everything. Even six years later, Katherine still makes excuses to drive by it whenever she can: the old brick building just a few miles up the road where they once lived in a spacious two-bedroom apartment as a family of three.

"It's for sale?"

"Not technically. I'll have to buy up all the individual apartments. But I'm planning to make them offers they can't refuse."

I laugh, delighted by this. Teddy could buy practically

152

anything he wants right now. He could get something a thousand times nicer, a hundred times bigger. But this building means something to them, and my heart swells because this is the Teddy I know.

This is the Teddy I love.

"I want to wait and surprise my mom once everything's settled," he says, "but I already have a bunch of ideas for how to fix it up. Want to see?"

I follow him back to his room, where his new computer is lying open on his bed. He flops down beside it, leaving room for me, but for a second all I can do is stand there, thinking about the last time I was here, that single charged moment between us.

Teddy's face is serious as he begins to type, his eyes reflecting the light from the screen and his hair still slightly askew. Watching him, I want nothing more than to rewind the past six weeks, to bottle the way he looked at me that night, to capture the lightness I felt the next morning when he spun me around, to memorize the taste of his lips when we kissed. I want to do it all over again, even if the outcome would be the same; even if there's no chance of a future, I still want this little piece of the past.

Though the truth, of course, is that I want more than that too.

Together we sit on his bed—Teddy sprawled out and me perched on the very edge—as he shows me a series of floor plans and layouts. "This one used to be ours, remember? There are eight units total, and my plan is to knock down the walls between them and turn the whole building into two giant apartments. One for me, and one for my mom. I'll take the lower half, since I want to make the basement into a game room—"

"Naturally," I say with a grin.

"Then I'm gonna build my mom her dream apartment upstairs." He looks up at me, beaming. "All these years without her own room, and now she's gonna have two whole floors to herself. Can you believe it?"

He looks so proud right now that my eyes unexpectedly fill with tears. "You're going to make her so, so happy."

"I hope so," he says. "She deserves it."

"So do you," I tell him. "You manage to hide it pretty well sometimes, but you're a really good guy at heart, Teddy McAvoy."

He gives me a crooked smile. "Well, I do have my moments."

When it's time to start working on the project, we move to the floor. His room has started to look like one of those stores that sells gadgets and electronics, the kind with massage chairs and fish tanks and noise machines. There are toys and boxes everywhere: game consoles and tablets, a remote-controlled car that looks a lot like the life-sized one parked on the street below, something with wings that seems suspiciously dronelike, and even a robot, which is standing stiffly beside its box, watching me with a blank stare.

"So what," I ask, shoving a model helicopter out of the way as we attempt to make room on the floor, "did you raid the mall or something?"

"I went on what you might call a shopping spree last week," Teddy agrees, kicking aside some Bubble Wrap. "It's possible I got a little carried away."

"You think?"

"Hey, I've had enough bad luck to last me a while. So have you, by the way. The world owes us. I'm just the only one smart enough to cash in."

I look around at the piles of screws and batteries, the tangles of cords and plugs. "I'll bet you a million dollars you never end up putting any of this stuff together."

"You don't have a million dollars," he reminds me, "which is your own fault. And the only thing I'm worried about putting together right now is our boat. So where should we start?"

"With this," I say, pulling out the instruction sheet for the project.

He studies it for a second. "Okay, well, I don't want to rock the boat, but—"

"Cute," I say, making a face at him.

"If you like that one, I've got about a hundred more."

As we start in on the calculations, working through a formula for buoyancy that we learned in class, Teddy's attention keeps drifting.

"Should we do this in the other room?" I ask, watching him fiddle with what appears to be either an alarm clock or a handheld video game. "I think there are too many distractions in here."

He sets it aside. "No, I'm with you. Floating: good. Sinking: bad."

"Teddy," I say with a groan. "If it's all the same to you, I'd rather not fall into the pool in front of everyone we know. Plus, this is fifty percent of our grade, and I'm still waiting to hear from Stanford."

"You'll get in," he says, but he sounds distracted. I follow his gaze to the bookshelf, where the stack of applications I printed for him sits untouched. "Here's what I've been thinking, though. If the point of college is to find a job afterward, and the point of a job is to make money . . ."

"No," I say quickly, realizing where he's going with this. "The point of college is to meet new people and learn new things and figure out who you are."

"And to find a job."

"Right," I say grudgingly. "To find a job that you love."

"But mostly to find a job where you make enough money to live. And now I have enough money to—"

"Hey," I say, feeling a little panicky. "Come on. Don't be an idiot. You're obviously still going to college. I mean . . . you can go even sooner now. No more measuring shoe sizes or inflating basketballs. You can get your degree and go right into coaching."

Teddy is looking at me with amusement. "I don't need a *degree* anymore."

"Yeah, you do, if you want to coach—"

"Who knows if that's even what I still want to do," he says dismissively, though this is all he's talked about ever since I've known him. "I can do anything now."

I stare at him. "But you want to be a basketball coach."

"Al," he says, like I'm not understanding the situation. "Things are different now. You must know that. I could *buy* a basketball team if I wanted. I could call them Teddy and the Terrifics and nobody could stop me from being head coach and assistant coach and ball boy all at once. What in the world would I want to sit through college for?"

"I just figured now that you don't have to take out loans . . ."

"No," he says, so starkly, so matter-of-factly, that I reel back a little. I rub my eyes with the heels of my hands, feeling the situation slipping from my grasp.

"Teddy, c'mon," I say. "You can't just *not go*. Please don't be that guy."

He stiffens. "What guy?"

"The guy who fritters away his days buying meaningless things and sitting around just because he can afford to do nothing."

When he looks up at me, his eyes are cold. "Why do I feel like you've been waiting to say that to me?"

"I haven't—" I start to say, then stop, realizing he might be right. "It's just . . . it's a little hard to recognize you right now." I glance around the room. "Especially with all this stuff."

"I like all this stuff."

"Sure, but it's . . ." I pause, trying to collect my thoughts. "Well, remember how your dad used to bring you all those presents when he was on a winning streak?"

He glares at me. "This isn't the same."

"I know. I'm just saying maybe there are other things you could be doing, other ways you could be spending the money. I mean, what about philanthropy? You haven't even mentioned giving some away—"

"Give me a break," he says. "I've had the money for, like, two days. I'm obviously gonna donate some eventually. You're just annoyed that I haven't asked *you* about it. Because you think anything having to do with charity is your territory."

I press my lips together. "Well."

"Well, what?"

"Well, I've been volunteering since I was little. It was what my parents—"

"Exactly," he interrupts, and I go tense.

"What's that supposed to mean?"

He sighs. "You only do it because you feel like you have to. For them."

"That's not true," I say, my heart thudding. "I do it because—"

"You're still looking for their approval."

He says this as if it's an undeniable fact, a simple statement of truth, something we've discussed a thousand times before, and I feel a quick burning anger, because is this what he's really been thinking the whole time? That I'm just going through the motions, trying to follow in my parents' footsteps? Is that what everyone thinks?

"That's not true," I say coldly. "I do it for me too."

"It doesn't matter," Teddy says, shaking his head, and

I clench my teeth, because of course it matters. All of this does. But he continues, his voice steely and his eyes hard. "The point is that it's not fair for you to be disappointed in me already."

"It's not that—"

"Especially since I offered you half." He practically spits the words at me. "So if you had so many opinions about how this money should be spent, maybe you shouldn't have been so stubborn about it. Then you could've been doing it all yourself."

This is true, but hearing him say it now, just moments after invoking my parents, a new fear washes over me. Because for all my worries about that snap decision—what it might've meant for Aunt Sofia and Uncle Jake, and Leo too, what it might've changed between me and Teddy—I somehow hadn't thought once about my parents or what they would've done.

Or maybe I had, and somewhere deep down I wanted to believe they'd have made the same choice. But now I wonder if I'm wrong. Maybe they'd have taken the money and done something good with it, something big, something important.

Maybe that's what I should've done too.

My eyes prick with tears at the thought, and I bow my head so that Teddy won't see.

"But you said no," he continues, "and I'm not going to sit here like everyone else and pretend it's because you were being noble. You said no because you're a coward."

Each word is a jab that lands square and true. I open my mouth to respond, then close it again. My mind feels muddled and thick and impossibly slow. I'm not sure how we got here, and I wish I knew how to get back out again.

"You passed up the opportunity of a lifetime because you were afraid. And because you didn't have the guts to try doing something great with the money yourself."

"That's not—" I start to say, looking up at him again, but Teddy has too much momentum to stop now.

"You don't want it—fine," he says, his eyes blazing. "But you don't get a say in what I do with it. You don't get to sit there thinking I don't deserve it. And you don't get to judge me."

Something inside me snaps back at this.

"Yeah," I say quietly. "I do."

He looks surprised. "What?"

"You might be right about all that other stuff," I say, trying to keep my voice from shaking. "But I'm right about this. Nobody else is being honest with you. They're all too busy fawning over you or waiting for you to throw a few bucks in their direction." *Or laughing at you,* I almost say, thinking of the guys in the parking lot or the girls I overheard giggling about his updated wardrobe last week. "They all want something from you."

"And you don't," he says in a way that makes my stomach churn, because of course I do. It's just not what he thinks.

"I want this to mean something," I tell him. "And I want

160

you to be happy. And I don't want people taking advantage of you."

Teddy shakes his head. "They're not."

"Come on," I say, more gently now. "I know those basketball guys were the ones who convinced you to get a house in Mexico. And you must've noticed the teachers sucking up to you. Not to mention all the girls batting their eyelashes in your direction. And Lila—all of a sudden Lila's hanging out with you again?"

"It's not—"

"Teddy," I say, rolling my eyes. "I saw you guys at school today. She was stuck to you like a freaking barnacle."

"That's not—"

"And meanwhile, you can't even be bothered to remember kissing *me*."

I freeze. I hadn't meant to say that, and now that it's out there I immediately wish I could take it back. Teddy's face has drained of color, and he's staring at me with a slightly strangled expression. I can hardly bear to look at him, and as the seconds tick by I'm convinced this silence between us will never, ever end.

"Of course I remember," he says after a long moment, and I let out a breath I didn't even know I was holding.

"Okay," I say, wishing I could think of something better, but I'm too distracted by the pounding of my heart, which is loud in my ears.

"Yeah," he says, and we sit there for a little while longer, just stewing in the terrible awkwardness of the moment.

"So . . ."

He scratches at his forehead. "It's just . . . ," he says, looking pained. "The thing is . . ."

I nod like an idiot, my chest filled with a mounting dread.

"There was a lot going on that day, you know?" he says, his eyes on the carpet. "And I think maybe I got a little caught up in the excitement, which is why I didn't want to—"

"It's fine," I say, holding up a hand, even as all the air goes rushing out of me.

I want nothing more than to disappear right now.

I want the floor to open up beneath me.

I want to be anywhere but here.

It takes great effort to say the next words, to make them sound like a normal sentence rather than a pathetic attempt at walking back three whole years of feelings. "That's what I figured."

"It is?" he says, a trace of hope flickering on his face as I throw him this lifeline. "Good. I'm sorry if—"

"Nope," I say, shaking my head too hard. "It's fine."

"I should've said something earlier."

"Yeah . . . I guess so."

He frowns. "What does that mean?"

"Well," I say, grasping for my dignity, trying desperately to regain some footing, "it's just that you've obviously been kind of preoccupied lately."

"Ah," he says with a nod, his face clouding over again. " 'Preoccupied' being a fancy way of saying I've had my head up my ass?"

I shrug. "You said it, not me."

"You didn't have to."

"I'm sorry," I say again. "It's just . . . this isn't you. The way you've been acting ever since all this happened. It's just not."

Teddy's jaw twitches. "God, Al, of course it is," he says, his voice filled with frustration. "This is exactly me. I *am* that guy. I mean, look where I live. You give me a truckful of money, and *of course* I'm gonna go buy a robot and a house and a new car and everything else I've always wanted. And *of course* I want to go on talk shows. Are you kidding? I'd be amazing on TV. And you know what? There's nothing wrong with that. It's what pretty much everyone would do in my situation. Everyone but *you*." Without warning, he picks up an empty cardboard box and flings it against the wall. "This *is* me, Al. You just don't want to believe it. You never have. You always want me to be something more, something better. But maybe I'm not."

He stops then, breathing hard, and we sit there in silence, staring at the mess of papers between us, instructions for how to build the flimsiest of boats.

"I'm sorry," I say after a few minutes, so softly I'm not sure he hears me. "It's just that . . . you promised."

He's sitting with his head bent, but I see his shoulders rise as he takes a breath, and then he drags his eyes up to meet mine. "What?"

I'm almost afraid to say the words. "You promised that nothing would change."

Teddy shakes his head, then rises to his feet, scattering the papers between us.

"You know what your problem is, Al?" he says, and there's a look of great disappointment on his face. "You think that change is automatically a bad thing."

And then he walks out of the room.

# Twenty-One

The next morning, Teddy flies to L.A.

I don't hear about it until lunchtime, when Leo slides into the seat beside me and starts to assemble his usual meal: two slices of pizza smashed together to create a thoroughly disgusting sort of calzone. "Can you believe it?"

"What?" I ask, lowering my turkey sandwich.

He frowns. "Didn't he tell you?"

I don't have to ask who *he* is; I know instinctively that this is about Teddy. Lately everything is about Teddy.

I've had a knot in my stomach ever since I left his apartment last night. It wasn't just the fight, although that was awful, the worst we've ever had. It was the way he looked so panicked when I asked him about the kiss. The way he dismissed it as meaning nothing at all. The way he so efficiently punched a neat little hole in my heart.

"He went to L.A.," Leo says, and I frown at him.

"What?"

"I guess he's doing a couple interviews out there." He grins at me. "Looks like our Teddy's gonna be a star."

I watch as he begins to eat, tomato sauce dribbling down his chin. I was with him the first time he made one of his pizza sandwiches in front of Max, and I couldn't help laughing at the expression on his new boyfriend's face. But to his credit, Max immediately set to work making one of his own, and when he took a huge bite, their eyes met across the table and a smile broke across Leo's face.

"So when's he coming back?" I ask as he mops at his chin with a napkin.

"I think he's going straight to Cabo from there. Not a bad life, huh?"

I nod, but I feel suddenly exhausted.

"What?" Leo asks.

"We got into a fight last night."

"You and Teddy?" He shrugs. "It'll blow over."

"I don't know," I say, and it takes a great deal of effort not to cry at the memory of it. "It was a really big one."

"What was it about?"

I hesitate. "Everything," I say, and he nods as if he understands exactly what this means. Maybe he does.

"You two will be fine. You always are."

But I'm not so sure. Teddy texted to make sure I got home okay last night, which I suspect was more out of concern for his mother's instructions than concern for me. I wrote back a short *yes*, and he didn't respond after that. Even once I'd crawled into bed I kept glancing at my phone, wondering if it would light up again. But it remained dark and silent, and I knew deep down there would be no reply.

After school, on my way to the animal shelter—where I spend Wednesday afternoons walking a pack of cooped-up dogs who are heartbreakingly eager for the fresh air—I try texting him again.

*Break a leg,* I write. Then I wait a minute to see if he'll respond.

He doesn't.

When I come downstairs the next morning, I see that the small television in the kitchen is switched on and an overly cheerful morning news anchor is discussing unexpected uses for empty soda cans. Aunt Sofia normally hates these types of shows; we tend to listen to NPR over breakfast, the measured tones of world news filling the kitchen. But this morning is different.

"Did I miss it?" I ask, grabbing a piece of toast and sitting down across from Leo, who shakes his head.

"I always knew that kid was going somewhere," Uncle Jake says, opening the refrigerator. Beside him Aunt Sofia is making a pot of coffee. They'd have both usually left for work by now, but neither wanted to miss Teddy's segment.

"It's just a talk show," I say. "There'll probably be a piece on cat tricks right after him."

"I don't know," Aunt Sofia says. "I think this could be big for him. He's so charming, you know? And such a good-looking kid."

Leo makes a goofy face at me across the table and I smile gratefully.

"Plus, he's insanely rich," Uncle Jake adds, walking over with his plate. "There's a recipe for stardom if I've ever heard one."

"It's just Teddy," I say, but with less certainty this time.

A commercial break comes to an end and the jaunty theme song of the show returns, then Teddy is suddenly on-screen. He's sitting stiffly on a green couch, his hands folded in his lap, and seeing him there—that familiar set of his shoulders and the nervous twist of his mouth—is enough to send my heart up into my throat.

"And we're back now with Teddy McAvoy," says a chipper anchorwoman. "He's the youngest lottery winner in U.S. history, still a high school senior and already a millionaire many, many times over."

Teddy gives her an *aw, shucks* smile. He's wearing a pale blue button-down and a pair of khaki pants. On someone else it might look normal, but on Teddy—who usually wears jeans and plaid—it just makes him seem older and very, very far away.

"So, Teddy. Tell us. How does it feel?" she asks him, crossing her legs and leaning forward. "You won 141.3 *million* dollars. That's no small chunk of change."

"No," Teddy agrees. "It's kind of mind-boggling, actually. I'm still trying to get my head around it."

"Now, this happened the day after your eighteenth birthday, right?"

"Right. The ticket was actually a birthday gift. From a friend."

I feel suddenly dizzy. From across the kitchen Uncle Jake gives me a thumbs-up.

"Wow," the anchor says. "A hundred-and-forty-one-million-dollar present. That's a pretty nice friend you've got there. Will you be sharing the winnings at all?"

Teddy shifts in his seat. My heart drills away at me as I wait for his answer.

"We're still working that out," he says after a pause. "But I hope so. It's an incredible gift. One that's already changed my life. I'd like to be able to thank her in some way."

I lower my eyes, afraid to know whether my aunt and uncle are looking at me.

"Well, there are always diamonds, right?" the anchor says, smiling with all her teeth, and Teddy lets out a bark of a laugh. It's the first genuine moment from him since the interview began, and I suspect it's because he's imagining me in diamonds. It's enough to make me want to laugh too, though I know it doesn't fix anything between us.

"Maybe," he says to the anchor, still chuckling. "We'll have to see."

"Well, either way, you've got a pretty good friend there."

Something changes in Teddy's smile then, and there's a flatness behind his eyes. All at once I feel cold down to my toes.

"The best," he says finally, a note of false cheer to his voice.

"So what are your plans now?" the host asks. "That's a truly life-changing amount of money. Enough to make all your dreams come true, right? So what are they?"

"Well, first I'm going to Disney World, obviously," Teddy says, which makes her giggle in a way that's all out of proportion to the joke itself. "No, I'm still thinking about what to do with it. It's a big responsibility. I'm going to have some fun, of course—"

"Of course," she says with a knowing smile.

"But I also want to make sure to do some good with it, if possible. And I want to do some nice things for my mom too."

"That's so sweet," the host says, putting a hand over her heart. "Like what?"

"Well, if I said it on national television, it wouldn't be a surprise, so . . ."

She's positively glowing now. "Too right. But I'll tell you this: she's lucky to have a son like you."

"Well, I'm lucky to have a mom like her."

"Do you have a girlfriend?" she asks suddenly. "Because I have two daughters . . ."

Teddy gives an easy laugh, and he looks so handsome right then that it makes my heart bobble. "No girlfriend," he says. "Maybe one day."

"Well, I can imagine there will be quite a few applicants for the job," she says, reaching out to shake his hand. "Teddy McAvoy, thanks so much for being here with us this morning. I'd wish you all the best of luck, but it seems like you have luck to spare."

Teddy is still grinning into the camera when Aunt Sofia points the remote straight at his head and the screen goes dark. None of us say anything for a few seconds. On the table the coffee is going cold, and the square of light from the kitchen window is lengthening. It's well past time to leave for school, but nobody moves.

After a minute Leo begins to laugh, and I stare at him.

"What?"

"It's just . . . ," he says, shaking his head. "Remember that time in third grade when he peed his pants in front of the whole school?"

Everyone is silent for a moment, then—all at once—we burst out laughing too, and once we start it's hard to stop, our eyes filled with tears at the memory, so starkly different from the version of Teddy we just saw on national television.

"I have a feeling," Uncle Jake says eventually, still trying to catch his breath, "that you might need to remind him of that at some point."

# Twenty-Two

The following evening, Leo drags me to a discussion on digital animation at the Art Institute. For two hours he's completely enthralled, leaning forward in his seat as if willing himself closer to the stage. But I have a harder time paying attention; my mind is elsewhere.

This morning I found out I got into two schools: Northwestern and Colgate. When I texted my aunt to tell her the good news, she sent back a chain of exclamation points so long they filled the screen. Northwestern is her alma mater, and though she knows I have my heart set on Stanford, I suspect there's a part of her that's been hoping I might end up closer to Chicago.

But the person I most wanted to tell—the person I always want to tell everything—is still the only one I haven't. Instead I watched this afternoon as he sat amid a group of women on yet another talk show, joking about his terrible estimation skills.

"If you give me a jar of jelly beans and ask me to guess how many," he told them, "I'd probably say, like, two million. I was never much of a numbers guy."

"And now look at you," one of the hosts said with a smile. "I'd say the numbers have definitely worked in your favor."

I switched it off then. But for too long I stayed there in front of the TV, looking at my own reflection in the flat blackness of the screen.

When the panel discussion is over, Leo and I walk out onto the steps of the museum. Across the street is a white granite building that's part of the college and we stand facing it, the gusty breeze from the lake at our backs.

"You'll get in," I say, and he looks over at me distractedly.

"What?"

"To the Art Institute." I nod at the building. "You'll get in."

He doesn't answer. Instead he walks down the rest of the steps, then pauses in front of one of the enormous stone lions—which stand guard at either side of the entrance—and gives it a salute, the same way he's done since he was a kid. The motion is subtler now, and he seems almost embarrassed to be doing it, but it's more superstition than tradition at this point. The lion regards him stoically in return, then we head off down Michigan Avenue, our path lit by an endless constellation of red taillights.

"When do you hear from Michigan?" I ask as we walk.

173

It's meant as a peace offering. From his stony silence I assume he's annoyed that I mentioned the Art Institute, so this is my attempt to balance it out, to show him that I'm supportive no matter what, that even if he goes off to Michigan next year I'm still on board. But this strategy only gets me another slightly irritable look.

"Are you okay?" I ask as we turn a corner, heading away from the crowded streets of the Magnificent Mile.

"I'm fine."

"You seem a little . . ."

"What?"

"I don't know," I say. "Grouchy."

This makes him smile. "I think I'm nervous about seeing Max tomorrow."

"Really?" I ask, surprised.

"This is the longest we've ever been apart. And lately it's just been hard. I think the distance is getting to us."

"You guys will be fine," I say, but he looks over at me sharply, and I can tell he doesn't want reassurances right now. So instead I slip an arm through his, and together we cross over one of the bridges that span the Chicago River, our feet making hollow sounds on the metal grates.

At our favorite burger joint, we take the stairs down to the entrance. Inside, it has a greasy smell to it, and the jukebox is playing too loudly. We slide into a corner booth and shove aside the menus, which we haven't looked at in years.

Once the waiter takes our order, Leo continues as if we hadn't stopped talking. "He's been really pushing me about Michigan, which is stressful, because I'm not sure

that's what I want." He hesitates. "But I love him. He's . . .
he's . . ."

"Max," I say, and Leo smiles. Max is his first boyfriend.
His first love. He's as outgoing as Leo is serious, a wildly
talented guitarist who plays in two different bands and is
officially the only person on record to ever persuade Leo to
dance. He has a big laugh and irresistible curly hair and he
loves Leo enough to have watched every single Pixar movie
with him more than once.

"He's Max," Leo agrees. "But I don't know if we can
handle four more years of long distance. It's the absolute
worst."

I nod, but I'm also thinking that nearness can be awful
too. Being so close to someone you love without them knowing it. Without them ever returning it. That's another kind
of terrible.

"You're lucky you know where you want to be next
year," Leo says. "I hate that it feels like I have to choose
between Max and—" He gestures out the window, which
I take to mean: Chicago, the Art Institute, his dreams. "It
just kills me."

"You have to do what's right for you."

He scowls. "What does that even mean? How am I supposed to know if I'm doing the right thing? All I do is worry
I'm screwing everything up. And then I start worrying that
all this worry is going to somehow jinx us, you know?"

"That's not how the world works," I say. "That's not how
*love* works."

"How do you know? You've never been in love."

175

His words are unthinking, but they still have a bite to them, and once they're out there they have a kind of volume too: for a few seconds they sit blaring like a siren on the table between us, so loud it feels like the whole restaurant must be staring at me.

"Sorry," Leo says. "That was mean."

"No, it was true," I say, shaking my head. "Well, half-true."

"What do you mean?" he asks with a frown.

I drop my head into my hands. "God, Leo. Don't make me say it."

"What?" he asks, sounding genuinely confused.

"You must've noticed. We're always together, and—"

"Teddy?" he says softly, and I brave a glance at him. When he sees my expression, he nods. "Aha."

I sit up straighter. "You don't seem that surprised."

"I wasn't totally sure," he says. "But I had a feeling."

"Why didn't you ever say anything?"

"Why didn't *you*?"

"Because it's humiliating," I say miserably. "To love someone who doesn't love you back."

"You don't know that."

"I do, actually. It came up during our fight the other night."

Leo's eyes get big behind his glasses. "It did?"

"Yeah, because we kissed—"

*"You did?"*

I laugh, but it comes out bitterly. "The morning we found

out he won. But it didn't mean anything. To him, anyway. He was pretty clear about that."

Leo reaches across the table and gives my hand a pat. "I'm sorry," he says. "Would it make you feel any better if I listed some of the worst things about Teddy? I can do it chronologically or alphabetically. Your choice."

"Thanks," I say, giving him a watery smile. "That means a lot. But I don't think it would help."

He nods gravely. "It's incurable, then?"

"I'm afraid so."

"Can I ask you a question?" he says, and I nod. "I know you can't choose who you love, but . . ."

"What?"

"Well, how can you have so much faith in someone—especially someone who lets you down as much as Teddy—when you have so little faith in the world?"

I frown at him, and then without thinking I say, "How can *you* be so superstitious about everything when nothing bad has ever happened to you?"

We blink at each other, both a little stunned. The jukebox switches over to a new song, and the waiter sets our plates down with a clatter, whisking off again without asking whether we still need anything, which is just as well, since it's a question I have no idea how to answer right now. It could fill the room, what we still need right now. It could fill the city.

Neither of us touches our food.

"That's *why*," Leo says eventually, his voice choked.

"That's why I'm so superstitious. *Because* nothing bad has ever happened to me."

"Leo . . ."

"I know you might find it hard to believe, but it's totally nerve-racking, having everything in your life be *fine*. Especially when you know it's not supposed to be like that. I've had it so much easier than you or Teddy. . . ." He pauses, tipping his head back so that all I can see is his throat, his Adam's apple bobbing up and down. "It doesn't seem right."

"Hey," I begin, but when he lowers his chin to look at me there's something so bleak in his gaze that I stop again.

"Maybe it'd be different if you guys weren't in my life," he says. "Maybe it'd be easier to ignore all the terrible things that can happen. But I can't. Because none of it's happened to *me*, and that means I'm overdue. It means the bottom's gonna drop out at some point. It just is."

"That's not necessarily true."

"Think about it," he continues. "My life's been pretty smooth sailing. The hardest thing probably should've been coming out, but even that wasn't as dramatic as you'd expect."

I nod, remembering when he first told me. It was the summer before freshman year, though by then I'd already sort of guessed as much. We were eating ice cream in Lincoln Park, and I was talking about my blinding crush on Travis Reed, and he gave me a look of such genuine surprise that I lowered my spoon. "What?"

"I like him too," he admitted, and we stared at each other a second, then both burst out laughing.

In the end it turned out Leo was more Travis's type; not long after that, they had their first kiss in the school parking lot after the fall formal. And a couple months later Leo decided he was ready to come out to his parents too.

"You'll be fine," I told him as he paced in front of me that morning, rehearsing what he planned to say. "Your parents love you. And they're the best people I know. Plus, they're Democrats, which means they're practically required to be on board, right?"

"Right," he mumbled, though he didn't sound convinced. Even with parents like his, there were no guarantees. But an hour later he returned with a dazed expression. And before I could even ask, he said with a look of immense relief, "It went . . . weirdly well."

Now, though, he looks almost disappointed by the ease of it all. "That was my one big obstacle, and it turned out fine. I mean, sure, it took me a while to get there, and freshman year was a little rough, but let's be honest: it could've been so much worse."

"Well, there *was* that time your parents hung a poster of the U.S. men's soccer team above your bed."

In spite of himself, Leo laughs. "That will never not be embarrassing."

"They were just trying to be there for you."

"Exactly," he says. "That's what I mean."

"What?"

"I've been really lucky. Too lucky. It can't go on like this forever. Something bad is bound to happen."

"That's not—"

"You and Teddy are my two best friends," he says, his brown eyes intent on mine. "And you guys have been through so much. Too much. It doesn't seem fair. Especially with you. You were dealt the worst hand ever, and you deserve more luck than anyone, and it just makes me feel even more guilty that I—"

"Leo," I say gently. "I don't think there's a big tote board somewhere. I don't think it has anything to do with keeping score." I pause. "I don't think the world is necessarily fair."

"But what if you're wrong?" he asks, leaning forward. "Look, Teddy got screwed in the dad department, right? Then he wins the lottery. Maybe that's the universe making it up to him."

"I think you're giving the universe way too much credit."

"But what if I'm not?"

I give him a hard look. "Then what about me?"

"Well, it would obviously mean you're due something good," he says, then adds, "something *great*."

"But that's the thing," I say, trying to keep my voice even. "I kind of hope that would be true even if something horrible *hadn't* happened to me. I hate to believe you have to pay for the good things with something bad."

"So you think it only works one way?"

"I don't think it works like that at all," I say, exasperated. "If it was possible to store up enough good karma to save you from anything bad happening, then it wouldn't be so hard to find volunteers at the nursing home on a Saturday night."

"Well, if there were bonus points for that," Leo says, allowing a small smile, "you'd have enough stored up for a lifetime of good luck."

I roll my eyes. "Now you know the truth. I'm only in it for the karmic credit."

"No," he says, picking up his water glass, "you're in it because of your parents."

"And because of me," I say quickly, automatically, thinking about how Teddy said this very same thing. Maybe that's how it had *started,* with me trying to do what my parents no longer could. But it's not about that anymore.

At least I don't think it is.

At least not entirely.

It's not.

I say this last part out loud: "It's not."

"It's not what?" Leo asks with a frown, and I blink at him.

"It's not only because of my parents. It's about helping people, and doing something good, and making a difference."

He nods, but he doesn't look quite convinced. He slides his fork back and forth on the table, his mouth twisting. "Anyway, I'm sorry about what I said before."

"What?"

"That you don't have faith in the world."

I consider this a moment. "It's not that, exactly. It's just . . . the world hasn't done much for me lately. I guess I'm still waiting for it to impress me."

Leo gives me an odd look. "It should've been you."

"What?"

"The ticket. The money. It should've been you."

"No, that's not my dream," I say. "That's Teddy's. Even if he doesn't know it yet."

"So what's yours?"

I think of that night so long ago, standing outside the door to Leo's room with my toothbrush in hand while he asked his mom if I was an orphan. She told him that I was, but that I would be other things too.

*Like what?* he asked then.

*Like what?* he's asking again now.

It's been nine years, and I still don't have an answer.

I wonder if I ever will.

"I don't know yet," I tell him, and then I pick up the lukewarm burger and take a bite before he can ask me anything else.

Afterward we pass a newsstand outside the restaurant and Leo stops short. When he pulls a glossy magazine off the rack, I see that there's a smiling picture of Teddy in the top right corner. Underneath it, in bold letters, it says THE BIG WINNER.

Leo stares at it in astonishment, but I only shake my head.

"The universe really outdid itself this time," I say.

# Twenty-Three

It's the second day of spring break and I'm up to my elbows in dirty dishwater.

Beside me Sawyer is drying off cups with a checkered towel, but otherwise the kitchen is empty. They were light on volunteers this weekend, so the two of us offered to take cleanup duty, which wasn't very popular tonight since the dishwasher was broken. But I didn't mind. It wasn't like I had anything else to do.

I scrub hard at a patch of crusted cheese on one of the plates, gritting my teeth as I attempt to pry it off, and Sawyer looks at me sideways.

"What did that poor plate ever do to you?"

I drop it into the soapy water, stepping back to avoid the splash. He reaches over and hands me a scouring pad.

"Here," he says. "Try this."

"Thanks," I say, blowing a strand of hair out of my eyes.

"If you insist on going to battle with that thing, you might as well have a good weapon."

This makes me smile. "Sorry. I feel like I'm not great company tonight."

"You're always good company," he says. "Though the cutlery might not agree."

"I'll go clear the rest," I say, wiping my hands on my apron, then heading back out into the other room, where a few stragglers are still sitting at a table in the corner.

"Hey, Alice," says Trevor, a regular here ever since I started volunteering. He's wearing the green woolen cap I got him for Christmas last year, pulled low over his eyes so that all I can see is his gray beard. Sometimes I run into him at the homeless shelter too, especially when the weather is bad. When he's not there I worry about him, but his answer to my questions is always just "I get by."

Now he's flipping through a newspaper as two of the other guys finish their bowls of vanilla pudding. When I walk over, I realize they're looking at an article about Teddy. "Big winner," Trevor says, studying the photo. "Just a kid too."

"I shoulda bought a ticket," says Frank, one of the other men, and the third, Desmond, shakes his head.

"I *did*."

Frank looks up. "Did you win?"

"Don't think he'd be eating this slop if he had," Trevor says, then winks at me. "Sorry, Alice."

"It's okay, I'm just on dishes tonight," I tell them. "But

I'll see what I can do about some chocolate cake for this weekend."

Trevor grins at me. "I'd come here for that cake even if I *was* a millionaire."

"Glad to hear it," I say, but as I carry a stack of dishes back into the kitchen I'm thinking about Teddy and that money, about how his mom has spent six years sleeping on a pullout couch in the living room of a tiny apartment in a crumbling building on a terrible block, and nobody could ever say they didn't need it. But then to hear Trevor and Desmond and Frank joke about winning only reminds me there will always be others who need it even more.

As soon as I drop the dirty dishes into the sink, my phone buzzes in my pocket and I pull it out to see that Leo's sent me a photo of Teddy from a gossip website. The headline reads LOTTERY HOTTIE MEETS PAPARAZZI.

With a sigh I set it down on the counter and turn back to the sink. I can feel Sawyer's eyes on me, but he doesn't say anything as I begin to scour the dishes, scraping at dried noodles and hardened sauce until my elbow is sore.

"So," he says eventually. "You wanna talk about it?"

I pass him a glass. "About what?"

"Whatever it is that's got you so fired up." He wipes down the cup, then sets it on the counter beside the others. "There's only so much dish-related brutality I can watch before intervening."

I stop what I'm doing and turn to him. The sponge in my hand is dripping into the sink, making fat splashes in the soapy water. Sawyer is watching me with those blue eyes of his, looking half-amused and half-nervous, and I find myself thinking about how different he is from Teddy.

I'm about to shrug off his question, to say that there's nothing wrong, to pretend everything is fine. But I'm suddenly desperate to talk to someone. Yesterday Leo left for Michigan, and Teddy is probably on his way to Mexico right now. Not that it matters, because how could he be the solution when he's already the problem?

I tip my head up to look at Sawyer, who is watching me closely.

"My idiot friend," I tell him, "has gone viral."

He raises his eyebrows. "Teddy?"

"Yes," I say with a nod, relieved to finally say it out loud and surprised to discover that I'm dangerously close to crying. I bite my lip.

Sawyer looks confused. "And that's a problem because . . . ?"

"It's not a problem. It's just that . . . the guy does a couple of interviews and all of a sudden he's like this Internet sensation?"

"He won the lottery," Sawyer says. "People are curious."

I shake my head. "He's everywhere. There are clips of him all over the place. He's even a GIF! And there are all sorts of fan sites already. I mean, it's only been a couple days. How fast do these people work?"

"It actually doesn't take that long to build a—"

"I don't get it," I say, cutting him off. "How can you have fans if you haven't done anything? What are they fans *of*?"

"Just one of those things," Sawyer says. "You know how it is. People online get excited about really random stuff."

"But he's not a cat eating a cheeseburger or a monkey making friends with a goat. He's just a guy who had some good luck."

"Human interest story, I guess. Young, good-looking guy from a not-so-great neighborhood wins the lottery. It's like a fairy tale."

I place both hands on the edge of the counter, leaning forward to watch the whorls of soap and grease in the water.

Sawyer tosses the towel over his shoulder. "Are you and Teddy . . . ?"

I look over at him sharply. "What?"

"Are you guys together?"

"No," I say without hesitating. The word comes out forcefully, echoing around the empty kitchen. I shake my head and say it again: "No."

Sawyer nods slowly, like he isn't quite sure whether to believe me. "Okay."

"We're not," I say, blushing. "Really."

"Okay," he says again.

"We're just friends. Or at least we were."

He folds his arms across his chest, waiting for me to continue.

"This lottery thing has made everything kind of weird," I admit. "We've always been . . . close. And then this huge thing happened, and now everything is different."

"And it feels like you're losing him."

I go still. "I didn't say that."

"Yeah," he says. "You sort of did."

When I turn to look at him he holds my gaze, and it should be weird, this moment between us, but for some reason it's not.

"Do you want to go out with me sometime?" he asks.

"Like, for cocoa?"

"Like, for dinner."

"Like, a date?"

He grins. "Exactly like a date."

"How about tomorrow?" I say, and I realize I'm smiling too.

# Twenty-Four

When I stagger into the house the next afternoon, Uncle Jake—who is working from home today, his computer balanced on his lap and his feet up on the coffee table—looks over.

"What in the world . . . ?" he says as I cross through the living room and toward the basement stairs, lugging a huge bundle of cardboard. I'm breathing hard and sweating. It's already been an enormous hassle to get this from the store to the bus and now home, and I'm so aggravated at having to do it all by myself that I can hardly see straight.

Uncle Jake jumps up from the couch and jogs over, slipping on the wooden floors in his socked feet. "What are you doing?" he says, taking the cardboard from me and leaning it against the wall. "I would've helped you with this."

It didn't even occur to me to ask him. It's not that he

189

isn't helpful when it comes to these sorts of things. Over the years, he's assisted in the making of too many macaroni necklaces to count, continued to dye Easter eggs with us even after the great purple stain incident, and learned how to braid strings into bracelets when it was all the rage among sixth-grade girls and nobody else would make them with me.

But I was so focused on the fact that I was going to have to build this boat without Teddy—so bitter about it—that I didn't even think to mention it. And now the word pops into my head again, entirely unbidden: *island*.

"It's for physics," I explain, leaning against the wall alongside the slabs of cardboard. I kick off my sneakers, still panting. "We have to build a boat."

Uncle Jake raises his eyebrows. "*We* as in . . . you and me?"

"*We* as in me and Teddy."

"Ah," he says, rubbing at his chin. "So . . . *we* as in you and me."

I start to shake my head, to tell him I'm fine on my own, because that's what I always do. But then I stop myself, thinking: *peninsula*. Thinking: *at least that*.

He eyes the cardboard, then peeks inside the plastic bag I've set down beside it, which is filled with rolls of tape. "This is it? All you can use? Seems less than ideal."

"Well, I wouldn't want to have to cross the ocean with it," I tell him, "but hopefully it'll be enough to get us to the other side of the pool."

"You and Teddy both? In a cardboard boat?" He laughs. "I'd pay to see that."

"Lucky for you, admission is free."

"Then we'd better get to work," he says, clapping his hands, and when he picks up the cardboard I feel immediately lighter, realizing how grateful I am for the help.

The house is all ours—Aunt Sofia is at work and Leo is in Michigan—but even so we decide the basement is the best place for this, so we send the cardboard thumping down the stairs, where it lands in a heap on the unfinished concrete floor.

"So," Uncle Jake says as we cut the twine. "What have you got so far?"

I stare down at the oversized rectangles in dismay. "You're looking at it."

"Right," he says. "So you haven't . . . ?"

I shake my head.

"And Teddy hasn't . . . ?"

"Nope," I say. "Not even a little bit."

He walks over to grab a notepad off the dusty desk in the corner. The basement is mostly just pipes, concrete, and extra storage space, and the walls are lined with boxes, many of them filled with things that used to belong to my parents, reminders of my previous life. Which is why I don't come down here very often.

"Teddy's got a tough road ahead of him," Uncle Jake says as we settle down on the floor, which is hard and cool. "That kid just got catapulted up to the moon. And you can't travel that far and that fast without some motion sickness, you know?"

I duck my head. "I guess."

"But," he says, his voice firmer now, "it's no excuse for disappearing on you either."

"He didn't disappear, exactly. He's in Mexico. For spring break."

"Yeah, well, I imagine he could've worked on this with you before he left."

"Teddy's always taken more of a last-minute approach to things," I tell him. "Though it's gotten a little worse lately."

Uncle Jake is watching me with something like sympathy, his blue eyes clear and direct, and I have to look away, because those were my dad's eyes too, and my chest goes tight with the familiarity of his gaze. "Must be hard."

"What?"

"All of it."

I shake my head, not sure what to say. "It's fine," I tell him after a moment, picking up a pen and turning back to the pile of cardboard. "We'll make it work."

I know that's not what he meant. He wasn't talking about the boat at all. But I can't think about Teddy anymore right now, and Uncle Jake seems to understand this too. So instead we get to work. He grabs his toolbox while I sketch rough diagrams, and we discuss the principles of flotation, things like density and balance and buoyancy.

And for a while I'm fine. For a while it's easy to forget about Teddy and the fact that he's spending spring break on a beach in Mexico while I'm spending it in our dimly lit

192

basement, working on a project that we're supposed to be doing together.

"You're pretty good at this," I say to Uncle Jake, who is making clean slices in the cardboard, following the outline I've drawn of the base of the boat.

He glances up at me with a smile. "I've built a few boxcars in my day."

"What's a boxcar?"

"It's not all that different from a box boat. We used to race them."

"Who?" I ask, still bent over my diagram, not completely paying attention, but when the silence lengthens I look up. My uncle is watching me with an unreadable expression, his mouth screwed up to one side.

"Your father," he says, and though the words sound casual, I can see in the set of his jaw what this costs him. He never talks about my dad. At least not to me.

For a few seconds we stare at each other. Behind him a thousand specks of dust are floating in the light from the window, making everything dreamlike and indistinct, and I'm almost afraid to breathe, like it might shatter the moment, like it might signal the end of something that I wasn't even sure—until now—I wanted to begin.

"He always used to beat me," he says again, his voice gruffer this time. He bows his head and rubs at the back of his neck. "Drove me nuts to see my little brother whizzing past me year after year. But I swear that kid could've made a rocket ship out of two toothpicks and a paper clip."

"He was always building stuff," I say, smiling at the

193

memory. "When we went out to a restaurant, he'd be piling matchbooks on the table the whole time. He couldn't help himself."

Uncle Jake's eyes are watery. "He was something, your dad."

My mind is humming, moving so fast my thoughts are tripping over themselves. I hesitate, wanting to be sure of myself, then push forward before I can think again. "I'd love to hear more."

Uncle Jake seems surprised. "More?"

"About my dad," I say, suddenly nervous. "Not just when you were kids, but later too."

It's been forever since I asked this of him. For so long now I've just assumed this particular door was sealed shut. But maybe time doesn't make it harder to get through; maybe it makes it easier. Because now I find myself turning this new piece of information over like candy on my tongue: once upon a time, my dad used to build boxcars. It's not much, but even such a tiny sliver of knowledge feels like stumbling across something rare and precious. And I find I'm not ready to let go of it just yet.

"Alice," Uncle Jake says softly, looking apologetic, and my heart sinks.

"I know it's hard for you to talk about him," I say before he can go on. "It is for me too. But . . . it's also getting hard for me to remember him sometimes. And that's so much worse."

He looks stricken by this, and for a long time he just

watches me, as if weighing something invisible to the rest of the world. Then, finally, he shakes his head.

"Maybe," he says, but it doesn't sound like a maybe. It sounds like a no. It sounds like the closing of a door.

I want to say something more. I want to ask him a thousand questions. I want to lie on my back on the basement floor and listen to all his stories.

But instead I just give him a feeble smile, trying to hide my disappointment as he turns his attention back to the scattered pieces of our hapless boat.

# Twenty-Five

That night, Sawyer insists on picking me up at home, which gives my aunt and uncle an excuse to hover near the windows on the second floor, trying—and failing—to be nonchalant as they keep watch for him. When he finally comes into sight—tall and thin and lanky, his blond head bent, his eyes on his sneakers—they both let out a shout.

"Have you guys ever heard the expression *be cool*?" I ask, unable to keep from laughing at the two of them with their noses pressed to the window.

"He's never been cool a day in his life," Aunt Sofia says.

Uncle Jake frowns. "Neither has she."

"This isn't a big deal," I say for what feels like the hundredth time. "I don't even know if I like him."

"But he's so cute," Aunt Sofia says, still peering through the window.

"And punctual," Uncle Jake adds with a note of approval.

"Unlike some people," she adds under her breath, and it makes me want to burrow under the floorboards, because they can only be talking about Teddy, which means I've obviously done a much worse job keeping my feelings hidden than I thought.

"He's a junior," I say as below us Sawyer turns up the walk. "And I'm graduating soon. What's the point?"

"What's the point of anything like this?" Aunt Sofia says. "You date. You enjoy each other's company. You have fun. Maybe you make out a little."

"Sofe!" Uncle Jake says, leaning back from the window to glare at her.

"Well," she says with a smile, but then her face rearranges itself into something more serious. "All I'm saying is that it doesn't have to be complicated. This is supposed to be the fun part, you know? So go have fun."

As if on cue, the doorbell rings.

"I'm not inviting him in," I inform them as I start to head downstairs. I'm still wearing the same worn jeans and plaid button-down I've had on all day. I'm determined not to think of this date as a big deal. Because as much as I like Sawyer, and as clear as it is that nothing more will happen with Teddy, it still feels somehow dishonest. My heart is a balloon on a string, and I'm not ready to let go of it entirely.

"What," I hear Uncle Jake call as I hurry down, "are you embarrassed by us?"

"Yes," I say emphatically, though really it's just that I've never had a guy pick me up here before—at least not like this, not in a way that feels so oddly formal. We don't live in the suburbs, where it's easy to cruise over in a car and honk a few times. In the city, going somewhere usually means taking public transportation, and it tends to be more convenient just to get there on your own. Teddy comes over all the time, but if we had plans to go out in an entirely different neighborhood, it's almost impossible to picture him showing up on my front porch beforehand just to personally escort me there.

This doesn't exactly bother me. But it does make me a little sad. Because Sawyer is different.

Sawyer is here.

And when I open the door and see him blinking at me as if I'm wearing a prom dress and not my rattiest pair of jeans, I realize it doesn't matter whether I consider this a big deal. Because it is to him.

"You look beautiful," he says, though all he can see is my usual quilted jacket, my jeans—which have a hole in one knee—and my scuffed black Vans. Even my hair is just tied back in a messy bun. If Teddy was here, he'd probably raise an eyebrow and ask if I'd just gotten up. But it's Sawyer who is standing before me, looking flustered.

"Thank you," I say, and he beams at me. "So what's the plan?"

"Well, it's choose your own adventure, actually."

"Is this going to end with me walking the plank of a pirate ship?" I say with a laugh. "Somehow I always ended up getting eaten by a crocodile in those things."

"I promise that's not one of the options," he says, then

rubs his hands together. "So here's choice number one: bus, taxi, or walk."

I can tell he thinks I'm going to opt for a taxi, but it's unseasonably warm tonight, the first hint of spring in the air after so many months of cold and snow.

"Walk," I say, and he nods, steering us away from the house, where I can practically feel Aunt Sofia and Uncle Jake still watching through the window.

"So how's your break so far?" I ask as we start to stroll, and Sawyer laughs.

"Super nerdy. I've mostly been at the library for a history paper."

"This whole history thing of yours . . ."

"I don't know," he says. "I just love it. There are so many different versions of the past. It's like you can never find out enough. I know it's kind of—"

"Charming," I say, and he smiles. "So what about the ancestry stuff?"

He shrugs. "Well, we moved here last year when my grandpa got sick, and it made me realize I should probably know more about my own history too. And that I should be asking him more questions while he's still around."

I consider my own family tree, how few branches are left and how few people there are to tell me about them. Aunt Sofia tries; she hangs ornaments that belonged to my parents at Christmas and makes cupcakes on their birthdays. But Uncle Jake is like a lock without a key. And how can I blame him, when I understand better than anyone how hard it can be to talk about them?

But that still doesn't make it any easier.

"Anyway, it was my grandpa's side of the family that had a castle near Aberdeen, which is where I want to—" Sawyer stops abruptly and looks over at me. "You know what? I probably shouldn't start talking about castles or I'll never stop."

"No, it's interesting," I say. "I barely know anything about my family history. And the closest I've been to a castle is one of those bouncy ones at birthday parties."

He laughs. "Slightly less historical but way more fun."

We pass under the metal scaffolding of the L train, where a man is playing his guitar, something slow and sweet and full of soul.

"So," Sawyer says. "Next choice: fancy bistro, hole-in-the-wall Mexican place, or grab a slice of pizza and eat it in the park."

"Pizza in the park," I say without hesitation.

"I'm sensing a theme with you," he says, but he looks pleased.

Once we get our slices, we find a wooden bench beneath a towering oak tree. In the distance a game of kickball is coming to an end, and the paths are busy with evening joggers and couples holding hands.

"This isn't a complaint," Sawyer says, opening up the pizza box and offering it to me first, "just an observation. But . . . you don't have very expensive taste."

"That's true," I say cheerfully, taking a bite.

"Is that why you didn't want any of the money?"

The question catches me off guard. I lower my pizza, unsure what to say, wondering how he could possibly know that.

"Sorry," he says. "Is this not okay to talk about?"

"No, it's just . . . why do you assume . . . ?"

"Well, you said the ticket was a birthday gift," Sawyer explains. "And Teddy seems like a pretty stand-up guy, so I just figured he must have offered you some of it. And if you'd accepted, I probably would've heard about it on the news."

"Right," I say, picking at the crust. "That makes sense."

"So I guess I'm just curious. What makes someone turn down millions and millions of dollars?"

I stare out into the darkness, wondering how I can even begin to answer this. "I don't know," I say finally. "I think it scared me a little."

"It's a lot of money," he agrees.

"Teddy's whole life has changed."

"Some would say for the better."

"And some would say for the worse. I wasn't sure I wanted that to happen to me."

It takes a great deal of effort to bite back the word *again*. But I'm pretty sure he doesn't know anything about my past. Everything between us is still a blank canvas, and there's something refreshing about that.

Sawyer nods, but he still looks troubled.

"What?" I ask, glancing at him sideways.

"It's just . . . well, I've seen you at the soup kitchen. My grandma says you're their best volunteer. And I know you do a bunch of other stuff like that too. So wasn't there a part of you that was tempted to take it and, I don't know, do something good with it?"

Once again I feel a wrench of sadness at this, because I know it's what my parents would've done, and there's nothing worse than feeling like I'm disappointing them even after they're gone. I tip my head back, trying to sort through my cluttered thoughts.

"Honestly? It was just instinct, turning it down. It seemed like the right thing to do, so I did it. And most of the time I'm glad. But of course there's a part of me that wonders . . . I mean, I can hardly walk into the soup kitchen without thinking of what that money could do. Or what it might've done for my family. I feel guilty *all the time*. But I also feel insanely relieved that I didn't take it, which only makes me feel even *more* guilty. And then I start wishing I never bought the stupid ticket in the first place, which is also awful, because it means so much to Teddy and his mom. So yeah. You could say I'm second-guessing myself. At this point I'm second-guessing my second guesses."

Sawyer shakes his head. "I'm sorry. I had no idea."

"It's fine," I say with a shrug. "Really. This is just kind of a weird time."

"Well, hey, maybe Teddy will end up doing something really great with the money, and that'll solve everything."

"Yeah," I say, aware of the doubt in my voice. "Maybe."

"Are you cold?" he asks, and it's only then I realize I'm shivering. I shake my head and zip my jacket up higher.

"I'm fine. It feels good to be outside."

"I know," he says, looking out over the park. "I moved here from California, so I still haven't really gotten used to the Chicago winters."

*California*, I think, closing my eyes. Even after all this time, when I hear the word, my first thought is still: *Home*.

"Me too," I say quietly, and he looks at me in surprise.

"You're from California?"

"Yes," I say, trying to make the words sound effortless, "I lived in San Francisco till I was nine."

He laughs. "That's so crazy. I'm from San Jose."

"That's close to Stanford, right? I really want to go there next year."

His face brightens. "That's awesome. It's such a good school. Definitely on my list too. They have a great history program."

"Yeah?" I say, thinking how nice it is to talk to him about this, when it's so hard to have the same conversation with Leo and Teddy.

"I actually had a job at the library there last summer," he says, "which I know isn't *quite* the same as going there, but I really loved it. Have you ever been?"

"Just once," I say, remembering that long ago day when my parents and I explored it together, my mother as wide-eyed as an incoming freshman. "My mom got into a graduate program there when I was little, so we went to see the campus."

"Did she like it?"

"The campus? Yeah. It's beautiful."

"No, the program."

I hesitate. This is the part where I'm supposed to tell him my sad story. Where the look in his eyes will change into something more sympathetic, something closer to pity. And I don't want that to happen. Because I like the way he's looking at me now. For once, I don't feel like lugging my tragic history into the conversation. So I don't.

"She didn't end up going," I tell him, simple as that.

"Well, hopefully you will," he says with a smile. "When do you hear?"

"Tomorrow, actually."

"Are you nervous?"

"Yes," I admit. "I've wanted this for so long. To go back. To go home. Not that I don't love it here, because I do. But I miss the way things used to be. When I moved here, it was sort of . . . abrupt. So it sometimes feels like I left a piece of myself back on the West Coast. And if I was to move back out there . . ."

"You'd feel whole again," he says. He doesn't press for more of my feelings on the subject, like Leo would. And he doesn't try to crack a joke so that I'll smile, like Teddy always does. He just sits there, considering this, then nods. "I think I get that. When you move, it's like your life gets split in two. So you never really feel at home in either place."

I smile. "Exactly."

"Plus," he says, "I really miss the tacos out there."

"Totally," I say with a laugh. "They were so much better."

We sit there swapping stories until it's time to make the next choice: bowling, a movie, or an arcade. I pick the arcade, and we spend the next hour playing Skee-Ball and fishing for cheap stuffed animals with a useless metal claw.

At one point Sawyer nearly gets one; he snags a plush penguin by the very tip of its floppy wing. As he's trying to reel it in I jump up and down and hit him on the arm a few times, excited all out of proportion to the prize, and in a fit of enthusiasm the words come flying out of my mouth before I can stop them: "C'mon, Teddy!"

It's automatic, nothing more than a habit, like accidentally calling your teacher *Mom*. But still I freeze, and so does Sawyer, his hand bobbling on the machine so that the penguin falls out of the claw and back into the soft pile of his stuffed friends.

Our eyes meet briefly, then we both look away again.

"Sorry," I say. "I didn't mean—"

He shakes his head, though I can see his blue eyes are full of hurt. "I know."

"I'm just so used to yelling at him," I say with a smile, but Sawyer's face is still serious. "Should we try again?"

"Maybe something different," he says, scanning the room distractedly. I follow him over to a wall of video games, neither of us speaking, and we spend the next twenty minutes steering Pac-Man and his wife through their pixelated maze. And because it's easier than talking about it, and because it's preferable to figuring out what it meant, I find myself being overly flirty with him, as if that might be enough to erase the sound of Teddy's name. It feels a bit desperate, even to me, but it seems to work, because after a while the awkwardness starts to melt away, and by the time we walk back outside into the chilly March night, things feel normal between us again.

When we finally turn onto my street, Sawyer stops short of our house, pausing a few doors down.

"I'm just over there," I say, pointing at the brownstone.

"I remember," he says with a smile. "But I figured your parents might still be keeping an eye out the window, so . . ."

It's been so long since anyone made that mistake, and the way it sounds coming from Sawyer—so normal, so obvious, because *of course* the pair of adults I live with should be my parents—I can't bring myself to correct him. "You saw that, huh?"

"Hard to miss."

"So what now?"

"Well," he says. "Now you get three more choices."

"Oh yeah?"

He reaches out and puts a hand on my waist. I'm surprised to find this sends a shiver through me. "Option one," he says. "I walk you to the door and say good night."

I inch closer to him. "What's option two?"

"Well," he says, looking bashful. "Option two is . . . I kiss you now."

"Interesting," I say, putting a hand on his chest. "And option three?"

"You kiss—" he begins, but before he has a chance to finish I stand on my tiptoes and press my lips against his, and just like that he's kissing me back. When we step away again, he smiles at me with such tenderness that I feel a little shaky.

"Good choice," he says.

It isn't until afterward, as I walk back toward the house, that the fluttering in the pit of my stomach gives way to something more hollow. When I'm sure Sawyer is out of sight, I pause for a second, pulling in long breaths of cool air, feeling oddly panicky. I know it isn't because the kiss wasn't great (it was), and it isn't because Sawyer's not wonderful (he is).

It's because—quite simply—he's not Teddy.

And suddenly I'm furious with myself. Because what in the world am I doing? What am I waiting for? It's like Aunt Sofia said: this is supposed to be fun. So why am I so miserable?

And right then I hate Teddy for it too. Because Sawyer is here, and he's not. Because Sawyer looks at me in a way that I know Teddy never will. Because Sawyer wants me, and Teddy doesn't. Because he planned a whole night in triplicate and picked me up at my front door, and Teddy— who ditched me to go off to Mexico with his friends, who is probably living the high life on some white-sand beach, sunburned and happy and utterly delighted with himself— would never do any of those things.

My head is spinning as I hurry up the walkway toward the front door, suddenly freezing and anxious to be inside, my eyes on the loose stones of the path, so I'm nearly on top of him before I realize someone is sitting on the porch steps.

I stop short, my heart flying up into my throat, and for a moment I think I must be seeing things.

Because there on the front stoop—impossibly, miraculously—is Teddy.

# Part Four

APRIL

# Twenty-Six

It's after midnight, and the first thing I think—however illogical—is that this must be an April Fools' joke. I'm about to say as much, but then Teddy lifts his head, and his face is so unexpectedly solemn that I drop onto the steps beside him without a word.

This is the first time we've seen each other since our fight, and it's almost physically painful, being this close to him. The silence between us—usually so comfortable—is now prickly and tentative, and it just about breaks my heart.

I'm sitting only a few inches away from him. But it feels like miles.

"So what happened to Mexico?" I ask when he doesn't say anything.

He shrugs. "It's still there."

"Well, that's a relief," I say, attempting a smile, but his

face remains impassive. There's a stillness to him right now that's disconcerting. Teddy is normally all motion and restless energy; there's this fast-burning spark inside him that always seems to be just barely contained, like at any minute he might combust. Like at any minute there might be fireworks. But not now. "What about everyone else?"

"They're still there too."

I wait for more, and when it doesn't come I ask, "So why aren't you?"

"Because," he says, finally looking at me, "my dad's back."

I close my eyes for a second, trying not to telegraph my concern at this news. But there can only be one reason Charlie McAvoy is here, and I know Teddy well enough to know he won't want to believe it.

"My mom called last night to tell me."

I nod, still absorbing this. "Is she okay?"

"I think so. I mean, it's not like they haven't been in touch at all. But I can't imagine what it must've been like for her to open the door and see him there, just totally out of the blue." He lets out a breath. "He's coming by again tomorrow morning."

"To see you?"

He nods. "Is it weird that I'm sort of nervous?"

"Not at all," I say, wishing there wasn't so much space between us. "Did she say why he's here?"

"He's in town on business. For some meetings, I guess."

"So you don't think he's here—"

"No," he says before I have a chance to finish. But we both know what I was about to say: *because of the money.* "He told my mom he didn't even know about it."

"Teddy," I say softly, but he shakes his head.

"He told her he has a real job now," he says, his tone brisk. "A good job. He hasn't gambled in almost a year, and he's been going to meetings every week."

He already sounds so defensive that there's nothing to do but drop it. "Okay," I say, wanting to believe that. But it just feels like too much of coincidence, too big a leap of faith. "It's good you came home."

Teddy nods, though I can tell he's holding something back; then I notice his backpack slumped against a flower-pot, half-hidden in the shadows.

"But you haven't actually been home yet."

"I don't know what's wrong with me," he says, rubbing his eyes. "I got into a cab at the airport, and when he asked where I was going I gave him your address. It was just auto-matic. I don't know. Maybe it's because I've been thinking about you so much."

My heart lurches, and it takes everything in me to fight back a surge of hope. I used to think the hardest thing was him not knowing that I loved him. But now, after he dis-missed that kiss, I understand there's something far worse: him not caring. So I do my best to tuck it away again, that feeling of possibility I've been carrying around with me for so long. I fold it once, then twice, then again, trying to make it small enough to forget about entirely.

"I feel awful about everything I said that day," Teddy says, shifting to face me. "It was terrible. All of it. And I'm so sorry. I really hate fighting with you."

I nod, but what I'm thinking is that I wish I could've fallen for someone else. Anyone else. It seems wildly unfair that this had to happen with my best friend, because I still need him for that, and it would be so much easier if these other feelings of mine weren't quite so tangled up in it.

"Me too," I say after a moment, and he looks relieved.

"That was a really bad one."

I nod. "The worst."

"Let's never do that again."

"Deal," I say, and he leans into me, resting a shoulder against mine so that we're tipped toward each other like two sides of a triangle. Beneath us, the stone steps are cold, and the small patch of grass in front of the brownstone ripples in the breeze. In the distance, I can hear the screech and pop of a bus, and there's a siren somewhere not too far away. But here on this block, everything is blue-dark and eerily quiet.

"How long have you been out here?" I ask, and he shrugs.

"I don't know. A couple hours, maybe. I knocked earlier, and Sofia told me you were out."

I stare at him. "Why didn't you just wait inside?"

"I wasn't planning to stay," he says. "But I can't seem to leave."

Without thinking about it, I reach over and take his hand. It isn't until he curls his fingers around mine that I realize what I've done. But by then we're knit together again the way we used to be, and the sting of it—of wanting him, of missing him—is replaced by a powerful sense of relief.

There's still an *us*. It might not look the way I hoped it would, but there's something familiar about it, something comforting.

It's not everything I want, but maybe it's enough.

Maybe it has to be.

"I know this is such a little-kid thing to say, but I don't really want to be home when my mom isn't there," he says. "Because what if he comes back and things are weird? Or what if he doesn't? What if he just leaves again? It's been so long that I'm scared to see him, but I'm also scared *not* to. Does that make any sense?"

I nod, dropping his hand and picking up the other one, rubbing his frozen knuckles. He inches closer to me and we sit there like that for a long time, not talking. I wish Leo was here, because he'd know exactly what to say. This is the thought that's running through my head as he walks up, almost as if I've conjured him out of thin air, as if this is a brand-new superpower of mine, as if the world has suddenly become a place where you only have to wish for things to make them so.

I'm the first to spot him turning up the path, a duffel bag slung over his shoulder, and for the second time tonight I'm completely dumbstruck. He looks serious, maybe even a little upset, and my pulse quickens with worry—because he's supposed to be in Michigan; he's supposed to be with Max—but then he sees us too, and his face rearranges itself, and he lets out a strange bark of a laugh.

"What are you doing here?" I ask, shooting to my feet as he drops his bag with a thump. But his gaze shifts to Teddy, who looks up at him with a frown.

"What happened to Michigan?" he asks, and Leo shrugs.

"It's still there. What happened to Mexico?"

"Still there too," Teddy says with a smile.

I stand there looking from one to the other, then shake my head.

"You two," I say, and I'm about to continue, to say something more, but I'm so happy to see them, to have all three of us together again—in spite of whatever circumstances there must be—that I simply leave it at that.

# Twenty-Seven

In the morning, there's an email from Stanford admissions.

I'm still bleary-eyed from lack of sleep—we stayed up talking until nearly four—and I squint at my phone, letting my thumb hover over the message. But I don't click on it. Instead I roll out of bed and stumble out into the hallway, but it's not until I'm standing outside Leo's room that I realize this might not be the best idea.

If it's good news, it might just make him feel worse about everything. Though if it's bad news, we'll *both* have an excuse to lie on the couch all day and eat ice cream in our pajamas.

Last night, after we'd come inside and made popcorn, which Teddy burned, then made a second batch, which Leo knocked over, then finally a third, which we managed to carry into the living room without incident, Leo broke the news.

"It's over," he said, but I'd known it even before then, since the moment he'd emerged from the darkness like some sort of melancholy ghost. Now, though, it was suddenly a fact, and the way he said it—the words set down like they were something heavy, like a suitcase he'd been carrying for far too long—broke my heart.

Teddy, who had clearly been too distracted to guess at this, immediately froze, his hand still shoved into the metal bowl of popcorn. Slowly, carefully, he extracted it, then shifted to face Leo.

"You and Max?" he asked in astonishment.

Leo nodded.

"But . . . why?"

"I don't . . . ," he began, then paused, his eyes swimming. "I don't think I want to talk about it right now."

Teddy and I exchanged a look.

"That's fine," I said quickly. "Maybe tomorrow."

And so we let it go. For the next few hours, we watched movies and ate popcorn and made Teddy tell us all about his big television debut and the hundreds of messages he'd gotten since it aired, including three marriage proposals. "I only considered one of them," he joked, ducking as I threw a pillow at him. I told him about how Uncle Jake and I had started the boat, and he swore we'd finish it together now that he was back, and Leo promised to buy us floaties in case things went terribly wrong.

We didn't talk about Max. Or Teddy's dad. Or even Sawyer.

For a few hours we just ignored all the rest of it.

But now it's morning; now it's tomorrow. Teddy is probably still asleep downstairs, and Leo is just a knock away, and what was so easy to avoid last night no longer seems to make sense in the light of day.

I glance down at the phone in my hand once more, then I knock. On the other side of the door, there's a grunt. "Leo?"

"Go away."

I pretend not to hear him. "Can I come in?"

"No."

"Great," I say as I fling open the door. The first thing I see is his green duffel bag, which is lying in the middle of the messy floor, and I feel a pang of sadness when I remember watching him carefully pack it only a few days ago.

"What?" he asks, poking his head out from under the covers, and it's hard not to laugh at his rumpled hair and grumpy expression. I sit down on the edge of the bed.

"I wanted to see if you were up."

"Clearly I'm not," he says, throwing the quilt back over his head.

"Well, now you are, so let's talk."

He groans and rolls over onto his back, reaching for his new glasses on the bedside table. "I don't know if I can talk about it yet."

"You said tomorrow."

"*You* said tomorrow."

"What happened?" I ask, unable to help myself. "What did he do?"

219

Leo props his pillow against the wall behind him and sits up, a look of annoyance flashing across his face. "Why do you assume it was him?"

"Because you're you," I say, expecting to draw a smile out of him, but instead his expression darkens.

"Yeah, well, I'm not sure Max would agree anymore."

I'm afraid to hear whatever's coming next, but I ask anyway. "Why not?"

"Because," Leo says in a small voice, "I'm the one who broke up with him."

"Oh," I say softly, the word landing heavily between us.

"It was inevitable," he says with a shrug, almost eerily calm now, as if he's talking about someone else entirely. "All we've been doing is fighting about next year. Then I go up there, and I see him with his new friends and his new band and his new life, and I realized we've been holding each other back."

"But you love him."

"I want to go to art school," he continues, as if he hasn't heard me. "I just do."

"Okay," I say. "So go to art school."

"Whenever I thought about Michigan, I started to feel claustrophobic, like I was being pushed into it. And that's because I sort of was. And I just didn't want to go."

"So you told Max that?"

He lowers his eyes. "No, I told him about how I never applied."

"*What?*" I stare at him. "But I thought—"

"No," he says flatly. "I couldn't do it."

"Leo . . ."

"I know," he says in a tight voice. He speaks slowly, as if trying to keep the words from spilling out at once. "I filled out the application. I just never sent it. It was like, as soon as I decided not to, this huge weight came off me. But I didn't want to lose him—"

"Because you love him."

He ignores this. "So I was gonna wait to tell him. I wanted to have one more week together without having to think about all this, but then I got up there, and he was so excited to show me around campus, and after a while, I just couldn't keep lying to him."

"Because you love him."

"And then we got into a huge fight about all of it, and I realized that everything had been building up, and it just felt like too much." He looks down at his hands, blinking a few times. "So I ended it."

"But you still love him."

"It's not that easy." He shakes his head. "I messed everything up."

"Yeah, but you—"

"Yes," Leo snaps, and something seems to crack in him, his eyes filling with tears. "I love him, okay?"

"That's not nothing," I say softly, unable to keep from thinking of Teddy. "To love someone and have them love you back."

"I don't think it's enough." He takes off his glasses and rubs his eyes with the heel of his hand, and it strikes me how sad it is, the way a relationship can be so unexpectedly fragile. If two people who love each other as much as Leo and Max can fall apart so easily, what hope is there for anyone else?

"I was reading about the curse of the lottery on the bus ride home," Leo says, slipping his glasses back on. "Do you think it extends to friends and family too?"

"Like a phone plan?" I joke, but when he doesn't smile I shake my head. "I don't think so. I don't believe in curses."

He gives me a funny look, and I know what he's thinking: that with a past like mine, choosing not to believe in curses is a pretty impressive piece of magical thinking.

But it's not that.

Bad luck exists; I'd be crazy to think otherwise. But what I believe in—what I have to believe in—is randomness. Because to imagine that my parents died as a result of curses or fate or the larger workings of the universe, to imagine it was somehow meant to happen that way—even I don't think the world is *that* cruel.

"There are so many articles," Leo continues, "about winners whose lives got completely ruined by it. Suicides, overdoses, family rifts. And a lot of them went broke too. It didn't matter how much they won. Somehow it all ended in disaster."

"Those are just stories," I say, but I'm thinking about Teddy and everything that's already happened, how I'm the one who put it all in motion, for better or worse.

Leo leans back against his pillows with a sigh. "I think I need some ice cream."

"Are you sure you don't want to—"

222

"Ice cream," he says firmly, and I nod.

As he hops out of bed, he catches me glancing at my phone and raises his eyebrows. I give him a sheepish look. "I got an email from Stanford."

"*The* email?"

"I haven't opened it yet," I tell him. "I couldn't do it alone. But I wasn't sure if you'd be in the mood."

"Just because I broke up with my boyfriend, who hates me, and only applied to one college, which I probably won't get into, and will most likely still be living in this room for the next four years, stuck letting Teddy pay every time we go out, and—"

"Stop," I say, holding up a hand. "You're going to be fine. You are."

"You don't know that."

"Yes, I do. You're an amazing person. And you have the biggest heart of anyone I know. Whatever happens next, you'll be fine."

"When did you get to be such an optimist?"

"I think it's your fault."

"I think it's Teddy's."

I laugh. "It's usually one or the other."

"So," he says, eyeing my phone, and I pass it to him. He glances at my inbox, then lifts his eyes to check with me once more, and when I nod he taps at the screen. For a few long seconds, his face is impossible to read, but then a smile moves from his eyes down to his mouth, and I breathe out.

"Really?"

His grin broadens. "Really."

"Wow," I say, feeling almost weak with relief. I blink fast as I think of my mom. I know she'd be so proud of me. I know they both would. But this is one of those times when I really, really wish they were here to tell me that themselves.

"So, California, then," Leo says, handing back my phone.

"I guess so," I say, and we both stand there for a moment, imagining what it will be like to be so far away from each other, half a country apart, just like it used to be, like all these years in Chicago never even happened.

"Maybe we should go downstairs and tell the others," he says, and I have a feeling he's not just talking about Stanford; he's talking about his own news too.

"Can I ask you something?" I say, and he nods. "Were you ever really going to apply to Michigan?"

He hesitates, looking uncertain. "Yes," he says, then changes his mind. "No. I don't know. Maybe."

I nod at this; I'd expected as much. "It's not a crime, you know."

"What?"

"That your head and your heart are in two different places. I mean, you were trying to psych yourself up to spend the next four years in the most un-Leo-like place in the world just so you could be with Max. That's a lot of love."

"You're making me sound way more selfless than I am," he says, pointing at the back of the door, which is covered in printouts of his digital animations. "My heart is in this stuff too. That's the problem. That's probably why it feels so broken."

"It'll get fixed again," I say. "Eventually."

"Is yours?" he asks, and I don't know if he's talking about Teddy or if he means what happened with my parents. But either way, the answer is the same.

"Not yet," I tell him.

# Twenty-Eight

Downstairs, Uncle Jake and Aunt Sofia are sitting in the living room with mugs of coffee, already dressed for work and reading different sections of the *Chicago Tribune*. They both look up when Leo and I appear in the doorway. "What are you doing here?"

"I live here," Leo says, flopping onto the second couch, his hands folded neatly over his chest like a mummy.

Aunt Sofia frowns. "We weren't expecting you back till this weekend. Did something happen?"

"Yes," he says, but when he doesn't say anything else both of them turn to me, their faces full of questions. I shake my head, and Uncle Jake just stares harder, but something clicks with Aunt Sofia and she covers her mouth with her hand, her eyes big.

"Where's Teddy?" I ask, because it's clear that Leo doesn't want to talk about Max. At least not yet.

Uncle Jake still looks confused. "Mexico?"

"No, he came back early too. He was asleep on the couch when we went up last night."

"So that explains why there's popcorn everywhere," he says, brushing a few crumbs off the cushion where Teddy was sitting just a few hours ago.

"Leo," Aunt Sofia says, setting her mug down on the coffee table and leaning forward. "Is everything okay?"

"You should ask Alice about Stanford," Leo says without looking over, and once again their gazes shift in my direction, then back to Leo, their eyes moving between us as if they're watching a particularly slow-moving tennis match.

"I got in," I tell them, and before I can say anything else they're both up and off the couch—Uncle Jake's coffee splashing, Aunt Sofia's reading glasses falling to the floor—and they have me wrapped in a hug that's noisy with the sound of their celebration. From where I'm smashed between them, I can't help smiling.

"That's incredible," Uncle Jake says, and Aunt Sofia is nodding hard, her eyes wet with tears. Behind them, I can see Leo stand up from the couch, then head off toward the kitchen, presumably to get some ice cream. He gives me a wink as he passes by.

"I'm so proud of you," Aunt Sofia is saying. "And you know your parents would've been proud too."

I swallow hard. "Thank you."

"We've got to celebrate tonight," Uncle Jake says. "I'll make dinner."

We both stare at him, an uncomfortable silence settling over the room as we contemplate his terrible cooking.

"Fine," he says, holding up his hands. "We'll go out."

"Good idea," Aunt Sofia says, turning back to me. "So what are you thinking?"

"I don't know. Maybe Italian?"

"No, about Stanford," Uncle Jake says with a laugh. "Though for the record, I'm fully on board with Italian."

"Oh," I say, surprised by the question. "Well, I'm going. Obviously."

Aunt Sofia nods, but there's something strained about her smile. "When do you have to let them know?"

"Just by May first. But I'm obviously—"

"We should at least talk about some of the other options before you accept. Just so you can see what else is out there. I know you've always wanted this, but . . ."

I frown at her. Last fall, when my early application to Stanford was deferred, Aunt Sofia had encouraged me to apply to a range of other schools. But I always thought this was just in case I didn't ultimately get in. Now that I have, how could she think I might pass up the chance to go to Stanford? After all these years of hoping and planning, how could she imagine I'd choose anywhere else?

"Fine," I say impatiently, suddenly anxious to escape the living room, which feels too small and too warm right now. "But it's not gonna make a difference."

"That's okay," she says. "I just want to make sure you

consider everything. Maybe it would even help to go spend a few hours at Northwestern this weekend—"

"I'm going to Stanford," I say, not bothering to hide my exasperation.

"I know that. But just humor me, okay? It can't hurt to check it out before you commit to anything. At least think about it."

I sigh. "Fine. But can we finish talking about this later? I've got to go, or I'm gonna be late for tutoring."

"With Caleb?" Aunt Sofia asks, glancing at the clock. "It's not even nine a.m."

"Spring break," I say, and Uncle Jake laughs.

"You party animal, you."

On the bus I try calling Teddy twice. I'm eager to tell him about Stanford, but more than that I'm dying to know how it went with his dad this morning. He doesn't pick up, so I text him, just to make sure he knows he's supposed to call me back.

When I get to the library I head straight to the children's section, where Caleb is waiting for me like always, hunched over a table that's shaped like a cloud, beneath the watchful eye of the children's librarian. He's in second grade, but he's small for his age, and he looks much younger, his feet still dangling off the tiny blue chair.

"Hi, buddy," I say, sliding into the miniature seat next to him, where my knees come up halfway to my chin. "How's it going?"

His round eyes are very serious as he considers the question. "Okay."

"Just okay?"

This gets a little smile out of him. He fidgets with the drawstring of his hoodie, then shrugs. "Good."

"C'mon," I say. "You can do better than that."

He scratches at his forehead. "Excited to read?"

"Bingo," I say with a grin. "Me too."

When I decided to volunteer with the program, which pairs foster kids with reading buddies, Caleb's was the first profile I considered. As soon as I saw that his parents had recently been killed in a car accident, I moved on to the next one. The word *orphan* still unnerves me more than it probably should, and the prospect of working with a kid in a similar situation to mine seemed an awful lot like holding my hand against a flame.

But as I was scrolling through the next profile, I couldn't stop thinking about the way my dad used to read Harry Potter to me before bed and how my mom would lean against the doorway, laughing as he did all the voices.

I've now spent the past couple of months reading story after story with Caleb. But I haven't told him my own yet, or how much I can relate to his. This hour we have, it's his escape. It's a time for wizards and mice, spies and magicians. A time when the only orphans are the ones between the pages, and they usually end up being the heroes.

Now he pulls a copy of *Charlotte's Web* out of his backpack.

"One of my favorites," I tell him. "Do you know the story already?"

Caleb shakes his head.

"You're gonna like it," I say, but even as I do, it occurs to me that this is a book about death as much as about talking pigs and spiders. Although so is everything, I guess, once you've been through what Caleb's been through.

We open to page one, and he places his finger beside the first line. "'Where's Papa going with that ax?'" he reads, then turns to look at me from beneath his dark lashes.

"That was great," I say, giving him an encouraging nod.

"Why does he have an ax?" he whispers, alarmed.

"It's okay," I tell him, because it will be in a few pages. At least for a little while.

We keep going, both of us breathing out when Fern manages to talk her father into rescuing the tiny runt of a pig. Caleb even offers up a smile when Mr. Arable announces that he only gives pigs to early risers.

"'. . . and Fern was up at daylight,'" he reads slowly, his finger moving across the page, "'trying to rid the world of . . .'"

He pauses, and I lean closer to see the word. "Injustice," I say quietly, bracing myself, because I already know what his next question will be.

"What does that mean?"

"It means something that isn't fair."

His head is lowered, but I see him shift as he thinks about this, and I want to tell him that I understand; that even though it will never stop hurting, what happened to him, it *will* get better someday; with the right amount of time and the right combination of people it will still burn like crazy, but the heat of it will come in and out like a radio signal and he'll learn to live in the spaces in between.

But I don't. Because it won't mean anything to him—not yet. I know this, because people tried to say it to me. Instead I watch him consider this a moment. Then, when he's ready, he turns the page.

Afterward we sit on the steps of the library, waiting for his foster mom to pick him up. When he sees the car, he gives me a wave, then trots down the rest of the stairs, the book tucked under his arm.

"See you next week," I call after him.

Even once they've driven off, I don't move. I just sit there as it starts to rain. There's something gentle about it, a drizzle that gets shifted around by the breeze, moving this way and that like a great curtain. The air is heavy with it, a smell like mud, like spring, and I breathe it in, listening to the insistent thrum on the sidewalk.

When I dig my phone out of my bag, I find a voicemail from Sawyer, asking if I want to hang out tonight. But there's nothing from Teddy, which means either things with his dad are going really well or else they went really badly.

I stand up and walk down the rest of the rain-slicked steps. At the bottom I take a left, heading toward home. But as I do a bus pulls up to the stop right in front of the library, windshield wipers squealing.

It's pointed in the direction of Teddy's apartment.

Before I can change my mind, I climb on.

# Twenty-Nine

There are three photographers outside Teddy's building; their eyes follow me as I hurry through the rain toward the entrance. I don't have an umbrella, so I'm relieved when someone pushes open the glass door just as I get there. I step into the vestibule and do my best to shake the water off my fleece. My shoes squeak on the linoleum floor as I jog up the stairs to number eleven. I knock three times, the way I always do. But when the door swings open, it's not Teddy who is standing there. It's his dad.

I blink at him, caught off guard. It's been six years since I've seen Charlie McAvoy, but he looks about twenty years older, his jaw softened by gray stubble, his face scrawled with deep lines. To my surprise he's wearing an expensive-looking suit and tie instead of the jeans and old flannel shirts that used to be a uniform of sorts.

He smiles at me. "Alex, right?"

"Alice."

"Sorry," he says, holding the door for me. "It's been a while."

Inside, Teddy is sitting on the couch, and when our eyes meet, he grins. He's holding a small dog-shaped robot in his hands, which he was obviously showing his dad, and it makes him look just like a kid on Christmas.

"Hey," he says. "I didn't know you were coming over."

"Well, you weren't answering my calls."

"Sorry," Charlie says. "We were busy catching up."

I kick off my damp shoes, glancing around the apartment, then at Teddy. "Where's your mom?"

"Grocery store," he says, still fidgeting with the control panel on the robot.

"So how have you been, Alice?" Charlie asks as he gets himself a glass of water. He looks completely at ease here, though this has never been his home—this is, in fact, the place his family was forced to move to because of everything he did. "It's nice to see you two are still pals. And who was your other friend? The skinny kid with glasses?"

"Leo," Teddy says, then looks over at me. "Is he okay?"

"Fine," I say, which isn't exactly the truth, but I don't really want to talk about it in front of Charlie. This whole thing is so surreal, all of us acting as if barely any time has passed, as if he didn't ruin their lives. I turn back to him. "So you live in Utah now?"

"Salt Lake City," he says, nodding. "I bounced around a

bit after . . . well, you know. I was in Tulsa, then Minne-
apolis, and now Salt Lake. It's a good little town." He looks
over at Teddy and winks. "And no gambling there."

"And you're here on business? What do you do now?"

"Well, I got out of the electrician game," he says. "Turns
out flexible hours weren't great for me. Something I learned
at my meetings." Again he glances over at Teddy, who
smiles back at him encouragingly. "So now I do sales for a
tech company."

"What kind of tech company?"

He laughs. "What are you, like, a budding reporter?"

"No," I say without smiling. "Just catching up."

"She thinks," Teddy says from the couch, "that you're
here for the money."

I turn to glare at him. He's dead right, of course, but I'm
stunned that he's outed me so casually. "That's not—"

"No," Charlie says, holding up his hands. "I get that. I
do. With my history, and the timing of it all, I'm not surprised. But honestly I didn't even know about it till I got
here. I just had some meetings in town, and it seemed like
maybe enough time had gone by that Katherine would be
open to letting me come see my son."

Teddy is giving me a look that says *I told you so,* and
Charlie is watching me with such sincerity that I feel a little uneasy.

"Anyway, I heard you were the one who bought the
ticket," he says. "And I wanted to say what an amazing gift
that is. I wish I could've been the one to do it for them, but

it means a lot to me, knowing that Teddy and his mom will be taken care of now. So thank you." He presses a hand to his chest. "From the bottom of my heart."

"You're welcome," I manage to say, and he beams at us, which only makes me feel more off-balance. It's hard not to fall under his spell.

"And Teddy was telling me they're moving back to the old neighborhood now . . . ," he says, like he doesn't remember why they had to move out of it in the first place.

"Oh," I say, turning to Teddy with a frown. "So you got it?"

I'm not sure why this news should make me feel so unsteady. But the idea that he could've bought a building—a whole building!—without mentioning it to me is jarring.

"Well, I made the offers," he says. "But it might be a while before I hear."

"I think we've got a real estate tycoon in the making here," Charlie says with obvious pride, then he glances down at his watch. "Hey, you know what, T? I've got to get going. Can't keep my clients waiting. But I'll see you tomorrow, right?"

"You bet," Teddy says, hopping up to give him a hug, and my heart goes soft again because I know he's waited such a long time for this.

"Hope to see you again too, Alice," Charlie says, then pauses near the door. "Where's the best place to find a cab around here?"

"Just on the corner," Teddy says, reaching for his wallet and pulling out a thick wad of twenties. "Here. This should cover it."

236

Charlie waves his hands. "Not necessary. Really."

"Just take it," Teddy insists, holding out the money, but Charlie demurs again with a cheerful smile.

"My son," he says, winking at me. "The millionaire."

Once the door closes behind him, Teddy and I are both silent. My back is to him as I try to figure out how to say what I need to say. But before I can, he flops back onto the couch and says, "I know what you're thinking. But you're wrong. He's different. We spent the whole morning talking, and he's got his life together now."

I turn around, unsure where to begin. "Teddy," I say gently. "There's just no way the timing is coincidental."

"You heard him. He's here for work. I mean, he's staying at the Four Seasons."

"That doesn't mean anything."

"Of course it does. Look, when all that stuff happened when I was a kid, he couldn't even afford a plane ticket home. We had to borrow money from your aunt and uncle to get him back from Vegas. He was a total mess. It was awful. All of it."

"I remember," I say quietly.

"So it makes sense that it took him some time to get back on his feet," he says. "It's not like he's showing up here claiming it was magic. He had a bunch of setbacks along the way. But people can change. He's been going to meetings regularly, and he hasn't gambled in a year. It wasn't instant. He's been working on it. And now he just wants to see me for a few days while he's in town, and you automatically assume—"

"What does your mom say?"

237

"Well, she's not as paranoid as *you*."

"But?"

He scowls. "She knows it's only for a few days, and she said it's okay if I want to see him. That it's my decision." He says this last part defiantly, his chin up, and I have a feeling this isn't all she said. "And that's what I want."

"Okay," I say. "I just want to make sure you're—"

"Stop. That's enough, okay? He's my dad, not yours," he says, and there's a heat to his words. "You don't know what it's like."

I know he doesn't mean it that way, but it still feels like a kick to the stomach, and I drop my eyes to the floor, unable to look at him. Even so I can feel him recoil, equally surprised by what he's said.

"I'm sorry," he says quickly. "I didn't mean it like that."

"It's fine."

He sighs. "It's just . . . it's really nice to see him again, you know?"

"I know," I say, walking over and sitting down beside him. I fall back against the cushions, suddenly weary.

"He wants to come to the boat race on Monday."

"He'll still be in town?" I ask, and when Teddy nods I tighten my jaw. "Just be careful, okay? You've always been really trusting—it's one of the best things about you. But now that you have all this money . . ."

"Honestly, Al. I swear that's not why he's here."

I'm still not sure I can believe this, still not sure I can bend my imagination far enough—or generously enough—to allow for the possibility that he just happened to be in town so soon after the son he hasn't seen in six years won a hundred and forty million dollars. But pressing the point obviously isn't getting me anywhere. So I nod.

"Just be careful," I say again. "You have something that people want now, and a lot of them will be happy to take advantage of you."

"I know," he agrees, but I can tell how badly he wants to believe otherwise, how determined he is to refuse this way of thinking.

"Well," I say, "if he's planning to come to the boat race, that means we should probably finish building the boat."

"That might help."

"All Uncle Jake and I did was draw up the plans and cut the pieces. So this is where you come in."

"Armed with tape."

"Exactly."

"How about we work on it tonight?"

"I can't," I say, shaking my head. "I have dinner plans."

Teddy raises his eyebrows. "With that guy?"

"What guy?" I say, though we both know exactly who he's talking about.

"The one you were making out with last night," he says, and though his tone is teasing, there's something serious in his eyes.

My face goes prickly. I didn't realize he saw us. "We weren't making out. He just kissed me good night."

"That was more than a good-night kiss."

I sit there for a few seconds, thinking about my kiss with *him*, reminding myself that it didn't mean anything, that he said so himself. I clear my throat, anxious to change the subject. "No, actually, my aunt and uncle are taking us out, if you want to join."

"How come?"

"Because," I say with a small smile, "I got into Stanford."

Teddy half-turns to face me. "You did? And you didn't tell me?"

"I just found out. That's why I came over."

He slings an arm around my shoulders, the way he always used to before things got complicated between us, and I burrow into the crook of his arm, resting my head on his chest, and we stay there like that—our breathing syncing up, our hearts beating in time—and it feels like coming home again.

"That's awesome, Al," he says, his breath warm against my cheek. "Congrats."

"Thanks."

There's a pause, and then he asks, "So I guess that means you'll be moving to California?"

"Probably," I say, happy that I can't see his face, because this would all be so much harder if I could. "But you never know. Aunt Sofia's dragging me to Northwestern this weekend. She wants to make sure I consider my options."

"Yeah, but that won't happen. We all knew you'd go back there eventually. California's always been home, right?"

I nod, but sitting here now, tucked under his arm in this little apartment in the middle of Chicago, the rain beating against the window and turning the afternoon sky the color of a bruise, it seems strange to me. I've been away from California for nine years now, which is just as long as I lived there in the first place. There's nothing waiting for me there. Everything I know, everyone I love, is here now.

So why does it still have such a hold on me?

I push the question out of my mind, pressing myself closer to Teddy, and we sit there together for a long time, until the rain slows, and then stops. Until, finally, the light comes back again.

# Thirty

It's Sunday morning and the Northwestern campus is quiet. It rained again last night, so the paths that cut between buildings are slick with wet leaves. We pause beneath a metal arch near the entrance, and Aunt Sofia lets out a happy sigh.

"This place," she says, shaking her head. "Best four years of my life. Just don't tell Jake that. I didn't meet him until after I graduated."

I give her a smile, but I don't want to be swayed by nostalgic stories of her college days or the clusters of castle-like buildings with their high-gabled roofs and spires that stretch into the low gray sky. Not when I've already settled on Stanford.

"I can't believe I've never taken you here before," she

says, looking around. "I should really come up more often myself. I always forget how close it is."

"We've been to football games," I remind her. "Just not for a while."

She laughs. "Not since that time you and Leo got into a fight and spilled your drink on the guy in front of you."

"We weren't fighting," I say with a frown. "Were we?"

I remember the drink getting knocked out of my hands and landing on someone's lap: an enormous guy who stood up to glare at us, soda dripping from his purple sweatshirt. But it's harder to imagine that Leo and I could have been fighting. We used to squabble all the time, the way any siblings do. But we never fought for real.

"Oh yeah," Aunt Sofia says as we head toward the sprawling green of the quad. "He was worked up because you were off to visit your grandma the next day without him. You'd only been with us about a year, and I think he'd gotten a little too attached."

A dim light switches on in a dusty corner of my memory, and I can picture Leo—red-faced and teary-eyed—trying to explain to Aunt Sofia that I belonged to *them* now, which meant I should be spending Thanksgiving at home rather than in Boston. This was before my grandmother on my mom's side passed away, my last remaining relative outside of the little family I'd recently joined.

"And you couldn't stop talking about the trip," Aunt Sofia is remembering, "so Leo just kept getting more upset, and you two started arguing, and he knocked the drink out of your hand. It was a total disaster. We had to leave in the middle of the second quarter. Last time we ever took you troublemakers to a game with us."

"Wow," I say, blinking. "I didn't remember that."

Aunt Sofia gives me a sideways glance. "Well, memory can be a tricky thing." It seems as if she's about to say more, but then she looks up and spots a huge, blocky building up ahead and her face breaks into a smile. "My home away from home."

"The library?"

"How'd you know?"

"Lucky guess," I say, watching her closely. "You really loved it here, huh?"

"I really did," she agrees. "Though it took a little time. I almost left after the first semester. The cold really got to me. All I'd brought was this flimsy jacket, and there was a big snowstorm at the beginning of October that year. It was brutal."

"I can't imagine coming here from Florida," I say. "It was a rough transition even from San Francisco. Why'd you apply in the first place?"

"The plan was to go back to Buenos Aires for university. It was where I was from, and we still had family there, and whenever we visited I fell in love with the city a little more. It wasn't home, exactly, but—well, you know what it's like."

"What?"

"To spend your life wondering about a place like that,"

she says. "To always feel like you have one foot in and one foot out."

I feel my face grow hot under her gaze. "So what happened?"

"I ended up getting a scholarship here," she says, sweeping an arm out. "And my dad thought it was too good an opportunity to pass up. They'd sacrificed a lot to come to this country. He really wanted me to go to school here."

"Do you ever regret it?"

She shakes her head. "I came to really love it after a while. And eventually I fell in love with Chicago too. And Jake."

"But what about—"

"Argentina will always be my home in some ways. Florida too." She smiles. "It's possible to have more than one, you know."

We walk in silence for a few minutes. Above us the sky is threaded with light, the sun pushing its way through the silver clouds. Between buildings I can see flashes of Lake Michigan, the water blue-gray and tipped with white.

"I know what you're trying to do," I say, breaking the silence, and Aunt Sofia glances over at me, her face untroubled.

"What's that?"

"You want me to pick Northwestern over Stanford. You want me to be closer."

She stops walking. "Alice."

"I just don't get why," I say, speaking fast now. "I always thought you guys were on board about Stanford, but the minute I finally get in you bring me here? I know you love it, but Northwestern was never part of the plan, and—"

"Alice," she says again, her voice full of patience, but I can't stop. Not yet.

"And Stanford, it's . . . it's what my mom wanted."

The words come out with more force than intended, and when Aunt Sofia doesn't say anything, when she just continues to look at me with a mixture of worry and understanding, something heavy washes over me.

*She did,* I want to say, suddenly eager to be understood. *She wanted it.*

And if she couldn't do it, then shouldn't I?

The sun moves behind the clouds again, and the world grows dim. I pull in a shaky breath. Taking my arm, Aunt Sofia steers me gently over to a bench. The wood is damp and cold, but we sit down anyway, and I stare out at the too-green grass of the quad, wondering why my insides feel like they're splitting open.

"Hey," she says softly. "It's okay."

"It's not that I don't want to be close to you guys," I say, my voice trembling. "It's just . . ."

"It's what your mom wanted," she says. "I get that. I do. And I can't imagine how hard this must be."

"What?"

She looks surprised. "Well, not having her here for this. It's such a big decision."

"She would've wanted Stanford," I say firmly.

"Right. Of course." She nods. "It's just . . . I want to make sure that's what you want too."

"It is," I say automatically. "I want . . ."

I stop. Then pause. Then try again.

"I want . . ."

But I trail off, because the truth is I'm not totally sure what I want. And if I'm being really honest, I don't know what she'd want either.

The last time I saw my mom—looking small and pale in a hospital bed—college was still half a life away for me. Her worries must have been so much more immediate than that: who would leave notes in my lunch box when she was gone and who would talk to me about boys one day, who would make faces out of blueberries on my waffles and who would bring me soup when I was home sick.

I'm sure she knew my dad would try his best. But she couldn't have known that he'd follow her so soon, just over a year later, and that Uncle Jake and Aunt Sofia would have to be the ones to step in, to fill those gaps the best they could.

And they tried, all of them. For that first year she was gone, my dad left his own notes in my lunch box with little doodles of penguins across the bottom, the only thing he knew how to draw. And later it turned out Leo was pretty good at making funny faces out of breakfast foods. Aunt Sofia was the one to tell me what I needed to know about boys, and whenever I was sick Uncle Jake would stay home from work to bring me bowl after bowl of chicken noodle soup.

This brand of kindness, this closing of the circle around me, it's more than just love. It's a kind of luck too, to have these people in my life.

But it's not the same as if my mom was here. How could it be?

And now—now I have to do this without her too.

I swallow hard, pressing my hands together in my lap. Aunt Sofia is still watching me, her eyes steady and warm, but I can't seem to finish the sentence.

*I want* . . .

*I want* . . .

*I want* . . .

It's like something inside me has crashed, and to my horror the words bubbling up in my throat, desperate and unbidden, are these: *I want my mom.*

But I don't say it.

"I want Stanford," I whisper instead, and Aunt Sofia nods. Across the quad, a tour group is moving slowly in our direction. The guide walks backward, gesturing with his hands, trailed by even sets of eager-looking parents and bored-looking kids. We watch their halting progress for a little while before she turns back to me.

"It's no secret that we'd love to have you closer," she says, her eyes shining. "I only have two little ducklings. And even though they're not so little anymore, I'm always going to want to keep an eye on them. You have to know that."

All I can do is nod; to my surprise I feel a tug of sadness at this. In all my daydreams about Stanford, I've thought only of going home again. Somehow it didn't fully sink in that I'd be leaving home too.

"But if Stanford is what you want, then we're behind

you," she continues, reaching over and placing a hand on top of mine. "Always."

"Thank you," I say, feeling dazed.

"And I want you to know I didn't bring you here to make a case for Northwestern, though I do think you'd love it. They have amazing programs in philosophy and literature and . . ." She stops abruptly. "Well, that's not the point. I just wanted to make sure you saw that there are other places out there. Other options. Other ways to be happy. Because that's all we want. For you to be happy."

I'm reminded of the days right after my dad's funeral, when Aunt Sofia was the one to stay behind, packing up the house and tying up all the loose ends because Uncle Jake couldn't bear to do it. Those first few nights she'd wait on the other side of the door while I cried, her voice muffled as she spoke to me. She never said *You'll be okay* the way so many other adults did. Instead it was always simply *You're okay,* as if this was an inarguable fact, as if she knew something I didn't.

And I find myself repeating this now, though I have no idea whether it's true. Even so, I try to say it like she used to, like it's a certainty, a fact. "I'm okay."

She smiles, and I realize then why it's been so hard to ask her about the money. It's because I know she'll tell me the truth.

"Aunt Sofe," I say, looking at my hands. "Can I ask you a question?"

She nods. "Of course."

"Were you guys upset when I didn't take the money?"

First she looks confused. Then her expression shifts into something more startled, before finally settling into amusement. "The lottery money?"

I nod, unable to meet her eye. "I turned it down without even asking you and Uncle Jake, and you guys have done so much for me, and paid for everything all these years."

"Alice," she says, scooting closer so she can put an arm around me. "I hope you know that not only do we not expect or want anything from you, we'd happily pay to keep you. It's been a privilege having you with us."

I laugh with relief, but it comes out wetly, like a sob.

"And you know," she continues, "that you're as much my daughter as Leo is my son. Maybe I don't say that enough."

"No," I say quietly. "You do."

"We always wanted more kids," she says, and when I look at her I'm surprised to see that her eyes are damp. "Always. But after Leo, it just never happened for us, and then after so many years of hoping and trying, you came along."

"A total mess of a nine-year-old," I say with a smile. "Just what you wanted."

Aunt Sofia shakes her head. "That's the thing. You were *exactly* what we wanted. I mean it, Alice. Losing your parents was unbearable for us too. But there was also this hole in our family, and you were the one to fill it, and that's always weighed on me, because—" She hesitates. "Well, it's not easy, you know? To get the thing you want most in the world in the worst way possible."

Her words buzz through me, filling my head like static.

I'm not sure what to think; I'm half-reassured and half-devastated by all this, half-comforted and half-wrecked.

"So," she continues, taking a long breath, "I've always tried to make sure you don't feel like we're trying to replace them. But even though you don't call us Mom and Dad, you should know that's how we think of ourselves. You're their daughter, and you always will be. But we hope you feel like you're ours too." She dabs at her eyes with her finger. "And it's never been a burden, financially or otherwise. In fact, it's an honor."

I nod, my throat too thick for words. Because right then, I don't feel like an island or even a peninsula.

I feel utterly landlocked in the best possible way.

"Anyway," she says, wiping her eyes, "my concern with the money has nothing to do with me and Jake. It's about you. I just want to make sure you've really thought hard about it, and that it won't be something you'll regret later on. Because it's a lot."

"I know," I admit. "Leo thinks I'm nuts."

"That's because Leo would take it in a heartbeat." She raises her eyebrows. "Honestly? So would Jake. So would most people."

"What about you?"

"It's hard to say. I guess you never really know until you're in that situation."

"But?" I ask, tilting my head.

"But," she says, "I think my instinct would've been the same as yours. It just seems like a lot, doesn't it? And it must come with an awful lot of strings attached."

"Yes," I say, feeling a rush of gratitude, because that's

exactly what I said to Leo, exactly what I've been thinking ever since Teddy and I dug the ticket out of the garbage that snowy day. I didn't know what a relief it would be, to talk to someone who doesn't think my decision was a monumentally stupid one.

"When my parents came over from Argentina, they made a life out of nothing," Aunt Sofia says. "And Jake and I have worked really hard to make a life for you and Leo. I'm proud of what we've accomplished. And I happen to think it's a pretty good life. Even without millions and millions of dollars."

"Me too," I say, and I mean it. I feel lucky that my parents left me enough money for college, and maybe for a few years beyond if I'm smart with it. But I realize now that I don't want a safety net. At least not a financial one. I want to make it on my own too.

"I know you had your own reasons for turning it down," Aunt Sofia says. "And I totally support whatever you want to do, as long as you're sure."

"I am," I say, then hesitate. "I think I am."

She looks at me carefully. "You think?"

"I don't want it myself," I say. "I really don't."

"But?"

"I guess I wish Teddy was doing something more with it," I say, the words tumbling out in a rush. "Something better. It's so much money. Even a little bit of it could help so many people, so it's just hard to—"

"Oh, hon," Aunt Sofia says, shaking her head. "You can't do that."

"What?"

"He's a kid whose family has had some pretty rough financial problems, and he just won an ungodly amount of money. You can't expect him to do everything right. Or to do everything you would do. Because it's not you. It's him."

"I know," I say. "It's just hard."

"It's not your job to worry about it," she says, drawing me close again. "Your only job is to be his friend, which I already know you can do."

I don't say anything. All I do is nod, hoping she's right.

# Thirty-One

The race doesn't begin until eighth period, but all of Mr. Dill's physics students are excused from afternoon classes so we can put the finishing touches on our boats. The rest of the seniors always grumble about this, since they only get to skip one period to watch, but as I stand at the edge of the swimming pool, the air warm and stuffy and thick with chlorine, I'm starting to suspect they have the better end of the deal.

Around us the concrete edges of the pool are lined with boats, which range from the impossibly professional to the downright raftlike. Some of them look like they could make it through the Bermuda Triangle, others like they might crumble under the strain of a light drizzle. Some are painted brilliant reds and yellows and greens, with elaborate cardboard sails and rudders, while others could easily be mistaken for oversized pizza boxes.

Ours is somewhere in between. It's squat and square and covered with tape, but it looks sturdy enough. We didn't have time to paint it, but last night, as we finished shoring up the sides, Teddy decided we needed to give it a name.

"It's bad luck if you don't," he insisted. "How about the *Teddy*?"

I groaned. "I think we can do better than that."

"Nobody can do better than the *Teddy*," he joked, but when I rolled my eyes at him, he shrugged. "Okay, how about the *Sink or Swim*?"

"A little too close to home."

"The *Sea You Later*?"

"Too cute."

"*Row, Row, Row Your Boat*?"

"Too long."

"I've got it," he said finally, his eyes lighting up. "The *Lucky Duck*."

"Don't you think it's kind of tempting fate to put the word *lucky* on it?"

"I thought you didn't believe in that stuff," he said. "Besides, I just won the lottery. If I can't throw around the word *lucky* after that, what's the use?"

But now, seeing the painted letters on the back of our boat makes my stomach twist. Because if there's one thing I know, it's that luck can change in an instant.

Teddy pulls off another piece of tape to reinforce one of

the corners, and I watch him stick out his tongue in concentration as he folds it carefully around the edge.

"So is she seaworthy?" I ask, sitting down on the bleachers beside him.

"You tell me." He pats the side of it, making the whole thing shudder. "You designed it."

"Then you *re*designed it," I remind him, because though he held up his end of the bargain—we spent much of the weekend working on the boat together—he also made about a thousand suggestions for subtle improvements on my plans, insisting that it would increase our speed.

"Winning isn't the point," I told him. "We just need to make it across."

He only frowned at me. "Winning is always the point."

Behind us two girls from our class walk by, and I hear them whisper something about a yacht, then start to laugh. I can pretty much guess the rest of it, and I suspect Teddy can too, because he stiffens but doesn't say anything.

The air around the pool is heavy and damp, and all the many voices of our classmates bounce off the tiled walls, making everything feel too loud and weirdly distorted. Already other students are filing in through the blue double doors at the other end of the bleachers. Teddy rips at the tape with his teeth, then spits out a stringy piece.

"I think it's almost time," I say, and he nods, but I can tell he's distracted by something over my shoulder, and I turn to see two of his friends from the basketball team, J.B. and Chris, walking over, one of them sunburnt, the other wearing a Hawaiian shirt. They look like they just stepped off the beach. Teddy watches them with a dazed expression; it must be the first time he's seen them since Mexico.

"Dude," says J.B., extending a fist, which Teddy bumps dutifully with his own. "I can't *believe* you missed the rest of the week. It was awesome. I could've lived on that beach forever. I almost didn't come back."

"Well, we sort of had to," Chris says, "since we ran out of funds after you took off."

Teddy frowns. "I left you guys a credit card."

"Yeah, well, you know how it goes, man," J.B. says. "The tab just kept growing and growing—"

"And growing," admits Chris, who at least has the decency to look a little embarrassed by this. "Things got kind of out of hand."

"We ended up maxing out the card," J.B. says, "which really sucked. For the last two days we had to give up all the top-shelf stuff and start eating tamales from that cart by the pool. It was pretty rough."

"Sounds like it," I say, and they both look over at me as if they didn't until that moment realize I was there.

Teddy's gone slightly pale. "You maxed it out?"

"Well, Mikey crashed the Jet Ski, which didn't help, and we got table service at a few of the clubs, and there was the whole thing with the jeep we rented—"

"Sorry, dude," J.B. says, giving Teddy a slap on the back. "But it's just a drop in the bucket for you these days, right?"

"Right," Teddy mumbles, his eyes on the turquoise surface of the pool.

"Anyway, good luck with"—J.B. gestures at our boat—
"this."

"It's no Jet Ski, but I'm sure it'll do," Chris says, and they
both laugh as they head off to join the rest of their friends
in the bleachers, which are filling up fast.

"They're jerks," I say, turning to Teddy once they're
gone.

He looks away. "It's fine."

"It's not fine," I say, suddenly outraged on his behalf.
"They're taking advantage of you, and—"

"It's fine," he says again, more firmly this time.

He looks up at the bleachers then, and I follow his gaze to
where his father is lifting a hand to wave at us. He's wearing the same suit and tie, but he's shaved, and without the
stubble he looks more like Teddy, an older, thicker version
of the boy sitting beside me.

"He came," Teddy says, clearly relieved. "I wasn't
sure . . ."

There's no need for him to finish that sentence. We both
know the part that's been left unsaid: he wasn't sure if
his dad would actually come, wasn't sure if he'd still be
in town, wasn't sure he'd actually follow through with a
promise for once.

But he has, and I can see the flush of color in Teddy's
cheeks as he turns his attention back to the boat. It doesn't
matter how badly he's been disappointed in the past. It
doesn't matter that he's spent six years being alternately
heartbroken and furious. It doesn't matter that his dad
has missed a hundred football and baseball and basketball

258

games. It only matters that he's here now, and I can tell by the set of Teddy's jaw that he's newly determined to win this race.

"You ready?" he asks, and for his sake I muster a smile.

"Ready," I say, wondering if this is true.

# Thirty-Two

By the time it's our turn, not a single boat has sunk, and you can almost feel the crowd waiting for it. They're tired of watching a series of makeshift cardboard contraptions successfully bob across the high school swimming pool. What they want is fireworks. What they want is a catastrophe. What they want is a show.

As Teddy and I step up to the edge of the pool, a murmur passes through the bleachers. The audience has been growing increasingly noisy all afternoon, but this is something different. There's only one other boat in our heat, a sleek-looking vessel that Mitchell Kelly and Alexis Lovett have painted to look like a submarine, periscope and all. But I know instinctively that the shift in energy has nothing to do with them. This is about Teddy, and it's clear from the set of his shoulders that he knows it too.

A jeering voice breaks clear of the din: "Last time *you'll* have to paddle, Moneybags!"

This is followed by a roar of laughter, and Teddy hunches down further, looking bewildered. All his life he's been the good guy, the unlikely hero, the one everyone roots for on the football field or the basketball court.

Now his story has shifted. He's no longer the underdog. Instead he's suddenly the luckiest guy in the room, in the school, maybe even in the whole city. He's the luckiest guy anybody knows, and there's no need to root for someone like that to win. There's nowhere for him to go but down, and that's where they want to take him. Because guys like that—lucky guys, fortunate guys—they don't need any support. And the audience knows it.

I'm crouched at the edge of the pool, one hand on the boat, which seems flimsier now than it did in our basement. My eyes are already swimming from the chlorine, and the back of my neck prickles; I can almost feel the way the crowd has turned, can feel their impatience for the balance of the world to right itself again, even if it's just in something as inconsequential as a failed science project.

I scan the bleachers for Leo because I could really use a thumbs-up from him. But when I finally spot him, his head is turned, watching something higher in the stands. I raise my eyes to see two men on their feet, talking angrily.

One of them is Teddy's dad.

I whip back around to see if Teddy has noticed and find that he's squinting up in that direction too, his arms slack at his sides, his face a study of indecision.

"I'm sure it's nothing," I say, but he doesn't answer me.

The rest of the crowd is getting quieter now as their attention shifts, and the voices of the two men are audible. Charlie shakes an arm off his shoulder.

"Just pay up, man," the other guy says, and my heart sinks as a gym teacher steps in, trying to appease them both. It's almost completely silent now, more than a hundred people watching the spectacle unfold as if they were in a theater.

"I'm not leaving," Charlie says to the teacher. "I'm here to see my kid."

I glance at Teddy again; his ears are turning pink as he watches. From across the bleachers, I'm relieved to see Uncle Jake pop up. He's been sitting beside Aunt Sofia and Katherine—who is watching all this with a horrified look— but now he dashes past the rows of rapt students and over to Charlie, who is still shouting.

"I'm a parent too!" he yells at the teacher, gesturing toward Teddy. "Of a student. Of *that* student."

The silence is beginning to turn into whispers and murmurs and muffled snickers. Uncle Jake finally reaches Charlie, and when he does he bends his head to speak to him in a low voice. To my great relief, whatever he says does the trick. Charlie sweeps his eyes across the crowd with a look of slow comprehension before landing on his son, who turns away. Finally he sighs and allows himself to be led out into the hallway.

"Good luck, kid!" he shouts vaguely in Teddy's direction, and the minute the door slams shut behind him the bleachers fill with noise. The other man follows him out a second later, but by then nobody is paying attention.

*"Good luck, kid!"* people begin to yell, cupping their hands around their mouths and shouting the words. "Do it for your pop!"

I turn back to Teddy, who is staring at the too-blue water of the pool, his back to the crowd. With a burst of static, Mr. Dill speaks into his megaphone: "Pardon the interruption, folks. But it looks like we're ready for the next race now."

"Hey," I say to Teddy, so softly that I'm not even sure he hears me over all the many voices. "Are you okay?"

He inclines his head, just slightly, and I can see that his mouth is set in a thin line. Without answering, he bends to push the boat into the water, holding it steady while I climb into the front. I fold my knees underneath me and grab one of the paddles, which are made from cardboard tubes. Then he gets in behind me, the boat tipping wildly from one side to the other before righting itself. I'm alarmed by how low we've settled into the water; my calculations had us riding a lot higher. But test runs were against the rules, so this is our maiden voyage, and it's all a bit of a guessing game at this point.

I grip my paddle hard, waiting for Mr. Dill's whistle to split the air. To our left, Mitchell and Alexis are staring straight ahead, their faces rigid with focus, and behind them the bleachers are a blur of people and noise.

"On your marks," says Mr. Dill, who is sitting in the life-guard chair at the halfway point, a clipboard balanced on his lap. "Get set. . . ."

Then the whistle sounds and we're off.

Teddy lunges forward so quickly that he knocks his head against my shoulder, and I immediately drop my paddle. He reaches for it before it can float away, shoving it back into my hand, then begins to row frantically. But he's much faster than me, and instead of moving forward we start to spin in circles.

He groans, then pulls his paddle out of the water to bring it to the other side and help me, but he manages to bonk me on the head in the process and I drop mine again. By the time he fishes it out, we're already a few lengths behind, the other boat splashing ahead of us, our two classmates somehow as synchronized in their movements as members of a crew team.

"Faster!" Teddy yells through gritted teeth, and I lean forward, paddling as hard as I can. I'm so focused on catching up that it takes me a minute to notice there's water in the bottom of our boat, at least an inch of it, soaking my knees and my bare feet. I turn to give Teddy a panicked look, but he just shakes his head at me and says it again: "Faster!"

The crowd is clapping hard now, half of them laughing and half of them booing as they watch us flounder in the middle of the pool.

The water in the boat gets higher, and I can feel the bottom start to bend.

"Teddy," I say, whipping around, but his eyes are hard and he doesn't even seem to see me: he's looking past me to the finish line.

The noise is now deafening, the voices ringing off the tiled floor and the concrete walls. The other boat has made it to the finish line, and we're still rowing fast but we don't seem to be getting anywhere, sinking deeper into the turquoise water.

Still, Teddy continues to paddle, unwilling to give up, and so I do the same in spite of the soggy cardboard, in spite of the rising water, in spite of the jeering crowd.

We're three-quarters of the way to the finish line when the whole thing collapses. There's no surprise to it by that point, no dunk tank moment; I'm already half-soaked, and the edges of the boat are starting to bow. It's like a blanket being folded in half, all four corners drawn inward, and just before it happens, before the bottom gives out entirely, the whole thing caving in at once, I manage to close my eyes and hold my breath. And just like that we're plunged into the deep end of the pool.

It's still something of a shock: the water is cold and the fall is sudden. For a few seconds I remain underwater, suspended in the muffled quiet. But when I open my stinging eyes to search for Teddy I don't see anything, so I kick hard and let myself drift back up to the surface just in time to catch him hoisting himself out of the pool.

"Teddy!" I shout, but it's lost to the sound of our classmates, who are stomping their feet, hooting and laughing and pointing.

*Better luck next time, kid!*

*Can't win 'em all, Moneybags!*

*Where's your yacht when you need it?*

Beside me our crumpled boat is still bobbing in the chlorinated water like something dead, the bottom already beginning to break apart, so I grab the edge and start swimming toward the shallow end, dragging it behind me.

I look up just in time to see Teddy disappearing through the door to the locker room without a backward glance, and suddenly I'm angry. I'm angry that we lost, angry that we failed. Angry that Teddy changed the design after contributing nothing for so long. Angry that he left me with the battered boat and the sneering crowd.

Angry that he left me at all.

By the time I make it to the end of the pool the next heat is lined up and ready to go, and I stand there, waist-deep in the shallow water, dripping and shivering and tugging at my clinging T-shirt as I look around for someone to help me pull the sodden cardboard mess out of the pool. But nobody seems to care. Mr. Dill is marking something down on his clipboard—probably our failing grade—and the audience has shifted its attention to the next race, no doubt hoping for an even more spectacular fail.

I start to heave the damp remains of the boat over the concrete lip of the pool, but it's unwieldy and surprisingly heavy, and I'm relieved when someone reaches down from above and pulls the whole thing out at once, hauling it onto the blue tiles, where it slumps to the floor like some sort of beached animal.

When I look up, I'm surprised to see that it's Sawyer who has come to my rescue. Only seniors are excused to watch the races, which means he must have cut class. "What are you doing here?" I ask as he reaches out a hand. But I wade over to the ladder and climb out on my own, eyeing him as I wring out my dripping shorts.

"I wanted to cheer you on," he says, handing me a towel from a stack sitting on one of the starting blocks. I wrap it around my shoulders gratefully.

Behind us the whistle sounds and the next race begins, a flurry of splashing and shouting. Sawyer puts a hand on my shoulder, steering me toward the locker room, and I follow him, relieved to have someone pointing me in the right direction.

"You're shaking," he says, and I realize that he's right. But at the door to the locker room I'm suddenly weary of all the high-pitched voices of my classmates from inside, many of them laughing, probably still about Teddy and me.

Instead I turn around and walk out into the hallway, my bare feet leaving wet footprints on the floor as Sawyer trails behind me. When we reach a small empty corridor between the nurse's office and the gymnasium, I slide down the wall and onto the ground, tipping my head back against the cool concrete. My clothes are still soaked, and the towel is draped around my shoulders like a cape, and my hair is dripping onto the floor. But I'm grateful for the sudden quiet.

Sawyer sits beside me, leaving a little space between us, and I'm not sure why but I feel oddly guilty as I wait for him to say something.

"So did we win?" I joke, but his face doesn't change.

"You like him, don't you?"

My first instinct is to say *Who?* to buy myself some time, or maybe just to avoid the conversation altogether. But I can't do that to him. Not after all the nice things he's done for me. He was the one who took care of the boat. The one who gave me a towel. The one who offered me a hand.

He was the one who was there for me today.

And it's not fair to him to pretend.

"Yes," I say in a small voice, flicking my eyes back to the puddle I've left on the floor so I can feel rather than see the way he steels himself, can sense the hurt so close to the surface, the way it radiates off him with a kind of heat.

"I waited the other night," he says, pulling his knees up. "To make sure you got in okay. I saw him there on the stoop, and the way you guys were talking."

"Nothing happened," I say, which is the truth. Nothing happened then, and nothing ever will. Teddy has assured me of that much. Our kiss that morning in his apartment feels like it happened to two other people entirely.

Sawyer gives me a sorrowful look. "It didn't have to."

"We're just friends," I say, trying not to sound so disappointed by this. A drop of water slides down my nose and Sawyer lifts a hand to wipe it away, then changes his mind and lowers it again. But his eyes remain fixed on mine, and I can tell he wants to kiss me. Honestly there's a part of me that wants to kiss him too. But I know that wouldn't be fair, because I just don't feel the same way he does. I wish I did. I want more than anything to feel for him what I do for

268

Teddy, because everything would be so much simpler that way, so much better.

But I don't. And I can't help that.

So I pull back, just slightly, and his face clouds over. "Does he even like you back?"

It takes me a second to say the word, and when I do there's something hollow about it. "No."

"Because I do," he says, his voice gruff. "I like you, Alice. A lot. I think you're amazing, and if he can't see that, then—"

"Sawyer," I say, because I can't bear to let him finish. "I'm so sorry."

He gives me a hard look. "I know you like me too."

"I do," I say, my stomach twisting as his eyes fill with hope. "But it's just  it's different with Teddy. I wish it wasn't. I wish it was you instead. But I just can't seem to shake this thing with him."

"You two have a history," he says, like it's the worst thing in the world, though history is what he loves.

"We do," I say. "But it's not about that."

Sawyer sits very still for a minute, then rises to his feet, looking down at me with an unreadable expression.

"You know he doesn't deserve you, right?" he says a little angrily. "That's why this sucks so much. It's hard to watch you waiting around for something that'll never happen because he's too self-centered to notice what's right there in front of him."

I open my mouth, then close it again, unsure what to say to that. But it doesn't matter anyway. Sawyer turns and walks back down the hallway, the sound of his footsteps fading until they've disappeared altogether.

Even after he's gone I stay there like that, my heart sunk low, my eyes still burning from the chlorine, thinking about how the worst part of it all is that he's probably right.

# Thirty-Three

Later that evening Leo and I are standing outside Teddy's apartment.

"You know this is pretty much the last place I want to be right now, right?" I say, and Leo gives me an exasperated look.

"We have to make sure he's okay."

I frown at him. "We were in the same boat, you know. Literally."

"I'm not talking about the boat," he says as he lifts a hand to knock, and when Teddy opens the door he looks about as pleased as I am to find us there.

"What're you guys doing here?"

"We knew it was taco night," Leo says, waving to Katherine, who is slicing a tomato in the kitchen. She's wearing her scrubs, and I know she'll have to leave for work soon, which is just as well, since I'm still annoyed at Teddy for leaving me with the boat today and I don't want to have it out with him while his mom is here.

"Perfect. I'm just making seconds before I go, since this one never stops eating," Katherine says, nodding at Teddy. "So there's plenty for everyone."

Leo beams at her, and Teddy grudgingly steps aside to let us in, though he still refuses to meet my eye. We head over to the kitchen, grabbing extra plates and napkins, making ourselves busy so that we don't have to talk about anything else.

I notice a pile of newspaper clippings on the counter, tucked beneath the napkin holder. The one on top shows Teddy's smiling face under a headline that reads DREAMS REALLY DO COME TRUE. A speck of salsa has landed on his chin.

"I'm glad to see you dried out okay," Katherine says to me, glancing up from the cutting board. "That was a tough race."

Teddy doesn't say anything and neither do I.

"If it was a race to the bottom of the pool, you guys would've killed it," Leo says, but nobody laughs.

When she finishes refilling bowls of tomatoes and lettuce and cheese, Katherine wipes her hands on her scrubs and looks at each of us in turn. "You two are taking this way too hard," she says. "It was a cardboard boat. What did you expect?"

"Maybe some help getting it out of the pool," I say under my breath, and Teddy narrows his eyes at me.

"I came back for it. But what's-his-face seemed to be doing just fine on his own."

I glare at him. "That's because *you* left me all alone in the water."

"Oh, come on, it's not like you were drowning."

"Would you have noticed if I was?"

"I was pissed off, okay?" he says. "I just had to get out of there. We completely tanked in front of the whole school."

"I know," I say, practically spitting the words. "I was there too. Remember?"

Leo pops a tortilla chip into his mouth, looking half-amused by all of this. But Katherine claps her hands hard, and the noise of it startles us into silence.

"Okay," she says firmly. "I think it's time to change the subject."

"Yeah," Leo says with a grin. "That ship has definitely sailed."

I give him a withering look.

"Leo," Katherine says, spinning in his direction. "How was Michigan?"

All at once the smile slips from his face, replaced by the same blank expression he's adopted whenever anyone has asked him about this since he got back.

"Fine," he says.

Katherine tilts her head, waiting for more, and when it doesn't come she pushes on. "It must've been nice to see Max."

"Yup," he says, suddenly intent on fishing a fallen chip out of the bowl of salsa.

"Okay, I have to get going," she says, apparently giving up on us. She walks over and stands on her tiptoes beside

273

Teddy, who bends so she can give him a kiss on the temple. "Last night shift."

He smiles. "I've been telling you about this whole sleeping-when-it's-dark-out thing for years," he tells her. "I highly recommend it."

"Thanks," she says, laughing, then turns to me. "And thank *you*."

The words are so full of gratitude that I blush. "Of course. I'm so happy for you."

"It's a big night," she says as she picks up her bag. Then she fixes a stern gaze on Teddy. "Don't stay up too late. And no wild parties. And don't you dare buy anything bigger than a breadbox." She rolls her eyes at Leo and me. "Did you guys see the ice cream maker? And the jukebox? I'm going to have nowhere to sleep if he doesn't stop."

"Mom," Teddy groans.

"And listen," she says, her voice more serious now. "Whatever went on with your father at the race today—"

"I already told you," he says quickly. "It wasn't that. He promised."

Katherine sighs. "Teddy, your dad—he's not a bad guy. But he's also not the most—look, I get that you want to believe the best in him. I do. But I honestly don't know if his promises are worth all that much."

"This time is different," Teddy insists.

"Maybe," she says. "But I'm not sure he's the best influence for you anyway. He's a lot of fun to have around when there's money falling from the sky, but . . ."

"Mom," Teddy says. "It's fine."

Katherine nods, but she still doesn't look convinced. "Well, if he does come by, just . . . I don't know. Be careful, okay?"

"What's that supposed to mean?"

"Just use good judgment. I know you love him. But don't forget he can be really charming. A little too charming. And that makes it easy to lose sight of what he really wants, okay? So call if you need me."

Teddy nods.

"I love you," she says fondly, and he leans down to give her a hug.

"Love you too."

When she's gone he turns to us, clearly eager to move on. "Let's eat before it gets cold," he says, so we follow him over to the table, passing bowls of toppings in silence until the landline in the kitchen starts to ring. After a few seconds, the answering machine—which is ancient and hopelessly out-of-date—clicks on. If I didn't know the reason, I'd be surprised Teddy hadn't upgraded it yet. But there's an old message on there from his dad, calling from Vegas a couple nights before everything fell apart to wish him luck in a basketball game. Once, when he thought I was asleep, I heard him play it from the next room and it just about killed me.

"Hi there, Mr. McAvoy," says a nasally voice, "this is Errol Mitchell with Peak Performance Investments. I'm calling because I heard about your recent good fortune, and

I've got some inside information about an opportunity that might be very interesting to you, but we've got to move fast. So give me a call and we'll talk about your financial future. Congratulations!"

When it ends I look over at Teddy, who shrugs. "Happens all the time."

"I thought you changed your number."

"I did," he says. "Twice."

"And you still get calls?"

"Ten or twelve a day. More on my cell."

Leo whistles. "Wow."

"Yup," Teddy says, carrying his plate over to the kitchen to get more food. As he walks by he punches a button to delete the message.

On the table Leo's phone begins to jitter, and when he picks it up he freezes. I crane my neck to see the name on the screen: *Max*. When I look up again our eyes meet, and then Leo grabs the phone and scrapes back his chair.

"Be right back," he mumbles, heading for Teddy's bedroom. A minute later we hear the sound of the door clicking shut.

"Max?" Teddy asks from the kitchen.

I nod. "I don't think they've talked since . . ."

"That's a good sign, then," Teddy says, walking over to the table. Outside it's fully dark now, and I can see his reflection in the window. He's wearing the same shirt he had on the morning after his birthday, the one with the lucky shamrock, and his hair is sticking up in the back the way it always does.

When he sits down across from me, his face is serious. "I'm sorry," he says. "About today. And about our grade."

I nod. It's a relief to hear him say it—and even more than that, to know that he means it. "Thank you," I tell him, and I mean that too. "It'll be fine. I can't imagine they'll pull my acceptances on account of some soggy cardboard."

He nods. "I really am sorry for leaving like that. I just needed to get out of there."

"I know."

"It was a lot, with my dad and the guys, then the boat too. . . . It sort of felt like the whole place was laughing at me."

"At *us*," I correct, but he shakes his head.

"No, it was definitely me." He puts his head in his hands and rakes his fingers through his hair. "I don't know what's happening. It felt like more than just razzing. It felt like they really hated me." He looks lost right now, like all it took was a single afternoon to rattle so much of what he knows to be true. "How can they already hate me? I haven't even done anything yet except give them stuff."

I press my lips together, not sure what to say. Teddy's always been insecure about money, and it's obvious he assumed this windfall would change all that. But having too much money comes with its own set of problems.

"I didn't ask for this," he says, lowering his chin. "It just happened to me. So how could they possibly—"

"It's because you're different now."

"What? No, I'm not."

"You are," I say. "Or you will be."

"But nothing's changed," Teddy insists, his voice breaking on the last word. "Nothing important, anyway."

"What happened to you . . . it makes you separate from them in a way." I pause, chewing on my lip. "It happened to me after my mom died too, when we were still out in San Francisco."

Teddy looks up sharply, surprised to be invited into this part of my life.

"One day I was like all my friends," I say, trying to keep my voice even. "And the next I was the girl with the dead mother. Everyone tiptoed around me for a while, then they just kind of stopped playing with me. I'd come home crying every day and my dad thought it was because of my mom, which it was, partly, but it was also because of what was happening at school, and I couldn't tell him that, because it seemed so small in comparison, you know?"

He nods.

"But I kind of get it now. Everything was different, and they didn't know how to act around me anymore."

"That's awful," Teddy says darkly.

"Maybe. But that's just how people are. It's not really about you. It's about them. So don't let it get to you, okay?"

Teddy clears his throat. "I'm sorry your friends did that to you."

"I was in third grade," I say, waving this away. "I barely remember their names."

"Yeah," he says. "But still."

After a moment I nod. "Still."

He leans back in the chair, suddenly looking very tired.

"I didn't think it would be like this. I thought it would be more . . ."

"Fun?"

He nods.

"It was," I say. "For a while. But there were always gonna be hard parts too."

"See, I wish someone had told me that earlier," he says with a wry smile. "Here I was thinking it was just gonna be bags of money and dreams coming true."

"Money doesn't fix everything."

"I know," he says, nodding, and then some of the light comes back into his eyes. "But it *can* fix some things."

"Like what?"

"Well, it can be used for stuff like plane tickets and hotel rooms and . . ."

"Are you skipping town again?"

"Actually, yes," he says with a grin. "And so are you."

"What are you talking about?"

"We're going to San Francisco. Or, to be more accurate, we're going to Palo Alto. To see Stanford."

"You're joking," I say, staring at him hard, but he shakes his head.

"I'm not."

"You're serious?"

"I am."

"You and me?"

"Me and you."

"No way," I say, letting out a laugh, half-surprised and half-confused.

Teddy's eyes are dancing. "Look, I know you think I've gone a little too crazy with the money, and maybe you're right. But I want to spend it on things I care about. On *people* I care about. And that means you. So hopefully this is okay."

I'm not sure what to say. "Teddy—"

"You've had your heart set on Stanford forever, but you haven't actually been there in a million years, and I really think you should see it again before you decide."

I nod, slightly overwhelmed. The full impact of this is just starting to sink in, not only Teddy's thoughtfulness but what it means to be going back to California after all this time, to return to a place with so many memories, so many ghosts.

"I was worried it might be too hard," Teddy continues, speaking more carefully now, his forehead knit with concern. "Going back. But I figure you'll have to do it at some point, and wouldn't it be better if you had someone with you?"

"Much better," I say gratefully, and he looks relieved.

"I already talked to Sofia and Jake, and they thought it was a great idea," he says; then he pauses and the tips of his ears go red. "They just wanted to make sure we'd have separate hotel rooms, which we do. Really, really nice ones."

I feel my face flush, so I ask the first question that comes to mind, eager to move on. "When are we going?"

"This weekend. You busy?"

"I am now," I say, unable to stop smiling, because I can't believe this is actually happening, that after all these years

280

I'm finally going back to San Francisco, the city that still has such a grip on me—and not just that but I'll be going with Teddy, the two of us alone together for an entire weekend. "What about Leo?"

"He knows too," Teddy says, waving an arm toward the back of the apartment, where Leo is presumably still on the phone with Max. "He tried to weasel his way into it with some nonsense about wanting to see Alcatraz, but I promised I'd take him somewhere else once school's out. This one is just you and me." He hesitates, looking less certain. "Is that okay?"

"Yes," I manage to say. "Of course. I don't know how to thank you."

"How about you promise to hate Stanford so you won't be so far away next year?"

I laugh. "How about something else?"

"How about you let me give you a million bucks?"

"Try again."

"How about you refill the salsa bowl?"

"You drive a hard bargain, McAvoy," I say with a grin. "But you've got yourself a deal."

# Thirty-Four

I'm spooning salsa into the bowl when there's a knock at the door. Teddy and I exchange a questioning look. It takes a minute for the answer to register across his face, and when it does he scrapes his chair back so hard it nearly topples over.

I watch him rush over to look through the peephole, then he pulls open the door. "Hey, Dad," he says as Charlie appears, still wearing his suit, which is significantly more rumpled now. "Where have you been? I texted you after the race—"

"My phone was off," his dad says. He's standing with his hands on his hips, his eyes darting around the apartment. "Is your mom here?"

Teddy shakes his head. "No. What happened before?"

"It was nothing," he says, then his eyes land on me.

"Hey, Alice. Heard about your boat." He says this in a tone so grave you'd think we lost the *Titanic*. "Bad luck."

"It happens," I say with a shrug.

He pats at his suit pocket, then reaches in and pulls out a bag of Skittles, which he tosses to Teddy, whose face lights up.

"No way," he says, looking down at the package in his hand as if it was filled with precious stones rather than candy. He turns to where I'm still standing in the kitchen. "We used to play poker with these. Greens were worth the most."

"Yup." Charlie claps him on the back. "Greens were good. And you always managed to rack up a pretty nice little collection, if I remember correctly."

"You taught me well," Teddy says with a smile.

"So, hey," Charlie says, rubbing his hands together. "Listen. I'm sorry to do this. But I was hoping I could take you up on your offer now and borrow a few bucks."

I can feel Teddy's eyes cut in my direction, but I stare down at the bowl of salsa. I don't want him to see what I'm thinking, which is *I knew it.*

"Sure," Teddy says, already reaching for his wallet. "How much do you need?"

"Maybe like a thousand?"

He pauses. "What?"

"Yeah, it's stupid, really. I lost my wallet this morning and my credit card was in there, so I just need a little cash to get by until I figure it all out."

Teddy shakes his head. "I don't have that much here."

"C'mon, kid," Charlie says, his voice deliberately light. "You're a millionaire now. You must have some cash lying around. How about five hundred?"

"Dad . . ."

"Or, tell you what. Maybe you can just write me a check instead. Unless there's an ATM nearby?"

Teddy gives him a long look. "You were betting on the boat races," he says, and it's clear from the disappointment on his face that he suspected this all along, from the moment he saw his dad arguing up in the stands. He just didn't want to believe it.

I close my eyes for a second, feeling like I shouldn't be watching this unfold, shouldn't be bearing witness to something so personal. But they're right in the middle of the room, which means there's no way to leave without interrupting. So instead I just stand there, trying to make myself invisible.

Charlie runs a hand through his graying hair with a sigh. "It wasn't a real bet," he says. "Just a little side wager. The guy next to me was bragging about his kid's boat a few races before yours, and the thing looked like a floating shoe box, so I took the bet, but they ended up winning, and we went double or nothing on the next one, and . . . well, it's not like I was at the tables in Vegas or anything."

"You said you were done with all that," Teddy says, and he looks so forlorn that I wish I could walk over and take his hand.

"I was," Charlie says with a helpless shrug. "I am. It was just a onetime thing. A joke, really. Honestly it's not a big deal."

Teddy is chewing on his lip. "It kind of is."

"God, Teddy," Charlie says, impatient now. "What do you want, some kind of collateral?" He tugs off his jacket and shoves it at him. "Here, I don't need this. There aren't any business meetings. Is that what you want to hear?"

"You skipped them?" Teddy asks, and I realize he doesn't yet understand what's happening. There was never any job. There was never any business trip. There was only Charlie, hoping that by the time he patched things up with his son he'd have wrangled enough money out of him to cover the cost of it all, probably including the new suit.

"Come on," Charlie says with a sudden grin. "You really think I'd give up the glamorous life of an electrician?" He fishes a pack of cigarettes out of his pocket, then holds it up. "Okay if I smoke?" But when he sees the look on Teddy's face, he shrugs and puts them back. "Look, I saw you on the news and I thought I'd come out for a visit. It's not a crime to want to see my son, is it?"

Teddy blinks at him. "So you knew."

"I just—I saw you on TV and I was proud of you, so I—"

"For what?" Teddy asks, his voice cold. "I didn't do anything."

Charlie shrugs again. "Fine. Okay. I get that you're mad. I just figured now that you're the big winner in the family, you might be feeling generous."

285

Teddy tips his head back. "I actually thought you were different," he says to the ceiling, and I can tell he's trying to collect himself. "I thought you'd changed."

"It's not like that was the only reason," Charlie says, looking more contrite now. "You're my son. I love you. I've been wanting to see you for years. It's just—I kept waiting, hoping I'd kick this thing. Then one day I turn on the TV and there you are. And I just couldn't wait any longer."

Teddy shakes his head.

"C'mon, T," Charlie says, attempting a smile. "Do you have any idea how many lottery tickets I've bought in my life? And how many times I've lost? Then you win big the first time you ever play? You have to admit it feels pretty good, right?"

This makes me look up at him. Because there's a part of me that's been thinking of this money as magic, something that's been dropped into our lives out of nowhere like a pot of gold. But of course it's not. It comes from people like Charlie McAvoy who play all the time. People who probably can't afford to be buying ticket after ticket but still do.

Teddy draws himself up straighter. "I can't give you the money."

"Look," Charlie says, his face darkening, "I'm supposed to meet this guy in an hour, and I owe him five hundred bucks."

"You said a thousand before."

"What does it matter? It's nothing to you. Not anymore." He attempts a grin, but there's something elastic about it.

"You'll buy your mom a whole building, but you won't even loan your old man a few bucks?"

A muscle twitches in Teddy's jaw. "I can't," he says evenly, and without warning Charlie bangs a fist hard against the wall. Even in the kitchen, it's enough to make me jump, sending my heart slamming against my chest. But not Teddy. He stands there, unflinching, his chin held high.

From the back of the apartment there's the sound of a door opening, then Leo appears in the living room. He looks from Teddy to Charlie, then over to me. "Everything okay in here?" he asks with a frown.

"Fine," Teddy says, eyes still on his dad. "He was just leaving."

For a moment it seems like Charlie's going to protest. He stands there rubbing his hand, looking surprised to have found himself in this situation. "Okay," he says, adopting a gentler tone. "I get it. No more of this. Any of it. I swear—I swear—this will be the last time."

Teddy folds his arms across his chest, his face entirely blank. Leo walks over and joins me in the kitchen, resting his elbows on the counter. But though he looks relaxed, I can tell he's watching carefully, ready to spring forward if needed.

"Teddy, come on," Charlie says, sounding more desperate now. "At least just give me the five hundred bucks so I can square things away before I go. It's the least you guys can do." He shoots me a look, as if this whole thing is partly my fault. "I promise this'll be the last time. This is it, then I'll go back home and I won't bother you anymore."

"I'm not saying you should go," Teddy says. "It's been good to see you again. It's just . . ."

"I know," Charlie says miserably.

Teddy takes a small step closer to him. "Listen, I'll go to a meeting with you. Right now. We'll do this together."

"I don't need a meeting. I need money. All I'm asking for is a little help from my son, and you won't even—"

"Rehab, then," Teddy says, looking hopeful. "There must be some kind of program, right? I'll do some research and make some arrangements—"

Charlie's expression shifts again. "So you'll pay for that," he says, his eyes narrowing, "but you don't trust me to do it on my own?"

"It's not that, but—"

"Forget it."

Teddy shakes his head. "I'm sorry, it's just—"

"I can't believe how much you've changed," Charlie says with a scowl, and the words hang there for a second, because it's exactly what you'd expect a father to say to his son after this much time has passed—only not like this, not when it's hurled like an insult, bitter and spiteful and mean. "I thought I raised you better than this."

Something inside Teddy seems to break at that. "You barely raised me at all," he says. "You threw away our savings, our home, our *family* for a few rounds of poker. You promised to get help and you didn't. You promised you wouldn't disappear again and you did. You promised you'd never touch Mom's bank account and you wiped it out in one weekend. And instead of sticking around to fix it, you took off." His voice is rising, his eyes wet with tears. "It isn't enough to send a bunch of stupid presents when you win. Stuff we don't even need. We needed *you,* and you weren't there, and now it's too late. You know how many times you emailed me last year? Four. It takes like *three* seconds, and you couldn't be bothered. Not even on my birthday. So you can't just show up now and expect things to go back to normal. There is no normal. You made sure of that."

Charlie's head is bowed, and his tie is crooked, and he suddenly looks much older. "I'm sorry," he says. "I didn't mean for any of this to happen."

Teddy's face softens, just slightly. "I know."

"I swear it'll be different next time."

"Sure," Teddy says, nodding without much conviction.

"But maybe . . . ," Charlie begins, wincing even as he does, "maybe you could still give me at least some of the money. Just enough to cover this bet, you know?"

For a second Teddy doesn't move. Then he pulls out his wallet. "This is all I have," he says, handing over a stack of twenties.

"Come on," Charlie says, his eyes pleading. "There's got to be more somewhere. I know you're holding out on me."

Teddy only shakes his head, his shoulders sagging as Charlie's face twists again.

"When did you get to be so heartless?" he mutters as he heads for the door, stepping out into the hallway and slamming it behind him.

For a while none of us say anything. But the words continue to ring out in the quiet apartment, and when I glance over at Teddy it's to see him standing with a hand over his chest, right where his heart is, as if checking to make sure it's still there.

# Thirty-Five

On Friday morning, I'm waiting at the window when a limo pulls up in front of the house. It's not quite light out yet, the sky still dark at the edges, and I close the door softly behind me so I don't wake anyone. We already said our goodbyes last night, when Uncle Jake pressed some extra money into my hand, and Aunt Sofia made me promise to text at least three times a day, and Leo ruffled my hair and told me to be good.

Now the house is quiet and I feel an odd pang of loss as I walk away from it, like I'm doing more than just leaving for a weekend, like I'm somehow saying goodbye.

Which of course isn't true.

It's only a weekend away. I'll be back on Sunday night.

Still, when I glance back at the narrow brownstone, my chest feels tight with unexpected emotion and I hurry the rest of the way down the path to the limo, suddenly eager to get under way. The driver steps out to take my bag, then opens the door for me, revealing Teddy, who is sprawled out on the backseat with a small crystal bowl of candy in one hand and a bottle of sparkling water in the other.

"Welcome," he says grandly as I crawl inside, falling into the seat opposite him. He holds out the candy dish. "Mint?"

"I'm good," I say, glancing around at the sleek leather interior.

"Then sit back and relax. When you travel with Teddy 'Moneybags' McAvoy, you travel in style."

"So it would seem."

"Stop looking so tense," Teddy says, straightening up in his seat. "I know you're sitting there thinking about how much this costs and how many poor starving kids that money would feed, but I swear I'm going to feed some starving kids with all this money too. And in the meantime I want to make this weekend great. Plus, this is my first-ever limo ride. So let's just enjoy it, okay?"

"It's my first limo ride too," I admit, and Teddy looks overjoyed.

"Well, see?" he says, putting on his sunglasses, though it's definitely still too dark to need them. "This is gonna be fun. I promise."

On the plane I'm more surprised than I should be to find that we're seated in first class, which is another first for me. "You get free ice cream," Teddy whispers once we get settled in. "And hot towels. And real silverware with the meal."

"How do you know?"

"Spring break," he says, clearly pleased to be the seasoned pro. Without warning he lunges across me, reaching for the control panel on the arm of my seat, his shoulder brushing against mine, his face suddenly very close. "Watch this."

He presses a button and my seat slides back, a footrest popping up out of nowhere. "Very cool," I say as I move the seat upright again. "So . . . any word from your dad?"

There was no response from Charlie after he stormed out that night, and there's been no response in the days since.

Teddy sighs, more impatient than anything else. "Nope."

"I'm sure he's okay," I say, and he grunts, because that's not the point. Charlie is always okay. He'll turn up eventually in Salt Lake City, or maybe Vegas, and eventually, when he's ready, he'll resume his usual pattern of spotty communication.

But this is the first time in six years he's actually shown up in person. And because it ended so badly—because it was such an epic failure of a visit—there are no guarantees Teddy will ever get another chance to repair whatever might still be repairable between them.

When he doesn't say anything else, I try again. "Has your mom—"

"She left him a bunch of messages."

"And she hasn't heard—"

"Nope."

"Well, what if—"

"Let's talk about something else," he says abruptly. "How's Leo doing?"

I stare at him in frustration. "I'm not sure. But they talked again last night."

"Was it better this time?" he asks, his face brightening. "Or just more fighting?"

"More fighting, I think. He won't really talk about it. He just keeps changing the subject." I give him a pointed look. "Kind of like how you keep changing the subject whenever I ask about your dad."

He raises an eyebrow. "Kind of like how you've spent nine years changing the subject whenever I ask about your parents?"

"Kind of like that," I agree, smiling ruefully.

"Look," Teddy says. "This week was the worst. But now we're on vacation, so I think we should forget about all that stuff, at least for the next few hours. There are like sixty movies on this plane, and if we don't get cracking we'll never get through them all."

I laugh. "How long do you think this flight is?"

"Long enough," he says, punching the screen in front of him.

For a while we flip from one movie to the next, counting to three before pressing play so that they'll start at the exact same time. But when Teddy falls asleep, I turn to look out the window, gazing out over the endless sweep of clouds below us.

Later, as the plane starts to descend and San Francisco Bay comes into view beneath all the fog, I glance over to see that he's awake now, watching me.

"Hi," I say.

He smiles. "Hi."

"Hi," I say again, then we both start to laugh. But for some time after that—until the flight attendant comes by and asks us to make sure our seats are upright—he keeps looking at me and I keep looking at him.

A black car collects us at the airport and we head straight to the hotel, which is definitely the nicest place I've ever stayed and possibly the nicest place I've ever been. The lobby has antique mirrors and ornate couches and so many flowers it looks like a garden, and when we step up to the desk to check in, the woman raises her eyebrows at the sight of us: two teenagers with backpacks in jeans and flip-flops, both of us trying to play it cool in spite of being slightly wide-eyed at our surroundings.

As she searches for our reservation, I keep waiting for her to call us out, or ask to speak with our parents, or tell us there's been some kind of mistake. I think a part of me has been waiting for this the whole time. Because in what parallel universe do we take limos and fly first class and stay in luxury suites?

But she hands over our keycards without incident, and we head upstairs to drop the bags in our rooms, which are next door to each other. When I walk into mine, I let out a surprised laugh. It's enormous, as big as an entire floor of our brownstone back home.

"This is like a ballroom," I say when Teddy comes to get me. "You could throw an actual ball in here."

"Well, you'll have to save me a dance," he says. "I'm too hungry to think about anything but lunch right now."

"What else is new?" I say, and he makes a face at me.

"So where do you want to go?"

"I have an idea," I tell him as we walk back out the door.

When I was little my parents used to take me to the farmers market at the Ferry Building on weekends, where we'd wander the tents and stalls, buying bread and cheese and fruit, then make a picnic of it on one of the benches overlooking the bay.

Until now, I wasn't sure I'd want to go back there. Or to any of the places I remember from my old life. It's one thing to dream about coming home to San Francisco and another to actually do it. I didn't know if I could stand to visit all our favorite spots, retrace our steps, see our old house again—the place where we lived for so many years as a happy family—without further damaging my already-shattered heart.

But then, on the ride from the airport, I could hear the sounds of the foghorns and smell the saltiness of the water, and to my surprise I felt a sudden longing to stand on the pier and look out over the Bay Bridge the way we so often used to do.

So that's where we go.

First I take Teddy through the Ferry Building so I can show him the huge vaulted ceilings and rows of shops. It's crowded with people buying coffee and flowers and jars of honey, browsing the bookshop and carrying bottles of wine. Teddy can't resist stopping for ice cream, even though we just had some on the plane.

"Vacation," he says, flashing me a smile as his cone drips onto his shoe.

Outside, the fog has mostly burned off and the air is sharp and cool. I pause for a moment to breathe it all in, and Teddy comes to a stop beside me.

"You okay?" he asks, looking worried.

"Yes," I say, and for once I mean it. It feels good to be back after so long, like time has slowed and stretched, like all these years in between never even happened.

We walk over to the farmers market, where vendors in endless rows of tents sell berries and wine, cookies and bread. "Something smells really good," I say as we weave through the stalls, and Teddy points at a tent with rotisserie chicken.

"Lunch?" he says, and I nod as we fall in at the end of a very long line.

He finishes his ice cream as we wait, and I hum, "If you're going to San Francisco," like some kind of dopey tourist, but I can't help myself. I feel sort of giddy being back, and I'm in such a good mood by the time we step up to the booth that it takes me a few seconds to register that the woman behind the counter is trying not to cry.

"Hi there," she mumbles, her eyes full of tears. "What can I get you?"

Teddy and I exchange a look. "Are you okay?" I ask, and she lifts her chin, pulling in a jagged breath.

"I'm fine," she says. "Thanks."

"Are you sure," Teddy says, "because—"

"Fine," she says again. She sets her notepad down and wipes her trembling hands on her blue apron. She's young— probably in her midtwenties—and her dark hair forms a curtain over her face as she tries to collect herself. Over her shoulder, rows of golden-brown chickens are rotating slowly above a flame, and behind us a long line snakes out past the next booth, where they're selling bunches of lavender.

"I just got some bad news, that's all," she says, blinking at us. "Sorry to be . . . here, I should really just take your—"

"It's okay," I tell her. "If you need a minute, we can wait."

Teddy jabs a thumb at me. "Me and her," he says with a sympathetic smile, "we're pretty well acquainted with bad news."

The woman's face crumples at this, and she grabs a napkin from the stack beside the cashbox. The man behind us cranes his neck impatiently and I shoot him a look.

"Thanks . . . it's just, I found out my mom has to go into hospice care, which we knew was coming, but on top of everything it's so expensive, and I'm already working two jobs, and . . ." She trails off, looking suddenly horrified. "And I can't believe I'm telling you all of this. I'm so sorry."

"Don't be," I say, shaking my head. "Really. I'm so sorry about your mom."

"Me too," Teddy says. Out of the corner of my eye, I see that he's already pulling out his wallet, and I hit him with my elbow, because the least he can do is let her finish before we carry on with the business at hand. But she clearly notices too, because she uses the end of her apron to dab at her eyes, then sniffs once and straightens.

"Sorry," she says again. "What can I get you?"

"Just an herb-roasted chicken," I say, feeling terrible, and she grabs one of the brown paper bags the chef has lined up on the counter beside her.

"That'll be fourteen fifty."

Teddy passes her a twenty, waving her off when she tries to give him change.

"Good luck with everything," I say, grabbing the bag and turning to walk away. Just before I do, I see Teddy slip something into the tip jar, a red plastic cup filled with coins and a few wrinkled dollar bills. When we're far enough away I glance over at him.

"What's your problem?" I say, failing to hide my annoyance.

"What?"

"You took out your wallet in the middle of her story, which is pretty much the universal sign for *hurry up*." I shake my head. "I hope you at least left her a big tip."

"I did."

Something about the way he says this makes me stop. "You did?"

He nods, unable to keep from grinning.

"How much?"

"A thousand dollars."

I stare at him. "You did?"

299

"I did," he says again.

"So when you took out your wallet . . ."

"I was just seeing how much cash I had to give her."

I open my mouth, then close it again. Suddenly I'm so proud I want to hug him. Instead I let out a laugh, shaking my head in wonder. "You're a really good guy, Teddy McAvoy. You know that?"

"Thanks," he says, putting an arm around my shoulders as we walk over to one of the benches. "But you don't always have to sound so surprised about it."

# Thirty-Six

There's a knock on my door in the middle of the night.

It starts out quietly, a soft thumping that works its way into my dream. But then it gets louder and my eyes snap open. The clock on the bedside table says it's 3:24 a.m., and I squint into the darkness for a minute before remembering where I am.

"I'm coming," I murmur, swinging my legs out of the bed. At home the nights are punctuated by streetlamps and stars, which sneak in through the slats of my blinds. But here in the hotel the heavy curtains blot out everything, so I switch on the desk lamp as I make my way across the massive room, blinking fast at the sudden brightness.

At the door I stand on my tiptoes and look through the peephole, where I'm surprised to see a fun-house mirror version of Teddy: his nose too big and his forehead too small. He hops from one foot to the other, knocking every so often.

"What's wrong?" I ask as I fling open the door. For some reason he looks just as surprised to see me as I am to see him.

"Oh," he says, as if this were an odd question. "Nothing."

I widen my eyes at him. "Then why are you knocking on my door?"

He pushes past me and into the room without answering. He's wearing plaid pajama pants and a Chicago Bears hoodie, and there are still creases from the pillow on one side of his face. When he spins around I can see just how jittery he is—he's tapping his fist against his open palm as he paces—and it occurs to me that there aren't all that many reasons to show up in someone's hotel room at three-thirty in the morning.

The idea that it could be the obvious one is both thrilling and terrifying, and my heart flops around, fishlike, as I turn to him, thinking *maybe,* thinking *hopefully,* thinking *finally.*

But then he stops moving long enough to meet my eye, and I can see in his face that it isn't that—of course it isn't. There's nothing romantic in his gaze, only a kind of frantic wakefulness, a jangly excitement that I've only ever seen in him one other time: the morning we found out about the lottery.

"Are you okay?" I ask, sinking down on the bed, trying not to feel so deflated.

He nods. "I know it's really late, but I've been going over

this again and again in my head, and I just couldn't wait till morning."

"What is it?"

"I have," he says, walking over to sit beside me, the bed dipping beneath us, "the best idea in the entire world."

"Wow," I say, distracted by his knee brushing against mine. "Okay."

He looks disappointed. "I was kind of hoping for a bigger response."

"Well, maybe if you tell me what it is . . ."

"Right," he says, clapping so loudly that I flinch. He hops off the bed and resumes his pacing. "So remember the chicken lady today?"

I stare at him. "What?"

"The chicken lady," he says impatiently. "The woman who sold us—"

"I know who you're talking about. I just don't know if she'd love being called a chicken lady."

"Not the point," he says, crouching in front of me as if he's about to give me a pep talk, which he sort of does. "Stay with me, Al, okay? This is important."

I rearrange my face into a more serious expression. "Okay."

"So," he says, shooting up again. His bare feet make shallow indents in the plush carpet as he walks back and forth in front of me. "I haven't been able to stop thinking about that all day. Or obviously all night."

"It *was* really good chicken."

"I'm not talking about the chicken, you ding-dong. I'm talking about the tip. It felt really good to be able do that for her, you know?"

"I bet," I say with a smile, because I do know, of course I know, and it's such a relief to see it in Teddy now too.

"And here's the thing: it wasn't just about the money. It's that I got to hear her story, and I know exactly what that money could do for her. And the best part is that she had no idea. She wasn't some jerk leaving a thousand messages asking me for cash, or my idiot teammates wanting handouts. And she wasn't some big, faceless charity—"

"Yeah," I say before he can go on, aware of the defensive note in my voice, "but big, faceless charities get money to small, helpless people."

Teddy holds up his hands. "I know," he says. "I do. They obviously do amazing work. But ever since I got this money, I've been having a hard time getting excited about a cause. Because I know I'm supposed to give a bunch of it away—"

I raise my eyebrows.

"And I also *want* to," he adds quickly. "I mean, this is more money than I ever dreamed of. And more than I know what do with. And besides . . ." He sits down next to me with a smile. "You're the one who bought the ticket, and I know how important this stuff is to you. So of course I want to use it to help people. Of course."

I nod, my heart swelling, because this is what I've been waiting to hear, and I was starting to doubt it would ever come. "So what's the idea?"

"I want to give it to people like her. People who need

it but aren't expecting it. Can you imagine what her face must've looked like when she saw all that money? I would've *loved* to see that. I know it's not life-changing the way other things can be. But there's something pretty cool about giving people a boost when they need it, just a little here and there to make their lives easier."

"Random acts of kindness," I say, and he smiles.

"Exactly."

It seems obvious now that he's saying it. Teddy is a people person; he lives for connection and thrives on being around others. He wants everyone around him to be happy—he always has—and now that he's armed with such a crazy amount of money, that instinct could actually make a real difference.

I think again about that woman, and how unlikely it was that we'd be the ones to step up to her booth at just that moment, when so many people probably could've used a helping hand in that crowd and so few were probably in a position to offer it.

As soon as the thought flashes across my mind I feel a quick spark of excitement. *This could work,* I think, struck by the possibilities of it, the potential. Because right then it doesn't feel the way it so often does, like an inheritance or a legacy.

It feels like something closer to magic.

"So?" Teddy asks, sitting down with a hopeful expression. "What do you think?"

"I think," I say quietly, "that it's brilliant."

His face lights up. "Yeah?"

"Yeah."

"But?"

"But it would be a lot of work," I say. "A lot to figure out. It couldn't just be you wandering around giving out really big tips."

"I know," he says, though the way he says it, so uncertainly, I can tell that's exactly what he had in mind. "I haven't worked everything out yet."

"Right," I say, nodding. "Like, would you have a team out there looking for people, or would they write in to ask for help? And would it be a nonprofit? Would all the donations come from you, or would you make it a foundation so others could get involved too? And would—"

"I don't know," he says, slightly irritable now. "I literally just thought of this tonight."

I bite my lip, studying him in the dim light from the desk lamp, and I realize with a sinking feeling that I already know what's going to happen. It's what always happens with Teddy. It doesn't matter whether it's cardboard boats or college applications or even girls.

He gets swept up in the moment, caught up in the idea of something.

And then, just as quickly, he loses interest.

Sitting here, I feel a bitterness rise up into my throat at the thought. Maybe it's because it's late now and I'm jet-lagged, my head swimming and my eyes burning. Or maybe it's because we're sitting here together on a hotel bed in the dark, and the idea of kissing me couldn't be further from his mind.

Or maybe it's because I'm one of his abandoned projects too. Because he kissed me like he meant it. And then it turned out he didn't.

He's still waiting for me to stay something, and I study my hands, trying to collect my scattered thoughts. "I really do think you're onto something here," I say eventually. "And it could be completely amazing. So I hope you're serious about it. But if you're not, can you please just tell me now so I don't get my hopes up?"

My voice wobbles as I say this, and Teddy frowns at me, confused.

"Al," he says, shaking his head. "C'mon. It's the middle of the night. Can you maybe cut me a little slack?"

"That's the thing. Everyone's always cutting you slack."

"So let me get this straight: you've been annoyed at me for ages because I wasn't doing enough with the money, and now that I think of something I actually want to do, you don't think it's good enough?"

"I told you," I say more softly. "I think it's brilliant."

"Then why are you being so hard on me?"

"Because it could be something really special."

"So you're trying to bully me into it?"

"I guess maybe I'm trying to *challenge* you into it."

"Well, you're being kind of mean about it."

"Someone has to be," I say with a smile, and he rolls his eyes.

"Really nice of you to volunteer."

"It's the least I can do. Especially since this is all my fault."

"What is?"

307

I shrug. "That you're in this mess."

"What mess?" he asks, looking genuinely confused.

"This," I say, and gesture at the hotel room, with its soft carpeting and heavy drapes, its crystal chandelier and bland oil paintings.

"I wouldn't exactly call this a mess," he says, but there's something forced about his smile.

"Yeah, well, none of this would've happened if it hadn't been for me," I say, and my tone is unmistakable: we both know I'm not talking about the five-star hotel or the first-class plane ride or even the building he's buying for his mom. I'm talking about all the rest of it: his dad coming back and the guys at school and the reporters outside his house and the incessant messages on his phone. I'm talking about the blogs and the talk shows and the extra lock on the door to his apartment. I'm talking about the curse.

"Well, you," he says finally, "and the good folks at the Powerball lottery."

"Right," I say. "But those guys are a lot less likely to hassle you about your work ethic in the middle of the night."

"That's true," he says, and his eyes linger on me a moment. "I guess it's pretty lucky I have you, then."

I smile. "You have no idea."

# Thirty-Seven

We drive down to Stanford the next morning. It takes a little finagling before we're able to head off in the small silver sedan—you're supposed to be at least twenty-five to rent a car here, but it turns out being really, really rich works too.

We decide to take the scenic route, though it's twice as long, and for most of the trip the car is silent. Teddy doesn't mention his late-night visit to my room and neither do I. Even the memory feels pulsing and dim this morning; there was an idea, and there was a discussion, and now all we're left with is this:

Teddy, afraid he might have gotten my hopes up.

And me, worried I might've put too much pressure on him.

This isn't our usual dance; we're not normally so delicate with each other. Nevertheless, awkwardness fills the car, and after a few miles I open the windows to let it stream out, watching the ocean scroll past, bottle-blue and flecked with white.

When we see the first sign for Palo Alto, my heart picks up speed, and as if he can sense it, Teddy glances over at me. "You okay?"

I nod, not quite trusting myself to speak, and without a word he reaches out and takes my hand. I give him a grateful smile, and just like that the tension from last night disappears. Just like that we're a team again.

When we pull into the parking lot, Teddy steps out of the car and raises his arms in a stretch and I put on my sunglasses, surveying the campus—this thin slice of my past, this possible piece of my future—through the amber-tinted lenses.

"No tours," I say, thinking of all those even sets of parents and kids I saw marching across the quad at Northwestern.

"Just wandering," he promises.

As we start to explore, I realize I don't remember very much of my last trip here, and what I do might just as easily have come from all my many visits to the website. It's so perfect it's almost hard to focus: the red-capped buildings and impeccably cut grass, the leafy trees and California sunshine.

"Does being here change your mind at all?" I ask, and to his credit Teddy doesn't even bother to pretend he doesn't know what I'm talking about.

"Not really," he says, looking around. "I mean, it seems

310

like a perfectly nice place to spend four years. But it's not for me."

"Well, that's good," I say, amused. "Because I doubt even 141.3 million dollars would be enough to make up for *your* transcript."

He jabs me with his elbow. "I meant college in general."

"I know," I say, and it takes a great deal of effort to leave it at that.

The paths are crowded with students, bags slung over their shoulders and books in hand. I try to imagine myself here next year. It doesn't seem like such a leap. But then it also doesn't seem so wildly different from Northwestern or any of the other colleges I've seen along the way. The backdrop changes from one place to another—red brick or white stone; parkas or flip-flops—but they're all pretty similar underneath.

It's not a lot to go on when you're choosing where to spend four years of your life, where you're meant to learn and make friends and figure out who you're going to be once you've been spit back out into the world.

If you pick one place, your life might go one way.

If you pick another, it will be completely different.

It's better not to think about it too hard or else the uncertainty will wreck you.

As we weave through the sun-soaked buildings, my head begins to pound, a tiny metronome just behind my temples.

"You're probably just tired," Teddy says. "I shouldn't have . . ." He trails off. *I shouldn't have come to your room last night.* This is what he says without saying it.

We come to a stop before an enormous bell tower, and I tip my head back, deep in thought. There's a fountain in front, low and wide and empty, the blue tiles baking in the sun. When I walk over to it a memory rushes up: sitting here when I was little, eating a half-melted candy bar while my parents talked nearby.

Only they weren't talking. They were arguing.

I sink down onto the edge of the fountain, and Teddy sits beside me. "Al?"

"I'm fine," I mumble, dropping my head into my hands as the world buzzes around me. I don't know what it is about this spot, this memory. But it's different from all the others that have climbed up and out of the past on this trip: flying kites at the beach or watching the sailboats on the bay, wandering the farmers market or taking evening walks up and down the steep hills of our old neighborhood.

Those happened, all of them.

But so did this: my parents standing just a few yards away, both of them upset, their voices lowered so I wouldn't be able to tell they were arguing.

I close my eyes. Is it that I have so few memories of them fighting, or that I never let myself think about them?

This one snaps into focus all at once.

"Maybe you can wait till next year," my dad said that day, looking pained as they stood in the middle of it all, the campus right in front of them but also somehow out of reach. "We just can't afford it right now."

"We could if you—"

312

"What? Got a real job?"

"I was going to say a better-paying job," she told him. "Just for a year. Just while I do this program. Then I'll be more qualified, which means I can get more funding, expand the center. Maybe we could even work on it together."

"Why is it that your causes are always more important than mine?" my dad asked, throwing his hands up in frustration.

"Because I'm trying to save *children*."

He raised his eyebrows. "And I'm only trying to save trees."

"Well," she said with a shrug.

The fight followed us back through the campus, into the car, and all the way home. But it's hard to remember what happened after that. My mom got sick just a few months later, so she never made it to grad school after all. And my dad had to get a better job anyway, to cover her medical expenses. When his car was struck by a drunk driver a year after she died, he was still passionate about saving the trees. But he was spending his days working at a call center where he answered people's questions about their malfunctioning coffeemakers.

All this time, I thought she'd missed out on Stanford because she got cancer—not because of anything as ordinary as finances, as mundane as a disagreement with my dad. And something about this shakes me.

Teddy bumps his knee against mine. "What's wrong?"

"Nothing."

"Al," he says, and for a moment, all I can think is: *Leo*. I wish Leo were here so I could tell him this story and not have to explain what it means. Leo would understand in an instant, and would know exactly the right things to say.

But then I look at Teddy, the way he's watching me, his eyes full of concern, and I remember what he said that night in his room: *You go to Leo when you want to remember. You come to me when you want to forget.*

Right now, Teddy is the one here, but I don't want to forget. Not this. So I take a deep breath. And then I tell him.

He listens quietly as I explain what happened—what I didn't until this very minute remember had happened—and when I'm finished, I expect him to say something like *wow* or *oh* or maybe just *I'm sorry, Al*.

But instead he says, "So they weren't perfect."

I blink at him. "What?"

"They were just people," he says, tilting his head to look at me sideways. "Really good people, but still just people."

"I know that," I say, but even as I do, I realize I'm not so sure. I'm still reeling from the force of this memory, wondering what else I'm not remembering, what else I might've missed.

"I think," he says slowly, cautiously, "that you sometimes see your parents as these completely selfless martyrs. You have them up on this impossible pedestal, and it's not really fair—to them or you. I know they did a lot to make the world a better place, which is really cool . . ."

I lift my chin, waiting for him to continue.

314

"But they also did those things because it was their job. Even people who are working to save the world are also still working for a paycheck. And at the end of the day, they're still just people."

I know he's right. They weren't perfect. They were just like anyone else. They fought and failed and disappointed each other. They were frustrated and tired. They snapped and groaned and muttered.

But they also laughed and teased and joked. They felt deeply and cared hugely. They tried to leave their mark on the world, with no idea they'd have so little time to do it. And they loved me. They loved me so much.

They were just people.

But they were also my parents.

"Yeah," I say to Teddy. "But they were pretty amazing people."

He gives me a long look. "Do you know how many people there are in the world who would've turned down tens of millions of dollars?"

I shake my head.

"Nobody," he says. "The answer is nobody. Just you, Al."

"Right, but you think I'm crazy."

"Maybe a little," he says with a smile. "But I think you're pretty amazing too."

I rest my head against his shoulder, the sun warm on my face. "I thought it would be different. Coming back out here. I thought it would feel more like coming home."

"It was only ever home because of your parents," Teddy says quietly. "Without them, it's just a museum."

I sit up to look at him, and he smiles at me, but there's something sad in it.

"I went to visit my old building the other day," he says, answering my unspoken question. "I had this crazy thought that I'd ask the architect to keep our old apartment the way it is." He shakes his head. "It was a dumb idea. It would mean the rest of the place would be brand-new, and then there'd be this one unit that's kind of a dump."

"Then why . . . ?"

"I got cold feet after seeing my dad," he says with a shrug. "That's where all my memories of him are, you know? I just couldn't imagine tearing it down."

I nod. "That must've been really hard, going back."

"It was," he says. "And it wasn't. It was like walking into a time capsule. The owners haven't done anything to it. Remember that crack in the ceiling that looked like an alligator? That's still there. So are all those tiles we broke in the bathroom." He pauses. "But it was good too. Seeing it. Because it didn't feel the same as when we lived there. *I* didn't feel the same. And now we can build something better in its place."

Somewhere along the way, we'd angled ourselves toward each other, our eyes locked, and now, slowly, almost involuntarily, Teddy tips his head to one side. Around us, the trees are moving in the wind, and the students are calling to each other, and the clouds are scudding across the too-blue sky. And all the while we remain like that, our heads tilted in opposite directions, watching each other intently.

I wait for him to snap out of it, to pull back again, but

he doesn't. Somehow, our faces are closer now, the distance between us smaller by half, and for a few long seconds, we're frozen there like that, stuck somewhere between a conversation and a kiss, a stalled overture that seems to last forever. Then Teddy's eyes widen, just slightly, and he gives his head the tiniest shake before leaning back again, taking all the air, all the hope, all the many pieces of my heart with him.

"Anyway," he mumbles, suddenly focused on his shoes.

I bob my head, not able to speak yet. But finally, I manage it too. "Anyway," I repeat, shifting away from him, my heart still ticking like an engine that's not quite cool. We sit there for another minute, staring out at the green grass and the orange buildings, and then I let out a long breath. "Can I ask you something?"

Teddy nods. "Anything."

"Can we go see my old house?"

"Of course," he says, looking relieved for the change of topic. "But are you sure?"

"Not really," I say with a small smile, but I stand up anyhow.

As we start to walk back to the parking lot, I glance over at him. He's wearing his old corduroy jacket instead of the new one he bought when he first won all the money. It's worn at the elbows and patchy in places, but I've always thought he looked handsome in it, and today is no different.

I don't know what that was, what just happened between us, the magnetic pull of it. But I know how he feels about me. And I don't want things to be complicated between us.

Not after all he's done for me. Not after dreaming up this whole trip. Not when we're finally *us* again.

"Hey," I say softly, slipping an arm through his. I feel him tense up, but I ignore it, determined to get back on solid ground, eager to show him that I'm not holding out hope, that I'm fine with things the way they are. "Thank you."

He gives me a wary look. "What for?"

"Just everything," I say, because honestly, there's too much to list.

His face relaxes into a smile. "You don't have to thank me," he says, but he seems pleased, and we walk the rest of the way to the car linked together like that.

When we're ready to go, he asks for the address to put into his phone, and I give it to him without hesitating, amazed that it could still be so close to the surface after nine whole years. But I suppose things like that get imprinted on you; they're not so easy to shake.

We take the more direct route this time, shooting up the ribbon of highway toward San Francisco, past the airport and through the city and straight to my old neighborhood, which sits high on a hill overlooking the bay.

Teddy parks a few blocks away, and then we walk up the steep incline together, past the playground where my parents used to take me, and the house with the beagle that always howled when I rode past on my bike, and the square of sidewalk where someone etched a heart with an arrow through it a million years ago.

The street looks exactly the same and entirely different all at once. I pause near the top, breathing hard, no longer used to the hills. After nine years in Chicago, it seems I've officially become a midwesterner.

"It's just over there," I say, pointing farther up the block.

"Do you want me to wait here?" Teddy asks, but I shake my head.

"No," I say. "Come with me."

When we reach the house, I steel myself, not sure what to expect. But it looks more or less the same: a tall, narrow Victorian with a gabled roof and a white porch. When we lived there, it was pale blue, but it's now painted a bright, cheerful yellow. Our apartment was on the top floor, and I can see my bedroom window from where I'm standing. Someone has hung a small piece of stained glass there, and it glints in the sun.

For a few seconds, I stare up at it, feeling numb all over. I've spent so much time thinking about it and not thinking about it over the years, trying desperately to remember it and even more desperately to forget it.

And now I'm here, and Teddy was right. It's just a museum. An exhibit from my past. A piece of my history.

All these years, I thought maybe this was where I belonged. I thought it was still my home. But it turns out it's just a house.

A feeling of emptiness crashes over me, followed by a sadness so big it fills every inch of my body, every corner of my heart. Because they're gone, really and truly gone, and

319

because I miss them, and because if they're not here in this place where we all lived together—where we sat on these front steps on summer nights and ate dinner behind that window and planted flowers right there by the porch— then where are they?

I don't even realize I'm crying until Teddy wraps his arms around me. For once, he doesn't say anything, doesn't ask if I'm okay or try to cheer me up. He just holds me as I bury my face in his shirt, and for a long, long time after that, he doesn't let go.

# Part Five

MAY

# Thirty-Eight

The envelope from the Art Institute arrives on the same day I have to let Stanford know whether I'll be accepting its offer.

It's there in the mailbox when we get home from school, and Leo doesn't even make it into the house before ripping it open. I stand below him on the front steps, watching nervously as he scans the letter. Then his face breaks into a grin and he lifts his hands in the air and goes tearing back down the steps and around our small patch of lawn, running in gleeful circles and whooping noisily, the letter held aloft.

I can't help laughing. "I take it the news is good?"

As an answer he stretches out a hand for a high five as he goes wheeling past me.

Inside he drops his messenger bag on the floor, peels

off his jacket, and pulls out his phone to call Aunt Sofia at work. I walk over to the refrigerator and grab an apple, then sit down at the table, a front-row seat to watch him share the good news.

Once he's told her, he hops up onto the counter. "I know," he says into the phone, giving me a wink. "I know. I'm a genius. I really am."

I roll my eyes at him.

"Yup, I can't wait," he says, and his smile dips just slightly, probably thinking about Max. There are a few beats of silence, then he looks over at me. "No, she hasn't let them know yet. I think she's holding out till the last minute for dramatic effect."

I take a bite of my apple, considering this. I actually have until midnight on the West Coast, which is two a.m. here. So there's still plenty of time. And it should be a no-brainer, the easiest decision in the world. But for some reason I haven't been able to do it yet: accept my place at Stanford.

Leo is still on the phone, and I know when he's done he'll want to call Uncle Jake too, so I give him a wave, then a thumbs-up, and head upstairs to my room.

My laptop is on my bed and I open it up to the Stanford website, staring at the sun-drenched pictures of those reddish buildings, thinking about the way Teddy and I sat on the edge of that fountain.

It's only been a couple of weeks since that afternoon, but it feels like much longer. We didn't talk about it again, what happened there on the street: the way I fell apart so completely, the way we stood pressed together for so long.

Something about the sight of my old house had split me clean apart, and there on the uneven sidewalk, on a peaceful hill in the middle of San Francisco, Teddy tried to put me back together again.

Once it was over, though, he didn't stop trying.

For the rest of the trip, he stuck close by my side. At another time, and in another city, this might have turned my eager heart to mush. But there was a watchfulness to him that made me uneasy, like he was scared I might go to pieces again at any minute.

When I tripped on a walk through the Presidio, he came jogging over with a look of grave concern. At the beach he worried my feet would get cold when I waded into the freezing bay. And at a bookstore he plucked a copy of *The Bell Jar* out of my hands. "I heard that one's really sad," he said, handing me *Little Women* instead.

I raised an eyebrow. "And you think this one's happy?"

"Why?" he asked, alarmed. "It's not?"

"You do know that Beth—"

"No spoilers," he said, taking the book back and shoving *Oliver Twist* at me.

"Dickens," I said. "Sure. He's always upbeat."

I knew he was just trying to cheer me up. He'd seen me crumble, had stood there and let me weep in his arms, and wanted to make sure it didn't happen again. But there was something almost feverish about his efforts, a desperation that solidified the worry that had lodged itself in the pit of my stomach.

That maybe it had been too much for him.

Since we got back he's been strangely distant. When I see him in physics, he always seems distracted. When I text him, he doesn't respond. And when I call it goes straight to voicemail. There's a reason I don't talk about my past very often. I hate the idea of anyone feeling sorry for me—especially Teddy. And now it feels like nine whole years of self-preservation has been drained away in a single weekend.

I turn back to the Stanford website with a sigh. It's especially hard right now, when all I want to do is talk over this decision with him. For so long California was the plan. But something shifted during our trip and now suddenly I'm not so sure.

I rest my fingers on the keyboard, and this time I find myself typing the word *Northwestern*. When the site comes up I stare at the homepage, remembering what Aunt Sofia said that day on campus: *I want to make sure that's what you want too.*

More than anything, I wish my mom was here. I wish it so fiercely I can feel the pain of it straight down to my toes. I wish I could ask her what to do. I wish I could know what my parents would think of me now, whether they'd be proud or worried, whether they'd see a girl trying to honor their memory or just a girl who is hopelessly lost.

I shut the computer and rub my eyes, feeling torn. I grab a piece of paper and draw a line down the middle. Then, before I can think too hard about what I'm doing, I write *Stanford* on one side and *Northwestern* on the other.

I blink at the words, knowing what I really mean is California versus Chicago.

What I really mean is past versus present.

There's a knock at my door and Leo pokes his head in.

"Mom wanted me to tell you we're eating out back tonight, so come down soon. I think she wants to have a little celebration." He raises his eyebrows at the list in front of me. "Any hints what we'll be celebrating on your end?"

"Not yet," I tell him, and he leans against the wall, his arms folded.

"One day on campus with Teddy," he says with a grin. "That's all it took to make you doubt Stanford?"

I laugh. "It's not his fault."

"Listen," Leo says, his face growing serious. "I'm gonna give you the same advice you gave me: You have to do what's right for you. Not for me. Not for Teddy. Not for my parents. And not for yours. For *you*."

I glance down at the piece of paper in front of me, my eyes bouncing between the two sides, two possible futures.

"We'll see you out there soon?" he asks, and I nod. When he closes the door behind him, I find myself turning back to the column on the left.

Before I can overthink it, I begin to write.

By the time I'm finished I can hear the sound of voices outside, and I stand up and walk to the window. Down below, the three of them are sitting around the wrought-iron table on the back patio, and as I watch, Aunt Sofia raises a glass in a toast to Leo, who does his best to look embarrassed even though he's beaming.

Once upon a time I might have seen this and crawled

back into bed, keeping a safe distance, sticking close to the edges. But not anymore.

When I got back from San Francisco and the limo pulled up to this house, with its glowing lights and cheerful flowerpots, my shoulders went slack with relief. Whatever had been roiling and churning inside me throughout those days on the West Coast quietly settled like the wind falling flat after a storm, like the finish line of some race, like familiarity, like peace, like home.

And for the first time in a long time, maybe even the first time ever, that's what it felt like, returning to Chicago: it felt like coming home.

Now, seeing the three of them gathered outside, all I want to do is go down and tell them I've made a decision. That I know where I want to be next year. But instead I wait for a moment, just watching them: Uncle Jake with his head thrown back in a laugh that carries up to my window, and Aunt Sofia looking so lovingly at Leo, who is telling a story with his arms outstretched, his face animated, his eyes dancing.

My family.

Beyond the rows of buildings behind us, the sun is sinking lower, washing everything in a soft yellow light; a few birds are perched on the telephone wires that stretch across the yard, looking down on the scene below, same as me.

There's a cake on the table, and from above I can see that it says *Congratulations, Leo and Alice!* Beside it there are three piles of napkins. One stack has cartoon lions on them, in honor of the larger stone ones that stand guard at the entrance to the Art Institute. The other two are solid colors: red and purple.

One for Stanford. And the other for Northwestern.

I can't help smiling at the idea that Aunt Sofia managed to recognize this possibility even before I did. That she somehow knows me this well, in spite of all the roadblocks I've put up between us. It's a nice feeling, like finding solid ground, like finally being discovered after the world's longest game of hide-and-seek.

I walk back over to my bed and sit down in front of the computer, staring at the website again, remembering my parents that day at the bell tower, the longing in my mother's voice when she talked about going to Stanford.

Then I think of Aunt Sofia and Uncle Jake, of Leo and Teddy, of what my parents would've really wanted for me after everything that's happened—to do what makes me happy and to be close to the people I love, the people who love me back—and I take a deep breath and make my decision.

When I get downstairs, I slide open the glass door that leads to the patio, and all three of them turn to look up at me, their faces asking the exact same question.

"So?" Leo says, and I smile.

"So," I say, sitting down to join them.

# Thirty-Nine

A few days later I'm dragging myself down the stairs, still not quite awake, when I hear a muffled yelp. I stand on the steps with my head cocked, listening. Then I hear it again, and I hurry the rest of the way down to see what it is.

In the kitchen Uncle Jake, Aunt Sofia, and Leo are standing around a cardboard box, which has been set in the middle of the table.

"What's going on?" I ask, and they step back to reveal the small brown face of a boxer peeking over the edge. He has floppy ears and a twitching nose, and his whole body is wiggling, the box swishing this way and that on the table.

"We've been puppy-bombed," Uncle Jake says darkly.

"What?"

"He just showed up," he says, waving a hand at the box. "Completely out of nowhere. *Puppy-bombed.*"

I look from him to Leo, who is fishing the squirming pup out of the box, laughing as it covers his face in kisses. "I don't get how—"

"And I'm allergic," Uncle Jake says indignantly. He gives Leo a pointed look. "Allergic! So don't get attached, because this little monster isn't staying long."

"Oh, come on," Leo says. "You haven't sneezed once."

Uncle Jake folds his arms across his chest. "But I will."

"He's fine," Aunt Sofia says. "He's not really allergic."

"You're *not*?" Leo and I say at the exact same time. We stare at him in astonishment. When Leo was a kid, this was all he wanted: a big-pawed, loose-limbed maniac of a puppy. But it was always a nonstarter because of his dad's allergies.

Uncle Jake shifts uncomfortably, casting a desperate glance in Aunt Sofia's direction. "Why are you blowing my cover *now*?"

"Because," my aunt says, taking the wriggling puppy from Leo and holding it close to her, "there's no way we're giving this guy back. He's way too cute."

"You weren't allergic?" Leo asks, shaking his head in disbelief. "Ever?"

Uncle Jake grins at this. "What can I say? You were always kind of gullible. I mean . . . you believed in the tooth fairy until you were ten."

"Eleven," I say, chiming in. Aunt Sofia sets the puppy on the floor and I scoop him up, resting my chin against his velvety head, feeling his little heart beating against mine. "I still don't get where he came from."

"Some guy just delivered the box," Uncle Jake says,

jabbing a thumb toward the front door. "He wouldn't say who it was from."

"It doesn't matter." Aunt Sofia is gazing fondly at the puppy. "He's ours now. The bigger question is what are we gonna do with him all day?"

"Well, you're the one who wants to keep him," Uncle Jake says, "so obviously you should bring him to your office."

"I'm in court today. You just sit behind a computer."

"My office is full of paper clips and staples," he says, sounding slightly hysterical. "It's a death trap!"

"It's fine," Leo says, holding up a hand. "I'll take a sick day."

Aunt Sofia shakes her head. "You're not taking a day off because of a dog."

"There are only a few weeks left of school, and I already got into college," Leo says. "I'm pretty sure it won't send my life skidding off the rails. And this way I can go to the pet store and figure out a dog walker and pick a name for him."

"I don't know if I trust you to pick out a name by yourself," I say. "You'll probably want to call him something nerdy like JPEG or Pixel."

"Actually, Pixel isn't bad."

I give him a look. "No naming him till we all agree, okay?"

"Okay, you poor nameless little dog," he says, looking down at the puppy, still in my arms. "It's just you and me today, pal."

Once I've transferred him back into the box we all head

332

out, leaving Leo to fend for himself. He lifts a coffee mug in farewell, looking pretty happy to be staying home, and I don't blame him. I was about to volunteer for puppy duty myself, but now that I've settled on Northwestern I'm desperate to tell Teddy. It feels strange to have made such a huge decision without him, and I'm eager to share the news.

All morning, I look for him in the halls. But it's not until physics, when I sit down behind his empty desk, that I realize for sure he's not here today. Again. This is the fourth time in the past couple of weeks he's skipped school. Teddy's never exactly gotten awards for perfect attendance, but still, it's a bit odd, and I'm disappointed not to see him.

As I walk out of class, I scroll through the unanswered texts I've sent him over the past few days, realizing there are twelve in all, messages like *Where are you?* and *Pick up your phone!* and *Are you okay?* and *Seriously, where the hell are you?*

Now I type out a thirteenth: *I miss you.*

But I can't bring myself to send it.

# Forty

After school I'm eager to go home and see the puppy, but I've got a reading session with Caleb, so I head off to the library instead. Yesterday his foster mom emailed to tell me they'd finished *Charlotte's Web,* which means it's time to pick out a new book. This is always my favorite part: wandering the stacks, pulling out books by their spines, watching as Caleb examines the covers and weighs his options.

Today, he lingers on *The BFG,* which I already know will be a hit. As we walk back to our seats, he's so busy flipping through the pages that I have to steer him through the shelves. When we turn the corner of the mystery section, I see that our usual table has been taken. And not just by anyone.

It's been taken by Teddy.

Caleb continues to walk over, still lost in the illustrations, but I remain standing there, unable to do anything but stare. I don't think I've ever seen Teddy in a library before—not even our school library—and it's a strange and unexpected sight.

When he looks up, he seems less surprised to see me.

"Hi," he says, leaning back in the too-small chair as we walk over. His backpack is propped beside his foot and it's half-unzipped, revealing several books and binders. On the table there's a notepad and a pencil, as if he's just settled in to do some work.

"Um, hi," I say, frowning at him.

Caleb slips into the other chair, setting his book on the table and gazing admiringly at the cartoon giant on the cover. Teddy leans forward to examine it.

"That's a good one," he says. "Who's your favorite character?"

"Wilbur," Caleb says automatically.

"Is that the giant?"

He looks at Teddy as if he might be slow. "No, he's a pig."

"The giant is a pig?"

"*Wilbur* is a pig."

"Oh," Teddy says with a knowing nod. "So the pig is a giant?"

Caleb giggles at this. "No, the pig is a pig and the giant is a giant."

Teddy grins at him. "Then who's Wilbur?"

Because this could easily go on forever, I clear my throat, and they both look up at me. "Can I borrow you for a minute?" I ask Teddy, who grabs his backpack, then holds out a fist for Caleb to tap his knuckles against.

"See you later, man."

"I'll be right back," I tell Caleb as I half-drag Teddy out into the hallway, where he leans against a poster of Harriet the Spy, his hands in the pockets of his fleece vest. "What are you *doing* here?"

"Working," he says with a shrug.

"In the children's section?"

"I like the ambience."

I frown at him. "I assume you're not doing something for school."

"That's true."

"So?"

"So . . . what?"

"Stop being such a weirdo," I say, punching him in the chest. "You can't fall off the face of the earth, then act like it's nothing. What's going on with you? Where have you been? And why are you hanging out at the library?"

Teddy rubs at the spot where I hit him, attempting a wounded look, but his eyes give him away: they're sparkling with laughter.

"I told you," he says. "I've been working."

"On *what*?"

"Just some stuff," he says, then does a quick sidestep before I can swipe at him again. "I can't tell you yet, but soon, okay? I promise."

336

I fold my arms. "Fine," I say. "But . . ."

"Yeah?"

"Are we okay?"

He nods. "Of course."

"I just mean . . . well, ever since we got back from the trip, you've sort of disappeared."

"I know," he says, and then does something he's never done before. He reaches out and tucks a loose strand of hair behind my ear, sending a shiver through me. "But we're okay. I promise."

I nod. "Okay."

"A little bird told me you picked Northwestern," he says with a smile. "That's big news. I didn't even know you were really considering it. Especially after our trip."

"I know," I say a little sheepishly. "It was kind of unexpected, but I ended up changing my mind."

He nods with approval. "You're allowed," he says, then clears his throat. "As you know, I'm not much of a fan of college myself—"

"Which we're not finished discussing."

"—but I'm a very big fan of the location." He looks like he's about to say more, then stops himself. "So congrats."

"Thanks," I tell him. "I'm really happy about it."

"Well, I'm happy you're happy," he says. "And guess what? My last offer in the building was just accepted. Which means I now own the whole thing."

"Wow," I say, widening my eyes. "Does your mom know yet?"

337

He shakes his head. "I just found out. I'm gonna tell her when I get home."

"I still can't believe you bought a whole building. I mean, I can . . . obviously. But a few months ago, this would've been . . ."

"Impossible," he says with a smile.

"So when do you get to move in?"

"Next month. There'll still be a bunch of construction going on, but the contractor promised at least one of the floors would be livable by then. I guess there's not really a rush, but I'm just excited. It feels like it's time for a fresh start."

I get the uneasy feeling he's talking about more than just the apartment. I think about his recent distance, wondering what it means and whether he's finally drifting away from me. The thought makes me want to grab his hand and refuse to let go.

He rocks back on his heels. "Anyway, I've got to run. But congrats again on Northwestern."

"Thanks," I say. "Congrats on the new place."

He gives me a wave, but as he starts to walk away something occurs to me. "Hey, Teddy?" I call out, and he spins around again. "This might sound weird, but . . . did you send Leo a puppy?"

His face splits into one of his trademark grins. "Maybe."

"Why?"

"Because," he says, as if the answer should be obvious, "it's what he said he wanted."

"Yeah, when he was *twelve*."

Teddy's smile widens. "Exactly."

I shake my head, amused.

"See you later, Al E. Gator," he says, waving over his shoulder.

It's been years, but even so, my response comes automatically: "I'll be there, Ted E. Bear."

When he's gone I head back in to Caleb, who is huddled over the book, his finger moving haltingly across the page. "Good so far?" I ask, and he points to the word *dormitory*. I say it out loud for him, but he still looks confused.

"What's a dorm-i-tory?" he asks, testing the sound of it.

"Well, it's a place where a lot of people sleep."

"But why does Sophie have to sleep there?" he asks, his eyes still on the page. "Where are her parents?"

"I think," I say cautiously, "that this dormitory is an orphanage."

"For orphans?" he asks in a small voice.

I nod.

"Like me."

"And me," I say. Caleb looks over sharply, his face screwed up like he isn't sure whether to believe me, like he's trying to figure out whether I belong in the category of adults who pander to him or the category who tell the truth.

"You?" he asks, and I nod again.

"Yes."

"You're an orphan?"

The word still has a sting to it, even after all this time. But I try not to let it show, because Caleb doesn't need to know that. He doesn't need to see that it still takes so much work to seem like a normal person, to maintain a hard enough shell around all that's gone soft inside you.

"Yes," I say, looking him square in the eye. "I am."

"Your mom died?"

I nod.

"And your dad?"

I nod again, and he considers me a moment.

"Mine too," he says, suddenly matter-of-fact. "It sucks."

I can't help laughing. "I totally agree."

For a few seconds we just look at each other. Then he turns back to the book, moving his finger to the next word on the page, then the one after that, murmuring them aloud in his slow and deliberate way. But I can't seem to focus on the story. I glance over at the far wall, where rows of posters hang above a low bookshelf. Some of them are just puppies and kittens sitting beside stacks of books, but others are more motivational. They're mostly clichés: FOLLOW YOUR DREAMS! and DON'T BE AFRAID TO COLOR OUTSIDE THE LINES! and YOU HAVE TO BELIEVE IN YOURSELF TO SUCCEED!

One of them has a black background, and each word is written across it in various bright colors. It says: IT'S OKAY NOT TO KNOW. IT'S NOT OKAY NOT TO CARE.

I stare at that one for a long time.

"Have you ever read Harry Potter?" I ask Caleb, interrupting him as he stumbles through a line about the witching hour. He glances up at me, confused.

"No, but I've seen some of the movies."

340

"So you know that Harry's an orphan too," I say, and he nods warily. "But when you think of him, what's the first word that comes to mind?"

"Wizard?" he asks, sounding just like Leo once did.

"Right. What else?"

"Quidditch player?" He pauses for a second to think. "Gryffindor?"

"Exactly. Harry was an orphan, but he was those other things too. Just like you're a lot of other things."

Caleb doesn't seem quite convinced. "Like what?"

"Well," I say, tapping my fingers against the cover of the book, "you're a reader." Then I point at his blue T-shirt. "And a Cubs fan."

He gives me a shy smile. "Yeah."

"What else do you want be?"

"A fireman," he says without hesitating. "Or a pig owner."

I laugh. "Both very good things."

"What about you?"

"Well, I'm a niece," I tell him. "And a cousin. And a best friend."

*And a daughter,* I think, and for once the word doesn't make me wonder whether that's actually true, whether you can still be a daughter without having parents. Instead it makes me think about what Aunt Sofia said that morning at Northwestern.

Instead it makes my heart feel very full.

"A tutor," I add with a smile, cuffing Caleb lightly on the arm; then I point to the open book. "And a reader."

He nods. "What else?"

I hesitate, because I'm already out of words and the list seems alarmingly short. I realize I don't know the answer to this question any better now than I did when I was nine, and there's something a little disappointing about that.

"I don't know," I say truthfully. "I'm still working on it."

# Forty-One

As we walk out of the library an hour later, Miriam, the librarian at the front desk, waves us over. She pulls a plain white box with a blue bow from behind the counter and peers down at Caleb. "This is for you."

He tips his head back, his eyes huge. "Me?"

"Who's it—" I start to ask, but Miriam just winks at me as Caleb tears the top off and lets out a shout. Inside there's a bundle of pink fur: a stuffed pig.

He hugs it fiercely to his chest. "Just like Wilbur."

"Just like Wilbur," I repeat as I scan the lobby. "Who dropped it off?"

"Some guy," Miriam says, still smiling at Caleb. "Isn't there a card?"

I check the box again, then shake my head. "No card."

"How odd," she says.

But as I lead a giddy Caleb and his new plush pig out to where his foster mom is waiting in the car, I'm actually thinking that maybe it's not so odd after all.

When I get home there's a similar white box on the front porch of the brownstone, and I'm not the least bit surprised at this either. I stand on the steps and peek inside to find a purple Northwestern hoodie. That's it. No note. No signature. No label.

There's nobody in the kitchen, which isn't unexpected, since it's still too early for my aunt and uncle to be home from work. But I was assuming the puppy would come hurling itself at me. As I make my way from room to room, calling out for Leo, waiting to hear the scrape of paws on the hardwood floors, I start to worry.

But then I hear the faint sound of barking from outside. Through the glass doors that lead to the deck, I see Leo with the puppy. And someone else too.

When I get closer I realize it's Max.

He's seated at the table with a can of soda, laughing as he tracks the dog—who is in hot pursuit of something, nose to the ground—and my spirits lift at the sight of him sitting there like he isn't supposed to be in Michigan right at this very moment, like he and Leo didn't just break up a few weeks ago, like nothing has changed at all.

"Max," I say as I slide open the door, and he swings his head in my direction, grinning, then hops up and pulls me into a hug.

"Alice," he says, kissing the top of my head. "Man, have I missed you."

From over Max's shoulder, I can see Leo watching us with an uncertain smile. I step back and put a hand on each of Max's shoulders, studying him. He looks a little bit taller than I remember, a little bit scruffier, but he has the same unruly brown hair and uneven dimples, and he's wearing the same canvas jacket he's had since his sophomore year.

"You look the same," I say approvingly, once I've had a chance to look him over. "Except for the stubble."

He laughs and rubs at his jaw. "That's just laziness."

"Well, it suits you," I say with a grin. "What are you doing here?"

"Leo needed some reinforcements to help with this guy," Max says, bending down to scoop the puppy into his arms.

"Seriously?" I ask, glancing over at Leo, who gives a sheepish shrug.

"I know he looks innocent," Leo says. "But trust me, he's all teeth."

"I grew up with dogs," Max says, shifting the puppy in his arms, "and I was looking for an excuse to avoid studying for finals, so I figured I might as well come see the little dude myself."

They're both looking at each other now, neither quite smiling, but also neither quite able to break away until the puppy cranes his neck up and bites at Max's ear.

"Ouch," he says, laughing. "He's like a piranha."

"Maybe *that's* what we should call him," I say, but Leo shakes his head.

"No," he says. "I'm still working on that."

"Well, I think I figured out where he came from," I say,

ready to tell them about the library this afternoon, about seeing Teddy and the box with the stuffed pig and the sweatshirt from Northwestern. But then Leo nods.

"Me too," he says with a look of amusement. "Teddy, right?"

"Right," I say, surprised that he figured it out too.

"It's what I said I'd want if I ever won the lottery," he says, answering my unasked question. "But that was a million years ago. I can't believe he remembered."

"Me neither," I say, though that's not exactly true. In fact I'm starting to think we might have underestimated Teddy a bit.

Max sets the puppy back on the deck, and we all watch as he balances on the top step, trying to work up the nerve to hop down. "You definitely need a name that captures that adventurer's spirit," Max says, and I laugh at this. But when I look over at Leo, his face has gone slack.

"Be right back," he mumbles, heading for the door.

"I'm just gonna . . . ," I say, and Max nods distractedly as he crosses the deck to grab the puppy again.

In the kitchen Leo is standing at the sink, his arms braced on either side as he stares out the window that faces the backyard.

I stop in the doorway. "Are you okay?"

"Fine," he says without turning. "I just . . . I can't believe he's here."

"Like . . . in a good way?" I ask hopefully, because I love Max, and, more important, I know Leo loves Max, and even

346

though he was the one to end it, it's obvious how much he misses him.

"I don't know yet," he says. "I have no clue what this means, and I'm scared to ask. The puppy was chewing everything, and I kept wishing I could call him, so I just sort of . . . did."

"Have you guys talked about anything else?"

"No," Leo says, shaking his head. "That's the crazy part. He borrowed a car and drove all the way down here. Five hours! But then all we've been doing is playing with the dog. And not talking. At least not about anything real."

I nod. "But he's here."

"He's here," Leo agrees, watching Max half-drag the puppy—who is clamped to the cuff of his jeans—around the yard. "I wish I knew what it meant."

"Well, it might help to start by talking to him instead of me."

He nods. "Yeah, but I'm just afraid if we start talking, we'll . . ."

"Jinx it?" I ask, and he gives me a sheepish smile.

"I know you think I'm nuts."

"I think," I say, watching him closely, "that the only reason you broke up with him was so that he wouldn't break up with you first."

"What?" Leo stares at me. "No."

"I think you were so busy waiting for something bad to happen that instead of getting blindsided, you decided to just go ahead and do it yourself."

He shakes his head, refusing to look at me. But I can tell by the color in his cheeks that I'm right.

"Listen," I say, more gently now. "Most terrible things that happen are out of your control. So it makes no sense to add some of your own. Especially not because you're scared, okay? You love Max. And he loves you." When Leo opens his mouth to protest, I stop him. "He does. Believe me, he didn't drive five hours just to see the puppy."

"Maybe not," Leo admits, his eyes drifting out the window.

"I don't know if it'll work out with you guys. Not everyone is that lucky," I say, feeling a familiar ache in my chest as I think of Teddy. "But don't screw it up for yourself. If it's gonna happen, at least let the universe do it for you."

He allows a smile. "I thought you didn't believe in that stuff."

"I don't," I say with a shrug. "But you do. So go out there and talk to him. Take a walk or get some coffee or something. I'll keep an eye on the puppy."

Leo smiles. "Lucky."

"Well, maybe not as lucky as you, but . . ."

"No," he says, laughing. "That's his name."

"What?"

"The dog. I think we should call him Lucky."

I stare at him. "You're joking."

"I'm not."

"Don't you think that's a little . . . ?" I don't exactly know how to finish this sentence, but it doesn't matter, be-

348

cause Leo isn't listening anyway; he's too busy watching Max roll around on the grass with the dog.

Here's what I know: it has nothing to do with luck, this moment, and everything to do with love.

But it's obvious Leo doesn't realize that. At least not yet.

"Okay," I tell him. "Lucky it is."

# Forty-Two

When Uncle Jake gets home from work, he drops his briefcase onto the kitchen table, where I'm working on my final essay for U.S. history, a halfhearted defense of Aaron Burr.

"Where is everyone?" he asks just as the puppy comes trotting over, all wrinkles and floppy ears. Uncle Jake peers down at him with an exaggerated look of menace. "Not you. I definitely wasn't looking for you."

"Aunt Sofia has to work late," I tell him, closing my laptop. "And Leo is with Max."

His eyes go comically big. "What?"

I laugh. "Yeah."

"He's here? In Chicago?"

"He came to help with the puppy. Supposedly."

"Well," he says, glancing down at the dog. "I guess you're not totally useless."

"They went out for coffee a little while ago, and they haven't come back yet. Which is either a really great sign or a really bad one."

"Let's assume great for now," Uncle Jake says, walking over to the refrigerator and opening the door. The dog trots after him, rising onto his hind legs to peruse the shelves, his nose quivering. "So it's just the two of us for dinner, then?"

"Three of us."

He grabs a beer, then closes the door and makes a face at the puppy. "Mongrel," he says, and the dog wags its tail cheerfully.

"Actually," I say, "he has a name now."

"You do know it's a lot harder to kick them out once you've named them, right?"

"It's Lucky."

"What's lucky . . . ?" he asks as he searches for the bottle opener; then he stops and looks over. "Oh, I get it. Cute. Sounds like Teddy's handiwork."

"Nope," I say, deciding not to tell him that the dog itself is Teddy's handiwork, since Uncle Jake might never forgive him. "Leo picked it."

"Well, I guess we're stuck with him, then."

"You'll get used to him."

"Yeah?" he says as he sits down across from me. "How do you figure?"

"You got used to me," I say with a shrug, and Uncle Jake's eyes snap up to meet mine. He looks surprised, and I am too. I hadn't planned to say that. I hadn't even known I was thinking it.

"Alice," he says, his face very serious. "You were hardly a stray dog."

I shake my head. "I know. I didn't mean to . . ."

"It's okay. I just don't ever want you to think . . ."

"I wouldn't ever . . ."

He holds up a hand. "Stop. Pause."

"No—" I start to say, but it's too late.

"I think," he's saying as he stands up from the table again, "that we're about to have a Conversation with a capital C, yes?"

I groan. "No."

"And you know what the rule is for those, right?"

"Chocolate," I say reluctantly.

"Right," he says as he walks over to the pantry and pokes his head inside. He rummages around for a minute, then leans back to show me a half-empty bag of chocolate chips. "I'm guessing we're not supposed to eat these."

"You guessed right."

"Well, this is an emergency," he says, dumping them into a bowl as the puppy dances around at his feet. He sets it in the middle of the table, then stares at me until I take a chocolate chip.

Uncle Jake is a firm believer that important discussions go better with a side of sugar.

"So," he says. "What's on your mind?"

I give him a look. "You're the one who wanted to talk."

"You're the one who compared yourself to the dog."

"That's not exactly what I meant."

He takes a handful of chocolate. "So what *did* you mean?"

352

"Nothing," I say, aware of the stubbornness in my voice. But I'm too caught off guard by his persistence to string any of my thoughts together. This is usually Aunt Sofia's territory. She's always on the hunt for hidden meaning in anything I say and has an uncanny ability to take a comment on something as mundane as the weather and somehow relate it back to my past.

But not Uncle Jake. He's good for a talk about financial responsibility or the importance of college, the many joys of fishing or which screwdriver to use in a given situation. But when it comes to conversations about what happened to me—especially those conversations that begin with a capital C—he's always been eager to avoid them.

"Look," he says now, pushing the bowl aside and leaning forward with his elbows on the table. His eyes—which look so much like my dad's—are fixed on me. "I know what happened in San Francisco."

I blink at him. This is not what I was expecting.

When I returned from the trip, my aunt and uncle peppered me with all the obvious questions: *What did you think of Stanford?* and *Was it okay being back?* and *How did it go with Teddy?* (Not to mention: *There wasn't any funny business, right?* And: *Right?* And: *But seriously, right?*)

I told them about the farmers market and the sound of the foghorns over the bay and how the city looked spread before us, all staggered buildings and steep inclines. About the beach and the bookstore and the Stanford campus, which had been even more beautiful than the pictures. But I didn't tell them about the rush of memories that afternoon on the quad or the emptiness I'd felt standing in front of the house, how that piece of stained glass in my old window had just about broken my heart.

"Nothing happened," I say, but Uncle Jake just gives me an even look.

"Teddy called us afterward."

I feel my face get warm for no particular reason. "He did?"

"Don't be mad at him," he says when he sees my expression. "He knew you were upset and that you wouldn't want to talk about it, and he was just trying to be a good friend." He tilts his head to one side. "So what happened?"

I'm about to say *nothing* again, but instead I try to think of what I *can* say, try to come up with some version of the truth that doesn't hurt so much, some route back there that isn't quite so treacherous.

Beside me the puppy is batting at a loose string on the carpet like the world's clumsiest cat, and I lean down to pick him up, pressing his warm body close to me.

"We went to the house," I say eventually, keeping my eyes on the scarred wooden table. "It was . . . hard. Seeing it again. You weren't there at the end. When Aunt Sofia was packing everything up. It was just the two of us and it felt so different, even then. Mom had been gone awhile. But it was like Dad just . . ." I hold up my hands and flick them open, making fireworks of my fingers. "Poof. Just like that. There, and then not."

I lift my eyes to meet Uncle Jake's, which are watery. He

takes a swig of beer, then sets the bottle down a little too hard on the table.

"Anyway, I remember Aunt Sofia put Post-it notes on all our stuff so she'd know where it was going: you know, like pink for the garbage and blue for charity and yellow for Chicago. Something like that. I came down one morning and the whole house was covered with them. They looked like decorations, like confetti. I haven't used one since."

Uncle Jake clears his throat. "Alice . . ."

"The house used to be blue. Remember?"

He nods.

"It's yellow now." The puppy begins to snore in my arms, a low rumble that vibrates through me. I watch his eyelids twitch in sleep, his paws moving in time with some unknown dream. "My dad was allergic to dogs."

"I know."

"For real," I add, which makes us both smile.

"I know," he says again. "And cats too."

"My mom was always bringing home strays, which drove him nuts."

"Well, in fairness, he could sometimes drive her pretty nuts too."

"It's funny," I say, the smile slipping from my face. "I'd kind of forgotten that."

"What?"

"That they used to fight a lot." I shift the puppy in my arms. Out the window it's nearly dark, and I can see our reflections in the glass. "That they weren't perfect."

Uncle Jake gives me a funny look. "I don't suppose it would help to tell you that nobody is."

"I know," I tell him. "People are just people. And a house is just a house, right?"

"Not always," he says, spinning his beer in circles. "That was your home. And honestly I think it was pretty brave of you to go back. It couldn't have been easy. I should've been the one to go with you. We probably should've done it a long time ago."

"It's okay."

"It's not, really. I'm sorry it's so hard for me to talk to you about this stuff."

"You talk to Aunt Sofia about it," I say, trying not to sound so wounded.

He nods. "Yeah, I do."

"So why not me?"

"Because," he says, his voice cracking, "you remind me of him."

"I do?"

"Of course you do," he says. "You're his kid through and through. The way you sneeze when you eat pepper. He used to do that too. And you make this face when you're concentrating that knocks the air right out of me. You look just like him. And his eyes. You have his eyes."

I realize I'm smiling. "So do you."

"The thing is," he says, "it doesn't seem like nine years ago. I know that's not an excuse, but it still seems like yesterday. And if it's that way for me, I know it must be even worse for you."

For some reason I think about Sawyer then, and his obsession with history. Sometimes, it feels like time is malleable, like the past refuses to stay put and you end up dragging it around with you whether you like it or not. Other times it feels about as ancient and far away as those castles. Maybe that's the way it's supposed to be.

There's a space between forgetting and moving on, and it's not easy to find. We're still searching for it, Uncle Jake and I. And that's okay.

"He'd be so mad at me. If there was one thing he loved, your dad, it was talking things out." He smiles, almost to himself, his eyes far away. "Man, that guy could talk."

I laugh, feeling something start to loosen inside me. "He once went out to get groceries and didn't come back for four hours. When he finally showed up, he brought this group of tourists he'd met at the store and they ended up staying for dinner."

"That's nothing," Uncle Jake says, grinning now. "This one time we were camping in the backyard, and our neighbors called the cops because of the noise. But when they showed up, your dad ended up talking their ears off, of course, and the neighbors came over to see what was going on."

"And?"

"And they ended up staying for s'mores."

I shake my head. "Sounds just like him."

"He could be kind of annoying that way," Uncle Jake says. "But it's why everyone loved him. Especially your mom."

We're both quiet for a moment, lost in our own separate

memories. Sitting here in the darkening kitchen, I'm struck by how different this feels. There's something blunt about the pain right now, something almost toothless. Maybe it's the fading light, or maybe it's the puppy in my lap. Maybe it's just temporary, or maybe this is what happens when you talk through something so that it starts to lose its knife-sharp edge, so that the corners get sanded down into something duller, something slightly less acute.

Maybe this is what it means to let time work its magic. Or maybe there's no magic to it at all. Maybe tomorrow it will all go back to normal.

Poof. Just like that.

But not now. Not yet.

"Hey," I say, and Lucky lifts his head. "I know it's really hard for you—"

"Yes," Uncle Jake says before I can finish.

"And it's not always easy for me either—"

"Yes," he says again.

"And honestly I'm not even sure I want to—"

"Yes."

"But I think maybe it could help. To talk about them more with you. So if it's okay—"

"Yes," he says, nodding. His eyes are rimmed with red, and he looks very tired, but he's smiling now. "You're right. I know you're right."

"And maybe it won't seem so hard if we stop thinking of them as Conversations with a capital C," I continue, watching him carefully. "Maybe it'd be easier if we just kept it all kind of lowercase for now. At least to start."

Uncle Jake looks thoughtful. "That could probably work."

"But?"

He points at the bowl in the middle of the table. "Do we still get to keep the chocolate?"

"I think I can live with that," I tell him.

# Forty-Three

I'm eating breakfast the next morning when Leo walks in with two cream-colored envelopes. The one on top has my name written in cursive across the front.

"Are you and Max getting married already?" I joke, dropping my spoon into the cereal bowl. "So nice of you guys to invite me."

Leo isn't really listening; he just walked Max out to his car—so that he can get back to Michigan in time for finals—and he still seems a little dazed. He sends one of the envelopes spinning across the table in my direction, but it skids onto the floor, startling Lucky, who has been dozing at my feet.

"What is it?" I ask, leaning to pick it up, then tearing it open. The paper is thick and expensive, and it has a pearly shine to it.

"No idea. Someone slipped them under the door."

His eyes are bloodshot this morning, either from too much caffeine or lack of sleep or just Max's sudden absence in the wake of his sudden appearance. Last night the two of them returned home hours after they left with matching smiles and a giddy, nervous energy about them. Uncle Jake paused the movie we were watching as they stood in the doorway of the living room, both bouncing on their toes.

"How much coffee did you guys have?" I asked, rubbing my eyes.

"Five cups!" Leo said, and Max gave us a manic grin.

"Seven for me."

Aunt Sofia had raised her eyebrows. "And?"

"And we talked," Leo said, looking at me as if this explained everything. Which it sort of did.

When they headed to the kitchen to get some leftover pizza, I saw Max reach for Leo's hand. They paused, their eyes locked and their hands knotted between them. They were just beyond the doorway, but from where I was sitting I could still see the look they exchanged, full of such obvious love that I actually let out a sigh.

But this morning Max is gone again, and even though he'll be back soon Leo is clearly in no mood for whatever is in these envelopes.

I open mine, then stare at the piece of paper in my hand, surprised to find a bizarrely formal request for us to appear at Teddy's apartment today at four o' clock sharp for a presentation. It's signed *Theodore J. McAvoy* with a funny-looking flourish.

"This can't be from Teddy," Leo says flatly, puzzling over his own invitation. "The guy barely owns a pen. There's no way he went to a stationery store."

"What are the odds this is a prank?"

Leo doesn't answer. He just shakes his head, turning the paper over in his hand. "What kind of presentation could it be anyway? 'How to Fritter Away Your Lottery Money on Needlessly Expensive Card Stock'?"

On the way to school we continue to speculate.

"Maybe it's more of an announcement," Leo says, walking with his fingers hooked into the straps of his backpack. "Maybe he's buying an island. Or investing in space travel. Or maybe he's gonna tell us he's off to explore the world."

A shiver runs through me at the thought of this last one.

When school is over I meet Leo near the bike racks, and together we start the walk to Teddy's. It's the kind of spring afternoon that makes you forget about the winters here, the sky so blue it looks almost fake and the trees crowded with brand-new leaves.

"So you and Max," I say, and he smiles involuntarily. "You're good?"

He nods. "Getting there."

"What happens next?"

"I don't know. He'll be home for the summer, so that's all I'm thinking about for now. After that I guess we'll have to see."

"Yeah, but what does that mean?"

"It means we'll see."

"Right, but—"

"It means," he says, "that I don't really know. Maybe it'll be good or maybe it won't. Maybe it'll all blow up again once we're apart next year. Maybe he'll break up with me, or I'll break up with him. Maybe we'll live happily ever after. Or maybe we won't." He shrugs. "I'm taking your advice and trying to pretend there isn't any sort of scoreboard. Which means it doesn't make sense to worry about it so much. Instead I'm just gonna try to live it and see how that goes."

I nod. "Well, I have a good feeling about it."

"Weirdly enough," he says with a smile, "so do I. And since I'm attempting to be more positive and operating under the assumption that I'm going to be spending more time in the Show Me State next year, I decided I'm gonna pick up some extra design work this summer so I can start saving for a car."

"You're going to be spending more time in Missouri?"

He frowns at me. "Michigan."

"I'm pretty sure the Show Me State is Missouri," I say, trying not to laugh, and he rolls his eyes.

"You don't have to be right about *everything*, you know."

"Just geography," I say agreeably. "And your love life."

As we near Teddy's building I look up toward his bedroom window.

"I wonder how long this will take. I'm supposed to be at the soup kitchen later."

"I think you'll be fine," Leo says. "We're talking about

the guy who set the record for the shortest oral report in South Lake High School history."

"Ah, yes," I say, trying not to laugh. "His four-second presentation on the subject of brevity. That was a classic."

When we reach the door Leo pushes the buzzer, then we both stand back and wait for Teddy's usual *hullo* to crackle out over the speaker. Instead there's a burst of static, then a voice, brisk and only vaguely familiar: "May I ask who's calling?"

Leo and I exchange a mystified look. He leans forward again, his mouth close to the speaker. "Teddy?"

"Yes?"

"It's, uh, Leo. And Alice."

"Welcome," Teddy says, his tone changing into something a bit more cheerful, but still no less formal. "Thank you both for coming. Even though you didn't RSVP."

"Oops," I say as Leo jabs the button again.

"Are you planning to let us up?" he asks, and as an answer, the buzzer drones loudly and the lock on the door clicks.

"Maybe the money's finally made him eccentric," I say as we trudge up the four flights of stairs. When we reach the top, it's to find the door to number eleven propped open with a chair. Inside, Teddy is standing in the living room in a neat black suit and striped green tie. He's wearing glasses, though he has perfect vision, and there's a pencil stuck behind one ear. He looks like someone playing the part of Businessman #2 in an old movie.

He also looks incredibly handsome.

"Sorry, was this supposed to be a formal presentation?" Leo asks, half-joking, but Teddy looks him over with a serious expression, taking in his sneakers and jeans.

"I suppose that'll do," he says, like some sort of robotic butler.

I glance over at the living room, where three blue binders are sitting on the coffee table, as if in preparation for a standardized test. Beside each, there are two neatly arranged pens and two sweating glasses of water on coasters. There's also a blank whiteboard propped on an easel in front of the TV and a fat black marker resting in the tray below.

"What's going on?" I ask, turning back to Teddy, who gestures in the direction of the couch in an overly grand and strangely formal way.

"Ladies and gentlemen," he says, though there are only two of us in the room with him. "Shall we begin?"

# Forty-Four

Teddy is clearly in his element.

Here in this living room that appears to be doubling as a boardroom, beneath this odd costume of his—the crisp suit and proper mannerisms—he's all shiny-eyed intensity and barely concealed enthusiasm.

"As you know," he begins, looking at us from over the rim of his fake glasses, "I've recently come into a lot of money."

"Yes," Leo says with a groan. "We know."

"Can you please take off those glasses?" I say, squinting at Teddy. "They're kind of distracting."

He pulls them off with a sigh, twirling them between two fingers. "And I've been trying to figure out what to do with it."

"Quite the burden," Leo says, looking pointedly around the room, which is littered with Teddy's recent purchases: an enormous LED TV, a brand-new sound system, a portable grill, and an authentic-looking samurai sword.

"I realize," Teddy says, following Leo's gaze, "that I haven't been the world's most responsible person so far. And I know you guys think I haven't been taking this seriously enough."

He pauses, as if hoping one of us might disagree. But when nobody says anything, he continues.

"Look," he says, raking a hand through his hair. "It took me a while to figure this out. There's no way to prepare for this sort of thing. When someone hands you a pile of money, you expect it to be all rainbows and lollipops."

"In fairness," I say, jabbing a thumb at the kitchen, where there are several boxes of bulk candy stacked on the counter, "you did buy an awful lot of lollipops."

Teddy smiles ruefully. "You know what I mean."

"I do," I agree, meeting his eyes.

"What I'm trying to say is that I don't exactly know what I'm doing. But I know I want to be better. I don't just want to be Teddy McAvoy: millionaire. And I don't want to be famous for not doing anything. I don't want to be the guy everyone's friends with because they want something from him." He bows his head and fidgets with his tie. "And I don't want people coming back into my life just because of the money. I didn't expect all that. I didn't sign up for it."

"Teddy," I say softly, but he shakes his head.

367

"I just . . . I want all this to mean something, you know?" His eyes find mine again, and this time it takes a few seconds for him to look away. "I want it to count."

On the wall behind him there are dozens of pictures in mismatched frames, a literal museum of his childhood. Looking from left to right is like watching a slide show, seeing Teddy grow into the version standing before us now: broad-shouldered and square-jawed, more serious than he was just a few months ago, with some of that old swagger gone, replaced by a sincerity that might've seemed out of place before all this, and that makes me love him even more.

"The thing is," he says, "I think I've been looking at this the wrong way. Like it was this crazy prize I won. But it's not. It's a gift, yeah. But it's also a burden. And I'm not saying that to be dramatic. Or because I want any sympathy. Because I don't. It's just that sometimes it can be really hard. It's like—it's like pulling a huge rock around. All the time. And I don't want to do that anymore."

Leo is looking at him with interest. "So what do you want to do?"

"Well," Teddy says, trying and failing to conceal a grin. He's talking to both of us, but he's only looking at me. "That's the thing. I want to smash the rock into millions of pieces. And then give most of those pieces away."

I laugh, partly out of surprise and partly out of relief. It's been weeks since our middle-of-the-night conversation in San Francisco, and he hasn't mentioned it since. So when I opened the envelope this morning, I didn't want to believe this could be it. I didn't want to get my hopes up. But now I shake my head, grinning right back at him.

"That's a lot of pieces," I say, and his smile widens.

Leo pushes his glasses up on his nose, considering it. The clock is ticking too loudly, and the dishwasher switches off with a hum, and Teddy is watching him closely, waiting for him to say something, because Leo is the one who can always tell whether an idea is crazy or brilliant.

"I mean, who needs a rock that big anyway?" he says at last, and Teddy lets out a breath.

"So . . . do you have a plan?" I ask, almost afraid to know the answer, but he sticks the pencil behind his ear again, claps his hands once, then points to the binders.

"Yes," he says with a little smirk, the same one he gets when I question whether he actually did his homework or studied for a test. "I have a plan." His overly professional voice returns. "If you'll please turn to page one."

"*Teddy*," we both say at the same time, and he laughs, immediately breaking character.

"Okay, okay," he says, holding up his hands. "I'll just tell you. Even though I spent basically all of last week at the library putting those things together."

"You went to a library?" Leo asks in mock astonishment. "Is it still standing?"

"I went to the post office too," Teddy says proudly. "And the bank, and the accountant's office . . ."

"Everywhere but school," I point out.

"I had bigger fish to fry. Which brings me to the chicken lady."

Leo frowns. "I'm lost."

"I still don't think you should be calling her that," I say to Teddy, who waves this away with an air of impatience.

"How about some quiet from the peanut gallery?"

"Peanuts, chicken, fish," says Leo. "Now I'm hungry."

"There's like fifty pounds of bulk candy in the kitchen," I remind him.

Teddy sighs. "Do you guys want to hear my idea or what?"

"Yes," I say, laughing. "Tell us."

And so Teddy explains to Leo what happened in San Francisco, about the impulsive tip he left for the woman at the farmers market, the way it felt to walk away knowing that money would make a difference in someone's life, all those things he told me so breathlessly later that same night.

He's pacing as he talks, scuffing his shiny shoes on the floor, tapping his pencil against the palm of his hand. But this isn't the same Teddy who burst into my room a few weeks ago. It's clear that this isn't one of his usual schemes. It's no wild idea or half-baked plan. This is no longer just a whim.

As I listen to him rattle off a speech that sounds surprisingly like a business pitch, I realize he's not just making it up as he goes along. It's obvious he's given this a lot of thought, that he's put a surprising amount of time and energy into it.

For once, he's not relying on charm. He's actually done the work.

"I want to start small," Teddy is saying, "with just the three of us. But eventually the idea would be to really grow this thing. To have a small army of people doing good deeds across the city, maybe even across the country."

"What," Leo asks, "like a tipping task force?"

Teddy shakes his head. "Not just tipping. I'm thinking so much bigger than that."

"Random acts of kindness," I murmur, and he swings to face me, his eyes bright with recognition.

"Exactly. The way I see it, we'd keep an eye out for anyone who could use a little help. Nothing huge. Just if they're having trouble paying for groceries, or could use a cup of coffee to warm up, or can't afford a birthday gift for their kid. The idea would be to lend people a hand in small ways that could make a big difference. We'd make it a nonprofit so others could eventually donate too, but my accountant tells me the seed money could generate enough interest to keep this going for a long time, especially if we're doling it out in small amounts. And I was thinking we could base it online so that people could write in with requests and suggestions, and . . ." He trails off, looking anxiously between us. "Well, I can tell you all the details later. But what do you think?"

Leo rubs his chin, his eyes on the table, deep in thought. After a moment he reaches for his water glass and raises it in the air.

"I think it's incredible," he says so earnestly that Teddy

laughs, a mixture of relief and delight. Then they both turn to me, their faces expectant. So I give them the only thing I can, the only thing I know to be true, the words that have been toppling around in my head since this conversation began all those weeks ago in a darkened hotel room on the other side of the country:

"This," I say softly, "is going to change everything."

I don't mean it the way I usually do.

I don't mean that change is hard or scary, though it's definitely both.

I mean only to say this: that sometimes, through good luck or bad, through curses or fate, the world cracks itself open, and afterward nothing will ever be the same.

All I mean is that this seems like one of those times.

# Forty-Five

There's still time before my shift starts at the soup kitchen, so Teddy suggests going to the Lantern for pie.

"To celebrate," he says, looking at us hopefully. "And to make some plans."

I agree to come along, but Leo's final paper—a critical look at the evolution of design in three of his favorite Pixar movies—is due tomorrow, so he needs to get home. As we walk him to the bus stop, he can't stop talking about Teddy's idea. "What if we also looked for people already doing something nice for others? Then we could reward them for that so they can do more. You know, pay it forward and all that."

Teddy bobs his head. "I love it."

"And I'll design the website, obviously," Leo continues. "We could even have a good deed of the week or something."

He reaches into his back pocket and pulls out his notebook, flipping open to an empty page. "And cards. We should make calling cards to hand out with the money so that people who get inspired can report back on the site. And a logo! I could totally do a logo too. We just need a name."

"I haven't thought of one yet," Teddy says. "You're the creative brains behind this operation, so I'm sort of hoping you'll come up with something brilliant."

By the time we reach the stop they've hatched a thousand more plans, and when we part ways Leo is sitting on the metal bench, already scribbling furiously.

At the Lantern, Teddy holds the door open for me, then pulls out my chair at the table, and I can't tell if he's still in fake businessman mode or he's just being unusually polite. We order two slices of blueberry pie from our usual waitress, then he sets down his menu and gives me a long look.

"I'm really sorry," he says, twirling his water glass.

"For what?"

"For not telling you sooner. I was dying to, but I wanted it to be a surprise. And I needed to get everything sorted out first: filing the paperwork, sketching out the business plan, meeting with the accountant, working out the—"

"Teddy," I say. "It's okay. I'm really proud of you."

The worry on his face disappears. "You are?"

"Of course. I think it's incredible. And I can't believe how far you've taken it already."

He smiles at this, then lifts a hand, almost as if he's about to reach for one of mine. But the waitress brings over our pie and he grabs his fork instead.

"Well, you were right," he says, tucking into his slice. "I guess I just needed to be challenged. Who knew?"

"I did," I say with a grin.

He winks at me. Teddy McAvoy is the only person I know who can pull off a wink. "So you're on board, right?"

"With what?"

"I want you to be involved," he says, taking a huge bite of his pie. "Especially now that you're gonna be here next year. I mean, I know you'll be busy with school, but you always manage to find time for this stuff, and now we'll get to do it together."

He finishes chewing and gives me a blue tinted smile. I open my mouth to respond but realize I'm not sure what to say, and as the silence lengthens, his face falls.

"I know I pushed you too much about taking the money," he says. "And I'm sorry. But this is different. It's the kind of thing you'd have done if it was you, right?"

When I nod, his eyes brighten again.

"So what do you think? It could be anything you want. Program director? Chief operating officer? Global head of good deeds?"

I open my mouth to say *yes*. To say *of course*.

But nothing comes out.

Instead I just stare at him, though he doesn't seem to notice. He waves his fork around as he chews. "It's kind of perfect, you know? I'll do all the big-picture stuff, and Leo will handle anything creative. And you'll be in charge of outreach, since I can't think of anyone better suited to figuring out how to give away a whole bunch of money."

I take a bite of my pie, but it sticks in my throat. When I've finally managed to get it down, I drink half my glass of water, then lift my eyes to look at Teddy. "It sounds amazing."

"Great," he says, beaming at me.

"But I don't think I can do it."

He blinks a few times. "What?"

"I can't do it," I say, nearly as surprised as he is.

"Why not?"

As soon as it's out there, the knot in my stomach unwinds. For some reason the image of the poster from the library flashes through my head, the one hanging in the children's section: IT'S OKAY NOT TO KNOW. IT'S NOT OKAY NOT TO CARE.

Teddy is still staring at me, waiting for an explanation.

"I never learned to play the guitar," I say, and the furrow in his brow deepens.

"What?"

"I always wanted to play. But I never had time to take lessons."

He sets his fork down, his expression still stark.

"You know how I've been saying that college isn't just about figuring out what you want to do—how it's also about figuring out who you are?"

He blows out an exasperated breath. "Not this again."

"I'm not talking about *you*," I say patiently. "I'm talking about me. Do you have any idea how much time I've spent volunteering over the years?"

He picks at his pie. "A lot."

"A lot," I agree. "And I'm not sorry about it, because I was able to make a difference to a lot of people, and I know I did a lot of good. And I loved it. I still do. But I'm not sure my reasons were always . . . my own."

Teddy's face softens. "I know."

"Actually, you're the one who sort of helped me realize that. And you were right. I've always put my parents on a pedestal, and I've worked really hard to make them proud. But they're not here anymore." My voice cracks on this, and I stare at the pie on my plate. "They haven't been for a long time."

He clears his throat but doesn't say anything.

"I don't want to let them down. But I also can't spend my whole life chasing after them. And I think the main thing they'd want is just for me to be happy," I say firmly, as much for myself as for Teddy. But I know it's true. It's all anyone wants for me, and I feel a surge of good fortune at the thought, and even more than that, a sense of peace.

Because it's what I want too.

I lift my eyes to meet Teddy's. "I think your idea is *wonderful*," I say, packing as much as I can into that last word. "And I'd love to help out with it here and there."

"But you don't want to run it with us."

"No." I shake my head. "I don't think I do."

Teddy sits back hard in his chair, as if absorbing a great impact. He looks more than just disappointed. He looks crushed, and a cold, heavy dread settles in my chest. All along I thought it was the money that would send us careening down different paths. But maybe it's this.

You pick one thing, and your life goes one way.

You pick something else, and it's completely different.

This thing he's about to do: I believe in it. But I've spent a lot of years trying to do the right thing for the wrong reasons. Now I want to try doing the right thing for me.

Still, it feels like I'm turning down more than just an opportunity to help launch a nonprofit. It's almost as if I'm losing something else too.

Even if that something is just a possibility.

Even if that possibility isn't even a very likely one.

He's still watching me from across the table, and after a moment he nods: once, then again. When he smiles, it doesn't quite make it up to his eyes, but I can tell he's trying. "Well," he says, picking up his fork again. "Maybe one day."

"Maybe one day."

He lifts an eyebrow. "After you've learned to play the guitar."

"And a few other things," I say, thinking again of what Aunt Sofia told Leo that night so long ago, when he asked what my other word might be.

*That,* she said, *is up to Alice.*

378

For the first time in a long time I feel electric with the possibilities. And this time, when the question arrives, I'm ready for it.

"Like what?" Teddy asks, and I grin at him.

"I guess we'll have to see."

# Forty-Six

On the way out, Teddy leaves a neat stack of hundred-dollar bills on the table for our waitress.

"I did promise," he says, his spirits clearly lifted by the prospect of seeing her face when she finds it. We linger in the vestibule, peering through the small window above the door, and watch her mouth fall open as she discovers the enormous tip.

He grins as we walk outside again. "You sure you don't want to be a part of that?"

"I do," I say, trying not to sound defensive. "Just not officially."

"Sorry," he says, relenting. "I know. You can do however much you want. Really. I'll have a pipeline of money ready just for you, so you can hand it out whenever you feel like it. I promise."

"Thanks," I say. "I've always wanted a pipeline of money."

He laughs. "I get that a lot these days."

We're still standing beneath the glow of lights from the diner, neither of us moving. Teddy's apartment is in one direction and the soup kitchen is in the other.

"I should get going," I say, glancing at my watch. "Will you be at school tomorrow, or are you still boycotting?"

"Nah, I'll be there," he says. "I figure I better finish up just in case I change my mind about this whole college thing at some point."

I can tell he's humoring me, but it makes me feel better anyway. "Maybe one day," I say, taking a few steps in the opposite direction. But he doesn't move.

I turn around and wave goodbye. Still nothing.

"I'll walk with you," he says, jogging to catch up with me. It's nearly dark out now, with only a low scribble of orange left in the sky. If I don't leave soon I'm going to be late for my shift, but I stand there for a second anyway.

"You don't have to. Really."

"It's a nice night," he says, already moving past me so that I have no choice but to follow him. The streets are still busy at this hour, filled with couples holding hands and children running ahead of their parents and groups of friends going out for the evening.

"I walk here by myself all the time, you know."

Teddy looks amused. "I know. I'm just being a gentleman."

"Yeah, but I'm fine on my own, so you don't have to be so . . ."

"What?"

"Overbearing."

He laughs. "I am not."

"You are. You were doing this in San Francisco too. You started acting like a mother hen the moment . . ."

"What?"

I frown at him. "The moment you saw me cry." As we pass beneath a streetlamp, his face flickers in the shadows. "And I get it. I fell apart. But that doesn't mean you need to treat me like I'm this fragile—"

He holds up his hands. "Whoa," he says. "That's what you think?"

"Well, what am I supposed to think? You spent the rest of the trip following me around like . . ."

"A mother hen?" he suggests with a smile.

I ignore this. "It obviously freaked you out enough to make you go AWOL the moment we got back—"

"I told you I was at the library," he says distractedly, glancing over at the stores lining the street, then he raises a finger. "Hold on a second, okay? I'll be right back."

"What?" I say, surprised, but he's already gone, jogging over to the bank on the corner, where he disappears inside the ATM vestibule. Alone on the sidewalk I lift my hands like *Can you believe this guy?* But of course nobody's paying attention, so I just wait there until he returns, tucking his wallet into the back pocket of his jeans.

"Sorry," he says, then without any sort of explanation he just picks up where we left off. "I didn't go AWOL. All that stuff this afternoon? Those binders you guys refused to even open? That took a lot of work. *That's* what I was doing. It had nothing to do with you."

There's a slight hitch in his step as he says this, as if he's about to stop walking, but then he ducks his head and keeps going, his jaw set.

This is the part where I'm supposed to let it go. To tell him it's fine. To give him the benefit of the doubt. But for some reason I can't. Not yet.

"I don't believe you," I say quietly. "I think you got scared. You say that you want me to be honest with you, that you don't just want to be the guy who cheers me up, but then you see me crumble like that, you get one glimpse of the real me, and—"

"Don't say that," he says in a low voice. "It's insulting."

I glance over at him, startled. "What is?"

"You can't act like I don't know the real you. We've been friends for nine years. And yeah, I know you've been through a lot, and I know you don't talk about it very often, but that doesn't mean I don't know you. I know you better than you think."

"Then you should know not to treat me like I'm breakable." The words have a bite to them that I didn't intend, but I'm frustrated and annoyed and a little bit angry, the way I only ever seem to get around Teddy.

He shakes his head. "I don't—"

"You do," I say. "And you of all people should know how much I hate that."

He frowns. "Why me of all people?"

*Because,* I want to say. *We've both been through things that should've broken us.*

*Because we both survived them.*

"Never mind," I say, walking faster. "It's just—"

Once more, he holds up a finger, and I stop midsentence.

"Just a minute," he says, dashing off in the direction of a drugstore. I let out an indignant sigh, realizing I'm definitely going to be late now, then spend the next seven minutes kicking absently at a mailbox and stewing over our interrupted conversation.

When Teddy returns he has a white plastic bag dangling from one hand, and he swings it in circles as we start walking again, turning left at an intersection and heading up a road lined with trees and houses and the occasional streetlight.

"That's not it," he says, as if he didn't just disappear without any sort of explanation, and it takes me a moment to remember exactly *what's* not it. We're nearly at the soup kitchen now, and my anger is starting to subside, replaced by something more desperate. The truth is, I hate fighting with Teddy. All I want is for things between us to be normal again. The way they were before the lottery. Before the kiss. Before all of it.

"I didn't get scared," he says. "I just had work to do."

"At the library," I say, rolling my eyes. "Yeah, you mentioned that."

He stops again. "Well, it's true."

384

I can see the church just up the street, its spire a navy shadow against the purple sky. There's a line of people along the side of the building waiting for the soup kitchen to open for the night. I'm too far away to make out any of the regulars, but I can see someone cup their hand and light a cigarette, the red dot rising and falling in the surrounding dark.

"I'm late," I say to Teddy, but when I look up at him I realize I've finally managed to barrel right through all his good-natured patience. At long last he looks annoyed with me too.

"If it felt like I've been avoiding you since we got back," he says through gritted teeth, "that's probably because I was."

I fold my arms across my chest. "O-kay."

"But it's not what you think. I was just trying not to put any pressure on you, okay?"

"About what?"

He groans, impatient. "About Stanford. Or . . . not Stanford."

"What?" I ask, confused.

"I mean, we saw what happened with Max and Leo, and I know it came from a good place—I know Max just wanted them to be together—but sometimes it shouldn't matter what you want, you know?" He says this so aggressively that it's hard to tell whether he's angry with me or Max. "It's what the other person wants. And yeah, I can admit now that I'm glad you won't be all the way out in California next year. Because being that far away from you for the next four years would be . . . I don't even know. Kind of unbearable, I guess. But I was just trying to make sure you had the space to figure that out on your own, so I'm sorry if that—"

"Teddy," I say, and he stops, blinking at me.

"Yeah?"

"Thank you. I think that's the nicest thing anyone's ever yelled at me."

In spite of himself, he laughs.

"Being that far away from you would've been kind of unbearable too."

"It wasn't just that, though," he says, his voice softer now. "And it wasn't just about the library or the nonprofit. I had work to do for myself too."

"You keep saying that, but I have no idea what—"

"It means," he says, a little impatiently, "that I don't think you're breakable. But your heart *is*."

"What?" I ask, not expecting this. I stare at him. "What are you talking about?"

"Look," he says. "I'm . . . well, I'm me. I screw things up. That's what I do. And I'm reckless with people. I don't mean to be, but I am."

I nod, though I still have no idea where he's going with this.

"But with you, it's different. I mean, even putting aside the whole friendship thing—which is a big thing to put aside—you've gotten pretty banged up, you know?"

"No," I say promptly. "I have no clue what you're—"

"You've been through a lot," he says, then before I can

protest again he hurries on. "You have. It's pretty hard to deny. And I didn't want to be just another thing that hurt you. I didn't ever want to be someone who does that to you."

*Does what?* I want to ask, though I'm too afraid—not because I know what the answer will be but because I know what I want it to be.

A car turns up the street, the headlights sweeping across Teddy's face. "So that's why I didn't mention it, what happened that morning after the lottery," he says, and I think he means the kiss, but everything is so jumbled right now it's hard to tell for sure. "But then we had that fight and I felt even worse, because the whole point was not to hurt you, and somehow I ended up hurting you even more."

"Teddy—"

"And then, yeah, I saw you cry in San Francisco. But it was a good thing, actually, because I got to see how strong you are. You let me in. That's not the same thing as crumbling. Not at all."

I stare at him, unable to think of a response.

"And it didn't scare me," he says with a smile. "It was just the opposite. I've always known how much you had to deal with, how awful it must have been. But being there with you . . ." He sucks in a breath, then shakes his head. "I can't even imagine how hard that had to be. How hard it must *still* be."

There's a certain tension that comes over me whenever anyone talks about my parents, an automatic stiffening in my neck and back, and it happens now as I stare at the cracked sidewalk. There on the pavement, my shadow overlaps with Teddy's, and for a second it almost looks like we're holding hands.

"So," he says with a note of finality, as if he's now explained everything. "I realized I had some work to do."

"Why do you keep saying that?" I ask without looking at him. "What's that even supposed to mean?"

"Al," he says, and when he reaches out and puts a hand on my shoulder, all the tension goes draining right out of me.

"What?" I ask, and my voice wobbles.

"I know I'm probably not saying this very well. . . ."

Without meaning to, I begin to laugh, because this is such a dramatic understatement of what's happening right now. But then I immediately feel terrible, because Teddy looks so serious, and for an awkward moment we both simply stare at each other. There's an undercurrent of something new between us, and though I'm not sure what it is, I can feel it all the same. It's making my heart thunder in my chest, making my hands shake, making every inch of me feel like putty.

"I have to go," I say quietly, but I don't move. His eyes have me pinned in place. To leave right now would be like walking out of a movie before the end. Like skipping the punch line of a particularly good joke. Like stepping away from a jigsaw puzzle when there are only a few pieces left to snap into place.

Instead I force myself to look up at him.

"I had a lot of work to do because of you," he repeats,

more insistently this time, like it's a message that's not coming through, a signal I'm not quite picking up. "You're the best person I know. And I knew I needed to . . . I wanted to be better too. Or at least *do* something better. Do you understand what I'm trying to say?"

I laugh and wipe away a tear that I didn't realize was there until it was halfway down my cheek. "Not even a little bit."

And then he kisses me.

Just like that.

He steps forward, and he leans down, and he kisses me.

It's not like the kiss after the lottery; it's not hasty or impulsive. This is a kiss that's been in the works for months now, maybe even years. It's something more durable, more lasting. It's those last few puzzle pieces clicking into place.

His hands are in my hair, on my neck and my back, and his lips are moving against mine with a kind of urgency, and all at once I understand what he's been trying to say, and I stand on my tiptoes, and put my arms around him, and kiss him back.

"Teddy," I say a little breathlessly when we finally break apart. We're still clinging to each other, his hand twisted in my jacket, my palms pressed against his shoulder blades.

He tips his head down to look at me. "Yeah?"

"You know you didn't have to invest millions of dollars and come up with a whole business plan just to kiss me, right?"

He grins. "I didn't?"

"I'm not *that* hard to win over."

"Yes, you are," he says, then he kisses me again. It's the kind of kiss you could vanish inside, the kind you could lose hours to, days even, and it feels like we do; it feels like we've been there forever, twined together like that, the rest of the world falling away, when the bag from the drugstore slips out of Teddy's grasp.

We both jump aside as the contents clatter to the sidewalk, and I stoop to gather them up again, my head spinning. Everything still feels off-kilter, which means it takes me a second to understand what I'm looking at.

"Why'd you buy so much deodorant?" I ask, grabbing one of them just before it can roll onto the grass. "You don't smell *that* bad."

"Thanks for that," Teddy says, laughing as he reaches for a package of dental floss. "But they're not actually for me."

I straighten up again, staring at him. "Wait."

"Yeah," he says with a smile. On the sidewalk there are toothbrushes and tiny bottles of mouthwash, a few boxes of Band-Aids, and even a couple pairs of socks. "I'll bring more next time, but I was just excited to get started."

"How did you know . . ."

He shrugs. "You're always talking about what sorts of things they need here."

"You were listening?" I ask with such astonishment that he laughs. But I can't believe it. I stare at the toiletries littered across the sidewalk. All this time, I've been underestimating him. All this time, I just assumed he wasn't paying attention.

"I brought some cash too," he says, patting his back

pocket, where he stuck his wallet after stopping at the ATM. "I know it's not enough, but I figure we have to start somewhere, right?"

I nod, still stunned. "Right."

"So?" he says, bending to pick up the bag, then glancing in the direction of the church. "You ready?"

I surprise myself by reaching out and taking his other hand. But I can't help it; he looks so hopeful right now, so earnest. I smile at him, and he smiles at me, and we stand there like that for a long moment. Then I nod, and together we make our way across the lawn, dazed and happy and eager to share our good fortune.

# Part Six

JUNE

# Forty-Seven

It's strange to see the apartment coming undone after so many years.

There are cardboard boxes everywhere, full of stacks of yellowing books, and dishes wrapped in newspaper, and piles of poorly folded clothes. On the walls, bright blue squares have replaced the many photos of Teddy, and below those the dust bunnies have come out of hiding, drifting across the wooden floors like miniature tumble-weeds.

I'm supposed to be packing a shelf full of framed photos, but I keep pausing to look around, astonished to see this place—which has always been so familiar, a second home of sorts—looking so completely different.

"Change is good," Teddy says, winking as he walks by with a box in his arms. He makes it a few steps past me, then backpedals until we're face-to-face and leans in to give me a quick kiss.

From across the room, Leo rolls his eyes.

But we're getting used to this now and it's easy to ignore him.

"Thanks," I say to Teddy, who gives me a lingering look, the kind that makes my heart beat too fast, then readjusts the box in his arms and heads off to stack it near the door.

*Change is good,* I think, testing the words, letting them roll around in my head like a pinball. Then I think it again, more forcefully this time: *Change is good.*

But I'm not quite there yet. Maybe I never will be. It's hard to imagine going through life convinced that all change is for the better. Too much has happened to me for that kind of optimism, that type of blind faith. But I'm trying.

*Change* can be *good,* I think, which feels closer to the truth.

The door swings open and Katherine walks in, shuffling through a pile of envelopes. "Mrs. Donohue's been hoarding our mail again," she says as she sets it on the counter. When Teddy reaches for one of the letters, there's a faint rattle. He tears it open and three green Skittles fall into his hand.

I laugh, surprised at the sight. But Teddy only stares at them.

"What are those?" Katherine asks, her face a picture of confusion.

"Skittles," he says. "Green ones."

She frowns. "I don't get it."

"Greens are good," he says, looking up at us with a smile. "But what does that—"

"They're from Dad," he says, and just like that she seems to understand. Nobody says anything; we're all looking at the candy in Teddy's palm as if it might hold some kind of answer. And for him I can tell it does. It's not much, but it's something: a sign that his dad is trying, that perhaps he'll even be okay. That they both will.

I think of the receipt I saw on Teddy's desk the other day for a donation to Gamblers Anonymous, and how hard it must be when the one person you most want to help in the world has no choice but to help himself. All you can do is wait. And hope.

But for now, green is good. And that's a start.

Teddy tips the pieces back into the envelope. Then he walks over to a box marked *Memories* and tucks it inside.

Katherine glances down at her phone when it starts to buzz. "Shoot," she says. "I'm supposed to be meeting with the contractor now. We're picking out cabinets today."

"Thrilling," Teddy says, and she laughs.

"Believe it or not, it is. To me, anyway. All of it is."

This makes him smile. Just last week Leo and I went with them to see the progress on the new place, the two of us hanging back as they stepped around piles of wooden planks to stand in the very spot where they used to live. I know they must've been thinking about the way their lives have unfolded since then, the way things changed for the worse, and then—just as suddenly—for the better.

"Thank you," Katherine said, drawing Teddy into a hug. Then she looked over his shoulder at me with tears in her eyes. "Thank you both."

Now she grabs the keys to their new home from the counter. "Don't forget I'm heading to the hospital afterward," she tells Teddy, waving as she closes the door. "But I'll be home in time for dinner."

When she's gone Leo turns to Teddy. "I thought she was cutting back her hours."

"She did. And no more nights." He shrugs. "I keep telling her she can quit altogether, but she doesn't want to."

"She loves what she does," I remind them. "She's lucky."

But Teddy is no longer listening. His attention has shifted to the TV, which has been on in the background with the volume turned low. It's tuned to a morning show, where the host, a man with jet-black hair and a deep tan, is doing an interview with a woman who sits nervously on the couch opposite him, her leg jangling.

"Turn it up!" Teddy says, so loudly and so suddenly that Leo drops the wooden spoon he was about to toss into a box. "Where's the remote?"

"I don't know." I scan all the usual hiding spots, which are in various states of disarray. "Why?"

"Because," Teddy says, dropping to his knees in front of the couch and fishing around underneath it. He emerges with the remote and aims it at the TV, punching at the volume button so many times that the people on screen are now practically shouting at us.

"Teddy," Leo and I both say at the same time, covering our ears.

"Sorry," he mumbles, lowering it again. "But *look.*"

I squint at the screen, trying to figure out what exactly I'm supposed to be looking at, but it's not until I hear the woman say *farmers market* that I realize who she is.

"Whoa," I say, moving closer to the TV. "That's the chicken lady."

"Do you really think you should be calling her that?" Teddy teases me, but I just wave a hand to shush him, moving closer to the screen.

"I thought it was a mistake at first, so I didn't do anything for a while," she's saying. She looks different with all the makeup, older somehow, more grown-up. But it's definitely her, and she's definitely talking about Teddy. "I thought someone left it by accident or that I'd get in trouble if I spent it, because they might want it back. I couldn't imagine anyone would do something like that for a complete stranger, you know?"

"You think she means you?" Leo asks, walking over to join us, so that we're all three standing in a row in front of the TV, arms folded, eyes trained on the interview.

"How many other people do you think left her a thousand-dollar tip recently?" Teddy asks, though he's smiling and his ears have turned pink.

"But then your mother took a turn for the worse . . . ," the host prompts her, and the chicken lady gives a slightly startled nod.

"Yes," she says, blinking. "She wasn't doing well, and I was having trouble paying for her hospice care, so I decided to use it." She ducks her head for a second, then looks up at the camera through glassy eyes. "She died a week later."

"I'm so sorry," the anchorman says, reaching out to pat her hand in a brisk show of sympathy. "But then something very special happened, didn't it?"

"Well, I decided to start volunteering at a hospice myself," she says, sitting up a little straighter, and the anchor purses his lips.

"Yes," he says. "Yes, of course. Which is so admirable. *So* admirable. But can you tell us what happened the morning after your mother passed?"

The chicken lady nods. "Right. Sure. Well, it had been a really hard night, and I needed to get out, so I drove to get some coffee the next morning. And even though I was sad, I kept thinking about how grateful I was that she got the care she needed that last week of her life, and how it wouldn't have happened without the kindness of that stranger, and I wished I could pay it forward somehow."

The anchor nods and gives her an encouraging look.

"But I don't have that kind of money, obviously, and the only thing I could think to do in that moment was to buy a coffee for the person behind me in the drive-through. So I did. It wasn't anything big. Nothing like that tip. But it was something, you know?"

"As it turned out, it *was* something," the man says with a thousand-watt smile. "Something pretty big. Because after you did that, the person behind you was so grateful that

400

they decided to do the same. And the person after that. And so on."

The chicken lady nods. "I found out later that over six hundred people kept the chain going all day long."

"Six hundred people!" the anchor says. "That's certainly a lot of coffee."

As they continue to marvel over the miracle at the drive-through, Teddy turns to us, his face lit with excitement. "See? It's already working."

"Yeah, coffee for everyone," Leo jokes, but Teddy shakes his head.

"No, did you hear what she said before that? She started volunteering. At a hospice! All because of that tip."

On the screen they're still talking about coffee. But the idea that this is only the beginning—that we're going to get to do more of this, that the ripple effect of such a simple act of kindness could be so boundless and lasting, longer even than the chain of cars in that drive-through—is enough to keep us standing there for a very long time.

# Forty-Eight

It's nearly noon when Leo stops what he's doing—which is sitting on the kitchen counter, systematically working his way through his third sheet of Bubble Wrap—and looks around. "Are you guys gonna be okay if I take off?"

"Why," I ask, "are those bubbles getting to be too much for you?"

He makes a face at me as he pops another one. "I'm supposed to meet Max for lunch," he says, surveying the sea of scattered boxes and overstuffed plastic bags. "But I feel a little guilty leaving. Though I guess you *are* a multimillionaire, so if you really needed the help you could've hired someone to do this."

"It's more fun making you guys do it," Teddy tells him. "Plus, it leaves more money for the people who actually need it."

"I think you've been brainwashed by Alice," Leo says, then holds up his hands in defense when he catches me shooting him a look. "Which isn't the worst thing. But while you're putting all this money aside for the nonprofit, don't forget to save a little for something fun too. It's not every day you win the lottery."

"He's right," I say, and Teddy looks over at me in surprise. "I mean, I'm really impressed with everything you're doing, and I'm really proud of you, but—"

"I think what she's trying to say," Leo interrupts, "is that it's good to be a little more like Alice. But don't stop being Teddy either, okay?"

"Well, I'm glad to hear you guys say that," Teddy says, dropping onto the couch, "because there's one thing I wanted to—"

"I knew it," Leo says immediately. "You bought an island."

"Not exactly," Teddy says with a smile. "But my twelve-year-old self would be pretty disappointed if I didn't at least try to make some of our childhood dreams come true. Which is why you're now the proud owner of a puppy. And why my mom has her new house. Which, incidentally, will have a pool table and pinball machine in the basement."

"Naturally," I say as I sit beside him on the couch, taking his hand in mine. It still feels so strange to be able to do this and to see his face soften when I do, his eyes resting on me with a focus that still makes me a little dizzy and probably always will.

"I got you a thousand colored pencils too," he says, turning back to Leo, who laughs.

"A thousand? Literally?"

"Literally," Teddy says. "I'd never short-change you on something as important as art supplies. You can even count them. I figured I'd wait and have them sent over to your dorm whenever you get assigned, since that's probably where you'll be doing most of your drawing from now on. Oh, and I took care of that too."

"Of what?"

"Paying for your dorm," Teddy says with a grin. "And your tuition."

Leo opens his mouth, then closes it, completely at a loss. "You did?"

"I did."

"Wow," he says, shaking his head. "I mean . . . wow. Thank you. Really. That's . . . so much better than an island."

Teddy laughs. "I'm glad you think so. I actually put some money aside for me too. Just in case."

"Really?" I ask, sitting up. "For college?"

"It wouldn't be till next year," he says quickly, "and that's only assuming I even get in somewhere—"

"I have a feeling you'll be fine," Leo says with a smirk. "You've got some pretty solid material for your personal essay."

"I'm gonna be really busy with the nonprofit," Teddy continues, clearly nervous that my hopes are already too high, "so it might not work out anyway. But I've been thinking about the whole coaching thing, and I guess there's still a part of me that wonders if maybe—"

"Teddy," I say, and he stops. "I think you'd make a great coach one day, if it turns out that's what you want."

He smiles, his whole face lit up. "Thanks," he says, then clears his throat. "Anyway, that's me and Leo. But you . . . you were the toughest to figure out."

I raise my eyebrows. "What do you mean?"

"Well, it's always been hard to get any wishes out of you," he says, and I smile, because all I've ever really wished for was this: family and friends, safety and love, the sun streaming through the window on a Saturday morning. Just this.

But Teddy twists to reach behind the couch, producing a package wrapped in newspaper.

"What's this?"

"Your wish," he says with a smile, and I hold my breath as I peel pack the pages of the sports section. When I see what it is, I burst out laughing.

"An ostrich?" I ask, holding up the stuffed animal.

"What can I say? Just trying to make all your dreams come true."

Leo is staring at us with obvious confusion. "I don't get it."

"Big ostrich enthusiast," Teddy says by way of explanation, which only makes Leo's frown deepen.

I turn the stuffed animal over in my hands, examining the glassy eyes and downy feathers. "Thank you," I say, thinking about that morning in the snow, the two of us talking as Teddy dug through the dumpster for the ticket that would go on to change everything so completely. "I love it."

"Oh, and one more thing," he says, pulling a folded sheet of paper out of his pocket and handing it over to me.

When I open it and see the word *Kenya* printed across the top, my throat goes tight. I scan the page, thinking about the photograph of my parents there, the setting sun and the lone giraffe and the way they were looking at each other, as if they were all alone in the quietest place on earth.

"Kenya," I say softly, waiting for the pang of it, the sharpness, that too-hot feeling that sweeps over me whenever I think of them, of the things they once did and the things they would still be doing if luck hadn't intervened.

But it doesn't come.

All I see is Teddy right now: his hopeful smile, the crease between his eyebrows that spells out his worry, the weight of his hand on mine.

"How did you know?"

"That picture in your room," he says. "I've seen the way you look at it. But I wasn't sure if it would be something you—"

"Yes," I say, and then I say it again: "Yes."

He grins at me. "Yeah? Good. Because we're gonna do a week of safari—hopefully we'll see some real ostriches at some point—and then a week of volunteering at a children's home over there." He pauses. "I took a wild guess that you'd probably be okay with that."

Almost without meaning to I let myself fall into him, and

he circles his arms around me so that I can hear the steady pulse of his heart. "I can't think of anything better," I say, smiling into his shirt, and he laughs.

"Even an island?"

"Even an island," I say, sitting up again.

Across the room, Leo slides off the counter. "Kenya?" he says with a kind of forced casualness. "Wow. That sounds like fun. A *lot* of fun. When do you leave?"

"Two weeks," Teddy says. "We're gonna stay in this awesome safari camp with these tents that look out over the savanna, and you get to see lions and giraffes and zebras and elephants and—"

"Fun," Leo says again. He stands and walks over to the door, kicking aside some newspaper to find his shoes, then tugging them on. "That's really, really fun. I'm sure you guys will have an amazing time."

"You know you're coming with us, right?" Teddy says, and Leo spins around again, his expression wary.

"I am?"

"Of course. How could we go to Africa without you and Max?"

Leo's eyes widen. "Max too?"

"Max too. If that's what you want."

"Seriously?"

"Seriously."

"This," Leo says, jogging over and tackle-hugging Teddy, "is going to be epic."

"It is," he agrees, laughing. "Now get out of here. Go tell Max."

Leo hops up again, practically bouncing on his toes as he heads over to the door, and I can't help smiling as I watch him, because I feel the same way: giddy and excited and wildly, impossibly happy.

"Hey," Teddy calls out, "how are you getting to lunch?"

Leo shrugs. "I don't know. Probably the bus."

"Here," he says, grabbing a set of keys from the coffee table and tossing them over to Leo, who stares at them.

"The convertible?"

Teddy nods. "It's all yours."

"What?" Leo asks, freezing.

"Take it."

"No way." He looks slightly panicked. "You love that thing."

"Yeah, well, it's not really my style anymore," Teddy says, half-turning to give me a sheepish grin. "Besides, if all goes well, you'll be needing a car next year, right?"

It takes Leo a moment to answer; he's too busy gaping at the keys in his hand.

"I know this is sort of a weird thing to say, considering everything," he says eventually. "But I kind of feel like I just won the lottery."

"Funny," Teddy says, his eyes finding mine again. "So do I."

# Forty-Nine

When I'm finished packing up the kitchen, the only thing left is the hippo-shaped cookie jar, and I stand there with a hand on its glassy head, lost in the memory of that blue-cold morning when the ticket was tucked safely inside, still a secret, still just a possibility, still only ours.

Now the midday sun is washing the room in honey-colored light, the cookie jar is once again filled with Oreos, and Teddy—the youngest winner in the history of the Powerball lottery—is in his bedroom, tossing his balled-up socks one by one into the box he's supposed to be packing, and the story of that ticket—of that morning—doesn't belong to us anymore.

It belongs to everyone.

Across town right now Uncle Jake and Aunt Sofia are eating a late breakfast in the quiet kitchen of the brownstone, the puppy snoozing beneath the table. A few miles away Katherine McAvoy is on her way to the hospital, where she'll spend the day comforting a seven-year-old girl with leukemia, not because she's getting paid to but because that's where she's supposed to be.

And Leo is driving to pick up his boyfriend in a red sports car, already thinking ahead to next year, to all the many trips he'll be making in it as long as his luck holds out. And Max is waiting to surprise him with tickets to the new Pixar movie, because he knows Leo better than anyone.

In Portland a woman is standing in front of a mini-mart thinking about the last time she was here, with her four kids in the car, and a sick husband at home, and a long day of work behind her. She closes her eyes, grateful for whatever it was that made her ask for a ticket that day while paying for her terrible coffee and overpriced gas.

Down at the very tip of Florida, an old man is lighting the candles on an enormous cake. When he picked his numbers all those months ago, he tried to play his grandchildren's birthdays, only he got one of them wrong. He was off by two days, which has sparked a new family tradition. Today, they're celebrating his youngest granddaughter's birthday for the second time this week.

And the man who was working the register at the convenience store that snowy night is opening a savings account for his two-year-old son, who will be the first in his family to go to college because of the prize money his father received for selling the winning ticket.

And one of the lottery officials is reading an article in a

glossy magazine about what someone as young and rich as Teddy might do after graduation, because even after twelve years of giving away giant checks, the man likes to keep tabs on the winners, to see which ones collapse under the weight of all that money and which use it to make the world a better place.

Sometimes he even makes bets with his wife.

On Teddy, he's about to lose.

In San Francisco the chicken lady is taking a shift at the hospice care center, listening patiently to a woman who sounds just like she did, with a sick mother and nowhere to turn, and she nods and pats her hand and opens a new file, knowing that now there's something she can do to help, which is the best feeling of all.

And Sawyer is dreaming of castles in Scotland, and Charlie is walking into a meeting, and Caleb is taking a nap at his new foster home, his arms wrapped tightly around his stuffed pig.

And the man who was behind me in line that day, who won exactly four dollars on his ticket, then immediately used it to buy another one, which got him nothing, is mowing his lawn, because his life didn't change at all. And who's to say if that's better or worse than what happened to Teddy, what happened to me?

Maybe it all would have gone this way no matter what.

Maybe it was always supposed to turn out like this.

Maybe it was never really about the numbers at all.

411

# Fifty

Teddy comes sliding into the kitchen in mismatched socks: one looks like a monster, with big teeth and googly eyes, and the other has tiny mustaches all over it.

"Look what I found," he says, coming up behind me and grabbing me around the waist. He buries his nose in my neck and I shiver, then swivel to face him. He looks down at his feet, wiggling his toes. "They were stuck under my bed."

"A perfect match," I say, and without warning he bends to kiss me. In an instant my head is swimming, and my ears are buzzing, and our hands are everywhere. It's still so new, this thing between us, even though Teddy is not, even though he's the most familiar thing in the world, and that makes it all so much better because it's the best of everything, and each time he kisses me—every single time—I get the feeling we might never stop, that we might just decide to live like this, lip to lip and hip to hip, bound together for the rest of our days.

But then he backs me up a few steps, and I bump up against the refrigerator, and we break apart, both smiling like crazy and breathing too fast.

"Hi," he says, which he does pretty much every time we stop, as if he's still surprised and delighted to discover that it's me he was kissing all that time.

I grin back at him. "Hi."

He leans forward, bracing his hands on the freezer, one on either side of my head, pinning me in place like he's about to kiss me again, but then he frowns and draws back.

"This thing is really old," he says, and I blink at him, confused.

"What is?"

"The fridge," he says, looking around. "And the oven, actually."

"That's what you were thinking about just now?"

He laughs. "Sorry, but . . ."

"What?"

"What if I surprised the next tenants by putting in some new appliances?" he says, suddenly excited. "Wouldn't it be cool if they just came in and saw it all here?"

"It would be very cool," I say, and I mean it. Whenever he talks like this, whenever he lights up at the thought of doing something kind, my heart starts to feel too big for my rib cage.

He stoops in front of the oven, opening the rusted door

413

and peering inside. The moment is clearly over, so I grab the brown garbage bag that's resting beside the sink.

"Don't throw away anything important," Teddy says without looking up, and I can hear the laughter in his voice.

"That never gets old," I say, hefting it onto my shoulder. "Never."

But as I step out into the hallway, I'm struck again by the memory of that morning, of how close we came to losing the ticket, of the way something so small—a missing slip of paper—could have changed things so dramatically.

Once I've sent the bag sailing down to the dumpster below, I take a long look at the brass numerals hanging on the door of the apartment beside the chute: 13. There was a time when I wished none of this had ever happened, when I wished the number thirteen hadn't been something I was quite so willing to hand over to the man behind the counter that day. But not now. It no longer feels like a trip wire or a land mine or a scar, that number. It's something else entirely: a memory, a dedication, a good-luck charm.

It's the thing that got me here.

And here is a pretty good place to be.

When I walk back inside, Teddy is standing in front of the refrigerator, his back to the door and his head bent, so it isn't until he turns around that I realize something is wrong. His hair is sticking up the way it does when he's been running a hand through it, and he looks a little pale. It takes me another few seconds to notice the card he's holding, and as soon as I do my heart falls so hard and so fast I feel like it might have escaped me altogether.

I stare at the refrigerator, which has been pulled out a few inches from the wall, then back at the card, which he's holding with both hands, then at his ridiculous socks: anywhere but his eyes, which I'm afraid to meet, because I'm afraid to see what's in them.

It's been so long since that snowy bus ride, so long since I borrowed Leo's pen and emptied my heart onto the page. So much has happened since that night. So much has changed. And now I've gone and ruined everything, just because of one stupid, careless moment a few months ago, when I made the mistake of writing on a birthday card the three words we still haven't said aloud to each other. If that's not enough to scare him off, to give him second thoughts about us, I'm not sure what is.

I should know better than anyone that luck is not an infinite resource.

And here, now, I might've finally used up what little I had left.

The silence lengthens. I'm still standing by the door, and Teddy is still standing by the fridge, and the distance between us is unbearable. The card is in his hand and I can almost see the words from here, though I've been carrying them around with me for so long that I don't need reminding. They're like a second heartbeat, steady and painful and true: *I love you, I love you, I love you.*

I'm bracing myself, waiting for the moment to tip one way or the other, waiting for everything to end or to begin. The stillness in the kitchen is airless and tense. A cloud passes by out the window and the room goes dim. Somewhere in the distance, a siren blares. And here in the quiet I let out a shaky breath before finally forcing myself to look up at Teddy.

I thought I knew all his smiles, thought I had them memorized and categorized. But this one is different. The way he's looking at me right now, it's like he's about to turn into someone else entirely. It's like his ship is about to come in.

It's like he's the luckiest person in the world.

It's like we both are.

# ACKNOWLEDGMENTS

I've never won the lottery before, but I often feel like I have, and that's because of all the amazing people in my life. This book wouldn't have happened without so many of them.

First, I owe a great big thank-you to my agent and friend, Jennifer Joel. We've been working together for over ten years now, and I can't think of anyone I'd rather have in my corner.

I feel incredibly fortunate to have landed at Delacorte, and I'm so grateful to my editor, Kate Sullivan, for the huge amount of time and love and energy she poured into this book. Thank you to Beverly Horowitz for making all my publishing dreams come true, and to Barbara Marcus for her incredible enthusiasm and support. My publicist, Jillian Vandall, is the absolute best. And I was thrilled to get to work with Dominique Cimina, Kim Lauber, Judith Haut, Adrienne Waintraub, Laura Antonacci, Cayla Rasi, Kelly McGauley, Kristin Schulz, Kate Keating, Hannah Black, Alexandra Hightower, Alison Impey, Christine Blackburne, Colleen Fellingham, Barbara Bakowski, and the rest of the wonderful Random House team. Thanks for making so much magic happen.

I couldn't do any of this without Kelly Mitchell, my sister and sounding board.

I'm very lucky to have friends who are not only amazing authors, but also thoughtful and generous readers: Jenny Han, Sarah Mlynowski, Aaron Hartzler, Elizabeth Eulberg, and Morgan Matson. I owe a huge debt of gratitude to Siobhan Vivian for coming up with the title, and to Jenni Henaux, Ryan Doherty, Anna Carey, Robin Wasserman, and Lauren Graham for all the guidance and encouragement along the way.

It's been a true pleasure to work with Rachel Petty, Venetia Gosling, Belinda Rasmussen, Kat McKenna, Bea Cross, and George Lester at Macmillan in the UK. I'm always grateful to Stephanie Thwaites, Roxane Edouard, Becky Ritchie, and Hana Murrell at Curtis Brown for all they do for me around the world. Many, many thanks to everyone at ICM, especially Josie Freedman, John DeLaney, and Sharon Green. And—as always—to Binky Urban, without whom none of this would've happened.

Lastly, of course, to my family: Dad, Mom, Kelly, Errol, and Andrew. Thanks a million.

# Say *hello* to another great read by Jennifer E. Smith!

"Over one epic evening, Jennifer E. Smith expertly captures every painful, perfect nuance of first love. I didn't want the night—or this book—to end."

—Sarah Dessen

"This latest stunner from Jennifer E. Smith will linger in your aching heart."

—Jennifer Niven

## Don't miss Jennifer E. Smith's other novels!

# Underlined

We <u>underline</u> everything
you need to know about
the best YA books, the coolest
authors, and the latest trends.

---

## WHEN YOU VISIT
## *Underlined*
## YOU GET:

- Personalized book recommendations, quizzes, lists, and videos
- Updates on trends, celebs, music, fashion, and more
- The chance to receive FIRST IN LINE perks such as early access to books, sweepstakes, events, and author content

---